Chaos

Paul Henke

To Jeff,

A merry christmas 2013
and
Welcome to TIFAT!

Paul Henke

GOOD READ PUBLISHING

Copyright © 2002 Paul Henke

The right of Paul Henke to be identified as the Author of
the Work has been asserted by him in accordance with the
Copyright, Designs and Patents Act 1988.

First published in 2002 by Good Read Publishing
A Good Read Publishing paperback

10 9 8 7 6 5 4 3 2 1

All characters in this publication are fictitious
and any resemblance to real persons, living or dead,
is purely coincidental.

A CIP catalogue record for this title is available
from the British Library

ISBN 1-902483-04-9

Typeset by Palimpsest Book Production Limited,
Polmont, Stirlingshire
Printed and bound in Great Britain by
Omnia Books Limited, Glasgow

Good Read Publishing Ltd
PO Box 1638
Glasgow
G63 0WJ

To Dorothy as always, and to our family
for their encouragement and support.

Acknowledgements

To Anne Buhrmann and Mary Young for their editing, proof-reading and pertinent comments. Thanks also to Brian Smith for his imagination and patience. To Wendy and the staff at Palimpsest – as helpful as always. To Keith Munro and Les Stevenson for their invaluable feedback. And last but not least to my friends Burg and Scott for listening to my ramblings over the odd bottle of wine.

Prologue

Bogata, Columbia

Sitting to one side of the audience Alleysia Raduyev displayed none of the nervousness she was feeling although she knew that the speech about to be made was the most important of her life. The most senior member working for her organisation rose to his feet and cleared his throat. To give her strength and to calm her nerves she conjured up her favourite memory of Alfonso, her late husband. She had loved him in her way. He had been so handsome and debonair. An impoverished Italian aristocrat he had made her smile with his winning ways and attentive gestures. When she had married him she had known he was weak, ineffectual. But she hadn't married him for his intellect. She had married him for his title and his good looks. She would have forgiven him anything . . . everything! And she had done, often. Until she had discovered that he was not only cheating on her but stealing from her as well.

How well she remembered the confrontation in her father's study and the doctored brandy. Alfonso had woken from his drugged sleep to find himself lying on the deck of her father's 50ft motor yacht, *The Black Narcissist*, tied with barbed wire that was fixed to a twenty-kilogram sinker. The pain of the barbs cutting into his flesh had penetrated his drugged mind even as the narcotic was wearing off. With infinite patience she had waited for him to fully understand what was happening to him. How imminent his fate. He began begging, crying and cursing her.

'This is to pay you back for all the times I pleaded with you

1

not to go to your whores,' she spat at him. 'Now you will see what it means to cross me.'

She signalled one of the seamen who turned the mechanism of the hand-crane, which lifted Alfonso to his feet, his arms above his head, the weight still on the deck. 'A moment,' she had ordered when he was standing. Stepping forward, she had put her hands on his face and kissed him. Hope had sprung up in his eyes. 'Will you be good? Stay faithful?'

'Yes, yes, *Cara mia*,' he had moaned. 'I have loved only you. I swear it.'

She had stepped back and signalled again. The crane turned outwards, taking him with it. The weight slid off the deck and hung beneath him, adding to his pain. He had screamed like a baby.

'Lower him slowly. Not so fast, I said slowly. Let me do it.' She had taken over, turning the handle barely a few degrees. He cursed, begged and then began to scream. A mere two metres to the waterline yet she prolonged his agony over an hour. In the early morning light she could see that his clothes were covered with blood from the barbed wire. He was semi-comatose from pain and fear.

When the water reached his waist he had looked up, pure hatred in his eyes. 'I curse you Alleysia Raduyev. May you rot in hell for all eternity.'

'You will be there a long time before me, my darling,' she had replied. He pleaded again. For a second she had weakened. She had contemplated letting him drop to the bottom and drowning. But then she had thought of all the private and public humiliations he had inflicted on her and she had steeled her heart.

It had taken a long time for the water to reach his neck. Tortured by the knowledge of his certain death Alfonso's emotions had surged from panic one second into drivelling hatred the next. His final, anguished scream when the water reached his mouth still brought a smile to her lips every time she thought about it. His attempts to prolong his life had been as useless as everything else he had done.

He had been her first blood but not her last.

*   *   *

'Shall I start?' A male voice whispered. The speaker was her right-hand man, King-Smith, who fronted her organisation.

Mentally she shook herself from her reverie. The audience consisted of only seventeen people, all men. Answering the question she nodded imperceptibly.

'I propose that our first venture as The Syndicate should be known as Operation Siren,' King-Smith began, speaking in an upper crust, English accent. 'Working together we will change the balance of power across the world. Unlike the Sirens of Greek mythology who lured only sailors to destruction on the rocks The Syndicate will lure entire nations. The cost up front is hundreds of millions but the rewards will be measured in billions . . .'

Guy Glover was a Central Intelligence Agency operative and had been for fifteen years. Most of that time had been spent in South America. He had painstakingly built up a cover story that would stand the closest scrutiny yet allowed him a great deal of freedom to come and go as he pleased. His company employed a dozen linguists who translated everything from contracts to novels. The business actually turned a profit, which Glover was allowed to keep. He used the money for bribes whenever he needed them. This last job had cost a small fortune. However, he had finally managed to establish a microphone in the room where the conference was being held. The so-called Colombian Summit Meeting. Discovering the meeting here in Bogota had been a stroke of luck but then that was the nature of intelligence gathering. Luck usually played the largest part.

The implications of King-Smith's speech left him aghast. Without doubt, this was the biggest case of his career. His priority was to get the information back to Langley at all costs. Switching off the recording machine Glover removed the cassette and slipped it into his inside jacket pocket. He straightened his tie, smoothed his trousers, a habit he had when nervous, and left the room. Glover was just under six feet tall, fit and tough. He could speak three languages fluently – English, Spanish and Portuguese. His swarthy complexion allowed him to blend in easily with the people of Colombia. Opening his hotel room door he peered out.

3

The corridor was empty. He had only stepped out of the room and was closing the door behind him when two men materialised from around the corner.

'Hey! *Quien está allí?*' one of them called in Spanish, drawing a gun.

Glover was unarmed and he stopped. 'Me? I am staying here,' he replied in the same language. The two men approached quickly and stopped less than a metre from him.

It was the wrong reply. 'This floor is fully taken. All rooms vacated. Hands up,' the man holding the gun said. 'Search him.'

The second man knelt at Glover's feet and began to pat his left ankle. Glover didn't wait. Lifting his right foot he brought it down with stunning force on the back of the neck of the kneeling man. Simultaneously he hit the arm of the gunman to one side and buried his extended knuckles in the man's throat. As the guard gurgled and collapsed the gun went off with a loud bang. Snatching the weapon from the man's hand, Glover hit the other assailant over the head with the butt, before running down the corridor.

Turning a corner he heard shouts behind him and accelerated. He took two flights of stairs three steps at a time and reached the lobby. In the middle of the foyer was a fountain with an ugly cherub spouting water from its mouth. Glover was walking nonchalantly past when he was challenged. Looking around him he saw four men closing in from different directions, each with a gun in his hand.

The gun Glover had taken in the corridor was in his coat pocket, resting in his hand. He did not waste time by attempting to withdraw it but fired though his coat. He killed two men before being hit from behind in the left shoulder. Turning to shoot the gunman he was dragging his own gun from his pocket when a second bullet smashed him in the chest. Flying back into the shallow water of the fountain, blood pumping out of him, he watched the two remaining gunmen approaching. There were screams and yells from the other occupants of the lobby but the men took no notice. Not even when an off-duty police officer drew his gun and ordered them to drop theirs. Instead they kept walking towards Glover, one of them raising his gun, pointing it at Glover's head. The officer called again but was contemptuously ignored as the gunman drew back the hammer of his pistol. The policeman shot him in the back. The second gunman whirled round, raising his own weapon to point at the officer who yelled again at the man to drop his gun. The gunman paused, dropped it, turned and ran into the crowd. The officer hesitated momentarily and the man was lost through the hotel's doors.

'Call police headquarters,' he ordered the nervous concierge.

The policeman walked cautiously across the floor to the fountain and checked the first killer was dead. Next he climbed into the water, annoyed at getting his shoes and trousers soaked. With a start he recognised the man bleeding to death.

'Guy.' He knelt by his side.

Recognising the police inspector Glover gripped his friend's arm. 'Tape. Langley,' was all he said before he died.

Vladivostock, The Russian Federation

All three nuclear warheads were being loaded into the back of a truck. The senior officer watching the evolution felt sickened by what he was doing. But, as he saw it, he had no choice. The money he would be paid would be used to start rebuilding the infrastructure of the city. Vlad, he thought, needed it desperately. With luck, the hard currency from the sale of the missiles would be sufficient to kick-start the process. Then, if he could persuade foreign investors to come in on the back of it, there would be a chance to rejuvenate the whole area. It was a faint hope, but it was all he had. To think a Russian Admiral would stoop so low as to be down amongst the carrion and the hyenas. He thought nostalgically about the good old days – under Communist rule. He shook his grizzled head in vexation. It seemed like a golden age but it wasn't. In truth the only difference was they'd had nothing to compare it with.

The three warheads were securely stowed in the truck. Its engine burst into life with a cloud of black smoke and it trundled away on worn tyres and broken springs. The Admiral returned to his office and poured himself a large vodka. One warhead, detonated in a major city, would wipe out millions of people and destroy billions, probably trillions, of roubles of property. He snorted sardonically. The rouble was valueless. The devastation would be counted in dollars. In reality, the final figure and the real damage to people would be incalculable. The area of the detonation would be bombed back to the Middle Ages. If the survivors were lucky. Well, that wasn't his problem. All he needed to do now was conclude the deal.

TIFAT Headquarters, Scotland

'We know that in the last year there has been a substantial increase in the amount of class A drugs flooding across Europe.' The American liaison officer from the DEA had been speaking for over twenty minutes. Each revelation was greater then the previous one. The figures were staggering. If profits from crime around the world were added up it would have a turnover that would be greater than the GNP of almost every nation with the exception of the USA and Japan. Europe's contribution alone made crime bigger than Scandinavia's Gross National Product.

The theatre could hold five hundred people. It was nearly half full. The men and women in the audience represented agencies from all over Europe. The Americans had called for the briefing, perturbed by what was happening.

'We have definite proof of the connection between the crime cartels and terrorism. We need to stop the flow of money to these organisations. Money is the lifeblood, the oxygen of terrorist cells. We stop one then the other dries up. It's imperative that we fight back collectively, across Europe, across the world. Let me explain.' For the next thirty minutes of the seminar an astonishing financial overview of the crime cartels was presented.

The fit looking, black-haired lieutenant commander sitting near the front was listening attentively. Like so many others, Nick Hunter was horrified by what he was learning. The speaker was keeping his words matter-of-fact. Somehow the bald information was worse as a result. The bleak picture he was painting was like something from a surreal nightmare, stark, terrible.

For Hunter the two-day briefing proved a defining time in his life. If he had ever had doubts about having joined TIFAT – The International Force Against Terrorism – then this briefing washed them away. The scale of the problem was becoming apparent as the hours unfolded and speaker after speaker added more pieces to the jigsaw. The presenters they had heard from were experts in defined areas. Astonishing amounts of opium were flooding out of Afghanistan via Iran. The Iranians, staunchly anti-drugs, were now suffering from massive addiction amongst their young people never before known. From there the drugs were sweeping across Europe. The cartels used extortion, prostitution, money laundering, drugs, gun running, immigrant smuggling and a host of other illegal activities to finance terrorism which caused the chaos that allowed the cartels to flourish.

The last session was a lecture on international law. It proved too much. The occupants of the room began talking among themselves, arguing and denouncing the inadequacies of the legal systems of the Western World.

General Macnair, the Officer Commanding TIFAT, allowed the debate to rage for a few minutes before stepping onto the stage. He held up his hand and after a few moments silence descended. 'Thank you, ladies and gentlemen. Let's get to the end. I know how you all feel. None of us realised the horror of the situation until we had the complete picture. Not even our politicians are aware of the full extent of what is happening. We are only now understanding the scale of the problem and that is in good measure thanks to the people who have taken the time to come here and brief us.'

Hunter whispered to his companion, 'It's unbelievable. I hadn't been aware how bad things had become.'

The American Colonel seated next to him nodded. 'Neither had I. This is a war we daren't lose.'

1

The sloop was a beauty, over two decades old, yet still graceful. Hunter turned the wheel two points to starboard and balanced the boat with the wind directly astern, filling the spinnaker. He set the autopilot, watched the compass for a few moments and then stretched out a hand to take the proffered cup of coffee.

'Thanks,' he smiled at Ruth. 'This is just what I needed. We should be set on this course for at least the next hour.' The two days they had spent together onboard had made him no less aware of his attraction for her. If anything his feelings had deepened. He watched as she brushed her dark hair from her face with the back of her wrist. She wasn't beautiful in the conventional sense but her wide mouth, always ready with a smile, her brown eyes and determined air gave her an appeal that Hunter found irresistible.

'I hadn't realised,' she said, 'that when I signed on as a crew member I was in fact giving myself into slavery.'

'Mutiny in the lower ranks?' Hunter paused with the mug to his lips, eyes sparkling and his voice filled with laughter. 'Are all your chores so difficult? So demanding and arduous?'

'Not all,' she smiled, remembering the night before. 'In fact some are reasonably enjoyable.'

'Only reasonably?'

'Well . . .' she drew out the word as she snuggled next to him on the transom seat. 'Nick, why did we have to leave so early? It's only six-thirty now. We've been up half the night already.'

'Not quite.' He put his arm around her shoulders and gave her a hug. 'Only since half past four.'

'That's half the night, considering the time we finally went to sleep.'

'You can have a lazy day. I wanted to catch the wind and get away to sea before daylight. The breeze will drop right away about dawn and then it will be at least two, maybe three hours, before it will pick up again. Only it'll be from the sea and we would be battling into it. That's hard work. This way we have a nice easy run before the wind while we have breakfast. Let me check the horizon and we can go below.' He stood up, lifted the binoculars to his eyes and scanned the dark sea.

It was the perfect time for sailing. Daybreak was half an hour away, the dawn a mere hint in the sky to the east. On his back the wind was warm and he knew that the forecast promised a lovely day. He was as content as his restless character allowed him to be as his eyes scanned the darkness, identifying lights and markers. There were two ships to port and three to starboard. Each ship was crossing either left to right or right to left and their bearings were drawing away accordingly. To port and starboard were the lights of La Capte and St. Mandrier respectively and astern the orange hue of Toulon, their departure port, glimmered hazily.

Le Beau Papillon, the Beautiful Butterfly, was a fifteen-metre sloop, unique in design. The hull was steel and in sound condition. The single mast was wood and her superstructure aluminium. She had been owned and lovingly cared for by one family. The mast had been tuned less than five months earlier in preparation for the sailing season and was angled backwards at five degrees. The rake of the mast compensated for the wind blowing downwards across the earth at an angle of about four degrees. All standing stays and shrouds had been adjusted to perfection and the previous owner had boasted to Hunter that she could sail faster and closer to the wind than any other boat of her class anywhere in the Mediterranean. After two days of trials Hunter believed him.

Known as *Papillon*, she was well equipped with the latest in electronic gear from sat-nav equipment to radar and radio. The main cabin aft, beneath their feet, held a double bed, en-suite

10

shower and head. On the starboard side was a huge saloon with comfortable furniture, a dining area and galley. There were two forward cabins, port and starboard, equipped with two bunks in each. Further forward was a shower room with another head. Forward again lay a well equipped workshop, which also doubled as a diving store. Finally there were lockers holding the many items required for safe and long distance sailing, sails and auxiliary equipment. The plush carpets, light stained oak and cupboards added to the feeling of luxury. *Papillon* was built to cruise the world in comfort.

Under the floorboards in the saloon was the engine compartment from where an eight-cylinder Peugeot marine engine propelled the boat along at a comfortable six knots.

Hunter checked the radar picture, set the alarm and joined Ruth below, reassuring her that if the radar detected another ship within five miles the alarm would sound and Hunter could be back on deck within seconds.

'I'll make breakfast,' he said, 'while you try and get the BBC World Broadcast. Let's find out what's happening.' In the short time they had been together Ruth had learned that Hunter was a news junkie, either listening to the BBC on the radio or getting BBC Radio 5 via the Internet. She, on the other hand, preferred listening to light classical music and, with a smile, she switched on the radio already pre-set to a French classical station. The warm sounds of an orchestra playing a Bach fugue filled the air. Hunter was about to protest, looked at Ruth's face and decided not to bother. He'd try and enjoy the music as well.

Cracking half a dozen eggs, he whipped them in a bowl with milk and butter, grated onion and cheese into the mixture, wiped away his tears and warmed oil in a frying pan before pouring the egg mix into it. As the omelette cooked, he poured beans into the coffee machine and made two fresh coffees. He flipped the omelette, received an ironic clap for his dexterity and made a mock bow in appreciation. Cutting the omelette in two, he served it with fresh bread he had put in the gas-fired oven prior to sailing.

Ruth took an appreciative mouthful and smiled happily. 'You'll make some woman a good wife one day,' she teased.

'Me?' Hunter laughed. 'I have a small but useful repertoire which ranges from various things done with eggs to spaghetti bolognaise and a rather hot chilli. All the staple foods of a bachelor. What about you? I haven't seen you cook yet.'

'Give me time.'

'I'm looking forward to it,' he smiled. In spite of knowing each other for only a short time they were at ease together.

They had met during an operation to stop Samuel Dayan, a right-wing Israeli industrialist, from causing a war in the Middle East. Hunter, as a Royal Navy Lieutenant Commander, diving and explosives specialist, had been a key player in the operation. Ruth, a Mossad agent, had helped him to grab success from the jaws of defeat. It was not putting it too finely to say that they had saved each other's lives on more than one occasion. After the operation Hunter had asked Ruth to join him on a sailing holiday. Their plans had been changed when Hunter was recalled to Scotland to attend the briefing. Although recently established it looked as if The International Force Against Terrorism was going to have its mandate extended to include the war on drugs. Hunter hoped that was the case. Meanwhile Ruth had returned to Israel and her duties, agreeing to meet Hunter whenever he could manage to get away. They had both arrived in Toulon on Midsummer's Day, two days earlier.

Ruth grimaced. 'The reason you haven't sampled my culinary delights is because we've eaten out almost continually since we arrived or we've had salads and cold foods for picnics. The fact is, I'm a rotten cook.'

Hunter laughed. 'In that case we had better invest in a good cook book.'

Ruth leant across the table and put her hand on his. 'So you don't think we could live off love?'

'Hardly. I need red meat and red wine.' The boat began a gentle pitching. Hunter said, 'I have to go up top. An ingrained naval sense of duty says I need to keep a watch. Can you bring up another coffee, please?'

'Aye, aye, sir.' Ruth gave a parody of a salute.

Minutes later they were sitting in the cockpit watching the

eastern sky turn from indigo to a pearly blue. The stars fled before the sun, only Venus lingering as the sun reached the horizon.

'I'm glad to hear things are settling down in Israel,' Hunter said. 'It was touch and go for a while.'

Ruth shivered. 'It doesn't bear thinking about. My father and the others are truly grateful. Dayan came very close to succeeding.' Her father was the Deputy Prime Minister of Israel and had nearly died at the hands of Dayan's men.

'It's our job to stop the madmen. The problem is there are so many of them, in all guises. Still, General Macnair's pleased. He was practically hailed as a hero when he got back to Britain. Which was a relief, I can tell you.'

'Why a relief?'

'We overstepped the mark. We operated without proper authority, although the General will argue that TIFAT's mandate gave him the right to act. Still, with Israel and our Arab friends all singing his praises there's nothing our political masters can complain about. Just thank God that the man in charge of TIFAT is prepared to act when necessary.'

'You're right,' said Ruth. She shuddered, 'Dayan came so close to winning it still gives me nightmares.'

Hunter smiled. 'If it hadn't been for you I probably wouldn't be alive today.'

'The same is true for me. I would have had to kill him. And even if I had I wouldn't have survived a second afterwards. You saved my life as well so we're quits.'

'Fair enough. Only, let's not make it a habit.'

'Of saving each other's lives?'

'Of placing them in danger,' he said with mock seriousness.

Ruth laughed ruefully. 'How did you wangle this trip? You never told me.'

'I have five weeks leave owing to me and for once I'm taking it. I'm not indispensable, nobody at TIFAT is.' He paused and then added, 'With the probable exception of the General. It's his baby. We owe our existence to his foresight and persistency.' He smiled. 'And you've got a month. So we have all this time

13

to enjoy ourselves. If we don't make it home we can stop off somewhere and leave the boat for another day. Or I can pay somebody to skipper it for me. It's not a problem.'

'Is anything ever, with you?'

'A problem?'

'Yes. You just seem to . . . I don't know. Sort anything out that needs sorting. It's as if you can just navigate around or over any obstacle.'

Hunter laughed. 'Hardly. I suppose,' he became serious, 'if you don't have to worry about the mundane things in life, like making a living, you can concentrate on the other things you need or want to do.' He shrugged. 'I've just always had a can-do attitude that's stood me in good stead all my life. Don't misunderstand, the challenges have been there. But a positive attitude of mind has always carried me through. Someday I suppose I'll really be tested. What about you? You're about the most positive person I know. Man or woman.'

Ruth smiled. In the gathering light Hunter's heart beat harder as he gazed at her. He knew he was in serious danger of falling in love. 'I suppose I've always thought anything's possible. In some respects it's the attitude that pervades all of Israel. My father has it to the nth degree. I guess I inherited it too.'

'Indeed you did. Okay, now to practical matters. Why don't you go below and get some sleep? I'll call you in about five hours. We'll try and get into a watch-keeping routine for the next few days until Gibraltar.'

'Right.' She stood up and kissed his cheek. 'You need a shave.' With that she vanished below.

Hunter drew a hand across his lean jaw and grinned contentedly. He took a bearing of the sun as its lower arc reached the horizon and for the next few minutes he amused himself calculating what the angle of the sun should be and comparing it to the compass reading. Both came to within a degree of each other, which satisfied Hunter. The compass was reading true.

When the sun rose he switched off the combined red and green lantern at the masthead and the white stern light. Scanning the horizon once more, he saw that the other ships had also doused their lights. He checked their position, felt the satisfaction of hitting his way point exactly and altered course twenty degrees to starboard. Resetting the autopilot he silently made his way forward to adjust the spinnaker. He let out the lazy brace and tightened the spinnaker sheet, moving the spinnaker round so that the wind continued to fill it. The breeze was a steady force four, the sea was now at red two zero, twenty degrees on the port bow, and the boat was gaily ploughing along at a steady nine knots. He adjusted the mainsheet and jib sheets and, finally satisfied, sat back in the cockpit. It was a wonderful day for sailing.

Rubbing a hand on his cheek he sighed and went below to shave in the forward shower. His expression in the mirror bore more than a passing resemblance to his maternal great-grandfather, David Griffiths. Not only had he inherited David's lean features and black hair but also his adventurous spirit. Like his great-grandfather, Hunter's dark blue eyes appeared to look on the world as a place of fun and excitement. The truth was he applied himself to whatever task he undertook and so enjoyed almost everything he did whether it was in his professional life or when he was relaxing. His hobbies were diverse. He enjoyed reading good books, drinking good wine and eating good food. But he thrived on action and whenever he could he would go scuba diving, skiing and para-sailing. Recently he had taken the decision to learn to fly. David Griffiths had been born a Welshman, Hunter was Scottish. Both, Hunter liked to think, had Gaelic blood in them. He lathered his face and contentedly began scraping his jaw with a razor.

A few minor course alterations saw him through to nearly 14.00 and he yawned, stretching his arms and legs. It was time to wake Ruth. Glancing around the horizon and satisfied it was all clear, he went below to make her a cup of tea. It was, she had told Hunter, the beverage of choice when first awakening.

When Ruth appeared on deck she carried a plate of baguettes with cheese and pickle and a bottle of cold water for Hunter. They ate in companionable silence, enjoying the warmth of the sun.

'Oh, look,' Ruth suddenly cried, 'a flying fish.' She pointed ahead of the boat. 'There are dozens of them. I didn't know you got flying fish in the Med.'

'Sharks too, although rarely this far from the Atlantic.' He stifled a yawn. 'I'm going below. Any problems stamp the deck and I'll come running. We should be on this tack for at least the next four hours. So the only potential difficulty would be if the wind shifts. Okay?'

'Okay.' Ruth gave a tentative smile. This would be the first time she had handled this or indeed any boat by herself. She had enjoyed being taught to sail by Nick. After two days he was satisfied that she could handle the yacht under normal conditions.

Hunter went into the aft cabin, stripped off, showered and collapsed onto the bed. Within minutes he was asleep.

Over the next two days they quickly established a routine they both enjoyed, giving them as much time together as possible whilst allowing them the sleep they needed when the other was on watch.

At 05.20 on their fifth morning at sea their idyll ended.

Seeing a contact on the radar, Hunter plotted its course as the two vessels converged. He frowned when he was unable to see any steaming lights and came to the conclusion that none were lit. *Papillon* had right of way but he was not so pig-headed or dogmatic to stand on into danger – especially against a large ship which could mow them down with barely a bump.

Sounding the foghorn in warning, he tried raising the officer of the deck on the ship, using channel 16, to no avail. He saw from the radar plot that if the ship continued on its present course it would hit the Spanish coast in about an hour somewhere around Palamós. Exasperated and angry at the dangerous seamanship of the officers and crew Hunter altered course and chased after the ship to identify her. The coaster was doing about six, maybe seven knots, while *Papillon* was pushing along at a good eleven.

Looking at her, he guessed she was about a thousand tonnes. Clearly she was old. Closing on her stern, Hunter used a hand-held spotlight to illuminate her hull. The name had been crudely painted out, along with the ship's port of registration.

Manoeuvring to get closer, he heard a gunshot followed by a scream and thought he saw someone falling into the sea.

With a stifled oath Hunter spun the wheel hard to port and the yacht's speed dropped away as she sailed into irons. Using the spotlight, he swept the water, looking for a possible body. The sea was running at about a state three, the waves between two and four feet high, the wind now on the bow at Beaufort Force three to four. Whitecaps were intermittent, making searching the sea for a body all the more difficult. The unusual and uneven movement of the boat woke Ruth and she appeared sleepily on deck.

'What is it?'

'A ship just passed. I heard a shot and a scream. I think I saw somebody falling off the ship but it seemed more imagined than real.'

'Look. Over there.' Ruth suddenly pointed. 'I thought I saw something. Yes. Look. There it is again – it's a face. Give me that while you steer.' She grabbed the light out of his hand and swept it in an arc across their stern.

'Got it.' Hunter saw the face and a hand held high in the air. Turning the ignition key, he waited a few seconds for the heating light to extinguish before pressing the starter button. He flashed up the diesel, engaging the gearbox and headed towards where he saw the figure disappearing under the waves. The hand appeared again briefly only a few metres away before sliding under the water. Hunter knocked the gear lever into neutral and dived over the side.

2

As the water closed over his head, Hunter opened his eyes and swam strongly down. The disturbed phosphorescence in the water as the body sank was clear to follow. Grabbing the body by the hair, he swam for the surface now some five or six metres above his head. He shifted his grip until he was holding the body by an arm and swam with one hand over his head lest he crash into the underside of the *Papillon* headfirst.

He broke surface, spat out the salt water and looked around him. The boat was only a few metres away.

'Ruth, over here,' he called.

She shone the spotlight on him causing him to shield his eyes.

He said loudly, 'Hang on. I'll swim to you.' He dragged the body with him to the transom. Ruth lowered the diving platform and Hunter quickly climbed onboard, pulling the body with him over the side.

Ruth knelt by the body checking the neck for a pulse. Nothing. Immediately she searched to see if a bullet was the cause or whether the person had drowned. Hunter knelt by the head and gave mouth to mouth. While looking for blood Ruth simultaneously pressed down on the body's chest five times in quick succession.

'I can't find a bullet hole,' she said. Ruth pulled open the coat and shirt to reveal a young girl's body. 'There's no blood so we keep giving resuscitation. Okay?'

'Agreed.' They fell silent, each concentrating on the job in

18

hand. Three minutes passed, then four, then five. 'Come on, damn you,' said Hunter. 'Live.' The words were barely out of his mouth when the girl groaned and seawater spilled out of her mouth. They turned her onto her side while she gagged and retched for a few minutes. As her heaves subsided her eyes fluttered open.

'Take it easy,' said Hunter. 'You're safe. What's your name?'
Silence.
'Can you speak? Do you understand me?'
Big, haunted eyes looked up at the two of them before tears trickled down her face and the girl began to shake.
'Take her below,' Hunter told Ruth. 'I'll get the boat sorted. See if you can get any sense out of her.'
Ruth helped the girl to her feet and took her to the galley. Hunter reset the sails, switched off the engine and, with the boat travelling at a brisk 10 knots, followed in the wake of the coaster. Sixteen minutes had elapsed since the shot was fired.
Hunter had no plan but he refused to allow the ship to escape until he knew more. He could not see the vessel but it was painting clearly on the radar screen. Setting the cursor he read the distance; just under two miles away. He switched to autopilot and went forward. On their present course, the spinnaker was more a hindrance than an asset and he quickly prepared to drop it. Returning to the cockpit, he untied the spinnaker sheet from the cleat and lowered the sail to the deck. In the bows, he unceremoniously stuffed the sail down the forward hatch. Back in the cockpit he adjusted the main and jib sheets and felt the boat heel over and inexorably pick up speed. A glance at the radar screen was sufficient to show him that they were closing the gap on the coaster.
As he doused the yacht's sailing lights the ghost of a plan began to form.
He went back to the bows and climbed down the hatch. Trampling the spinnaker underfoot, he rolled it up and stuffed it in a ready-use locker. In the workshop he opened another locker and lifted out a cleverly concealed panel in the bottom. Nestling in the steel container was a webbing set of belt and holster and

Paul Henke

a Glock 17 automatic self-cocking revolver. He pressed the magazine catch on the left side of the butt behind the trigger and ejected the magazine. To ensure there was no round in the chamber he pulled back the slide and pulled the trigger. Satisfied, he pushed the magazine back home.

From a cupboard he took out his grey combat gear and quickly changed. Strapping on the webbing, he put a commando knife down the special holder in the seam of his trouser leg and lifted down a spear gun as an afterthought. He found a coil of half-inch nylon rope and tied the end to a grappling hook. A few moments later he was back on deck.

The ship was now less than half a mile ahead. Ruth reappeared. If she was surprised to find Hunter dressed for action she didn't show it. As a Mossad agent her motto was hope for the best but plan for the worst. It had, she reckoned, stood her in good stead on more than one occasion.

'She's calmed down enough to tell me what happened.'

'And?' Hunter looked at Ruth while at the same time making a slight adjustment to the autopilot.

'She's from Kosovo. You know you were talking over dinner the other night about the connection between the immigrants pouring into Western Europe, drug smuggling and terrorism?'

'Sure.'

'It seems she was a part of the people trafficking. Unwillingly, but still a part of it. She speaks reasonably good English as well as German. Her name is Jana Avramovic and she is from a village near a town called Gnjilane. It's a poppy-growing region.'

Hunter nodded. 'Near the Macedonian border.'

'She was en route to Germany to join one of the Kosovo enclaves in Bonn as a heroin courier.'

'Germany? This is a long way round.'

'That's what I thought. Apparently the borders overland are too tightly controlled. Travelling through Spain is much easier. Anyway, when she refused, they threatened to kill her young sister and brother. She says that many hundreds of immigrants from her area have been targeted at Western Europe. Ten of them were taken to Tirane and smuggled onboard that ship.

20

They met dozens more couriers on board. Men, women and children. Some had volunteered because of the money but the majority had been forced into doing it. They've been at sea for three days with little food or drink. Yesterday condoms filled with heroin were stuffed inside their systems. An hour ago one of the young girls was suddenly taken ill. A condom had burst and pure heroin had entered her bloodstream. She was still alive when they threw her over the side.'

'My God.' Hunter was aghast. 'So, this girl . . . Jana? Is she carrying heroin?'

'No. She managed to get rid of the condoms. When they found out what she had done they took her on deck as an example. The shot you heard was intended for her, but she suddenly screamed and jumped over the side. The bullet missed. I have to say she's a very brave young lady.'

'She's certainly that.' Hunter looked at the radar. 'The ship is three cables ahead.' He could see the dark outline of the vessel. 'Ask the girl for as much information as possible – the whereabouts of the prisoners and crew. How many we're up against. It looks like fate has dealt us a hand here.'

Hunter checked the radar and adjusted their course while Ruth went below.

She returned very quickly. 'Their movements were restricted but the passengers, even the volunteers, are all down in a forward hold. The men and women are separated in two large cabins fitted with bunks and a few chairs. Too few for all of them to sit at one time. There are two disgusting slop-out loos and no shower facilities. A standpipe supplies cold water but it is only switched on for an hour in the morning and an hour in the evening. Few, if any, complain. Jana says that they endured far worse conditions during the war and so they are used to hardship. She says she doesn't know how many there are but it's a lot. She also thinks that there are a number of spies amongst them, keeping an eye on things, although she isn't sure. One or two of the women behaved oddly.'

'Makes sense, I guess. A mole would help to stamp out any unrest before it got out of hand.'

Ruth nodded. 'I agree. Why don't we send for some backup?'

'There's no time. Once I'm onboard, put a call into TIFAT HQ and tell the duty officer what's going on. Let General Macnair decide what to do. Okay, I'm going forward.'

The *Papillon* had closed to less than half a cable directly astern of the coaster. Hunter tied off the end of the rope he was holding to the forward cleat and led the rope through the fair lead and back on deck. 'Okay,' he whispered.

Ruth started the engine and opened the throttle full. The extra push closed the gap a little more quickly and at ten metres Hunter leaned over the starboard bow and swung the grappling hook in a vertical circle. At exactly the right moment he released it and heard the hook land on the ship. He pulled on the line and satisfied himself that the hook was safely snagged on the railings. Dropping the rope he returned to the cockpit. Ruth was already letting go the mainsail sheets. Hunter helped her to gather up the canvas. Seconds later they dropped the jib. The rope paid out and as the yacht yawed to port, her way falling off quickly, she was jerked round in the wake of the ship. As she careened to one side, Hunter knocked out the autopilot and the boat settled down to follow the other vessel. Hunter stopped the engine and relaxed for a minute.

'Right. Now I'll get onboard. Is the girl all right?'

'Not a peep from her. I think she's fallen asleep after all she's been through.'

'I'm not surprised. Right, here goes.' Hunter went into the bow, took hold of the rope and pulled the yacht up to the stern of the coaster. The deck was some five metres above his head and he waited as the yacht pitched down and then up again. At the top of the movement he reached up the rope as far as he could and swung off the boat, hitting the ship's side with his feet. He pulled himself up and got a hand over the railing then paused to look and listen. Apart from the sound of the ship's engines and the whistle of the breeze across the deck he heard and saw nothing. Climbing silently onto the deck he slung the spear gun from across his back. It was loaded, ready to fire and held three more shafts beneath the barrel. Until he knew what and whom he was up against he intended to operate as silently as possible.

The ship was indeed a rust bucket. Hunter could see that maintenance had been superficial for years. He was surprised that the ship had a seaworthiness certificate, let alone safety certificates to go with her life saving and fire-fighting equipment. But the hulk was ideal for the smugglers' purposes – What would be the best way to cover illegal activities if the authorities were after you? Sink an old rust bucket like this in deep water and hope for the best. Let any cargo go down with the ship. Including, he thought, any human cargo. Dead men and women tell no tales. A quick explosion in the bottom of the hull would fit the bill. Set off from the bridge most probably – coldly logical and utterly ruthless.

Hatred coursed through Hunter's veins for the vermin he was dealing with. It was a sentiment he could not afford to indulge. He needed his wits about him, needed to be as cold and calculating as the people he was up against. He took a deep breath, getting his emotions under control. His objective was to disable the ship and let the appropriate authorities take over.

Ahead he saw a match flame, heard voices and smelt the pungent odour of tobacco. He ducked down by the side of the starboard lifeboat davit and watched as two cigarettes were lit. Exploiting the smoker's instinct to look at the match and cigarette, spoiling any night vision they might have, Hunter stepped silently forward, the spear gun ready in one hand, his diving knife in the other. There was an oath as one of the men sensed his presence. Too late, Hunter saw that they both carried guns. He was at least three paces away as the nearest man swung a gun off his shoulder and brought it to bear. Hunter fired the spear gun and hit the target in the throat. As the man gurgled on his last breath, he staggered backwards and jostled the other crewman, spoiling his aim. A shot was fired, loud in the night, as Hunter clamped a hand over the top of the gun, pushing it to one side and rammed his knife under the man's chin. The angle and power cut the man's spinal cord in half and he hung dead on the end of Hunter's arm. From ahead and above him he heard anxious voices calling and although he did not understand the language, he guessed somebody wanted to know what the shooting was about.

'*Niecevo*,' Hunter called, instinctively using the Russian for "It's okay". No more was said. He shoved the body he was holding over the side, retaining the knife in his hand. Wiping the blade on the clothes of the other body he threw it overboard as well. There was a faint splash as the body hit the water. He didn't know if the men on the bridge had heard or if his Russian had fooled them. Picking up a machine gun that had been dropped by one of the men he recognised it as the ubiquitous Uzi. He checked the safety was off and slung the gun over his shoulder. Striding across the deck to the port side, he found a life belt locker, which he hid behind. Reloading the spear gun he settled down to wait.

All was silent. He was just beginning to think that nobody was coming to investigate when he saw figures sneaking along the deck. They walked slowly, dark images against the white background of the superstructure. There were two, no, three, of them. Listening intently, he was sure that he could hear others coming down the starboard side. With possibly six armed men heading in his direction, the odds were stacked heavily in their favour. The hand on his shoulder was totally unexpected.

3

Hunter whirled round to confront Ruth who was kneeling by his side. He stifled the oath that sprang to his lips. 'What are you doing here?' he whispered, his mouth close up to her ear.

'Rescuing you. When I heard the shot I knew it was all going wrong. I'd already changed and was ready to follow if you needed me. I've brought another spear gun and a knife.'

'Take the Uzi. You dispatch this lot when I tell you. A quick, loud job and then we go after the other three. Okay?'

'Okay.'

'Fire!' Hunter shouted. Ruth sprayed the three men and Hunter rapidly fired six rounds. The men died without returning a single shot, staggered by the fusillade of shots. There were yells of consternation and someone up on the bridge shouted what sounded like instructions. Hunter and Ruth moved forward, looking for better cover. They waited, hidden under the port lifeboat, behind a davit. After a few minutes there were more shouts from the bow and then figures began to appear. They were being herded along the deck, men, women and youngsters, the girls indistinguishable from the boys.

'What do we do now?' Ruth asked.

'Get out of here. Come on.'

Bent low they ran along the deck to the stern. Ruth swung herself over the guard-rail and clambered down the rope towing the *Papillon* twenty metres astern. Hanging onto the rope, she was dragged through the water. Hunter followed her, cut the rope and watched as the ship sailed away. They went hand over hand along the rope and back to the yacht, climbing onto the diving platform and into the cockpit. Hunter flashed up the engine, engaged the gears and opened the throttle. He turned the wheel and as they picked up speed, he headed at ninety degrees to the ship. In the dark of the night he could no longer see the coaster but it showed clearly on the radar.

'Damnation, I think she's turning.' He spun the wheel further and turned the *Papillon*'s stern to the coaster. The wind was now on their starboard quarter at about a force four. He needed the sails up in a hurry as he saw the gap between the ship and the yacht steadily close. It occurred to him that perhaps the old vessel had a hidden turn of speed when it was necessary.

'I'll get the mainsail up while you work the jib,' Hunter shouted. He hauled on the mainsheet, pulling the canvas up the mast, while Ruth tackled the jib. As the mainsail filled, Hunter adjusted the sheets and then manipulated the main boom to get the optimum speed out of the boat. He watched as their speed crept up to nine and then ten knots. Checking the radar, he saw that the coaster was now less than a mile away.

'Did you phone TIFAT?'

'Yes. I spoke to Lt. Napier. He was waking the General.'

'Good. I hope he's managed to call up the cavalry.'

'Why?' Ruth frowned.

Hunter looked at her and realised that he could see her features clearly. Dawn was fast approaching. 'Because I think we're in serious trouble. Look over there.'

Ruth looked over the stern. The coaster was only a hint in the gloom but there was no mistaking her as she ploughed towards them. Black smoke was belching from her stack as she steamed at full speed.

'Any ideas?'

'Right now, not many. Look at the radar. There's not another ship within ten miles. The coaster can either run us down or get close enough to fill us full of bullet holes. Either way we can't win.'

'It's not like you to give up,' said Ruth, sharply.

'I'm not. I'm just telling you the down side.'

Ruth looked astern and scowled. 'They're closing so let's hear the up side.'

'Send out a mayday – now, to all ships. Use the auto-alarm. They're chasing us so we can turn stern to the wind. I'll get the spinnaker up. It'll give us a few more knots.' Hunter turned the boat two points to starboard before he engaged the autopilot. Darting forward, he threw open the hatch and climbed below. Finding the spinnaker, he made sure it was running loose before he climbed back onto the deck. Within minutes he had the sail filling in the wind. He watched with satisfaction as the speed of the *Papillon* increased. The needle edged up to twelve and then thirteen knots. That was probably about as fast as she would go. Running before the wind and the sea, under other circumstances Hunter would have felt a surge of joy. As it was when he looked back at the looming hull of the coaster an icy dread gripped him. He needed to find a way out of their predicament. *Predicament?* He grinned mirthlessly. *That was a . . .*

He didn't finish the thought as the dawn was rent asunder by the harsh sound of machine gun fire. It stopped almost as soon as it had started and looking back Hunter could see why. They were still too far away to be in any danger. He studied the radar. The speed of closing was definitely slowing. Maybe they would be able to outrun the coaster after all. Surely the ship's crew would turn back? Surely?

Ruth reappeared. 'I've sent the signal and also phoned TIFAT. Lt. Napier said that General Macnair raised holy Cain with the Spanish authorities to get a coastguard cutter or a naval ship into the area. Apparently one is already on its way from Barcelona.'

'Barcelona is sixty miles away so all they will be doing is picking up the pieces. Unless . . .' Hunter scrutinised the radar. 'Unless we bluff them.'

'How?'

'Look, down there. A ship on the screen, that's . . . fifteen point six miles away. Dead ahead.' Hunter adjusted the cursor on the radar screen to check the distance before he picked up his binoculars and scanned the horizon. He could see nothing. The ship was too far away. 'Wait here.'

He dropped down the companionway into the main saloon and stepped into the chartroom. He picked up the VHF radio and broadcast, 'King Carlos this is *Le Beau Papillon,* I hear you loud and clear. I understand you are fifteen miles away and closing rapidly. There is a ship astern trying to run us down. They have fired a machine gun at us. Over.' Hunter paused as though listening to a reply, wondering if his bluff would work. He was hoping that whoever was onboard the coaster would be listening to channel 16, the frequency monitored by all ships at sea, at all times.

'That's affirmative,' he continued, giving an ambiguous reply. 'I believe that the ship is smuggling immigrants into Spain. The crew is armed and dangerous, so you should be prepared. Over.'

Again he paused, thinking what else he should say. He had one last idea. 'Roger that. I understand that a helicopter will be airborne in ten minutes and en route. Thanks. Out.' He replaced the microphone and went back to the cockpit. Staring bleakly aft, he mulled over another idea, one born of desperation.

'Look! The ship's turning.' Ruth pointed. 'Your ruse worked, Nick!'

Hunter grinned, staring at the stern of the ship as it disappeared in the gloom. 'Okay, let's get ready to go about.'

'What? Are you mad? We've only just escaped with our lives.'

'I know, but we can't just let them get away. We need to follow and when the Spanish navy does get here we can point them at the ship. We still have to stop the cargo that's onboard from being landed.'

Ruth gave a heavy sigh.

'Ready about?' Hunter asked.

'Ready about.' Ruth spun the wheel and Hunter manipulated the running rigging. A few minutes later they were settled on a new course, tacking back the way they had come.

Hunter studied the radar picture and used his binoculars on the departing ship before he announced, 'Something's happening. There's less smoke belching from the funnel and they appear to have slowed down on the radar. Go a point further to port so that we don't catch up on them too quickly. We just want to watch them not get within harm's way again.'

Hunter put the binoculars back to his eyes and looked intently at the ship. After a few moments he remarked, 'That's funny. They appear to be stopping completely.' He watched for a while longer. 'If I didn't know better I would say that they're launching the lifeboats.' He paused. 'They are. What on earth is going on?' Hunter ducked down the companionway and into the chartroom. Taking a sat-nav readout of their position, he plotted it. Land was fifteen miles away. Why would the crew put to sea in lifeboats so far from land? He was missing something, but what? He stared at the dark blue on the chart, deep in thought. It made no sense, unless . . . No! That was ludicrous. He looked again. Even as he did so a horrendous possibility dawned on him. He felt a slight tremor beneath his feet.

'Oh God,' he said aloud, leaping up the steps and into the cockpit. 'Quick, head for the ship,' he ordered.

Ruth was startled but turned the wheel to starboard as Hunter adjusted the sails to get the maximum speed out of the *Papillon*.

'They're getting rid of the evidence. They've set off explosives onboard.' He looked through the binoculars once more. 'They've stopped the ship over a deep trench. According to the chart it's at least five hundred and fifty metres to the sea bed just here. If they sink the ship with the passengers and heroin nothing can be proven against them.'

'Couldn't divers go down and find the proof?'

'The technology to reach the ship might exist but I doubt anybody would bother. It would be a massive operation, believe me. They'll get away and continue plying their vile trade. I spooked them all right but I didn't think they'd do this. Mass murder and it's my fault. We have to save them. Look, the lifeboat is heading away. They're escaping.'

'Let them go,' said Ruth. 'We need to get to the coaster.'

Hunter sighed. 'You're right. Let me take the wheel.' He adjusted the yacht's course by a fraction, hauled tight on the mainsheet and the *Papillon* keeled further to port. Her speed

29

picked up and they were flying along. Glancing at the indicator, Hunter saw that they were doing twelve knots. Looking ahead he could see the coaster settling in the water and he guessed that she was down by as much as a foot already. He gauged the distance to go and the course they were on through narrowed eyes. If they stayed on their present heading for another two or three cables and then jibed once more they could be within reach of the coaster. Hunter held the course and then yelled, 'Jibe-ho.'

Hunter spun the wheel, Ruth eased the main sheet, the boom passed across the deck and they were around and on a port tack.

Already the coaster was way below her Plimsoll line and sinking fast. Hunter could only guess at the fear and panic that was gripping the people who were trapped in the hold of the ship.

'Take the wheel,' he said. 'I'm going up forward. I'll tell you whether to turn port or starboard. I'll try and jump as we go past. Okay?'

'Sure. No problem.' The frown creasing her brow belayed Ruth's words.

Hunter kissed her cheek. 'Go into irons once you're past. We'll see what to do then.'

He went forward. The *Papillon* was pitching about three-quarters of a metre as she easily rode the waves towards the now stationary vessel. 'A few degrees to starboard,' Hunter yelled. Ruth did as she was bid and then he yelled, 'Do the same again.' The boat edged further over. The ship was now less then twenty metres away and closing fast. Hunter put one foot on the guard-rail and steadied himself on the forward lower shroud. As the stern of the coaster slid past he launched himself into the air, stretching to reach the deck which was now less than four metres above the water line. He grabbed the deck with ease and, barely pausing, swung his feet up to the deck while at the same time reaching up with one hand to the railing above. Within seconds he was on the deck and running forward.

Running, sliding on the uneven deck, he could hear hammering as the stern of the ship sank more quickly than the bows. On the fore-deck he stopped, appalled at what he saw. The main hatch was battened down with criss-crossing heavy hawsers each one attached to a shackle, which in turn was screwed onto a deck clench. One look told him that the hawsers had been specially made and the deck clenches welded on to fit exactly. The hatch was open about two centimetres and through it he could hear screams and the sound of water.

There were eight hawsers, four one way and four the other. He would have to unscrew eight or possibly twelve bolts before he could throw open the hatch. He ducked down by the side of the first one just as a bullet hit the ventilation inlet on the deck. Sprawling flat, he looked over the side. The crew's lifeboat had turned and was now on its way back. Somebody onboard must have seen him and decided to make very sure no one escaped. Only with no witnesses would they get away with it.

The lifeboat was an old cutter, with five people onboard, two of them women. Hunter held his fire. The angle and distance meant he was a difficult target so he rolled next to the hatch and fumbled with the first of the bolts. He was grateful to see that, unlike the rest of the ship, the hawsers and clenches were well maintained. The bolts were greased and the first one moved easily in his hand. The clamouring became louder as the prisoners realised that somebody was trying to set them free. The cries and entreaties became increasingly pitiful as the water inexorably filled the hold.

Another shot flew close over his head and Hunter risked looking up to see where the cutter was. It had closed to two hundred metres and from the sound of the engine it too was well maintained. Hardly surprising, thought Hunter, as it was their escape route. He looked at Ruth who had taken the *Papillon* into irons and was now sitting with the sails down and the engine running. She had heard the shots and moved closer to the ship, hidden from the men in the boat.

Hunter stayed low, slithered across the deck and said, 'Go around the bows and when I start shooting, open up with the Uzi. Okay?'

Ruth circled her thumb and forefinger. She pushed the gear

lever into ahead and inched along the coaster, the Uzi slung over her right shoulder, cocked, ready to fire. Hunter undid another two bolts before a fusillade of bullets forced him to slide crab like along the deck to hide behind the lip of the hatch. When the boat was less than a hundred metres away he knelt on one knee, took aim and emptied the automatic at the boat. He had the advantage over its occupants. He was on a stable platform while they had been pitching up and down on a sea that was now running over a metre high. At the same time Ruth appeared from around the front of the freighter and opened fire with the Uzi, spraying the area around the cutter. Either Hunter or Ruth hit a figure standing up in the boat, for a man suddenly threw his arms in the air and pitched into the sea. The smugglers, in fear of their lives, turned and headed away at speed.

The moment Hunter saw the boat begin to veer away, he returned to his task and continued unscrewing the bolts. A fourth bolt quickly followed and he moved to the next four. Frantically now, as the screams became louder and the panic more endemic, he undid the fifth bolt. The hatch moved a few centimetres. With another bolt removed, the hatch opened sufficiently for a small, scrawny figure to wriggle through. It lay on the deck, sobbing. Another shackle sprang open and now the hatch was wide enough to let a few more small bodies scrape through. None of them came to help him as he started on the last shackle. In the hold the noises were becoming more sinister. He could hear desperate people arguing. A hand appeared but even as it did, it vanished again as that person was dragged back to let somebody else try and escape. The last shackle was a struggle. His hands were covered in grease and gripping the bolt was difficult. Two and then three people emerged, all adults. No one tried to help as they desperately looked around for a way of saving themselves. Two of them rushed for the lifeboat that was still hanging in its davits. Hunter ignored them, undid the last remaining bolt and threw open the hatch.

The sea was within half a metre of the deck and Hunter knew that at any second the ship could slip beneath the water, taking those still in the hold with it. Reaching down he indiscriminately grabbed a hand and unceremoniously pulled the person up and literally flung them to one side. He kept grabbing, pulling, freeing. Suddenly the ship lurched to one side, and he knew that he had only moments left and still the opening was alive with waving hands and shrieking mouths. Some grabbed the sides and pulled themselves out but Hunter was able to reach those in the middle and pull them through. The ship lurched again and began to slide beneath the waves. Even as the coaster sank, Hunter heard Ruth's voice above the noise shouting at him to jump clear. Instead, he kept pulling people free. With the water lapping at the deck others rolled clear and still Hunter was pulling bodies out. He was appalled. How many were there, for God's sake?

The hold was now full of water and at last it seemed that the number of hands in the opening was finally lessening. He grabbed them and pulled them free just as the ship went straight down. Grabbing the last two by their collars, scrawny youngsters, frantic with panic, he took a deep breath as the suction pulled them down. He kicked his feet hard, his head up, their struggling bodies growing limp by his side. The suction pulled them further down but at two metres the hydrostatic switch on the pencil-thin life jacket he wore around his neck clicked in. The jacket inflated and he felt himself rising, the pressure on his ears easing. Hitting the surface he spat out seawater, took a deep breath and awkwardly checked the two bodies he was holding. One gave a groan, gagged and chucked up seawater, gasping in air. The other stayed inert in his grip. He let go the one who was breathing, spun the other body around and put his arms around it. Holding tightly, he gave three body-wrenching squeezes, turned the body face to and began mouth to mouth. He pushed in six deep breaths and repeated the performance. This time the body convulsed and spewed water. The youngster began to thrash around in panic. Hunter grabbed him around the shoulders and swam towards the *Papillon*, easily pulling the slight body with him.

A scream broke into his reverie and he lifted his head. Two men were attacking Ruth. Letting go the youngster, he yelled,

33

'Swim!' and broke into a fast crawl, hitting the diving platform and launching himself into the cockpit. He went berserk.

Alleysia was content. With Glover dead her secret was safe. She had been forced to make an example of the man responsible for security at the hotel but it was necessary. His death would be a warning to the others that she would never tolerate sloppiness. Otherwise there was no doubt that the meeting in Columbia had been a great success. A voice interrupted her thoughts and brought her back to the present.

'Oh, Duchess,' she smiled at the plump, redhead. 'Forgive me, I was daydreaming. How lovely to see you again.' A flawless smile hid her unkind thoughts about the Duchess' frumpishness. Could it be true that she was now having an affair with an Italian count ten years younger than she was? 'What a wonderful gathering. The great and the good, all here for charity.' Alleysia's English had the merest hint of an accent. She spoke four other languages with the same ease.

The fashion show in Monte Carlo was being hosted by Princess Stephanie to raise money for children in need across Europe. The clothes exhibited were wonderful creations by the world's top designers, which, if valued by their weight per ounce or gram, would be the most expensive items in existence. Alleysia hated such affairs but knew they were necessary. Networking provided many useful contacts and she heard a lot of important gossip. The trivial ramblings of empty-headed wives had proven very useful in the past when blackmail was called for. She could think of two judges and half a dozen European politicians who had learnt that fact – to their cost.

'It was very generous of you to pay so much for that dress.' The English Duchess prattled on while Alleysia tried to tune her out of her thoughts. If she had to be there at least she could use the time sensibly by planning ahead. She particularly wanted to think about her trip to Vladivostock. She wished the damn woman would go away and leave her in peace. Alleysia's smiling mask revealed nothing of her thoughts.

4

General Macnair's mood was bleak as he sat in his office at TIFAT headquarters and looked down at the River Forth glinting in the distance. Although he had been woken early with a report on Hunter's skirmish in the Mediterranean his low spirits had another cause – the Colombian summit. The transcript of the CIA agent's tape had been very useful – crucial. Now Macnair's paper had been finished and forwarded to the relevant agencies all he could do was wait and see. Let it be read with an open mind, he prayed. No doubt he would be labelled a xenophobe but he could deal with that. The statistical proof was overwhelming. The recent DEA briefing had shown that.

When the details of the Colombian summit meeting had been forwarded to him, Macnair had known that it was time to put his head above the parapet. The report he had written was the result. The meeting between the relevant senior government ministers had already taken place and he was waiting to hear their decisions. What would be the outcome? Orders to disband TIFAT or to remove him? Or would his conclusions and recommendations carry the day? They were shared by every senior policeman, heads of intelligence organisations and senior officers of every branch of the armed forces across the free world. A veteran, Macnair had mustered all the back up he could. Support had come from surprising quarters. Every revolution needed a spark. Now all he could do was wait.

The phone rang. 'Macnair.' At the sound of the voice on the other end the hand holding the receiver trembled slightly with tension. He listened and then said in a calm tone, 'Thank you. I'll get on to it right away.' He broke the connection and dialled an internal number. 'Jim? My office, now, please.'

A few moments later Major Jim Carter, TIFAT's quartermaster, appeared. He stopped in the doorway when he saw Macnair was smiling. A sight he hadn't seen in days.

'We won the argument. Just. In accordance with the American Secretary of State's policy speech, World War III has been declared. Only we shan't be telling the public for a while.' The Secretary of State had declared in a recent speech that WW III had started – the war against terrorists and the drug cartels.

Carter returned his boss's smile. 'Excellent. They won't know what's hit them.'

Macnair nodded. 'No quarter is to be given. The intention is that there are to be no trials unless it is unavoidable and mandatory thirty-year sentences will be handed out. You know, Jim, a lot hinged on that tape. Luckily, the man Glover spoke to before he died was a rarity in Colombia – an honest policeman. The tape was water logged and badly corrupted but Langley received it within forty-eight hours and the transcription has proven very useful.' He paused and added, 'I'd like to know what was missing though. Langley said they'd continue working on it but didn't hold out much hope of learning any more.' Frowning, he tapped a tattoo with his fingers on his desk before saying, 'Recall Hunter. I need him here.'

'But, sir! This is the first leave he's had in nearly a year,' Carter protested. 'And even when he's on leave he gets involved with a drugs bust.'

Macnair nodded. 'All right. Give him another three days. Then I want him back. And no arguments.'

Hunter knew now that he was in love with Ruth. He would do anything in the world to protect her. Seeing her being held by one man and beaten by another, his anger knew no limits. He hit the stern of the yacht and came over the side all in one smooth movement. The man hitting her felt a heavy hand on his shoulder, a smashing blow to his arm that left it numb and then he was flying through the air into the water. The other man who was holding Ruth still had his mouth open in surprise when Hunter turned on him. Grabbing him by the throat, Hunter smashed a fist into his face and broke his hold on Ruth. The man was heavy set, at least three inches taller than Hunter, a mountain of a man turned to flab. Two fast blows to the belly had the man doubled over. Hunter grabbed him by the hair, lifted his face and hit him across the jaw. At the last second Hunter had changed the blow. Instead of using the palm of his hand into the nose and sweeping the cartilage into the skull, a deathblow, he had moved to incapacitate the man instead. Ruth's assailant staggered backwards, tripped on a deck cleat, fell heavily and hit his neck across a hatch surround. His neck broke with an audible crack.

The other man was hanging onto the side of the yacht with his good arm and Hunter knelt down, grabbing him by his collar. 'What were you trying to do?' he snarled, his face inches from the other man's.

The man said something in a language Hunter couldn't understand.

'Speak English, *Deutsch* or *Francais*,' Hunter said.

'*Nichts, nichts,*' the man answered in German.

'*Sprechen Sie Deutsch?*'

'*Ja. Ja. Kann ich. Ein wenig.*'

'What were you doing?' Hunter asked in fluent German. 'Why did you attack Ruth?'

'It was a mistake. We thought she was one of them.'

Hunter looked into the other's eyes and could see that the man was lying. Disgustedly Hunter let go of him and left him hanging there. By now the boat was surrounded by swimmers, some trying to climb on board while others yelled pitifully for help. A catastrophe was in the making. The *Papillon* rocked alarmingly as people clambered aboard. Hunter had no time to ponder on the man's last words. He picked up the Uzi and fired into the air. The pandemonium subsided to sobs and whimpers and the men, women and children stopped trying to climb onto the yacht.

'Does anybody speak English?' he shouted.

'Yes.' Voices chorused back at him.

'Right, translate what I tell you. I will shoot anybody who tries to climb onto this boat without my say so.' He waited while his words were interpreted. 'There is a danger of capsizing.' Again he paused and listened, not understanding the languages being used. He was sure that the people in the water represented at least three different countries. 'Children under fifteen swim to the back of the boat and come aboard. Go straight down below.' He looked into the companionway to see Jana's white, fearful face looking up at him. 'Jana, come up here and show yourself.' She did as she was told and there were gasps from some of the people still in the water. 'Jana will help you. Come on, hurry up.'

The youngsters swam to the back of the boat and began to clamber onboard. They stepped over the body still lying on the deck without a second look. They had all seen dead people before. 'Ruth, find towels and any spare clothes we have. It doesn't matter whether they fit – they need to get out of their wet things.' He helped the youngsters aboard. One man swam forward and pushed his way onto the diving platform. Hunter hit him across the side of the head with the Uzi and he fell into the water, stunned. He surfaced spluttering, spitting out water and invective in a language Hunter did not recognise. When Hunter cocked the gun and aimed it, the man shut up.

'Perhaps I did not make myself clear. I will shoot. We have to save you all and we cannot do so by allowing the boat to be swamped. That's it. Nice and easy,' he smiled and spoke softly to the children as they clambered aboard. 'Down you go.' He turned to Ruth. 'Find as many life jackets as we have and give them to the poorer swimmers amongst the women.'

One woman called out and the woman next to her translated. 'She is pregnant. She can't swim for much longer.'

'Tell her to come aboard. How many have gone below?' he asked Ruth.

'I think twenty-two. They're sitting on the deck to lower the centre of gravity. I told them to sit quietly as we are too heavily laden.' Even as she was speaking Ruth was opening the life jacket locker and throwing out jackets to those women she thought were in greatest difficulties. In all she threw eight overboard.

'Good.' Hunter did a rapid head count and guessed there were still as many as thirty to thirty-five people in the water. The pregnant woman climbed onto the diving platform and into the cockpit. She looked big enough to have almost gone her full term.

Ruth was addressing those to whom she had thrown the lifejackets. 'Pull it on over your head and press the buckles together on either side. After that pull the toggle.' Even as her words were being translated, she could see that those in the water were grouping together in small numbers and she guessed that they were probably families and friends. As the life jackets were inflated she could see the relief on the faces of others as they held on to the jackets as well.

'Can you take her below and see she's all right, please?' Hunter asked Ruth, who nodded in reply. 'Okay,' he raised his voice, 'the rest of you swim over to the boat and hold on to the sides. Those who have life jackets on,' he continued, picking up a coil of nylon rope, tying one end to an aft cleat and throwing it across the sea, 'catch hold of this rope and stay with the boat. Those of you who can, hold on to somebody wearing a life jacket. Don't drift away, whatever you do. We won't be able to help you.' Some semblance of order was beginning to take shape. Now that the children were safely onboard, the grown-ups appeared resigned to their situation. Nobody was fighting or arguing. They realised that to survive they needed to do what Hunter told them. Taking the opportunity, Hunter bent over the body still on the boat and checked the pockets. Inside he found a wallet and, to his surprise, a bible. Frowning he flicked through the wallet. It was empty. The bible he threw onto a seat, unable to bring himself to throw it away. Had he killed a religious man? Shaking his head he didn't for one second believe it. Grabbing the body by the shoulders he pushed it under the guard-rail and into the water. As the clothes became waterlogged it sank from sight.

One of the women holding on to the side of the boat said, 'Please, sir. I ask you something?'

Hunter nodded. 'Sure. Ask away.'

'We want to know what is to happen. We cannot stay like this much longer.'

'No, of course not. The Spanish navy is already on its way here.' He looked at his watch and did a mental calculation. 'I would think in the next two hours. I shall radio them and find out exactly when they will arrive.'

She translated what he had told her and a man asked another question. 'Please, sir,' he spoke ingratiatingly, 'what is to happen to us then?'

Hunter shrugged. 'You will be taken somewhere warm and safe in Spain and the authorities will deal with you.' He hoped he sounded reassuring. If they knew that he was aware they were carrying drugs and that they were going to be arrested they might attack him and Ruth and hang the consequences. He watched their faces as the woman translated what he had said. Some had tentative smiles, others scowled and glowered at him. He had been thinking about using channel 16 to call the Spanish navy but their expressions convinced him that it would not be a good idea to leave the cockpit. He saw a few of the men muttering and glancing darkly at him and he guessed that they were looking at ways of overpowering him. There were half a dozen or so cluttered around the starboard side. They looked to be a rough lot. One of them moved a hand and Hunter realised that they were surreptitiously moving along the boat, trying to work their way past the others to get nearer to him.

'Ruth, go and call on channel 16. Give the Spaniards our lat and long and explain our situation. See if they can get a helicopter in the air and search for the other boat. Ask for an E.T.A. and if they are going to be more than two hours ask if somebody can drop a couple of life rafts.' He smiled at her. 'If you hear any shooting ignore it.'

'What?'

'Trouble's brewing and I need to nip it in the bud. That's all. Nothing to worry about.'

'I'm not worried about you,' she smiled back. 'I'm worried about them.' With that she went below.

Hunter stared at the man he had thrown off the yacht who had now moved past two others on the boat and was less than a metre away. He looked up at Hunter who took a pace nearer to him. Smiling calmly down at the upturned face, Hunter smashed the butt of the Uzi on the knuckles of his left hand. The man screamed in pain as Hunter swung the gun around and pointed it at his head. He then pointed it at each of the individuals he suspected of being privy to their action. When he got to the last man, Hunter altered his aim, flicked the safety to single shot and fired just over the man's shoulder. There were screams and yells. He fired again and shouted. 'Shut up. You six,' he looked at them and he could see that some of them understood. 'If you move again I'll kill you. Do I make myself clear?' The men glowered their hatred at him. 'Do you understand?' he yelled at them. They nodded nervously. None of them doubted his sincerity.

Ruth reappeared, took in what was happening with one glance and reported, 'They'll be another three hours at least. The ship was late in departing Barcelona. A helicopter is being sent from the ship with life rafts and will be here in twenty minutes. Another two are being despatched to look for the cutter. The authorities are being alerted along the coast so there is a possibility those that got away will be picked up.'

'I wouldn't hold my breath if I were you,' said Hunter, aware of the casual attitude of the Spanish authorities from previous encounters. 'But I'm willing to be pleasantly surprised. The kids down below – are they okay?'

Ruth shrugged. 'They're a strong lot. They've been through so much and seen such a great deal already, they need to be tough just to survive. I thought we were tenacious and stubborn in Israel but this lot . . .' She shook her head in amazement.

'You're right. I think we need to be on our guard.' He nodded at the men who were trying to cause trouble, making it clear that they were talking about them. 'Watch them like a hawk. If they try anything either call me or shoot one of them.' Hunter pointed two fingers at one of the men and moved his thumb in the age-old gesture of a gun being fired. He wanted them to be absolutely clear as to what would happen if they tried anything. The man didn't even flinch but sneered openly at him.

From astern, one of the people hanging onto the rope called, 'Please, sir. What is happening? I cannot hold on for much longer.' The man was holding on to the rope with his hand on the life jacket worn by a woman alongside him. He was looking haggard, his strength waning.

'Listen everybody,' Hunter shouted. 'A helicopter is on its way with life rafts. They'll be here any minute. When they're dropped, climb inside where you should find food and drink.' Even as he spoke a droning sound became louder and a few seconds later a helicopter came into sight. Hunter recognised the Lynx Mk. 95 that had been modified with the Racal tactical data system and sold to the Portuguese and Spanish navies only a few years earlier.

Hunter waved and the helicopter dropped into a hover less than half a cable away. The down wash from the blades churned up the water and the people swimming turned their heads away. Two yellow objects tumbled out of the open door in quick succession and the helicopter accelerated away, taking its down wash with it. The two heavy objects sank two metres under the sea where the water pressure released the hydrostatic catches. The life rafts rapidly inflated and popped to the surface, floating there like yellow boils on a blue skin.

'Swim over to the rafts. Go on,' Hunter yelled. The people clung where they were, afraid to let go of the relative safety of the boat to swim across the open sea to the much greater safety of the rafts. 'Go on. You'll be all right.'

Those with life jackets let go of the rope and began to swim towards the nearest life raft, towing one and sometimes two others with them. A few of the braver souls holding on to the sides of the *Papillon* let go and also began to swim away. Once these few started the rest followed, and with relief Hunter felt the yacht float a bit more easily in the water. The last to go was the man who had been causing all the trouble. He looked Hunter in the eyes, said something and spat in the water.

Hunter smiled coldly at him and said in German, 'I don't know what you said but I'd like to meet you again.'

'My name is Stavios.' The reply was in good, but heavily accented English. 'I will look forward to it.' His lack of knowledge of the language had been a pretence all along.

By now most of them had climbed into the covered life rafts and were breaking out the high protein food and fresh water they found in the pockets. There was a flare up of tempers and one person who was trying to climb aboard was pushed off and into the sea. Somebody screamed, there was a loud slap and the scream turned into sobs. As much as he itched to, there was nothing Hunter could do. He looked at Ruth who shrugged wearily. She sat down in the cockpit and relaxed for the first time in hours.

'There's never a dull moment around you, my darling, that's for sure,' she said.

He smiled at her. 'I was about to say the same thing to you.'

Ruth laughed. 'What's that Chinese saying? May you live in interesting times?'

'Actually, it's a Chinese curse. I prefer Helen Keller's motto – Life is a daring adventure.'

'That I can believe. So what do we do now?'

'We just wait until the navy gets here. You know, there's a certain irony to getting caught up in all this so soon after the briefing I had.'

'I suppose so. But considering the scale of smuggling perhaps its not so unusual after all. What is unusual is the fact that you saw it, as opposed to an ordinary, law-abiding citizen.'

'You mean I'm not law-abiding?' he teased.

'Hardly,' Ruth replied, dryly. 'Why was there so much hostility from that man, I wonder?'

Hunter shrugged. 'I think he's one of the spies. A nasty piece of work.' Picking up the bible he'd found he flicked through its pages. The fact that it was written in English surprised him. In Joshua, chapter 15, verse 47, he came across the word Ashdod underlined in pencil. Continuing to flick through the book, he changed the subject. 'Have the kids below been given anything to drink?'

'Yes. Jana saw to that almost as soon as they were onboard. She told me she was training to be a doctor before the war.'

'What? She looks too young.'

'That's more a sign of your age, Nick. She had two years of her course behind her. Now she can't finish it. It's such a shame. What will happen to them do you think?'

'They'll be taken to a detention centre and processed. After that, God alone knows. To be honest, I don't know what will happen. They might be deported or, if they can prove a good case, be allowed to stay.'

'What sort of case?'

'Usually they have to prove that their lives are in danger should they be sent back. In many cases that isn't so. However, for some it is. It's the difficulties in separating the bogus asylum seekers from the bona fide cases that cause the problem.'

'What about Jana? Her life genuinely seems to be in danger.'

'I agree. I've been thinking about her. Why don't we save her a lot of time and trouble? Ask her to come up here just in case some of the others understand English. Tell her she can stay on and we'll help her.'

'Before I do, where did you get that bible?'

'I found it on one of the men I killed. There are a few words underlined in pencil but I can't see anything else special about it. And the words don't make any sense. Oh well,' he shrugged, throwing the book down again. 'It's probably nothing.'

Ruth nodded. 'I'll get Jana.' She called down and a few seconds later Jana appeared. 'Nick and I have just been talking. When the ship comes for the others, you stay below out of sight. We'll take you ashore and sort something out.'

Jana smiled tentatively and said, 'That is kind of you, but I do not have anywhere to go and nobody to help me. When I was on the ship everything was arranged. Now I will have to go back to Albania.'

'Is that what you want?' Hunter asked.

'No. I wish to study and become a doctor. Then I would go back and help my people.'

Hunter frowned. 'Do you have a passport?'

'No. It was taken from me on the ship.'

'Okay. That's still not a problem. We'll take you to Gibraltar. From there you can fly to Britain and resume your medical studies.'

'What are you saying?' said Jana. 'How can I go to university? I have no money. I will not be allowed into Britain without a passport.'

Hunter put his hands on Jana's shoulders and looked at her squarely. 'You will go to Britain and attend a university, I promise you that. You will become a doctor. You will not want for money. Leave it to me.'

There was something about the way that he spoke that filled Jana with hope. 'You mean this? You do not joke?'

'I mean it. My family has a trust that pays out to deserving people, those who otherwise couldn't afford a proper education. Mainly it is used for people from the third world, India and Africa in particular, but I'll make a case for you. So don't worry. You can finish your education and become a doctor. There's only one condition.'

'What is that?' she was suddenly wary.

'You become a good one,' he smiled.

Jana laughed, clapping her hands together with joy. 'Oh yes. I will become a very good doctor. But first,' she looked down below, 'I must try and help these people.' She went into the saloon while Hunter started the engine and turned the boat into the sea. The rocking motion turned into a more comfortable pitching and he sat down to rest.

Ruth was looking at him wonderingly. 'Can you really do that?'

'What? Oh, sure. No problem. And if I can't get the money out of the trust I'll pay for it myself, though Jana will never know. It'll just be easier if she has an official offer of a Scottish bursary. That way she'll have no trouble getting into Britain. She'll need to improve her English but she seems bright enough and a few weeks of cramming will help.'

'Nick, you're incredible.'

'I am?' Hunter was startled. 'You mean . . .' he raised his eyebrows suggestively and Ruth smiled.

'No. I mean the dichotomy of your personality. You're a kind, considerate man who can kill without compunction.'

He shrugged. 'I actually think that if we don't do something soon the world will go to hell in a basket. If we keep turning the other cheek, if we don't stand up to be counted, the bad guys will win. Look at the way drug dealers are targeting our schools. And not just secondary schools but primary! In the sixties and seventies it was the universities. Now look what's happening.'

'We don't have the same problem in Israel,' said Ruth. 'We are too concerned with the everyday need to survive. It's wonderful how such a requirement focuses our minds on the important things.'

'It makes you think. Maybe a good war would sort out the west.'

'Nick! You're kidding aren't you?'

He smiled. 'Of course I am. But we need to do something. The drugs industry world wide has a turnover ten times bigger then the GNP of Israel.'

'Good Lord.' Ruth put her hand to her throat as the enormity of it all sank in. 'Surely something can be done? What about the United Nations? Nato? The upholders of law and order? Anybody.'

'At the moment, it's a police matter. Right now we don't have the go-ahead to do anything. The criminals are arrested and brought to trial. Oh, and we must remember these people have *human rights*. The victims don't, but the criminals do.' He shrugged. 'We can't win playing by our rules. We have to play by theirs. TIFAT was set up to do just that but we still have to be given instructions to operate. Macnair is working hard to be given the green light. What I learnt at last week's briefing is that by comparison to the enemy, we are under financed, under resourced and under manned.'

The transom loudspeaker in the cockpit burst into life.

'*Le Beau Papillon, Le Beau Papillon*, this is warship channel 16, over.'

'I'll answer it,' said Hunter. He went below into the chart room.

'Warship, this is *Le Beau Papillon*, over.'

'This is warship. Go to channel one two.'

'Roger. Going down.' Hunter turned the dial and re-established contact.

'We have you on radar and will be with you in twenty minutes. Over.'

'Roger, warship. Twenty minutes. Listening channel one six. Out.' He stepped out of the chartroom and stood there for a few seconds. The saloon was full of faces looking at him, some fearfully, some defiantly. The door behind him opened and one of the girls came out of the master cabin, adjusting her clothes. He heard Jana behind her call something and another girl stood up. She looked embarrassed. She ducked her head and went quickly into the cabin and closed the door behind her.

Intrigued, Hunter knocked on the door. It opened and Jana put her head out, saw Hunter and started guiltily. 'What's going on?' he asked.

'I'm . . . I'm sorry. I have to help them.'

'Help them? How?'

'By getting rid of the drugs. The authorities must not find them. They will go to prison for many years. I have to help them. They cannot help themselves. Everybody is carrying drugs. You know, inside them.' She pointed at her vagina and backside.

'Why don't they just take a box of the stuff ashore along with the people?'

'It buys them time. If they are caught with the drugs on them they will go to a heavily secure prison to await trial. If they are taken along with the rest of us as immigrants we go to camps which we can just walk out of. By the time the authorities discover the truth the men behind it are far away, taking the drugs with them.'

That made sense. Hunter was about to argue that the authorities should take the youngsters as well, but reconsidered. They were only kids, after all. More exploited than bad. He nodded. 'All right, but you had better make it quick. The Spanish will be here in less than twenty minutes. What about the grownups? Will they be doing likewise?'

'I don't know. They have no reason to believe that the Spanish will be searching them. So they probably hope that all is well and they will be treated sympathetically after what has happened to them and they will be allowed into the country.'

'In that case,' Hunter said grimly, 'they are in for a shock.' With that he returned to the cockpit. He scanned the horizon with his binoculars and easily saw the looming grey outline of a frigate steaming at full speed towards them. He thought for a second and then returned to the chartroom and made contact with the frigate again. He had a brief but satisfactory conversation with the first lieutenant Pedro Gonzalez, who would be coming over in the ship's sea boat.

A short while later the ship hove to and a boat was launched. It carried a fully armed complement of men.

5

All the children except Jana were ferried to the frigate. She stayed down below, out of sight until the ship departed.

Soon the frigate was behind them as they headed south-west towards the British protectorate of Gibraltar. In the evening Hunter heard the boat's name being called on one three two megahertz and went below to answer it.

'Nick, it is I, Lt Cdr. Gonzalez. Over.'

'Hi, Pedro. Reading you loud and clear. What do you have for me? Over.'

'The adults were full of heroin. We have collected nearly ten kilos in all. The adults have been arrested but I do not know what is intended. None of the children were carrying anything so they will be transported back home as soon as possible. Over.'

'Good. Thanks for the information and well done. Over.'

'It was nothing. You did all the work. Unfortunately we did not find the occupants of the boat you told us about. I'm sorry. Over.'

'Thank you for that, Pedro. It doesn't matter. The effort is much appreciated. I may see you again one day. Over.'

'Roger, Nick. Out.'

'This is the *Papillon*, out.'

Hunter used his binoculars to scan the horizon, matching ships' lights to the radar picture. Jana appeared, carrying a mug of soup and a sandwich. She held it out to him and he took it gratefully.

She paused. Hunter looked at her. She evidently wanted to say something. 'I want to thank you. For everything.'

'It was nothing. Anybody would have done the same.'

'Anybody may want to do the same,' she corrected him, 'but few,' she groped for the words in English, 'could have done it. You not only save my life but you are offering me my dream. Words aren't enough.'

'Sure they are,' said Hunter. 'Just work hard and make your parents proud.'

Tears appeared in Jana's eyes, reflected in the pool of light from the companionway and the loom of the overtaking light on the stern. 'They are dead. Killed by the Serbs.'

'I'm so sorry. I should have realised.'

'Since a year ago now.'

'No other family?'

'A brother and sister. If I do well I can take care of them.' Hunter realised for the first time how utterly vulnerable people like Jana were and how easily they could be exploited by ruthless men, like those who ran the drugs cartels. He wondered what threats some of the adults had been subjected to before they agreed to work for the criminals. It was easy, he thought, to condemn without understanding. Rounding up the drugs carriers, the mules as they were known, was practically a waste of time. They needed to get the big-time operators, the men who gave the orders and used coercion and fear to achieve their ends.

Sailing through the night Hunter sat peacefully at the helm, the bible he'd found intruding on his thoughts. They arrived at the outer wall of Gibraltar harbour at 03.00 and went in through the southern entrance. They tied up on the South Mole astern of a Type 42 destroyer. He had been given permission to enter the dockyard as opposed to the yacht marina thanks to his rank. They were met by a duty military policeman, who checked Hunter's identity card, saluted, refused a drink and left them to a quiet night. The sound of the boatswain's call at 08.00 woke Hunter. He listened to the eight-second single high note with a smile.

'What's that whistle?' Ruth asked, sleepily.

'It's a bosun's call. The ensign is being hoisted. Listen.' There sounded a single second high note and a single second low note. 'That's the "carry on". Now the hands will turn to and get to

50

work. While I,' he snuggled under the duvet, reaching for Ruth, 'have a better idea.'

She giggled delightedly.

In the middle of the morning Hunter was taking the inflatable dinghy across the harbour when he had to avoid a large speedboat that was travelling too fast in the confined waters. Stifling his irritation and natural response he watched it head out to sea. He noticed the red eye painted on the stern and the name, *An Evil Eye*. Tying up near the dockyard gate he was walking away from the boat when he stopped, frowning. He knew that name from somewhere. Where? He thought for a moment, returned to the inflatable and headed back to the yacht. Sitting in the cockpit onboard *La Papillon*, he sipped a fresh coffee while he flicked through the bible. Grabbing a pen, he wrote down the words he found underlined. There it was. St. Mark, chapter seven, verse twenty-two. An evil eye. Finishing his coffee he climbed back into the inflatable and looked to the North Mole where a marina had been built a few years earlier. Scanning the boats through his binoculars an idea crystallised into a certainty.

Returning in the inflatable, he tied up near the dockyard gate and went ashore, walking up the hill to Main Street. There, at the southern end, was the Governor's Residence, originally a Franciscan convent built in 1531. He asked to meet the military attaché. Hunter's name, rank and the name of TIFAT saw him ushered in within seconds. The man behind the desk was a dapper major from a Scottish regiment. He held out his hand and welcomed Hunter.

'Sam York. What can I do for you, Commander?'

'Call me Nick.'

'I'm Sam. So what can I do for you?' he repeated.

'I picked up a young lady two days ago.' He saw the look on the other's face and hastily added. 'No, no, nothing like that. I'm giving her a lift. She's lost her passport. This is her bursary confirmation that was faxed to the boat this morning. She is on her way to Edinburgh University. Can you get her on a flight and let immigration at the other end deal with her?'

'Sure. I'll get a copy made and forwarded to London. What about air tickets? Will there be anyone to meet her?'

'Yes. The air tickets will be waiting for her at the BA desk and somebody will meet her from Griffiths & Co, the merchant bank. They run the bursary.'

'Okay. I'll arrange a temporary travel permit. When she gets to London she can go to her own embassy and get another passport.'

'Thanks, Sam. It's much appreciated. In return would you like to join me for dinner? My treat.'

'That's kind. Did you see the *Manchester*?'

'Yes. I'm berthed directly astern of her.'

'There's a cocktail party on board this evening. Why not come? We can go to dinner afterwards.'

'Excellent. I'll enjoy that. I have someone else with me. My girlfriend.' It was the first time Hunter had used the word to describe his relationship with Ruth. It felt good.

'No problem. She's invited as well.'

'Thanks.'

'When is the other young lady due to fly out?'

'This afternoon. That's why I came to see you. Hoping you could short circuit matters.'

'Take her to the airport and I'll have the papers waiting for her at the BA desk.'

'Thanks. Let me ask you something. What's the drug situation like around here? Is there much smuggling going on?'

York frowned. 'A lot more than we care to admit. Why?'

Hunter briefly related his experience.

'It doesn't surprise me. Cocaine is the really big problem, of course, but heroin is definitely on the increase.'

'Why of course?'

'It's somehow the respectable end of the drugs market. Well,' he paused, 'not respectable exactly. It's the well heeled who use it. The jet set. So a blind eye is often turned to the problem. Nowadays if you claim personal use in Spain you aren't even arrested. If you're caught dealing then that's different. Heroin is treated differently again. Even a user ends up in court.'

'Do you know the names of the boats in the marina? The visitors?'

'I don't, but I can easily find out. Why?'

Hunter explained his theory.

'Give me a second.' Lifting the telephone he dialled an outside line. Moments later he was speaking to the manager of the marina. Replacing the receiver he said to Hunter, 'There's a fax on its way with a list of the names of the boats that are visiting. Can I get you a coffee in the meantime?'

They swapped stories about their respective careers for a few minutes until a knock came on the door. A secretary appeared carrying a sheet of paper. She placed it on the desk and left. York handed it across to Hunter who quickly scanned it. Nothing showed of the excitement he was feeling. Without a word he handed across the list of names he had compiled from the bible.

York compared them and sat up straight. 'They're all here. Every one of them.'

'There could be some more.'

'Can you leave this with me? We've got sniffer dogs at the barracks. Let me speak to the senior policeman. He's a Chief Superintendent from London. He and I were discussing the problem a few nights ago. There's a lot more heroin appearing. And I don't just mean here on the Rock but right along the coast of Spain. I'll arrange something for the morning. Want to come along for the ride?'

'Sure. I wouldn't miss it for the world.'

With those words Hunter left to return to the *Papillon*. Main Street was the main shopping street and as Hunter emerged he met Ruth and Jana laden down with shopping.

'We've been indulging in a little retail therapy, haven't we, Jana?'

'Ruth has been very kind. I never owned so many wonderful things in my life.'

'Good.' Hunter did not enlighten her as to where the money came from. After all, why be a member of one of the richest families in Britain if you couldn't indulge your whims now and then? He was delighted to see Jana smiling. She would make a good doctor some day, if her compassion for the children on the yacht was anything to go by. She had admitted to throwing more than twenty condoms of heroin over the side, a fortune by anybody's standards.

He told them his news about Jana's flight but instead of it being greeted happily Jana looked saddened and pulled a face.

'We had been planning a special dinner for tonight,' said Ruth. 'But it can't be helped. We'll do it some other time in Scotland. Nick, take these.' She handed him the bags she was carrying and then took some from Jana. 'We'd better get back and get organised.'

In the middle of the afternoon they said farewell to Jana. Boarding the plane, she glanced back. Her eyes conveyed her apprehension at what lay ahead yet they were also bright with expectation.

They returned to the *Papillon* where Hunter spent a pleasant few hours repairing and working on the yacht. There were crinkles to fit to canvas and ropes to fit with soft and hard eyes. While working with his hands, his mind was in over-drive. He had an idea for the morning, which he would pass on to York.

In the early evening he and Ruth showered and changed. Hunter wore a cream suit with a blue shirt and the London Naval Officer's Club tie with its gold crown motif, while Ruth's black dress suited her to perfection. They stood on the quayside and watched as the cars drew up and disgorged the good and the great of Gibraltar society.

Arm in arm, they strolled towards the forward gangway. The ship had been decorated for the occasion with various flags and bunting to give her a festive look. Awnings had been erected as soon as the ship had docked. In the evening sun there was a gaiety about her that belied the fact that she carried more armament than a squadron of ships of her size fifty years earlier. Hunter let Ruth walk up the gangway ahead of him. As he stepped onboard he automatically saluted. He had expected to have to give his name but was pleased to see that the Officer of the Day, responsible for the running of the ship while in harbour and wearing the white ice cream suit, as it was disrespectfully known, was an old friend.

'Robbo,' said Hunter with a grin, holding out his hand.

'Nick,' the grin on Lt Cdr John Robertson's face was equally wide. 'It's good to see you.'

'Let me introduce Ruth. Ruth, this is Robbo. What are you doing here?'

'I'm PWO. It's a good job as we are Captain "D" for the squadron.' A Type 42 was normally commanded by a three-stripe commander, "D" would be a senior four-stripe captain. A good report from such a senior officer could do wonders for promotion from lieutenant commander to commander. Commander was recognised as the first rank of self-respect by the officers of the Royal Navy. It was the first promotion earned and not given automatically. The Principal Warfare Officer was the man who literally helped the Captain to fight the ship. 'Got here just before work-up and then we came on this deployment. Look, go ahead and I'll catch up with you after I've seen the last of the guests onboard.'

Hunter led the way forward. As they stepped onto the fore deck, a steward holding a drinks tray offered it to them and Hunter said to Ruth, 'G and T or a Horse's Neck?' He indicated the different coloured drinks on the tray.

'What's a Horse's Neck?'

'Brandy and ginger ale. Very refreshing,' he added, helping himself to a gin and tonic.

'I'll try one,' she said. He handed her a glass and she took an appreciative sip. They wandered into the crowd, Hunter meeting a few other officers he knew until he came to a stop, a wide grin on his face. 'The last time I saw that profile was on *HMS Dryad*,' he said.

The lieutenant commander with the red colouring between her stripes turned, gave a squeal of delight and threw her arms around him. 'Nick, how wonderful! What on earth are you doing here? I didn't see your name on the guest list.'

'Hullo, Jacqui. I wangled an invitation this afternoon. Jacqui let me introduce Ruth. Ruth, this is Jacqueline Turner, a dentist by profession.' The last time the two of them had met was whilst serving at the naval shore base, *HMS Dryad*, in Hampshire. Hunter had been in charge of a clearance diving team and Jaqui had been the base's dentist. Their friendship had never been more than platonic, a fact that Hunter regretted at the time.

The two women eyed each other warily. Jacqui was a blonde who had received more than her share of wolf whistles in her time – usually from behind her back and usually from politically incorrect naval ratings.

'How do you do?' Jacqui said.

Ruth nodded and coolly returned the greeting.

'So what are you doing here?' Hunter asked.

'I'm on the Rock, at the hospital. I followed Jeremy out.'

'Are you and he . . .' he trailed off.

Jacqui lifted her hand to show him. 'Twenty-four carat. The wedding's in six months. I'll make sure you get an invitation. He's on-call otherwise he'd be here.'

'I'll look forward to it,' said Hunter and then added unexpectedly, 'Make the invitation to both of us.' He wasn't sure who was the more surprised, Ruth or himself.

Jacqui looked at him in shock and then said with a wide smile, 'Wow. Nick Hunter! I would never have thought it possible. Ruth,' she smiled warmly at her, 'we'd better go and have a chat and you can tell me your secret.'

Ruth, delighted and dazed at the same time, let Jacqui lead her away from Nick. He stood there looking after them, suddenly aware of peals of laughter from Ruth. He wondered what Jacqui was telling her.

Hunter replenished his glass and wandered over to a group of people including York, the military attaché. He nodded to Hunter, murmured an excuse and both men moved away. 'I've made arrangements with the police and it's a go. Incidentally, I spoke to General Macnair. He's endorsed the operation. He said to say good luck.'

'Thanks.' Hunter nodded his appreciation.

'I did a search on the bible using the computer. These names all appear in it one way or another.' He took a sheet of paper from his inside pocket and handed it to Hunter who took a cursory look.

Hunter glanced down the list. 'Let's talk about it over dinner. May I keep this?'

'Certainly. Come on, let me introduce you to a few people.'

For the next hour or so, Hunter circulated, talking to a mix of old acquaintances and strangers. It was a pleasant, typical naval cocktail party. Halfway through he and Ruth met up and they circulated together.

'What has Jacqui been telling you?'

Ruth smiled impishly up at him. 'Just girl talk.'

When Robbo Robertson caught up with them Hunter took him to one side and confided, 'Tomorrow there's going to be a raid on the marina. The local police will co-ordinate it but our military police handlers and dogs'll back them up. I expect there to be ructions and a number of boats will attempt to put to sea. Is there any chance of you asking the old man to supply a couple of raiders to block the entrance?'

Lt Cdr. Robertson looked surprised. 'I guess so. What's your involvement?'

Hunter related his tale once more. 'I've spoken to York and he's fixed things with the police. However, I think it is going to be tougher than it looks. If I'm right, then there's every chance matters will turn ugly. I've told York but the best the police will agree to is that they will wear bullet-proof vests.'

'You're suggesting we use armed men?' Robertson was aghast.

'Yes. I think there are as many as twelve boats working together. I believe them to be manned by some of the most vicious thugs that walk and I think they are armed and dangerous.'

The lieutenant commander looked thunderstruck. Give him a war situation and the relative comfort of the operations room and he was in his element. Few could do a better job. But ask him to step outside his training and he was at a loss. He lacked imagination – which made him an ideal middle or even senior ranking officer in almost any of the services. Except TIFAT.

'Look. Introduce me to the Captain, will you? I'll have a private word with him.'

Paul Henke

Robertson took him to meet Captain Matthew Myers, DSC and Bar, Royal Navy – a tough looking individual. Myers had won the Distinguished Service Cross while serving onboard *HMS Antrim* during the Falklands war and the Bar while operating in Bosnia. Hunter knew Captain Myers by reputation and what he knew he liked. He hoped his judgement was not misplaced.

'Sir, it's a great pleasure,' Hunter said.

Myers nodded. He looked at Hunter from under bristling grey eyebrows, his brown, intelligent eyes summing up the man. Then he surprised him by saying, 'You're with Macnair's mob. Is that right?'

'Yes, sir.'

'It's about time we had an outfit like his. Malcolm and I met at Staff College a few years ago. He and I often discussed the very issues which led to TIFAT being set up. I just hope the bloody politicians leave him alone to get on with it.'

Hunter grinned. 'So does the General, sir.'

'I take it this meeting isn't an old fashioned courtesy call?'

'No, sir. Let me explain.' Hunter repeated the story he had told Robertson. He answered the half dozen questions the Captain threw at him, apparently to the Captain's satisfaction.

'I approve. Leave me to talk to York and the Chief Superintendent. In fact, the Chief Superintendent is having dinner with the Governor and I later. I'll sort things with him. Will that do you?'

Hunter smiled with relief. 'Yes, sir. And thank you very much.'

After the cocktail party it was customary for the unattached ladies to be invited to a private party in the wardroom. Hunter and Ruth were also asked but Hunter declined, using a prior engagement as an excuse. He made arrangements to meet at the ship at 06.00 and they departed with Sam York to a little bistro overlooking the harbour.

'Sam, back at TIFAT we've been working hard on the connection between terrorist activity and drug smuggling. We've discovered a series of coincidences covering the last five years which are too important to ignore.'

58

'What are they?'

'Hang on. I'll tell you after we order.' Hunter turned to the waiter who had approached their table and stood with a pen poised over an order pad. All three of them asked for steak, baked potatoes, a salad and a bottle of *Rioja*. After the waiter left Hunter began. 'The price of heroin on the streets of Europe has plummeted because the amount available has skyrocketed. We know most of it comes from Pakistan, Afghanistan, Turkey, the former Yugoslavia and other parts of Eastern Europe. Agreed?'

'Agreed. So what?'

'Statistically those are also the countries from which most immigrants have arrived. The list you gave me . . .' Hunter paused as the waiter returned with the wine. 'Just leave the bottle, thanks,' he said, smiling at the teenager. 'The list is very interesting. Look at the nationalities of the people on the boats with biblical references.' He took the sheet of paper from an inside pocket and showed York.

The major nodded and said, 'I see what you mean.'

'There'll be trouble tomorrow. We are certain that terrorist organisations protect the drug cartels, who in turn finance the terrorists. They coerce or bribe the mules to bring the drugs into Western Europe. I suspect that tomorrow we will find drugs and maybe guns. Probably both.'

'How can you be so certain?' Ruth asked reasonably.

'I'm not but the coincidence is too high.'

The bistro was filling up and as the food was delivered to their table they began to speak of more pleasant topics. The disastrous showing of the English cricket team in the Ashes left Ruth cold, but Israel's success in the Eurovision song contest a few years earlier gave them all a laugh. It wasn't late when they left. They wanted an early night, knowing what the next day could bring.

6

Hunter was dressed in his grey combat fatigues. He wore his webbing and holster with his Glock and said to Ruth, 'If you position yourself where I suggested you'll be able to see what's going on.'

'Are you sure I can't come with you?'

'Quite sure.' He put his arms around her and kissed her gently. 'If it was up to me there'd be no problem but the navy has an old fashioned idea about women in danger.'

'Huh!' She pushed him away. 'I think some of that has rubbed off on you. However, I won't argue. Take care.'

'I will,' he smiled and climbed up to the jetty. He walked briskly along the quay to *HMS Manchester*. Two rigid raiders were already in the water and standing on the quarter-deck was a contingent of marines in fatigues. To Hunter's surprise Robbo Robertson was there, dressed for battle.

Captain Myers appeared, the marines were called to attention and both Hunter and Robertson saluted the senior officer. 'Stand the men at ease,' Myers said. When Robertson gave the order the Captain said, 'This officer,' he nodded at Hunter, 'will have operational control. I am led to believe that there is a possibility of danger. As a result the police and customs officers will not only wear flak jackets but will also be accompanied by armed men from the regiment. Your task is to stop any boat from trying to escape. Good luck. That's all, PWO, dismiss the men.'

'Aye, aye, sir.' Robertson saluted, called the men to attention and dismissed them.

They quickly climbed down into the raiders – flat-bottomed, fibreglass boats. Each man carried a Sterling machine gun, standard issue throughout the UK's armed forces, capable of firing single and automatic shots. The gun was the L34, a silenced version that was as quiet as falling rain when fired. Two men carried Accuracy International L96A1 rifles, British made sniper's rifles of incredible accuracy. Again Hunter could see that they carried the "Moderated" version with integral silencer. Myers was taking no chances.

A corporal sat at the wheel on each boat, the engines idling. Five men climbed into each one, with Hunter in one boat and Robertson in the other. They cast off and the boats headed towards the harbour entrance. In the still of the morning they clearly heard gunshots.

Chief Superintendent Alex Cairney had mustered his men at Southport Gates, a couple of kilometres from the marina. There were to be four teams, each consisting of two armed police officers, one customs officer, a handler and his dog and two armed soldiers. The police carried side arms, the soldiers had machine guns held at the ready across their chests. Cairney thought it was over-kill but was prepared to go along with the preparations after talking to York, who was now standing with him, dressed in battle fatigues.

'Right. Let's go,' said Cairney.

The men climbed into army Land Rovers and headed to the marina. It was a large, purpose built haven for privately owned pleasure craft. There were boats berthed at the pontoons worth as little as two or three thousand pounds while others were gin-palaces, ranging from four or five hundred thousand to well over a million pounds. The boats identified as part of the drug smuggling ring were in the latter bracket.

Although the Chief Superintendent expected to find drugs, he did not expect any armed resistance. As a result, he refused to wear a flak jacket like the remainder of the men. The gate leading to the pontoon was shut with a combination lock but he had taken the precaution of getting the number within a week of arriving on

Gibraltar. They knew where the target boats were berthed. In the early morning light, as dawn was breaking, the teams appeared, frightful apparitions moving quietly along the wooden pontoons. They split up and arrived at the first four boats.

When they were in radio contact and he had the report that they were all in position Cairney commanded, 'Go, go, go.'

Stepping onto the large after deck of a beautiful yacht, Cairney hammered on the glass door. 'Open up. Police. This is a raid. Open up, I say.'

Onboard three other boats the same procedures were taking place. Bleary-eyed occupants opened the door to be shoved unceremoniously onto a seat and told to stay where they were. The questions were the same on every vessel.

'Who else is onboard?'

'Are you the owner?'

'Where was the boat registered?'

'What was your last port of call?'

'What is your nationality?'

The first dog found drugs two minutes after she had jumped on board. Cairney handcuffed two men and two women and hustled them off the boat. One of the men broke free and began to run along the pontoon yelling at the top of his voice, waking up occupants of other boats. A soldier ran after him and quickly caught him, rugby tackling the man onto the wooden slats of the pontoon. The man's hands were behind his back and he fell heavily, hitting his chin hard and knocking himself unconscious. But it was too late. Engines were flashing up with a roar, as men used to acting quickly understood that something was amiss.

Cairney left a policeman with their four captives and ran as fast as he could along the pontoon. With a young corporal right behind him, he approached a large gin palace – one of their targets. The corporal, seeing that a gun was being aimed at them and with far quicker reactions than the older man, shouldered Cairney into the water just as the machine gun opened fire. The bullets missed except for one. It hit the corporal in the middle of the chest. His Kevlar jacket stopped the bullet killing him but the shot cracked three ribs and left a bruise as big as a dinner plate. The corporal followed Cairney into the harbour and came up spluttering beside the senior policeman whose life he had saved. With the operation falling to pieces around him, Cairney knew that Hunter had been right in all particulars.

Three boats tried to escape. One was stopped when an over-anxious woman turned the wheel in the wrong direction and smashed the boat into an empty finger pontoon, holing the boat at the water line. The other two, nearer the sea, sped towards freedom.

The rigid raiders came around the corner, hidden by the wall of the detached mole. Robertson picked up a loudhailer and announced, 'Halt or we fire.' The words echoed loudly across the basin but the boats continued to plough towards the entrance. One was already up on its plane and fast approaching twenty-five knots. Robertson hesitated. The boat was almost on top of them when Hunter, further back, drew his automatic and emptied it into the side of the boat. One of the marines, faster off the mark than the others, did the same with his machine gun. A bullet struck a can of petrol, which exploded in a ball of fire and the boat came to a dead stop alongside Robertson's raider.

Seeing what had happened, the driver of the other boat slowed, went astern, turned sharply and headed for the southern entrance, ramming the throttles into full ahead. Through the entrance the boat swung hard to starboard and sped towards the beach at La Linea, two miles away.

'After them!' Hunter yelled and the raider's throttles were rammed into full ahead. They shot past the burning boat where Robertson's men were vainly trying to put out the fire and rescue the occupants. In the strengthening light Hunter could see the boat reach the beach and figures leaping down.

'Sergeant, can you hit them?' he asked the sniper.

'Yes, sir.'

'Do it.'

'Yes, sir.'

The sergeant swept the rifle to his shoulder and, barely pausing to aim, fired the first round. There was a cough and the man running up the beach collapsed face down. A second shot followed and another man was down. The third man stopped and raised his hands, turning to face the soldiers. The raider hit the beach and the men jumped ashore. Hunter walked quickly towards their captive and then stopped in surprise. The man he was facing was Stavios, the troublemaker from the *Papillon*.

'You!' Stavios breathed, shocked to the core.

'So we meet again. I look forward to hearing what you have to say. How did you get away from the Spanish?'

The man broke into a torrent of a language Hunter did not recognise. 'Speak English,' Hunter snarled.

In reply the man cleared his throat and made to spit at Hunter who stepped forward and hit him in the face with the palm of his hand. The loud slap created a shocking sound as it turned the man's head. He made as if to retaliate and Hunter stood, hands on hips, smiling. Stavios thought better of it.

'I said speak English.'

'I will speak only my language. You will have to get an interpreter for the courts. I will deny all the charges against me. I will claim you murdered innocent men. You will be the one on trial.'

'Sergeant,' Hunter turned to the sniper.

'Sir.'

'Will you kindly take the boat over there back to one of the pontoons and have it searched. Take the bodies with you. We don't want to embarrass ourselves with the Spanish. I'm going for a spin in the raider. You,' Hunter faced the man, 'get in.'

'I will not. I . . .'

Hunter took out his automatic and this time hit Stavios on the side of the head. As he staggered, disorientated, in pain, Hunter hustled him to the raider and pushed him into the bottom of the boat. 'Corporal,' Hunter said to the driver, 'I'll take over. You help the others.'

'Yes, sir.' The corporal climbed out of the raider and pushed it into deeper water.

Engaging the gears, Hunter turned the wheel and backed slowly away from the beach. Once clear he pushed the throttles into ahead and as the gears engaged he shifted into full speed. The

raider took off like a rocket and out to sea. Keeping an eye
and his gun on the prisoner, Hunter throttled back and allowed
the boat to bounce in its own wash when they were about
four miles off-shore. Grabbing Stavios by his belt he dropped
him overboard. The man sank beneath the water and came up
spluttering.

'I want some answers,' said Hunter. 'Let me ask you again.
How did you get away from the Spanish?'

He got a mouthful of what Hunter guessed was abuse in the
same foreign language. Hunter knelt by the raider where the
man was holding onto the side, grabbed his hair and shoved
him under. He held Stavios there, struggling frantically, until
Hunter felt the man begin to weaken. When he pulled him to
the surface it took a few minutes of coughing and spitting until
he was able to speak.

'I told you to speak English.'

In reply Hunter was treated to the same torrent and so he
repeated the process. This time he held him down even longer
and when he pulled his head out, for a moment, he was fearful
that he had left it too late. But Stavios began to cough and splutter
once again until finally he groaned, 'Wait – no more. I speak
English. Escape was easy – I bribed a guard.'

'Good. That's better. I know that you are a part of the
smuggling ring that is bringing heroin into Europe. Where's it
coming from?'

'I don't know . . .' he got no further. Hunter shoved his head
under, but only for a few seconds.

He pulled it up and put his face close to the man's. 'Let me
explain something to you. I want to know how you came to be
on that ship, who blew it up and why. I also want to know why
you were trapped on board and hadn't escaped with the others.
I also want to know who is masterminding everything.'

'Masterminding? I don't understand.'

'The person planning it all. Who? What's his name? Start
talking now.'

Stavios reluctantly began to give answers. Ten minutes later
Hunter thought he had all that he was going to get and he grabbed

the man by the hair and pulled him on board. As Hunter turned to climb into the driver's seat, a blow to the head knocked him sideways.

Stavios jumped on to Hunter's back, got an arm around his throat, and with the other on the back of his head he began to strangle Hunter.

Hunter tried to jerk his head back but it was like being held in an iron vice. With rancid breath, the man snarled, 'You will take the knowledge you have to your grave.'

Grasping the side of the raider Hunter heaved himself into the water, the man with him. Immediately the grip lessened on his throat and Hunter broke free, now in his element. Breaking surface, he grabbed a lung full of air and swam down. He gripped Stavios's leg and took him with him. The man kicked frantically, trying to break free, while Hunter towed him steadily down into the depths.

Hunter had once free dived down thirty metres after a foolhardy bet with an American SEAL. At twenty metres he touched the bottom. The man was no longer fighting, no longer kicking. Hunter shifted his grip and looked into dead, staring eyes. It was time to get to the surface. Pulling the toggle on the green tubular life jacket, it inflated and he shot upwards. Hunter looked up to see that the surface was dappled yellow. The sun must have risen on another beautiful, Mediterranean day without him noticing.

7

A Commander in the Russian Navy, Yuri Voropaev showed his identity card to the guard, received a sloppy salute and walked onto the base. When he opened the door to the communications centre he found only a skeleton staff of two operators. They stood to attention at the sight of his uniform.

'Carry on,' he said, forcing a smile. 'I am checking the macro-transmitter.'

'It's in the office over there, sir,' said the duty petty officer. If he was curious as to why Voropaev wanted to check the transmitter he didn't show it. Officers were a law unto themselves in any navy, even a defunct Russian one.

Voropaev nodded his thanks and went over to the office closing the door behind him. It took only seconds for him to see that it was switched on. He prayed that what he was about to do would work. At the moment he saw no other solution. The set was the same as the one he had used when he had been the Commanding Officer of a nuclear submarine. He pressed two buttons simultaneously and the frequency changed instantly to the highest wavelength available. At a speed of five words per minute, slower than usual due to lack of practice, he began to punch out a message in Morse.

When he finished, he re-set the frequency and left. The two naval ratings in the Vladivostock base ignored him.

Hunter sat in the cockpit of the sloop enjoying the warm sunshine and sipping a coffee. York was with him. They were holding an impromptu debrief while Ruth was ashore buying supplies. Hunter had been about to take the sloop to the marina to top up the tanks with diesel and water when York had arrived.

'Is Cairney okay?' Hunter asked.

York nodded. 'He's lucky to be alive. If it hadn't been for the corporal's quick thinking Cairney would be dead now.'

'And what about the corporal? Is he all right?'

'Yes. He'll make a full recovery. The cracked ribs will heal normally and the bruising will soon go. I've recommended he be put up for a gong.'

'Good. Does Cairney realise how lucky he was?'

'I'm not sure. I think his confidence has been shaken. He has an excellent record as a copper, but it's the old fashioned kind. Arrest that man, it's a fair cop and all that guff. We are now up against vicious, organised and well financed gangs who will kill as easily as step on a cockroach. Men like Cairney are out of their depth.'

'If he doesn't adapt, he'll die,' said Hunter.

'I think Cairney knows that. Unfortunately, there are more Cairneys in European police forces than any other sort. Did you hear the latest on the final haul?'

Hunter shook his head.

'Every boat we raided had either heroin or guns or massive amounts of money and guns. Every last one of them. Cairney has sent a report about the operation to the Met and has suggested that they disseminate the information throughout the country and check every marina.'

'He has? You do surprise me.'

'He emphasised the need for caution. He even went so far as to say that we are fighting a new type of criminal, one that will shoot first and to hell with the consequences. Incidentally, I managed to persuade him to keep your name out of it. He wanted to give credit where credit was due, but I explained your desire for anonymity.'

'Thanks. Macnair would have my guts for garters otherwise. He's a great believer in staying out of the limelight as much as possible.'

When York left, Hunter started the engine, letting it warm through before moving. There was always the danger of a cold diesel motor cutting out unexpectedly if it suddenly went from forward to reverse.

He replenished his coffee while he waited. Earlier he had typed and encrypted his own report to Macnair. Despatching it via sat-nav telephone, he had included the meagre information he had gleaned from Stavios. Following a dispute with the ship's Captain, Stavios and his men had been forced at gunpoint into the hold. They had expected to be released when they reached Spain. Hunter had not learnt what the disagreement had been about. The only useful information he'd discovered was that the boss of a major drugs cartel appeared to be an Englishman. Hunter could make no sense of the fact that the cartel operated out of Russia, possibly Georgia. He had told no one else what he knew, figuring that it was up to Macnair to pass on the information.

Finishing his coffee, in bare feet and wearing only a pair of shorts, he let go the shorelines and put the gears in reverse. He spun the wheel hard over and the boat came slowly away from the wall. Putting the gears into neutral, he paused and then shoved them ahead. The sloop halted for a second and then moved slowly forward. Hunter relished the feel of the wheel in his hands, the breeze across his face and the gentle motion of the deck underfoot. God was in his heaven, he thought, but all was *not* right with the world.

Alleysia was in a towering rage yet her face remained an inscrutable mask. Her jet-black hair, straight and cut in a severe style around her face, remained immaculate. The only sign of her agitation was her fingers drumming on the arm of the chair, her nails, like her lips, scarlet like drops of blood. She stood up and walked across the room to the sideboard. Slim, her figure was perfectly proportioned to her five feet four inches of height. Her tailored black suit contrasted sharply with the porcelain white of her skin.

Pouring herself a glass of mineral water she quickly drained it. A strict regime kept her at peak physical fitness and health

– Alleysia never lacked control. To look at her she could have been any age from twenty-five to forty. She was, in fact, thirty-eight and the boss of the biggest and most powerful crime organisation in Russia. Since the death of her father, she had worked ceaselessly to consolidate her power and to expand her influence. For there was a dark side to the power she loved. Controlling, domineering, Alleysia exploited any hypocrisy, frustration or pain in those who crossed her, callously and manipulatively pulling strings with a hidden hand. A closed book, with no one privy to her motivation, she revelled in the knowledge inherited from her beloved father and rejoiced in the intellectual challenge of running a business . . . with so much power at her blood red finger tips.

The meeting of The Syndicate in Columbia had been a triumph. It had taken four years to finally bring it about, to persuade the cartels that it was better to work together than apart. The Syndicate was the first global, truly international crime organisation, operating just like any other multi-national company.

There was one significant difference of course. There were no legal disputes and no opposition was allowed to flourish. The world had been carved up between the cartels and the rewards were proving to be greater than she had ever dreamt possible. She looked through the window of her office at the screen that covered the whole length and height of one wall in the main room. Twenty metres by twenty metres, it normally displayed a map of the world, but now Gibraltar took up a big portion of the screen. Looking at the map she could imagine the events unfolding there.

She would teach them a lesson. Not only had she lost some good men but she had also lost ten million dollars worth of heroin and cocaine when the coaster sank. She had to make it clear that the world would be a safer place if she was left alone to continue her operations. The world wanted drugs; she would supply them. Didn't the fools realise that it was a question of supply and demand, like any other business? If they wanted to stop her then they could legalise the use of drugs. Until they did, they would be playing right into her hands.

Looking across the vast room, she watched the men and women hard at work, bent over their computer terminals. This was why she had become so powerful. She had been the first one to realise that it was a business, just like any other. Mentally shaking herself, she decided that her staff could deal with the logistics of running her empire. As Chairman of the Board – Chairperson, she corrected herself – it was her task to make the executive decisions. She pressed the button on her intercom. 'Come here,' she snapped at King-Smith. He was her right-hand man, her mouthpiece. He was fiercely protective of her, concerned only for her safety and well being. The deal with the Russians was taking too long. She had decided what she would do.

Hunter waited at the re-fuelling pontoon for Ruth. She appeared an hour later by taxi, laden down with fresh supplies of food and drink. Hunter was lying in a hammock he had slung across the fore deck, between the mast and the fore stay, a novel resting in his hands, thinking about her. She was beautiful, tough, intelligent and resourceful. She was also, he reminded himself, a dedicated member of Mossad, the Israeli secret service. So how would that affect their relationship in the long run? He opened his eyes to slits and watched as the taxi driver unloaded bags of groceries. Paying him, Ruth stood with her hands on her hips, looking at Hunter.

She suddenly smiled. 'I can see you're awake, lazy bones. Are you going to help me, or not?'

'Never any peace,' he grouched good-humouredly.

'None for the wicked, at any rate. We've been invited to Jacqui's for drinks and dinner. I accepted for both of us. Is that okay?'

'Sure. I look forward to it,' he replied as he clambered out of the hammock and padded across the deck. He slipped on a pair of canvas shoes and stepped onto the pontoon. Ruth was standing on the quay surrounded by the bags. She saw a two wheeled cart nearby and went over to get it. Hunter joined her and together they loaded the cart with the groceries. Neither of them noticed the two men sitting in a car, watching them through binoculars.

Ruth stowed the provisions while Hunter flashed-up the engine and prepared to move back to their berth, astern of *HMS Manchester. Le Beau Papillon* was now fully watered, fuelled and ready to depart Gibraltar for Lisbon, four hundred miles away. Hunter planned on stopping at the small fishing port of Estoril for one night. Then it was another four hundred miles to Corunna where they would stay for two days. Weather permitting, they would launch out across the Bay of Biscay, Brest another four hundred miles. Hunter had the journey planned in his head and was looking forward to the adventure.

That evening, when they left the boat, they took the inflatable straight across the harbour, saving a walk of about a mile and a half. They tied up next to a set of steps and strolled out through the main gate. A taxi was cruising past and Hunter hailed it. Inside Ruth gave the driver their destination.

For those personnel serving on the Rock, there were either married quarters or single sex blocks of small apartments available. Individuals who wished privacy or to co-habit without the "sanctity of marriage" had to find their own accommodation. Jacqui Turner and Jeremy Williamson had done just that in the area known as Rosia. Williamson was a tall, slim, intense man, his unruly black hair a sharp contrast to Jacqui's sleek blondeness. He was a plastic surgeon who had worked extensively with burn injuries, and had helped to pioneer some of the techniques that now existed. Hunter knew of one young soldier who had suffered eighty-percent burns when an incendiary device had exploded as he walked the streets of Belfast. His wife and daughter had just crossed the road and escaped the explosion. The soldier's clothes had burnt away and the flesh on his back had burnt down to his backbone. Thanks to Jeremy Williamson, the soldier not only survived, but eight months later was back on active duty.

There were two others present at the dinner, Sam York and a staff nurse from the hospital by the name of Susan Waterstone. Susan was tall, brown-haired and brown eyed, with a wide smile and a curvaceous figure. York was practically drooling over her.

The talk around the table was animated and informed. It

ranged from international politics to hospital politics and inevitably to the action that had taken place the day before. Hunter was circumspect with the information he disclosed but it soon became obvious that the three people from the medical profession possessed an understanding of the size of the problem although there was a sharp disagreement as to how to solve it. Hunter and York were all for fighting the smugglers with every means possible, while the doctor, dentist and nurse supported the decriminalisation of drugs. Caregivers, they argued from the standpoint of treating patients. Hunter and York's viewpoint favoured destroying an evil cancer eating into the heart of the civilised world. There was little agreement as to the best course of action.

'Why not,' suggested Ruth at one particularly acrimonious moment, 'try and do both?' All five of them turned on her.

At the end of the evening nothing had been solved but all agreed it had been an interesting debate. Hunter declined the offer of a night-cap pleading an early morning departure and accepted an offer from York and Susan to share a taxi back to town. It was a warm night. A full moon had just risen over the rooftops and bathed the area in a white light. They said goodnight to their host and hostess at the entrance to the apartment and walked down the three flights of stairs. Hunter, ever alert, stood in the doorway and glanced up and down the quiet street, looking for the slightest oddity. Something was wrong, but he couldn't put his finger on it. He was about to dismiss his thoughts as mere paranoia when he realised what had aroused his suspicions. The night was as silent as a crypt. Yet earlier, when they had arrived, there had been birds singing and squawking. He had mentioned it to Jacqui and she had said that the birds were a nuisance, chirruping well into the night. There had been complaints about them, but little done about it. After a few weeks they had become a background noise the couple no longer noticed, like traffic in a busy city street.

'Back,' Hunter said and stepped inside quickly before smashing the overhead light with a sweep of his fist. A fusillade of bullets swept into the foyer, shattering the glass, which sprayed all around them. Hunter and Ruth dived for the floor as York jumped on top of Susan and dragged her down too, covering her with his body. The foyer was pitch black. As suddenly as it started, the shooting stopped.

'Anybody hurt?' Sam York asked.

'No,' said Hunter and Ruth in unison.

'Susan?'

'I'm . . . I'm okay, I think. My dignity will never recover and, oof, you're squashing me to death.'

'Sorry.' York rolled off her.

'Are you armed, Nick?'

'No.'

'What about you, Ruth?' the Major asked.

'I've got a Jericho in my bag.' She felt around the bottom of her cavernous handbag and wrapped her fingers around its grip. 'Got it,' she announced.

'Sixteen or twelve rounds?' York asked, keeping the surprise out of his voice. He'd known she was Mossad but hadn't expected the answer she'd given.

'Twelve.'

'Okay.' The Jericho pistol, manufactured by Israel Military Industries, fired 9mm Parabellum rounds.

'Good. I've got a Spitfire.' Designed by John Slough it was one of the favourite police weapons in Europe and used extensively at competition shooting. It held fifteen rounds of 9mm Parabellum.

'What is it with you two? How can you be carrying guns in Gib'? It's not allowed,' said Susan, fear catching at her throat.

'Don't worry about it,' said Hunter. 'Susan, stay low and crawl upstairs to the flat. Listen!' In the distance they could hear the wailing of sirens. 'Go on! Now.' The urgency in Hunter's voice conveyed the message strongly enough for Susan to crawl on her hands and knees to the stairs and quickly mount them. As she went around the first corner she heard Hunter say, 'Here they come.'

Five men were darting across the street, each heavily armed with what appeared to be machine guns. In the bright moonlight they were easy targets but made no effort to conceal themselves.

The wailing sirens made speed of the essence. The attackers knew that they had nothing to fear. British men and women, even members of the military, did not carry weapons unless on active duty, which was rarely the case on British soil, even on Gibraltar.

'Wait until they get close,' York said softly. 'Ruth, when I say, you start from the left, I'll start from the right.' The men were ten metres away when he said, 'Fire.'

It was a turkey shoot. Ruth's first bullet hit the left-hand gunman in his stomach, the second his head. York hit his target twice in the middle of the chest. Ruth's next two shots went straight into the heart of the second man. York's second target went down with a head shot. The fifth man, standing in the middle, stopped in shock when he saw the others drop and was lifting his hands in the air when York and Ruth fired simultaneously. Their shots hit the man in each shoulder and flung him to the ground.

'Stay here,' said Hunter. 'I'll see if the coast is clear.' He ran outside, bent double and stopped by the side of the wounded man. Blood was pouring from gaping wounds and Hunter guessed he had only a short while to live.

'Who sent you?' Hunter asked, grabbing the man by the throat.

'*Was? Ich verstehe Sie nicht.*'

Hunter repeated the question in German.

'The devil's daughter. More evil than anyone the world has ever known.' The German clenched his teeth, arched his back in agony and died.

'Damnation,' Hunter said in frustration. The man had bitten into a cyanide capsule.

Two police cars drew up and a voice over a loudspeaker said, 'Put your guns down and raise your hands over your head.' A car mounted searchlight fixed Hunter like a moth and he raised his hands.

'It's all right,' Hunter heard Chief Superintendent Cairney say and he lowered them again. The bulky figure quickly shambled over. 'What's going on?'

'We were attacked. Look at their firepower.' He waved his hands at the guns lying on the ground.

'I can see that.' Cairney stood deep in thought and then sighed. 'This is worse than I believed. It's truly frightening.'

Hunter nodded. 'This looks like a revenge attack. How have they managed to react so quickly? And how did they know to come after us? Out of the six at dinner tonight, the only two people involved were Sam and I. Think how many others took part. So why pick on us?'

The answer dawned on them both simultaneously. 'Christ,' said Cairney.

'We haven't been singled out,' said Hunter, appalled. 'They're targeting the entire ship.'

'Look, I'll leave you here. I'll call for an ambulance to take the bodies away,' said Cairney.

A police inspector in uniform was approaching and he'd heard the Chief Superintendent. 'Sir, I must protest. This is the scene of a serious crime. We need to investigate. Get forensic here.'

Cairney turned to the hapless inspector and said, 'I used to think so too. There'll be no forensic. No investigation. These bodies will be cremated and their ashes thrown away.' He turned back to Hunter. 'Can you warn *Manchester*? I've got a lot to do.'

'What these people can do against a Royal Naval destroyer is beyond me,' said Hunter, 'but I'll warn the crew.'

'How about attacking any of the lads when they're ashore?' York suggested, as he approached.

'I think a general recall is needed. Can you get your lot working on that?' Hunter asked Cairney.

'No problem.'

'In the meantime, I'd better phone the Captain.'

Hunter led York and Ruth back to the apartment and while York told Jacqui and Williamson what had happened, Hunter telephoned the ship.

'Quartermaster, this is Lt Cdr Hunter. Can you get me the Officer of the Day? It's urgent. Thank you.' Hunter waited for a few moments.

'Officer of the Day.'

'My name is Nick Hunter, I'm . . .'

'Yes, sir, I know who you are. I've been told it's urgent.'

Thank goodness, thought Hunter, for a switched on OOD. 'I need to speak to Captain Myers but tell him to go to Bikini Red immediately. I've spoken to Chief Superintendent Cairney and he's about to arrange a general re-call. Go and speak to him now and I'll hang on.'

The wait seemed interminable though in fact it was only minutes. He heard the receiver being picked up and then Myers' voice. 'Hunter? What's going on?' In the background Hunter could hear the piped broadcast informing all hands that Bikini Red was now in force. The watch on deck was to be armed.

Hunter told the captain what had happened. 'We think that these people will stop at nothing to extract their revenge. The speed at which they've moved is frightening. We're concerned for the lads ashore. They're easy targets for anybody who wishes to take a pot shot at them. Or worse. A knife in the back would not be out of character for these people.'

'I agree. I'll put the ship in defence watches and close up the operations room. I'll also have armed patrols on the upperdeck and send patrols ashore to collect the crew. Luckily they don't wear uniform anymore.'

'True, sir, but Jack and Jenny still stick out a mile,' Hunter replied.

'I know,' the Captain said, bleakly. 'I'll speak to you later.' He broke the connection and turned to his First Lieutenant. 'Number One, we won't treat this lightly. I've spoken to General Macnair and if only half of what he says is true then we could be in trouble. We'll put to sea at the earliest possible time.'

'Sir?'

'We'll be safer,' was the bleak observation.

Hunter hung up the receiver. 'Okay. Time to go. Back to the *Papillon* and let's get the hell out of here.'

'Nick?' Ruth frowned.

'If they attack us what do we do? We were lucky tonight

77

because they didn't expect us to be armed. We won't have the same luxury next time. So I think we should get back to the boat and set sail.' He had come to the same conclusion as Myers.

A taxi disgorged them at the main gate to the dockyard and they said their goodbyes to York and Susan. Hunter was pleased to see the armed guard on the gate and the alertness of the police. During the ride they had seen a number of men and women being escorted to military vans and Land Rovers, their leave curtailed, their escorts armed and nervous.

Climbing into the inflatable, Hunter started the engine and they headed across the harbour. Hunter tied up at the stern of the *Papillon* and reassured Ruth, 'I'll just go and have a word with the captain of *Manchester*. Leave the boat and I'll haul it onboard when I get back.'

He jumped ashore and walked along the jetty. Patrols were moving along the deck, vigilant and nervous.

'Halt! Identify yourself,' a sentry at the bottom of the gangway called. Hunter noticed that the forward gangway had been removed.

'Lt Cdr. Hunter to see your Captain.'

'Come forward and be recognised.'

Hunter stepped closer, his hands in evidence. Just then he heard Robbo Robertson. 'It's all right. I can vouch for this officer.'

'Aye, aye, sir.' The sentry saluted and let Hunter up the gangway.

'What's going on?' Hunter asked.

'We're preparing for sea. The old man thinks it'll be safer and I can't say I disagree with him.'

'We're doing the same thing. We just got back and . . .'

'What did you say? Hunter – I saw you onboard half an hour ago. I was on the bridge wing. I didn't call down as I was going to come and say goodbye.'

'Hell's teeth!' Hunter was already running down the gangway. *Please God, no! Let me be in time.* But he had told Ruth to get ready to depart and she had probably gone below. Would it be on a timer . . . or a booby trap? The former wouldn't be any good as there was no guarantee when they'd be onboard.

The latter would be hidden where? The engine cover was the obvious place. Or the main hatch. There was always the chance that they would put to sea without opening the engine cover, but they would have to open the main hatch. That's where he would have placed the bomb.

He sprinted along the jetty and saw that Ruth, with the independence he loved, had pulled the inflatable onboard and secured it in its stowage. She had one hand on the sliding hatch and was pushing it open.

'No!' Hunter yelled. 'No!' He was too late.

8

Ruth pushed open the doors as she looked up at a frantic Hunter who was running as though he had the devil at his heels.

She looked bewildered as Hunter jumped onto the boat and landed with both legs bent under him. He had only one chance and he intended taking it. Milliseconds counted.

She was standing in the cockpit, looking at him in confusion. His next move seemed impossible, superhuman. Desperation lent him a strength he didn't know he possessed. Hunter grabbed her under each arm and leapt as if he were standing on a coiled spring. He lifted Ruth clear and threw her overboard, metres away from the boat. He followed, twisting in the air, his body tucking round like a ball to reduce the effect of the explosion. His back hit some standing rigging but he ignored the pain of the scraping wire as he flew through the air. He hit the water and came up spluttering, close to Ruth.

'What on earth! Nick! Are you mad?' She gasped, shaking water off her head.

Hunter drew breath, feeling the strength returning to his limbs. He looked around him, disorientated. 'Robbo said he saw somebody onboard and I figured if he was right they could have rigged . . .'

The explosion was huge. They had drifted a few metres away from the boat and the blast followed the line of least resistance straight up in the air. Even so, the shock and noise were stunning. *Papillon* had been berthed near the stern of *HMS Manchester*. Burning debris rained down on the aft deck of the warship where the ready-use petrol tanks for the rigid raiders and inflatables were stowed. They exploded immediately, sending fiery liquid in all directions.

'Dive!' Hunter yelled and, taking a deep breath, swam beneath the water. Ruth was right behind him as burning petrol showered the area where they had been treading water. They swam away, looking up, seeking a dark edge in the flames flowing across the water. With bursting lungs they finally saw the end of the inferno. Kicking frantically they swam as fast as they could towards the darkness. They hit the surface gasping, sucking in gulps of air, kicking the water, moving further from the heat and flames.

'Hands to Emergency Stations. Hands to Emergency Stations.' They could hear orders being piped onboard the *Manchester*. 'Fire, fire, fire. Fire on the quarter-deck. Hands to muster . . .'

Hunter tuned the announcement out and looked at the debris that had been his boat. Their boat. He looked at Ruth who, after her time in Mossad, was no longer shocked by anything. 'I hope you were insured,' she said.

Hunter laughed in spite of their predicament.

Already the continual practice that was a way of life onboard a RN vessel was paying off. Fire fighters had quickly mustered to get the fire under control. Foam was pouring from nozzles attached to fire extinguishers and smothering the flames. It looked as though the worst of the damage had been superficial. They had been lucky. If there had been anybody standing near the stern they would have been killed.

'Let's go.' Hunter turned his back on the carnage and began to swim towards the North Mole and the northern entrance. From there he intended to follow the harbour wall around to the beach at the north-west corner of the Rock.

'Shouldn't we let the *Manchester* know we survived?' Ruth swam alongside him.

'No. If everybody thinks we're dead we might just live long enough to get out of Gibraltar. So let's get going.'

Ruth followed resignedly in his wake. She knew that he was right.

It was a mile and a half swim. The entrance was less than a hundred metres away as they followed the wall around the northern perimeter. There was virtually no wind so the sea was flat calm. Forty-five minutes later they crawled onto a tiny beach and rested in the shadows for a few minutes.

'We can't walk through the town like this,' Ruth pointed out, reasonably. 'We'll stick out a mile.'

'I know.' Hunter looked at his watch and was surprised to see that it was only a few minutes past midnight. 'I don't suppose you've got your handbag with you by any chance?'

'By some chance you happen to be right. I don't. Why?'

'I've got my passport but we need one for you.'

'I've got mine as well,' she surprised him.

'You do? Where?'

'Nick. I'm Mossad. My passport and a credit card are in a special pocket in my skirt. All my clothes have a water-proof pocket to carry them. You never know when you'll need them.'

Hunter thought then how lucky he'd been to meet a woman like Ruth. Nothing seemed to faze her. He also made a mental note to pass the idea on to Jim Carter. It never ceased to amaze him that simple ideas were still to be found and used. 'I've also got my wallet with my credit cards and money. So we'll be all right once we leave Gib'.'

'How do we cross into Spain? Whoever did this may have people on the lookout for us. It's more than likely the border guards have been bribed as well.'

They were sitting against a low wall, talking quietly, the sand comfortable beneath them. In a cloudless sky with the moon now passing its zenith, the stars shone brightly.

Ruth snuggled against Hunter. Relief at their close escape welled up within her. 'I could enjoy this. Only . . . I haven't said thank you for saving my life.'

'Darling Ruth,' Hunter put his hand on her face and kissed her. 'I love you. There's nothing I wouldn't do for you.'

'I love you too, Nick. Now tell me, how are we going to get out of here?'

'I've been thinking about that and I have a plan, a cunning plan,' he said, mimicking a well-known television actor. 'Come on.'

'We don't have a weapon.'

'We'll manage without one. Come on.'

Standing up, he pulled Ruth to her feet and began walking along the beach. Near the end he found what he was looking for. Next to a small hut with a bar alongside were a dozen pedallos. A wire passed around their hulls and was padlocked to a bracket in the side of the hut. Hunter sat on the sand, braced his feet on the wall of the hut, took the wire in his hands and heaved as hard as he could. The bracket flew away from the partially rotten wood and he went flying backwards.

Scrambling to his feet Hunter unthreaded the wire from the first pedallo. He dragged it to the water's edge and walked back, scuffing the sand. He picked up the bracket and used a fist-sized stone to hammer it back in place.

'With a bit of luck,' said Hunter, 'nobody will realise a boat's missing. After all, I doubt anybody comes here and counts them but they'd notice if we leave the bracket off.'

They walked backwards down to the water, scuffing the sand, destroying their footprints. Ruth climbed on board while Hunter pushed the boat into deeper water. He clambered after it and settled in the left-hand seat. They both made themselves comfortable and started to pedal steadily, away from Gibraltar. Hunter rested his hand on the tiller and steered towards the lights he could see on the mainland of Spain, some two miles away. Ruth placed her hand on his and, in what passed for contented silence despite the trying circumstances, they moved slowly along.

'Take your shoes off,' said Hunter, pulling at his own. 'And let them dry out a bit.' She did as he suggested.

'See the flashing lights? That's the end of the runway. It sticks out about six hundred metres into the sea. We go round it before heading for Spain.

After a while Ruth said, 'This is peaceful.' The sky was alight with stars. There was only the gentlest of breezes, the sound of the water passing the hull and the steady, rhythmic beat of the paddles adding to a feeling of well being.

'Enjoy it while you can,' said Hunter. 'Because I think all hell is going to break loose.'

'Talk to me.'

'I've been thinking about the whole problem we're trying to confront. How do we tell friend from foe? Who's been bought off by amounts of money staggering to a normal person yet a pittance for the drug cartels? How do we fight the scum when every court in the world bends over backwards to look after their rights? Stopping individuals is a short-term solution. These cartels are like the Hydra of Greek mythology. Cut one head off and two grow in its place.'

'But the Hydra was eventually killed by Hercules, wasn't it?'

'Yes, using a firebrand. Maybe that's what we need.'

'I'm not with you.'

'We need the modern equivalent of a firebrand.'

'Something specific in mind?' Ruth asked, smiling at him.

He smiled back and shrugged. 'I'm damned if I know.' He paused and added, 'Yet. But it's appropriate, somehow, given our location.'

'How?'

'The Straits of Gibraltar used to be known as *Fretum Herculeum*. In ancient times the rock was known as Calpe and on the African side as Mount Abyla. Together they were called the Pillars of Hercules.'

'How come you know so much?'

'I was assistant navigating officer on a County Class destroyer named *HMS Antrim*. We spent six months around the Med. One of my jobs was to inform the ship's company where we were and where we were going. I used to put together all sorts of information out of interest.'

'Tell me more about the last briefing you attended.'

'At TIFAT?'

Ruth nodded and said, 'Can you say any more about it?'

'I guess so. As we seem to be caught up in the middle.' Hunter paused to gather his thoughts. 'One of the biggest problems we have is co-ordinating a fight against the drug cartels. The main reason for that is the diversity of the agencies that are tackling the problem. Ever heard of the INL?'

'No. Who are they?'

'The Bureau for International Narcotics and Law Enforcement Affairs, INL for short. Their mandate is to extend America's first line of defence through diplomatic initiatives and international programs that strengthen the commitment and abilities of foreign governments to deter the crime cartels. The cartels are involved in people smuggling, forced prostitution, drugs, money laundering and every other rotten thing you can think of. In America alone one billion dollars worth of cars are stolen and smuggled out of the country annually. Think of the consequences of that one single crime. Statistically, illegal narcotics in the States cost their society one hundred and forty billion dollars a year. Fraud, particularly against the elderly, runs to tens of billions. The cartels threaten the political and economic stability of countries that are important trading partners with the west. The INL provides law enforcement training to police officers, judges, prosecutors, customs and border officials. They run six hundred and ninety-six courses in more than ninety-five countries and spend about thirty million dollars doing it. When the Medellin cartel was targeted, it was estimated that thirty metric tonnes of cocaine a month was stopped from entering the USA alone. A ton is worth one hundred million dollars. That puts into perspective the amount we're spending fighting the problem against the resources the cartels have.'

'That's hardly fair. The INL is just one agency. Surely there are many others?'

'True. World wide there are over one thousand. Unfortunately their idea of co-operation is a meeting once a year to discuss any "progress" in the fight against the cartels.'

'You sound bitter.'

'Bitter?' Hunter paused and then continued. 'No, that's the wrong word. Disappointed, disillusioned, angry. All of those, but not bitter. We act within the law and hence we lose. The head of European Operations at the INL told us that the *modus operandi* of the cartels has changed significantly. It's been a gradual process but the upshot is there are no more turf wars in Europe. Believe it or not, turf wars were one of the main weapons the law enforcement agencies had in their armoury. Scum fighting scum. Going in afterwards and mopping up. To some extent it worked. In the last twelve months there has been a two hundred percent increase in mules.'

'That still doesn't amount to much.'

'That's only the ones we've caught. But that's not the point. We're so busy catching the small players that we miss the big ones. It's estimated that two million migrants are on the move across Europe. Many are illegal and pay vast sums to the cartels. Money they cannot afford or can't pay back. So they're forced into prostitution, slavery and drug smuggling. If arrested they suddenly only speak their native language, demand interpreters and clog up the courts for months. What punishment can be meted out? What's fair? How can you punish somebody for attempting to better their lives for themselves and their families but who are then caught up in a web of crime they can't escape? So it goes round and round. The increase in class A drugs in six months has been over eighty percent. In six months!'

Ruth placed her hand on Hunter's arm and gave a gentle squeeze. 'So we need to fight back,' she spoke softly.

'We do and we will. We also need to fight the corruption of the officials and judges that are making it all possible.' He paused, remembering. 'I met a very interesting Frenchman at the briefing. His name is Leon Sautier of the French Bureau of Investigation. He was telling me about the problems they're having with drug smuggling into the South of France from North Africa. About the corruption of the officials dealing with the situation. It was, quite frankly, scary stuff.'

'So it sounds.'

'However, we might get a chance to fight back. The intention is to give TIFAT the backing to attack whenever we can. Not through the courts, but more directly. There was a suggestion put forward to establish a clearinghouse of information from all agencies world wide that are fighting organised crime. Similar

86

to the El Paso Information Centre, but on an international basis. The scale of the problem is so huge that any one agency would be swamped. So the world is going to be cut up into areas and the information disseminated.' Hunter paused and then added, 'It's a start I suppose.'

They were approaching land again. They could hear the gentle surf rolling in. The pedallo crunched onto the sand and Hunter leapt ashore. Ruth followed right behind him.

'What shall we do with the boat?' she asked.

'I was thinking we could shove it out to sea and hope it drifts away. But we don't want a search and rescue operation to be called on the off chance that somebody is missing.' He looked around. 'There's the answer. Come on, back on board.' He pushed the pedallo back into the water and he and Ruth climbed back on. They pedalled a few hundred metres along the shore and again turned on to the beach. They dragged the boat onto the sand and placed it amongst the dozens of other pedallos that were strung out along the beach.

'Right. Let's have a shower and get going. There's a bather's shower just over there.' They stripped naked and let the cold water wash away their tiredness along with the salt. Their clothes had dried on them, although their shoes were still damp. Dressing quickly, Hunter checked the time. 03.40 – dawn was still a few hours away.

Walking away from the beach they arrived at a track which soon led to a road. It was the main coastal highway, deserted at that time of the morning. A signpost announced La Linea was five kilometres to the right and Algeciras eight kilometres to the left.

'We'll go left,' announced Hunter.

They jogged along and forty minutes later they were approaching Algeciras. Even at that hour the city was coming to life as the early morning denizens, those citizens needed to kick-start any town or city in the world, began work. These were the people who manned the markets for the shops to buy fresh produce, or delivered the morning papers and fresh milk to the shops and supermarkets, or parked their huge wagons in pedestrian only areas to unload some of the thousands of items needed and consumed on a daily basis.

'I could use a drink,' said Ruth, licking her lips. 'An ice cold carton of milk followed by a cup of coffee.'

'There's a problem,' said Hunter, 'we've no pesetas. Only Gibraltarian pounds. Wait a second. Stay here.' He slipped away and a few minutes later reappeared carrying two cartons of milk.

'Where on earth did you get those?'

'In that side street. I noticed a milk crate outside a coffee shop.'

'You stole them?'

'Hardly. I left a Gib' fiver for them. That's an enormous profit, so just enjoy.' As he spoke he pushed open a carton and handed it to Ruth. She hungrily drank the cold, refreshing liquid. Hunter did the same, feeling much better as a result.

'Let's follow the signs for the city centre. We're bound to come across a bank that'll like one of our cards.' At the fifth bank they found a cash dispenser that responded to Hunter's credit card. With a pocketful of pesetas they entered the next coffee house they found. Already other sleepy-eyed early risers were sitting at the tables, reading newspapers, smoking, having breakfast. Soon both Ruth and Hunter were enjoying a meal of freshly baked rolls and excellent coffee. They ate in silence, their mouths too busy to talk.

Finally, Ruth said, 'That's it. I'm full. Last night's excitement left me ravenous. Now what do we do?'

'Next, we phone Macnair and find a way back to the UK.'

'Isn't it ludicrous to think they'll be looking for us? Let's just go to the nearest airport.'

Hunter nodded. 'I agree it's ludicrous. However, how were we singled out? How did those men know to come after us? After Sam and me. These people are astonishingly well organised. What if, as a matter of course, our descriptions have been circulated? I'm not saying,' he added hastily, 'that it's likely. I'm just saying, what if? You know what Mossad would say.'

Ruth nodded. 'I know. And they'd be right. It's better to be safe than sorry.'

'Any ideas?'

'I think the best thing to do is to hire a car and drive to Seville. We can do it in a day, easily.'

Hunter paid the bill while Ruth used the restroom. In the street they found a telephone box and Hunter called TIFAT HQ in Rosyth. He was quickly put through to Jim Carter.

'Nick? Thank God. We thought . . .'

'I can imagine. We just managed to escape the blast.' He gave Carter a brief report and then added, 'We're hiring a car and heading for Seville. We'll fly from there.'

'Okay. Have you got everything you need?'

'Sure. We've both got our passports. I've got my driving licence so there's no problem hiring a car.'

'Good. I'll inform the General. He'll be delighted. Although,' Carter chuckled, 'he did say last night that you had more lives than a cat and we could expect you to turn up.'

'I'm glad he didn't worry too much,' said Hunter, dryly.

'He wants you back here ASAP. He was going to recall you today anyway.'

'It's academic now, but why?'

'We declared World War Three in accordance with our plans. The gloves are off.'

'Good,' replied Hunter. 'It's about time.'

Although there was a feeling of tension in the air, Alleysia was reasonably content. Her organisation had got the man on the boat and the woman with him. They had caused damage to the English warship, albeit superficial. The *Manchester* had sailed a few hours earlier. Closing her eyes, a red mist was forming in her thoughts and she fretted, shaking her head to clear it. The rest of the plan had not gone so well. The attacks she had ordered on the various people and places in Gibraltar had failed to materialise. Instead, members of her organisation had either been arrested or shot. Luckily, they were low-level types from the gutters of the world capitals and of no consequence. What was important, she thought, was the message. *I can get you, no matter what the cost in lives; whether your armies die or mine is of no consequence to me. I have the money and resources to do it.* She stretched luxuriously and decided that it was time to get out of bed. A knock on the door made her frown.

'Enter.'

A manservant opened the door and walked in carrying a silver tray on which lay a message. Angrily she snatched the piece of paper, knowing it signified bad news.

'Get out,' she screamed angrily, after she read it. 'Send Maria to me and give King-Smith a message. Tell him I expect this matter to be dealt with today.'

She screwed the transcript of Hunter and Carter's conversation into a ball and threw it on the floor. The huge investment she had made in the eavesdropping satellites was paying off.

Angrily she threw back the satin bedclothes. It was always the same. She could trust nobody but herself to do things properly. Even a simple operation in Gibraltar had been bungled. The demands of her organisation were never ending. Where was Maria? If she didn't hurry she would have her worthless hide whipped. She smiled. She might anyway. Just for fun.

At the Hire Company Hunter chose a BMW Z8 sportscar and told the counter clerk that he would return it in two days time. Walking out of the office, Hunter did not register the clerk making a telephone call. Speaking English, he whispered, 'Yes. I am sure it is the right man. The car registration? Certainly.'

Hunter drove out of the parking lot and stopped on a street corner. He put down the roof as Ruth jumped in delightedly beside him. 'I've always wanted to ride in a Z8,' she said. 'Gun it, James.'

Hunter smiled and pulled away from the curb. Soon they were on the N340, the coastal highway that stretched all the way to Tarragona, just south of Barcelona. It was infamously known as one of the most dangerous highways in Europe, with more road accidents than elsewhere on the continent.

'See if you can find either the BBC World Service or Radio America,' Hunter suggested.

Fiddling happily with the radio, Ruth was enjoying the wind in her hair and the sun on her shoulders. She glanced at Hunter out of the corner of her eye and her heart soared. He competently changed gear and pressed his foot on the accelerator as they passed the 50kph sign, blatantly ignored by the Spanish drivers. When she moved the radio dial, an English voice came and went.

'Go back a moment. I want to hear that,' said Hunter.

Ruth pressed the button and the medium wave, digital readout moved down the scale. It locked onto BBC World News. They heard the end of a broadcast and then a further announcement. 'Today, the governments of Western Europe hit back at drugs cartels and terrorist organisations across Europe. In a series of raids orchestrated by Interpol, hundreds of locations believed to be involved in drug smuggling were raided. Great success . . .'

'Switch it off or find another programme, please,' said Hunter. 'The raids are a smoke-screen.' Changing down a gear, he pressed the accelerator and passed a British lorry, probably bound for the UK.

'What do you mean?'

'I mean, it's not the real game in town.'

'What on earth are you talking about?'

'Jim Carter gave me some interesting information. Certain things are beginning to happen. Or, to quote Sherlock Holmes, the game is now afoot. TIFAT is going to rattle a few cages and dislodge a few rats. Then see where they lead. That announcement was pure journalistic hyperbole. Dozens, not hundreds of raids are planned and will be carried out while we still can.'

'What do you mean by while we can?' Ruth interrupted him.

Hunter scowled at the traffic, looked in the mirror, decided he was mistaken and answered. 'We're dealing with an incredibly powerful organisation. God alone knows how far its malign influence has spread. All we do know is that it's immense. The General needs to move fast before anybody tries to stop him. Worse, before anybody succeeds in stopping him.'

'Who would try and stop TIFAT?'

'Primarily the politicians and the courts. The operations General Macnair's instigating are designed to create fallout. But it may not be enough.'

The road was suddenly empty. They had just passed Estepona, twenty kilometres south of Marbella, when the car he had become aware of, a big Mercedes, suddenly filled his rear view mirror. He saw the guns appearing even as his foot instinctively pressed the accelerator to the floor.

9

Back at TIFAT HQ, Macnair pondered the political situation across Europe together with the reports he had acquired. Mentally he ticked them off. The Metropolitan Police inquiry into drugs and asylum seekers was explosive to say the least. Suppression of the report was a crime as far as Macnair was concerned.

Then there were the Swiss reports from the chiefs of police of each canton, which made grim reading. Over eighty percent of crime committed in Switzerland was drugs related and often the perpetrators were asylum seekers from Eastern Europe. The report had also been squashed but had been leaked to the media. The backlash explained the nationalist Swiss People's Party's amazing gains in the latest parliamentary elections. Twenty three percent of the vote had gone to the far right. Their campaign had been conducted on three platforms: tax cuts, staying out of the European Union and, most significantly, huge curbs on immigration coupled with the forced repatriation of any individual found guilty of committing a crime. Any crime. The party now had forty-four of the seats and was second only to the Social Democrats who held fifty-one seats.

His phone rang. 'Macnair.'

'Sir,' said Major Carter, 'we should be receiving the first reports any time now.'

'Thank you, Jim.' He broke the connection and continued his mental review of the European political scene.

In Austria the picture was the same. It had witnessed the biggest electoral win for a far right party anywhere in Europe since the Second World War. Austria's Freedom Party, led by Jörg Haider, had taken more than a quarter of the votes nation-wide. Haider was now negotiating with the socialist and conservative parties to be included in the government. His party stood for ultra-right wing economic and social policies. More significantly he blamed Austria's social ills on foreigners and asylum seekers. He was calling for the ban on all immigration and the immediate deportation of outsiders who broke the law.

France had been beset for years with the same problems but now the calls for action were becoming strident. Immigrants were being blamed for many of the problems and civil unrest was becoming rampant. Again, the police reports Macnair had acquired and sent off with his own were damning in the extreme. Ethnic minorities, the majority of whom had moved to France in the last five years, committed over sixty percent of all crime in France. In over ninety-eight percent of cases the crimes had been drug related.

In Germany the situation was far worse. The only factor keeping the far right out of political influence, if not power, was the memory of the Nazi atrocities. Even those memories were fading as current social problems caused unrest to sweep the country. The backlash was targeted against immigrants, mainly Turks and Yugoslavs and again, the police reports were damning in the extreme. As a percentage of the population, the immigrants were far more involved with drugs, particularly heroin, than any other section of society. The involvement of the so-called Russian Mafia made matters worse.

Macnair sat back in his chair, tired but satisfied and ran a hand through his thinning hair. The thought of getting a fresh coffee, the last one having gone cold in its mug, took hold. Weariness won and he stayed where he was. He closed his eyes for a few moments, reviewing everything they had set in place. For the past forty-eight hours teams of TIFAT operatives had been working across Europe with police forces, Customs and Excise and drug enforcement agencies. A huge concerted effort was underway, attacking suspected drug dealers from Greece to . . . He opened his eyes and looked at the electronic map of Europe filling one wall of his office. Marked on the display were red crosses with the name of the village, town, or city where an operation was taking place. It also showed the code name of each team. He glanced north, to Norway, no . . . Iceland. Another marina. This time at Akranes a few kilometres north of Reykjavic. Although they were targeting mainly marinas, they were also hitting suspected wholesale distributors in cities and small airfields. The information amassed and collated by Isobel, TIFAT's information technology boss, ably helped by GCHQ, had been disseminated to trusted senior officers of various services in thirty countries, including the USA. He had sent Colonel Hiram B. Walsh of Delta Force to liaise with the Americans. Not that they needed it, thought Macnair. The USA was the one country capable of dealing with the problem. It was the Europeans who required handholding. And butt kicking, Macnair thought ruefully.

His phone rang, galvanising him into action. 'Macnair.'

'Malcolm, this is Kurt Mithoff, GSG9.' Mithoff was in charge of the German Federal hostage release and anti-terrorist force. It was based on the Border Police because all other German police forces were regional and could not operate nationally.

'Kurt! Good to hear from you. What can I do for you?'

'I thought I would report personally.' The measured voice carried only a hint of an accent.

'That's very kind of you. Do you mind if I tape our conversation?'

There came a chuckle down the line. 'I assumed you would be, to transcribe it for our political masters. As I am doing.'

Macnair chuckled in return. 'Precisely.'

'The operation has been a great success. We raided four targets and, as you say, came up trumps in all four. We found one wholesaler in Hof, just as you predicted.'

Instinctively Macnair looked at the wall and spotted Hof immediately, a border town with the Czech Republic. 'Any trouble?'

'Yes. But we were ready for it. Your team did excellent work.' Again Macnair looked at the display. Team Amber. Captain Joshua Clements, seconded from the American Delta

Force, led them. 'We took out twenty-one of the enemy. My minister is delighted that we will not be bothering with a trial. Incidentally, we found in excess of one hundred and twenty-five million Deutschmarks worth of pure heroin and the same again in diluted form.'

'Have you been able to identify any of the bodies?'

'Yes, easily. We found a safe in the building. In it were ID cards and passports. All but two of the criminals were either Turkish, Czech or Chechnyan. The other two were German nationals from Berlin. We are now examining everything we can find in the hope it will lead us somewhere. We will follow the paper trail, as you suggested.'

'That was Isobel's idea. In her opinion the truth cannot be obliterated. It can be hidden, broken, obfuscated but never done away with. Will you be sending copies of everything you find, as I requested?'

'Of course, my friend. It is time we fought back. TIFAT is the obvious place from where to co-ordinate our war. I am waiting for the reports from the other three raids and as soon as I get them I will send them to you.'

'That's very kind of you, Kurt. I look forward to getting the rest.' They said their goodbyes and Macnair hung up.

Macnair looked at his watch. Noon and that was the first report. There were many more still to come. It would be a long day.

'Sir,' Isobel put her head around the door. 'I thought you would like to know that I am getting encrypted reports down the secure lines. So far I have received them from Stockholm, Bergen, Marseilles and Rome.' She handed Macnair printed copies of the reports, now in plain language.

He scanned them briefly and smiled happily. 'Excellent. If the remaining operations continue like these then we'll have dealt a nasty blow against the cartels.' Macnair noticed the dubious look on Isobel's face and added, 'Okay, I know and I agree. These people are low-level, maybe medium-level operatives. We need the bosses and we'll get them. They won't ignore us as we up the pressure.'

Isobel nodded. 'Gareth and Leo are working on a few things

now.' Since TIFAT's inception, her department had swollen to twenty strong but, as she acknowledged, her left and right hand men were Gareth and Leo. 'The indications I have, though we've no proof as yet, is that the leader of the cartels is an Englishman.'

Macnair nodded. 'Hunter said the same. Only I find it hard to believe.'

'Why, sir?'

'The cartels are strongest in Eastern Europe. How would he have been able to establish a power base there?'

'I don't know, sir. I'm just telling you what we've learnt.'

Jim Carter appeared behind her and she stepped to one side to let him in. 'Sir, there's a call on line four. It's Lt Napier, calling from Sweden.'

Macnair pressed a button on the telephone. 'Napier? General Macnair. You're on loudspeaker. Isobel and Major Carter are with me.'

'Hullo, sir. Just letting you know what's happened this end. As you know, we were involved in the raid on the marina at Helsingborg. Unfortunately, it was not as clean an operation as it could have been.'

'What do you mean?' Macnair asked with a frown.

'I explained to General Dansohn that we were dealing with armed and dangerous men . . .'

'I'd also done the same.' Macnair interrupted him.

'I know, sir. He told me. Frankly, he didn't believe either of us. He gave me a lecture on human rights and how things were done in Sweden.'

'What happened?' asked Macnair, knowing only too well how likely it was.

'We hit six boats in six teams. The only people carrying weapons were us. We covered four groups between us. The Swedes tried to make arrests.' He paused, swallowing, reliving it.

'Go on,' Macnair prompted.

'It was a bloodbath, sir. We reacted in time and protected our teams, although one Customs officer with me was injured and so was a policeman.'

'And the two teams without our back-up?'

'All killed, sir. Along with General Dansohn.'

'Dansohn was there?' Macnair was incredulous.

'Yes, sir. He went along to prove that we were over-reacting.'

'We?'

'Well, to be more precise, sir, you. That we were dealing with straightforward drug smugglers who would never gun down officers of the law.'

'Damnation. I warned him most strenuously.'

'Yes, sir, I know. So did I. At one point I thought the General was going to order us to leave our guns behind. I told him that if we were ordered to do that then we wouldn't be going on the raid. I warned him to reconsider his decision about being armed but he would have none of it.'

'What about protection? Vests?'

'Nothing, sir. Like I just said, they treated the whole thing like a routine arrest.'

'And now?'

'And now, sir, they're in shock. I'm at police headquarters debriefing with their second-in-command, Brigadier Lars Larson. He's as mad as hell. He wants as much information as we can give, no matter how unsubstantiated. He's declaring all out war across Sweden. Can you help?'

Macnair strummed the fingers of his left hand on the desk, thinking furiously. He looked up at Isobel who shrugged and nodded.

She said, 'I can see what we've got and pass it on. Let him decide if it's any good. We've enough to do as it is, so let the Brigadier get on with it.'

'It won't compromise our sources?'

'No, sir. No chance. We'll just send the information raw without any references or cross-check analysis.'

'Okay, do it. Did you hear that, lieutenant?'

'Affirmative, sir. What do you want us to do? Stay on here or come back?'

'RTB. We've more operations and I've got you ear-marked elsewhere.' Return to base was the order of the day for all the teams. 'Tell Brigadier Larson that he has my condolences.'

'Roger that, sir. Goodbye.'

Macnair broke the connection and frowned. 'Maybe now the fools will begin to believe me when I tell them how dangerous the situation is. Isobel, please send a flash message to everyone we're working with and give them the details of what happened in Sweden. It may save a few lives. Any news regarding Turkey?'

'No, sir. The last we heard Team Green was in Sarikamis.'

'That's Masters, isn't it?'

'Yes, sir,' said Carter. 'Don Masters, Badonovitch, McReady and Weir. A good team.'

'Yes, they are that,' said Macnair. 'How's Badonovitch?' The Spetsnaz had been wounded in a recent operation. A ricocheting bullet had lodged itself in Badonovitch's thigh and another had gashed his forehead.

Carter smiled. 'He's fine, sir. He's incredibly tough. The thigh wound has completely healed and his forehead is a thin red scar which is fast disappearing. The doctor declared him one hundred percent fit.'

'Good.'

Four time zones to the east, Team Green was in trouble. Masters' operation was unravelling fast. Everything had been textbook perfect from the time they had met Zim Albatha at Ankara and flown by internal flight to Trabzon on the Black Sea. From there they had transferred to a helicopter for the last leg to Sarikamis. The team knew Albatha from his involvement in the fight against the terrorist Habib. Albatha had been instrumental in supplying vital information, which had helped TIFAT in tracking the terrorist down. Having been recently promoted to captain in the feared Turkish State Security Organisation, Albatha had been given special responsibility in the fight against drugs. He was a mine of information, much of which he had passed to Macnair. A big man, 6ft 6ins tall, over 220lbs and sporting a handlebar moustache, Zim Albatha was as large as life.

He greeted each of the team with a bone-crushing handshake and a thump on the back. Speaking precise, heavily accented English, he smiled a lot, enjoying a private joke he shared with no one. He was one of those people who appeared to find the world a funny place. 'When this is over,' he said, 'please join me and my, how do you say? Intended? Is that right? The one you are going to marry?'

'That's right,' replied Don Masters in his Scottish burr. Masters was a REME sergeant and one of the army's foremost explosives specialists. He had proven that he could spend five minutes in a kitchen and, using ingredients found in its cupboards, concoct an effective bomb. The only ingredient he owned up to using was washing-up liquid. Very tough, he had been at TIFAT from the beginning.

By the time they reached Sarikamis they felt as though they had been travelling for days. They were on the border with Armenia. One hundred and fifty kilometres to the north was Georgia, and Azerbaijan was less than two hundred kilometres away to the east. Armenia was an important centre for poppy growing, heroin manufacturing and arms smuggling. There were more terrorists and drugs cartels per capita of the population than anywhere else on earth, with the possible exception of Columbia.

Sarikamis was a God-forsaken hole, 2,000m high, at the end of a valley which ran north-east to Armenia. It straddled the main road from Tbilisi to Erzurum. A hundred kilometres to the east, where the road crossed the border, were a customs post, a small army detachment and nothing else. The landscape was bleak and mountainous, hot and dusty in the summer, freezing and snow covered in the winter. The people were tough, independent and utterly without respect for authority. On the whole they were law abiding – by their standards – smuggling gold to India and counterfeit finished goods from the sweatshops of India and Pakistan back into Europe. They led hard lives – what was the harm of a little hashish grown locally or bhang from India, now and again? And if they sold some of the weed from time to time for extra money, what of it? But heroin – never! That was an evil trade carried out by evil men, as anybody in the district would say if they were asked.

There were few border checks although the Turkish army patrolled the area as rigorously as their limited budget allowed.

Unfortunately, there were far more trails across the mountains than there were patrols. The lot of the Turkish soldier was not a happy one. The pay was bad, the food was lousy and the conditions unbearable. A little baksheesh could always turn a man's eye blind and seal his mouth. If not, a bullet or a dagger could do so just as easily.

On the eastern edge of town, passing within a kilometre to the south, was a main smuggling route travelled by heavily laden convoys carrying heroin and arms. It was so well organised, and so large, it required the active help of senior local officials – political, police and army. Which was why Albatha was involved. Known to be totally incorruptible, his masters back in Ankara had sent him to clean up the area and to remove the scourge once and for all. Turkey was determined to prove its application to join the European Union was justified. On the ground, however, Albatha knew that he was losing the fight.

When the operation had been put together, only a handful of men had any idea what was going to happen. The original contingent of troops to carry out the attack had been twelve men, plus the team from TIFAT. Albatha had let it be known that the numbers were sufficient. He had then used his own sources and contacts. Troops had been brought in from other regions and bivouacked in a secret location away from the area. Utter secrecy had been the watchword for the whole operation. Masters had wholeheartedly agreed with his plan.

Team Green had carried out the surveillance for the attack. It was to be in a remote valley fifteen kilometres from the town. They had established their attack zones, forward areas and safe havens and briefed Albatha. He had made a number of useful suggestions. Having modified the plan they then settled down to wait. They knew approximately when to expect the next convoy, thanks to GCHQ sending real-time information to Isobel, who had forwarded it via the sat-nav phones.

They knew there were five lorries and six Land Rovers in the approaching convoy and that the Land Rovers carried machine guns with four fighters in each. Each member of Team Green was strung out along the attack zone together with a hundred other troopers.

'Green one, this is Green three, over.' Corporal Peter Weir used his personal radio to Masters.

'One, over.'

'Convoy sighted. Two minutes, over.'

'Roger that. Out.' Masters looked along the valley. He was well dug in, as were the others. Albatha had been up and down the line half a dozen times, checking and re-checking until he was satisfied. Every fifteenth man carried a Stinger missile launcher and Badonovitch and McReady each had the latest anti-tank weapon known as the Maggot. The Maggot had four rockets, each one as fat as a shotgun cartridge, half a metre long and packed with enough high explosive to penetrate the thickest tank and demolish it. It was aimed like a rifle and each rocket, once it had acquired its target, locked on and never let go. This was the ultimate in "aim-and-forget" technology. When fired, fins popped out at the front and back of the shaft, stabilising its flight. It travelled so fast that any occupants in a target had no time whatsoever to respond, even if they knew that a Maggot was on its way. Major Carter had purchased it on the open market before it became standard issue in NATO.

The convoy came into sight, moving sedately but steadily along the well-worn track. Masters frowned. There was something wrong. What on earth was it? He put his binoculars to his eyes and examined the lead Land Rover and then the lorry. It took a minute to understand. The occupants were far more vigilant than he would have expected. He stared at the first lorry and saw the canvas cover move as somebody inside fell against it. His every instinct told him it was a trap, as he realised the men in the cabs were scouring the skyline behind him.

They were in a steep-sided valley that stretched over a hundred metres wide. The valley walls rose hundreds of metres on the far side but behind them the skyline was a hundred metres away and only fifty metres higher. A great place for an ambush but an even better one for a trap.

'Team Green, this is one, we have trouble. I think it's a trap.

Zim, have every fifth man face the other way. Green three, when the last vehicle is over the explosives, then blow them. Green two, fire left to right and Green four fire right to left while I fire behind. Zim, did you get that?'

'Yes. If we have been betrayed somebody will pay.'

'Let's survive first,' said Masters.

Corporal Peter Weir was an Olympic standard marksman. He hit the marker with his first shot. The two hundred kilos of plastic explosive erupted and blew the Land Rover to smithereens, killing the occupants and damaging the lorry ahead. As the canvas covers were thrown back they revealed lorries loaded with fully armed men. The lorries were stopping and the men disgorging even as the army opened fire.

Masters was running away from the fighting towards the ridge. Bent double, he took hand grenades from a pouch. Although six feet two, broad shouldered and heavy, he could still cover ground quickly. He dropped flat at the ridge and looked over. What he saw shocked him to the core. The steep sided hill was covered with armed men, some of whom had reached the summit and were preparing to shoot into the backs of the soldiers. Pulling the pins from the grenades he lobbed four of them in quick succession amongst the climbers. As they exploded, Masters, using an Austrian Steyr AUG Para machine gun, opened fire. Highly accurate with a rate of fire of 700 rounds per minute, the magazine had been modified to carry fifty-two rounds of 9mm Parabellum ammunition instead of the normal thirty-two. The rate of fire was controlled by the trigger. The first pressure gave a single shot and further pressure changed it to automatic. Masters had also taped a second magazine to the first. He could eject, turn and continue firing in less than two seconds. In his hands it became one of the most formidable weapons in the world.

He ignored what was going on behind him. Instead he concentrated on the enemy in front. Holding down the trigger he sprayed across the ridge, killing and injuring the men who were preparing to fire into the backs of the soldiers. Many who were killed or injured slid down the precarious slope, taking others with them. Masters was causing complete carnage when a bullet hit him in the arm, throwing his aim wild. The bullet passed through the fleshy part of his underarm but Masters realised that it had come from behind. He whirled around to see a gun being aimed at him. Even as he brought his own gun to bear he knew he was too late.

Albatha had understood the betrayal and knew others were probably involved. Deliberately he did not join in the fighting, in order to keep an eye on some of his men. Immediately he identified two of the enemy within. In horror, he watched them kneel together and aim at the backs of their colleagues. Firing two snap shots before they could shoot, he had the satisfaction of seeing their heads being blown away. Another defector opened fire with a machine gun, missing Albatha. Peter Weir took the would-be assassin out with a bullet between the shoulder blades.

The man who had fired at Masters was less than five metres from Albatha. Even as the man was about to fire again, Albatha shot him in each shoulder and each leg. He wanted him to talk.

Masters saw what happened, waved his thanks and turned his attention back down the hillside. More of the army had reached the ridge and were now throwing grenades or firing on fully automatic into their attackers. Some of the criminals were turning and trying to escape as the hailing shards of steel cut them to ribbons. Then suddenly their nerve broke and the few still alive turned and scrambled down the hill, the scree sliding from under them, sending them careening downwards, in many cases to serious injury.

Seeing the battle won Masters turned his attention to their own ambush. He registered that a number of their men had been killed. The fight had turned into a stand off. He needed to do something to break the deadlock.

'This is Green one. Check, over.'

'Green two, okay,' said Badonovitch.

'Green three, okay,' replied McReady.

'Green four, fighting with a flesh wound,' replied Weir.

'Green one, fighting with a flesh wound. Four, you fire on anything that moves out there. Two and three go left and come up the valley. I'm sweeping in from the right. Zim, get ready to attack. Copy?'

They acknowledged their orders. Masters slipped over the ridge and worked his way carefully along the valley, keeping just below the skyline. When he was in position he radioed in again. Badonovitch and McReady were ready.

'Zim, you copied everything? Over.'

'Affirmative. We're ready.'

'Okay. Go!'

While Badonovitch and McReady moved in steadily from one side, Masters moved in from the other. Albatha and his men charged across the track, alternate men shooting on fully automatic and those in between throwing grenades as far and fast as they could. The Turkish army was renowned for having some of the toughest, bravest troops anywhere in the world. With Green Team coming in left and right and Peter Weir picking off anybody who showed face, the nerve of the drug dealers snapped. They turned and ran.

But there was no escape. The side of the valley was too steep to climb and when they tried to scramble up it the Turks picked them off, one by one. Those who tried to escape along the valley were stopped by Masters at one end and Badonovitch and McReady at the other. Half a dozen threw down their weapons and raised their hands in surrender. They were killed by the Turks.

Battle over, Albatha checked his men. Five killed and four wounded. He turned to Masters and said, 'We were, how do you call it? Set up?'

Masters nodded. 'Well and truly. It was a close thing. If you hadn't arranged the extra troops we'd never have survived.' Masters shrugged. 'We'll talk about it later. Now we need to examine the trucks and see if they were carrying any drugs.'

'Surely not,' said Albatha. 'This was purely an ambush to get us.'

'Maybe, maybe not,' replied Masters, stroking his chin with a callused hand. 'Think about it. They had what they thought was an overwhelming force to attack us. They expected to win and win easily. What better than to have a large supply of drugs go through at the same time? Come on, let's take a look.'

'Wait a moment,' said Albatha. 'Let the medic look at your arm. We don't want it going septic.'

Masters moved his arm, the pain and discomfort all but forgotten in the heat of battle. What had been a dull throb was becoming more painful by the minute. 'Okay.'

The medic had already seen to Weir who had sustained a flesh wound in the left arm. Masters' wound was more serious but not life threatening. The medic doused it with antibiotic powder and placed a field dressing front and back. The bleeding had almost stopped. Masters just hoped there would not be any lasting damage. When he arrived at the first lorry he stopped in wonder. The soldiers had pulled up the floorboards to reveal row upon row of pure heroin. It represented a huge fortune in the West, more money that the most avaricious person could dream of. Suddenly Masters was scared. How on earth could they fight wealth and power like this?

He looked at the faces of his men and could see that the same thought was going through their minds. The Turkish soldiers seemed impervious to it. They were happy to be alive, helping to gather the drugs in one pile. When the lorries were emptied, Albatha poured petrol over the mound and set fire to it. They stepped back as the acrid black smoke drifted into the still air and an estimated few hundred million dollars worth of heroin was destroyed.

While they stood there the medic came back to have a word with Albatha.

Nodding his thanks, Albatha turned to the men from TIFAT. 'My friends, one of the traitors is still alive. I need some answers, so if you will excuse me I will go and talk to him.' He walked away, stopped and looked back. 'I hate drug smugglers and traitors in equal measure,' he smiled.

The four members of Green Team joined some of the soldiers for a cup of tea and bars of high protein chocolate, an excellent food substitute after the adrenaline highs they had been on. Albatha returned after a while with a grim look on his face.

He gratefully accepted the mug of sweetened tea offered by Peter Weir.

He took a mouthful and wiped his moustache with the back of his hand. 'Ah, that's better. I'm afraid the traitor did not survive after all.' Albatha did not look in the least bit sorry. 'I found out what I wanted to know. Correction,' he paused and then went on. 'I had confirmed what I already suspected.'

Masters nodded. 'Governor Sakov?'

Albatha looked surprised. 'Yes. How did you know?'

Masters shrugged. 'It's obvious. Only the Governor of the region could have arranged matters so well. What are you going to do?'

'Finish it. Are you coming?'

Masters looked at the others and nodded. 'We've come this far, so we'll carry on. What're your intentions?'

'He'll be in Erzurum tonight. There's a banquet being hosted for a Japanese company thinking of setting up a car factory in the region. The Governor has been invited in appreciation of the help he's given to the Japanese manufacturers.'

'We'll come with you. Anybody else?'

'No, we'll keep it small. My fiancée, Alim, can help by arranging the clothes that we'll need. I'll send her details of your sizes.'

Knowing the precarious livelihood earned by any honest member working for the Turkish government and knowing that Albatha would never ask, Masters put a hand in his pocket and took out a wad of American dollars.

'Here, use this. It's what we've been given it for.'

'Thank you,' said Albatha, the relief evident in his voice. 'Let us ensure this filth,' he waved a hand at the smouldering pile of heroin, 'is fully destroyed and I will send my men on their way. We will need to see to the bodies as well. They must be buried in accordance with their preferred religion.'

'Zim,' said Masters. 'Please tell them that one thousand dollars will be paid to the families of each of the Turkish men killed. It is a TIFAT policy to look after those who are injured or, if they die, the families of those killed.'

Albatha nodded, gratitude evident on his face. 'So I've been led to understand. Thank you.'

He walked away to speak to his junior officers and to issue instructions.

'We'd better report in,' said Sam McReady.

Masters nodded and took out his sat-phone. 'I'll tell HQ what's going on.'

The Z8 suddenly accelerated like a rocket, its engine screaming in protest as the rev counter shot into the red. It accelerated from 90kph to 150kph in seconds. The occupants of the Mercedes were taken by surprise and Hunter drew away before the driver could respond. But the advantage was only seconds long as the big car inexorably closed the gap. At the speed the cars were travelling it was pointless for any of the gunmen to lean out and fire at the BMW, but one of them tried. Holding an automatic out of the window he emptied it to no effect as the wind buffeted the gun, throwing his aim off.

'What's the plan?' Ruth yelled to Hunter.

'I'm still working on it,' he called back.

'Well, you'd better think of something fast – they're gaining. And once they're alongside, the slightest nudge or a gun firing at us and we won't have much of a chance.'

'I know. There's a turning ahead for Ronda. We'll take that.' The car was now showing 210kph on the clock. Nearing the turn-off, he slowed down, letting the other car catch up. He switched from the right hand lane to the middle. His timing needed to be perfect. The Mercedes drew alongside, in the outside lane, and two guns appeared in the window. They couldn't miss. Ruth was not looking at Hunter but had her eyes on the car now only two metres away.

'Stand by,' Hunter yelled, hitting the brakes hard.

The BMW slowed rapidly and the Mercedes shot ahead, taking the gunmen by surprise. Hunter swung the wheel to the right. The car went careering down the slip road while he fed the brakes short, sharp hits, keeping control. He stopped the car at the intersection and turned left onto the 473, heading for the National Park of Sierra de las Nieves, the mountain range stretching ahead of them far in the distance. He accelerated too hard and the BMW's tyres squealed in protest, black tread melting into the road as Hunter fought to retain control, the back fishtailing. He over corrected and the car swerved dangerously close to the side barrier. Within seconds he regained control and they went flying onto the twisting, two-way road, narrowly missing an overloaded lorry trundling along on sagging springs. The startled yell of the driver and the blare of his horn were lost in the distance as the BMW sped away.

'I don't understand,' yelled Ruth, 'how they got onto us so quickly.'

Hunter nodded. 'I agree. They seem to have tentacles every-where.' He thought for a few seconds. 'It's the sheer power of their money, I suppose. Bribery or coercion will do it every time. We need to dump the car.'

Ruth nodded in agreement, busy with a map of the area she had found in the glove compartment. 'There's a mainline train service from Ronda that goes on to Seville.'

'We'll take it,' said Hunter. He slowed down for a German car crammed with youngsters crawling along ahead of them. The road now was a series of hairpin bends and he felt frustration mounting as he looked for a way to pass. He kept one eye glued to the mirror, expecting the Mercedes to reappear at any moment. 'How far was it to the next turn-off back there?'

Ruth looked at the map. 'Ten, maybe twelve kilometres.'

'That's what I thought.' Seeing an opportunity, he changed gear and rammed the accelerator to the floor. The powerful car took off, leaving the Germans behind as though they were parked. 'We need to get a move on, otherwise they'll catch us up. One advantage is we have far better road holding than a big Merc, so I'd better put it to good use.'

The beautiful countryside passed in a blur. The terraces of grapes, like regimented green soldiers, stretched along and up the hills on both sides of the road. This was an area of outstanding beauty and a favourite for visitors. Hunter used all his skill and concentration to pass slower moving cars and buses, lorries and vans, as he tried to put as much distance as possible between themselves and their pursuers.

The land around was changing. Approaching the Serrania de Ronda it became more barren. From time to time they saw an ibex, with long, recurved horns, the wild goat of Europe and Asia.

'When we get to Ronda we need to head for the new part of town. That's where the services are and, I suspect, the railway station. It's a pedestrian zone so we'll have to abandon the car before we get there.' Ruth was reading from a guidebook courtesy of the car rental agency. 'There are three bridges across the gorge, which I think we'll have to walk. The new town is the other side of the gorge and this road leads directly to it. Damnation!'

'What is it?'

'I'm wrong. The train station is to the north of the town. The line doesn't enter Ronda. It's been built to by-pass the buildings.' She studied the map further. 'We can go round to the east or we can drive straight through and dump the car in the old town. Down a side street somewhere. The town has the second oldest bullring in Spain and is a great tourist attraction, so there could be loads of cars and people about.'

'Sounds a good bet. We'll dump the car.' They were approaching Ronda and he eased up on the accelerator. 'Time to begin acting like law-abiding citizens,' he added.

The town's population of over thirty thousand almost doubled in the height of the tourist season. Now, at the start of the holiday period, there were plenty of people around and there was a festive air to the place. Situated in the Andalusian Mountains, the city was built on a triangular plateau. On the western side vertical rock faces reared over a thousand metres higher than the town.

As they reached the edge of the town Hunter turned left into the Virgen de la Paz and found a parking space. He didn't turn off the engine immediately but sat there, looking about them, checking if anybody was taking any undue interest in them. Once satisfied, he turned off the engine and threw the keys into the glove compartment.

'When we get to the airport I'll tell the rental agency where to find the car,' he said.

Closing over the roof, they climbed out of the car and walked towards the new town. They came to the gorge and crossed the Puente Nuevo – the New Bridge – built in 1788. In spite of their situation, neither of them could help but be impressed by the view a hundred metres down into the Rio Guadalevin gorge. They entered the beautiful Plaza Espana, dominated by an imposing town hall.

The streets were busy although not over-crowded. People were obviously enjoying themselves and had an expectant air about them. Hunter realised what was afoot when he saw a brightly painted poster and pointed. 'A bullfight this evening. Good. The more people the better.'

In the information office they discovered there was a train to Antequera where they needed to change for Seville. They would have enough time to catch the last flight to London but it meant staying out of sight the whole afternoon. They couldn't book a seat, nor could they learn if there were places on the plane. They would have to take the risk that seats would be available.

Leaving the information office they continued north. There were fewer pedestrians clogging the pavement as they moved further from the bullring. Hunter and Ruth constantly looked about them, like tourists. Except they were not looking at the sights, they were looking at the people.

Ruth spotted them. Passing the church of La Merced, she suddenly grabbed Hunter by the arm and stopped to stare into a shop window displaying fancy leather goods. 'Two men on the corner. They keep looking at their hands and at the people.'

Hunter glanced to his left and away again. 'I see them. Dark suits, coats buttoned and wearing ties. They stand out like sore thumbs. I doubt they've got photographs but it could be our descriptions they're checking.'

'I'm not so sure,' said Ruth. 'I've been thinking how they got onto us so quickly. The only answer I can think of is the clerk in the car rental agency gave us away.'

'And I noticed that the agency had a surveillance camera,' said Hunter.

'Exactly. So it's possible they've got photographs.'

'Come on, we'll go down this alley and try another way.'

The alley was narrow and relatively cool after the sunlight of the main street. Doors on both sides appeared to lead to private apartments. Looking up, Hunter could see four levels of balconies, close enough that you could lean over and touch your neighbour's. Halfway along they came to a small bar, not used by tourists but by the locals. Glancing in they saw that the half dozen tables were empty of customers.

Entering, Hunter said in poor Spanish, '*Buenas tardes. Dos cafe, por favor.*'

The young lady standing behind the counter immediately answered him in almost unaccented English. 'Certainly, sir. Do you wish for anything to eat?'

'Please,' Hunter replied. 'Ruth?'

'I'll have a baguette,' she pointed at one stuffed with cheese and salami. Hunter chose the same.

'I will bring them to your table,' said the young girl with a smile.

They sat where they could see the door, alert, ready for trouble. After a few minutes Hunter went through a door marked *Retrete* and checked if there was a backdoor. There was and it was open. They stayed there for nearly an hour, killing time. Finally, they decided they ought to leave. Any longer and the waitress would become suspicious. Throughout the time they had been there no one else had entered. When Hunter passed a comment to the waitress she had shrugged and explained it was the siesta.

The poster advertising the bullfight had said it would begin at 6pm and people were continuing to make their way in the general direction of the bullring. It was becoming satisfyingly busy but not busy enough to suit Hunter.

'Look at the corner,' he said, ducking his head.

'I see them. Both sides. That makes four of them. What shall we do?'

'In here,' he grabbed her arm and they went into another bar.

This one was for tourists and here the prices were more than double what they had just paid. The place had fifteen or so tables and was half full with people enjoying a drink and talking excitedly about the bullfight. From their accents it was clear that they were Americans. Hunter and Ruth sat next to the door marked *Retrete* at the back of the restaurant. For non-Spanish speakers it also bore the outline of a man and a woman.

'I'll check it out,' said Ruth.

She was back within moments. 'A short corridor, ladies to the left, gents to the right. There's a door at the end which is a fire door and guess what?'

Hunter raised an eyebrow and said, 'It's locked, bolted and chained?'

'Precisely. A lot of good it would be in an emergency. However, in the ladies there's a window that'll open easily enough. It's narrow but we ought to be able to squeeze through if we need to.'

'Let's hope it doesn't come to that. Hell! I spoke too soon. Outside, by the door. Two men in suits. They look like they might be coming in. Come on.'

Five hours after the attack, Green Team with Albatha and Alim, were in the main square of Erzurum, in Turkey. The city was a large conurbation of distinctive villages, each with their own ethnic identity. It made for an interesting place to visit but also a dangerous one if you strayed into the wrong area. Luckily, Albatha appeared to know his way around. The team was dressed in Turkish made suits, wearing white shirts and bright coloured ties, the badge of any self-respecting businessman in Turkey. Their weapons were well hidden but could be accessed easily.

They had split up. Albatha, Weir and Masters in one group, Badonovitch, McReady and Alim in another. If challenged, Albatha and Alim would do the talking.

They knew that after the dinner Governor Sakov would be staying at the Grand Hotel, situated in the square, the guest of honour of the Japanese. Masters reviewed what he knew of Sakov. A Russian by birth and a Turkish national by choice, he had bought his way to the governorship some three years earlier. Since then the whole area had been a byword for thievery and corruption. Masters was at a loss to explain why a reputable Japanese company would want to establish itself there.

All six were in contact using their personal radios, the microphones buried in their watchstraps, the loudspeaker-transmitters hidden in their ears. Their communications equipment was the very latest in micro engineering.

'Here's Sakov now,' Albatha murmured.

'The man wearing the dinner jacket, tall, grey-haired?' Weir clarified.

'The same,' hissed Albatha. 'The bastard.' He spat his displeasure into the street. From the reconnaissance they had carried out earlier in the day, they knew that the Governor had a large suite on the third floor.

Staying in their separate groups, they adjourned to a local restaurant for dinner. Neither group acknowledged the other by so much as a glance but sat around their respective tables, talking quietly, careful not to be overheard speaking English. It made for an uncomfortable meal.

It was midnight when they returned to the hotel. The foyer and bars were full of people, some from the banquet, others just revellers looking for a late night drink in pleasant surroundings. The piano player was playing old American blues songs, taking requests and accepting every drink he was offered. His playing was becoming more erratic as the night wore on.

In pairs they made their way to the third floor, using the stairs and separate lifts. At the corner to the corridor where the suite was situated Albatha took a careful look. 'Hold it,' he whispered, 'something isn't right. There should be at least one guard outside.' He moved slowly along the corridor. His pulse quickened when he saw that the door to the suite was open and positively raced when he recognised the red blotches on the carpet as blood. 'Close in. Be ready for anything.'

Albatha and Badonovitch came from one side of the corridor, Masters and McReady from the other. Alim and Weir stayed hidden to protect their backs. At the door, Albatha halted on one side and Masters on the other. They could see a trousered leg on the carpet. Looking closer, they could make out the rest of the body. Blood had seeped from the head and made a red halo on the thick carpet. Both men listened intently but heard nothing.

Albatha signalled to Masters and they entered the room quickly, going in different directions, guns drawn, ready for any eventuality. Except for the sight that met their eyes.

10

Governor Sakor had been garrotted, his oxygen-deprived tongue turned blue. The wire was still cutting into his neck, blood coagulating around the serrated metal. His hands were tied to the arms of a chair. His fingers had been sliced off and placed in a pile on an occasional table. His three bodyguards had been luckier. They had been shot.

'All dead,' said Albatha. 'No! Wait!' He darted across the room and knelt by the body of one man, lying on his back, whose eyes had flickered open.

Summoning up the last reserves of strength in his fast dying body, he gripped Albatha's arm and said, 'Georgians.' His head lolled back and he was dead.

Masters frowned. 'Does it mean anything to you?' he asked, quickly checking the other rooms.

'It may do,' replied Albatha, enigmatically. 'I need to speak to General Macnair.'

'Wait a moment, Zim,' said Masters. 'I want to know what's going on. Who did this and why? Right now we're up to our necks in manure and we're in danger of drowning in the stuff. We need a lot of answers and we need them fast. What do we do about this? If we report it we'll have to explain what we're doing here.'

'I agree, my friend. We will leave quietly and let the maid find this in the morning. Let the local police have the headache. We have much bigger fish to fry without being bogged down in explanations. Our objective has been achieved, albeit not as planned. However, there is good news.'

Masters looked puzzled. 'Right now I could use some.'

'This could be confirmation of involvement by a group I have been aware of for some time. If the Georgians were indeed responsible then their tentacles are reaching far further than I thought possible.' He frowned at Masters who stood with his head on one side, listening.

'Keep talking,' Masters mouthed, moving towards a large cupboard in the corner of the room. He had heard the faintest of noises. A scrabbling, a movement as somebody eased a cramped muscle. The warm blood still dripping from the Governor's finger stubs had been Master's first clue. Whoever had committed the atrocity had not had time to escape.

Stepping to one side of the cupboard he put his hand on the handle and tore it open. The man inside looked up in shock, raised a gun and blew his own brains out. The silenced weapon barely made a cough.

'Christ,' said Masters.

'There has to be somebody else,' said Albatha. 'No one man could have done this alone.'

Badonovitch and McReady stood either side of the door. Each man looked carefully around the room. There was nowhere else to hide.

'Try the other room,' said McReady.

A double door was set in the centre of one wall. Albatha and Masters approached it circumspectly, one each side. Albatha knelt down and gripped the doorknob and looked at Masters who nodded. Twisting the knob, he flung the door open. Nothing happened.

Masters crouched and darted inside. He was in a large, luxurious bedroom. The room was dominated by a huge four-poster bed, canopied with floral patterned curtains and big enough to sleep four comfortably. The old fashioned furniture was large and solid, two wardrobes and a chest of drawers. The two men quickly checked them but found nothing. A further door could only lead to a bathroom. It was the last place to look. The door was slightly ajar and Masters kicked it wide open, expecting a fusillade of bullets. Again nothing. Albatha quickly searched and found nobody.

They stood perplexed in the middle of the floor. McReady appeared in the doorway. 'Down!' he yelled. Masters acted immediately, pushing Albatha to the floor. McReady shot the man who was kneeling on the top of the canopy over the bed. The head shot killed the man instantly and silently.

They searched both bodies but came away empty-handed.

'We'll leave it to the pathologist's lab,' said Albatha. 'They may get some information from the clothes. If they have criminal records we might learn even more. But somehow, I doubt it. Let's get out of here. It is time to have a nightcap and I will tell you what I know about the Georgian cartel. If what I have heard is only half true then it is no surprise that they committed suicide rather than report failure.'

Alleysia Raduyev was so angry that she was unable to think clearly. Simpletons! Incompetents! She knew she had to dispel the mist. Taking deep breaths, her thoughts inevitably, as they always did at such times, strayed back to that life-changing day eight years earlier. Memories flashed by frame by frame. Her beloved father had been at his desk, using the telephone. She had just left the room to fetch him refreshments. They had been discussing their plans for their winter holiday. Every winter they went skiing. It was part of their ritual since her mother had died in the bomb blast meant for her father eighteen years earlier. For years she had analysed her feelings about her mother. She had tried to conjure up sorrow or remorse but all she had ever felt was relief and even happiness. Now she had Papa all to herself. As she had grown into womanhood Alleysia had taken more and more responsibility for her father's household until that most glorious of days when he had formally announced that she was in charge of all matters appertaining to their home. On that day he had given her the details of the bank, the wages for the staff and *carte blanche* to run the place as she pleased. Built in the eighteenth century the chateau boasted twenty-one bedrooms and eight public rooms. These did not include the servants quarters, whose many occupants fetched and carried for the two of them. They lived in total luxury, content in each other's company.

Until her father, anxious to exploit his impeccable European connections, had introduced her to that . . . that gigolo, Count Alfonso Palocco.

The memories flooded back. They had been married within three months. Her father thought he was wonderful. So charming. So refined. His title proved a great asset to them, allowing them to move in the highest echelons of European society. He took her maidenhood on their wedding night and didn't touch her again for a month. Once a month, only when drunk, did he bring himself to make love to her. The experience left her cold but she had no experience to judge it against. Until she had heard him degrade her on the telephone when she had mistakenly picked up an extension.

Alfonso likened their lovemaking to lying with a dead pig. On the other end a woman had laughed gaily at the description. Murmuring seductively, she begged him to leave Alleysia. Soon, he said. He needed more money.

The confrontation had come two weeks later. Her father had sent for her. He and Alfonso had been in the study, her father's sanctum sanctorum.

'Alfonso has informed me that he wishes to divorce you,' her father had said abruptly.

Although she had known it was coming it was still a shock. She looked at her father, tall, grey-haired and utterly distinguished. The head of the biggest criminal organisation in Georgia. Then she had looked at her husband. Dark-haired, flashy good looks spoiled by a weak chin and a greedy mouth. For all his connections, he was a stupid man, she had come to realise. She was about to discover just how stupid.

'Your husband has asked for a settlement of five million US dollars.'

She looked from one to the other. Her expression gave no indication of her inner turmoil. Her father's face was set like granite, her husband's had a supercilious twist to the sneering mouth.

'It is a fair sum,' her husband insisted. 'After what I have had to put up with. Papa's little girl – with not a spark of passion in her.'

'Silence!' her father bellowed, smashing his hand down onto

the desk, making them both jump. 'You are a pimp and a thief. I have let you into my house and into my daughter's bed. And how do you repay my trust? By fornicating with every trollop in the district. Oh, don't look so surprised. Do you think I do not know what goes on under my own roof? In my own area? I control it all. For hundreds of kilometres in every direction. Nobody farts unless I am told about it,' her father boasted. 'You have brought shame and sorrow to this house. Get out! Now! You arrived with nothing and you will leave with nothing.'

Alfonso settled back in his chair and smiled. 'I think not. Either we reach a settlement or your activities will be reported to the authorities. I will give them details of your drugs operations and your contraband smuggling, along with the details of your activities with illegal immigrants across Europe. I have amassed the information and sent it to my advocate in Rome. If I do not appear there in two days he knows what to do with it. You will be finished. I think five million dollars for what I have put up with is a fair price.'

Alleysia's father smiled and nodded. 'Is that your last word?' He spoke softly, a sure sign he was at his most dangerous.

'Yes. That is my final word.' Alfonso sat back in his chair, one leg over the other and smirked contentedly at her father.

Her father stood up, crossed to the sideboard and picked up a decanter of finest brandy. He waved it at Alfonso and said, 'Let us drink a toast. To the man who has outwitted me.'

Alleysia could not believe it. Her father was yielding to him. Her father who protected her from all harm. The God she turned to when she needed help. He was letting that . . . that carrion . . . that filth, walk away. She watched him pouring the liquid into the finest, antique crystal goblets. He picked up both and swirled the brandy around as he walked over to her husband and offered one to him. Alfonso took it, raised it in mock salute and downed a substantial mouthful. Her father had sat back at his desk, his own untouched.

'You are not drinking?' her husband queried.

'No. No, it would not agree with me.' Her father had pulled open a drawer of his desk and taken out a floppy disk and a pile of papers. 'This is the information you sent to your lawyer. It was returned to me within twenty-four hours of being delivered to Rome. Your advocate has been in my employ since you married my daughter. I made it clear to him that it was in his best interests to keep me informed.'

The crystal glass had dropped from Alfonso's hand and smashed to pieces on the wooden floor. He tried to sit up, to move, but seemed incapable. 'What have you done?'

'You have been drugged. Within minutes you will be unconscious.'

As the horror of his situation seeped into her husband's fuddled brain, tears had come to his eyes and trickled down his cheeks. 'Please, I beg you – I'm sorry. I'll stay. I will love . . .' He had slid unconscious to the floor.

Her father had pressed a button concealed under his desk and two armed men entered. 'Take this carrion away. Drop him in the lake.'

'Father – Father, please,' she had begun and then faltered.

'You do not wish me to spare him, do you?' her father asked, puzzled. 'For you, Alleysia – but . . .'

'No, father. You don't understand. I intend to deal with this. He is my husband. It is my responsibility.'

Her father had hesitated. His instinct was to protect his only daughter. But he was aware that if she were to inherit his organisation then she would have to prove to him and others that she was brave, resourceful and, most importantly of all, ruthless. He had nodded his assent.

She had followed them down to the boathouse. As she re-lived the memories of that night she smiled.

For five more years she and her father had been happy. Until the coup.

11

Hunter kept his face averted and went through the door, Ruth at his heels. The toilet window was at shoulder height. It was secured by an old-fashioned catch along the bottom. He pushed the catch up and shoved at the window. It was painted securely shut.

The door behind them opened.

'What, young man, do you think you're up to?' The blue-rinse was one of the Americans, a particularly vulgar specimen who spoke in the same shrill tone she had used when pontificating on bull-fighting.

Ruth came to the rescue. 'You saw those two men who just came in? Wearing suits?'

'What about them?' Suspicion oozed from every pore.

'They work for my husband. He . . .' Ruth faltered and then rallied. 'He beats me. This is my brother. He's helping me to get away. I want a divorce but my husband refuses. Please, don't give us away. I must get back to Israel where my father can protect me and I can get a divorce. My husband's Spanish – it is against the Roman Catholic Church to divorce.' She gilded the lily by adding, 'He has affairs, the hypocrite. I can't stand anymore.' From somewhere she mustered a tear and wiped it away with the back of her hand.

'Of course I won't say anything,' said the woman, thrilled to be involved. She couldn't wait to tell the others.

'Can you stand and guard the door while I open this window?' asked Hunter.

The woman stood with her back to the door and crossed her arms. 'Nobody'll get in while I'm here,' she announced.

Hunter took a Swiss army knife from his pocket, opened a blade and cut the paint around the window. He put his hands each side of the window frame and gave a series of shoves. On the fifth the window moved and one more sent it flying open. He caught it before it crashed back.

'Come on, Ruth. Up you get.' He cupped his hands and she stepped lightly into them. She wriggled through the opening and dropped feet first to the ground. Hunter tried to follow. He got half way through and became stuck. The lock catch caught in a buttonhole. He was hooked, unable to go further.

'Come on,' said Ruth. 'Hurry up.'

'I can't. Damn it, my coat's caught.' He grabbed the material, pulled hard and writhed furiously. Feeling the coat give, he pushed his hands in front of him just in time. He hit the ground awkwardly on his hands and somersaulted onto his feet. 'Hell,' he exclaimed as he came up against the opposite wall.

'Are you all right?' Ruth asked.

'I'll live. Come on, we'd better get going.' The tear in his jacket was not obvious and he tucked the torn cloth out of the way.

From the rear of the building a side passage led them back to the street. Hunter put a wary eye to the corner. The pavements had suddenly become far more crowded. 'Come on, we'll move slowly through the throng.'

'They're going in the wrong direction. They're all heading for the bullring. We'll stick out,' Ruth protested.

'We'll go very slowly. Try not to bring any attention to ourselves. There are men on both sides of the street up ahead and I think they're looking for us. When we get to the crossroads we'll go right and then cross the road further along and come back on the other side. Okay?'

'Okay. We can't hang around too long or else they'll notice us, even in this crowd.'

'Agreed. Right . . . now.' Hunter sidled around the corner as the two men nearest to them turned away to look at a couple approaching down the street.

Halfway along the side street they crossed the road and made their way back towards the junction. Now they were on the other side of the two men and walking in shadow. By now the crowds were teeming, jostling and shoving good-naturedly, heading to the bullfight. Hunter and Ruth paused at the corner. The men were looking uncertainly about them checking from face to face and frequently looking down at something they were holding in their hands.

'Let's go.' Hunter took Ruth by the hand and they stepped around the corner. Heads low, they walked more briskly, close to the wall, against the crowd, away from danger. At any moment they expected a yell, a challenge. Soon they were fifty metres away, then a hundred. Then the street curved around to the right and they could breathe more easily.

'It's not far to the station,' said Ruth. 'But the danger's not over yet.'

'True. Although they don't know we've abandoned the car. So they may not be looking there.'

'The resources of these people are frightening,' said Ruth with a shudder.

'I agree. The sooner we get out of Spain, the better.'

'I've been thinking,' said Ruth. 'I'd concentrate my foot soldiers at the railway station. There and the bus station.'

'Any ideas?' Hunter asked.

'A disguise?'

'What as? The back of a donkey?'

Ruth smiled. 'No, but . . .' she paused. 'We make ourselves obvious. Be loud.'

'Drunk?'

'Tipsy. We don't want to overdo it.'

'Clothes?'

'Let's buy Spanish,' said Ruth leading the way into a clothing store designed for tourists.

A short while later they reappeared, wearing sombreros and ponchos. They looked ridiculous. They wove along the pavement laughing, bumping into other pedestrians, apologising. They saw a further three pairs of suits watching, comparing faces and photographs. Hunter and Ruth hardly rated a second look.

Passing into the cool interior of the high domed station, Hunter made his way to the *Taquilla de billetes*. He bought two, first-class return tickets to Seville. The train was waiting to depart when Hunter and Ruth moved quickly along the platform. They paused at the first class, non-smoking carriage and climbed aboard. Hunter looked back in time to see two of the men in suits dashing across the platform and onto the train. A whistle blew and the train moved slowly forward, gradually picking up speed. The train they were on was an exprés rápido, a fast inter-city train with a restaurant and buffet car. There were at least a dozen stops between Ronda and Seville. At any one, reinforcements could arrive to back up the two men Hunter had seen climbing aboard.

The first class carriage was split into eight seated compartments. Hunter and Ruth had one to themselves. By European standards the train was spacious as the railway track was a wider gauge than elsewhere in Europe and first class reeked of old-fashioned opulence.

'Two men got on,' said Hunter. 'I think they're after us.'

'Will they wait for reinforcements?' Ruth asked.

'That's what I was wondering. I think they'll want to get it over with and get off at the next station. Problem solved. Undying gratitude is earned and given.' He looked upwards. The luggage rack was solid wood and nearly a metre deep. 'If you get up there we can take them by surprise. I'll pass you something. Up you get.'

Swiftly Ruth climbed onto the rack. Opening the door, Hunter looked out into the corridor. There was nobody in sight. He went back to the carriage entrance and, as expected, found a fire extinguisher. Having unstrapped it he returned to the compartment.

'Here. Hold it at right angles. I'll try and lure them into the compartment. You use this to take out one. I'll get the other.'

Hunter sat next to the door and craned his neck to look along the corridor. As expected, the two men were already approaching, peering into each compartment. They were hurrying, only seconds away.

'Here they come,' he said. Throwing himself across the compartment, he sat with his head bent, snoring. The door was flung open and a harsh voice said something in a language Hunter didn't recognise. He didn't move, his eyes watching the feet and then the legs of the first man as he came nearer.

Hunter didn't move until he heard the loud crash of the fire extinguisher smashing into the second man's head and falling with a clatter to the floor. As his partner spun around Hunter pounced. Grabbing the man's gun hand, he forced the gun down, away from Ruth, and hit the man across the back of the neck with the edge of his hand. The man dropped, pole-axed, his neck broken.

Ruth climbed down from the rack just as her target was beginning to recover. She snatched up the extinguisher and brought it down as hard as she could onto the man's forehead. It cracked his skull.

'What language were they speaking? Do you know?'

Ruth shook her head. 'I couldn't hear properly. Have you any idea?'

Hunter shook his head. 'It wasn't any of the Western languages. Russian with a strong regional accent may be a possibility but I'm only guessing.' Looking out of the window he saw that the landscape was changing as the train meandered northwards. The scenery was breathtaking but Hunter was too busy thinking to enjoy the view. 'We need to get rid of the bodies. Help me to search them.'

The two men carried no identity but each had an automatic. Ruth and Hunter were both relieved to be armed.

Luck was with them. A short while later the train entered a long tunnel and they were able to push the bodies out through the window, hidden by the darkness.

Looking at his watch, Hunter said, 'With a bit of luck we'll be in Seville on time.'

*   *   *

The members of Green Team sat in a quiet restaurant with Alim and Zim Albatha, having breakfast. Albatha was holding court.

'There is a Georgian cartel,' he began, 'that has been operating for decades. It started when Stalin was still alive and is well established in the region. Once Russia fell apart it expanded rapidly. Some years ago there was a coup, a bloodbath. The boss of the cartel was killed but an Englishman and the daughter of the boss finally put down the coup. Rumour has it that she inherited her father's crime business and put the Englishman nominally in control. She has a well-deserved reputation for brutality and quite sickening violence. We think it is the biggest crime syndicate anywhere in Europe.'

Masters let out a low whistle. 'That's some organisation.'

'They aim to control local and national markets – giving them power over entire regions – including their own legislation. The rumour is that it will become the biggest in the world. If not in personnel then in terms of turnover.'

'Turnover?' McReady queried. 'You make it sound like a legitimate business.'

'A business certainly,' said Alim. 'Legitimate, never. They deal in drugs, arms, slavery, and illegal immigrants. Anything that can make them a profit.'

'Or give them power,' added Albatha. 'They control enough wealth to change governments. Oh, and I don't mean banana republics. I'm talking Belorussia, Estonia, Latvia, Bulgaria, possibly even the Ukraine.'

Alim continued. 'We know that Slovenia and Croatia have political parties which the Georgians fund. They are beginning to make inroads into the new democracies. Think what that will do, only a stone's throw from Austria and Italy. What if they take over a country? Nothing will stop them except war. And who's going to fight them? Europe's stomach for war is waning fast.'

'How do you know all this?' Masters asked.

'We have been pulling together information for years,' replied Albatha. 'At first it was only of interest to us because of the proximity of Georgia and Chechnya to our eastern border. It was from there that they expanded into the west. They used

127

coercion, bribery and utter ruthlessness to achieve their aims.' Albatha paused, took a mouthful of food and swallowed some coffee. 'The problem is we haven't identified the Englishman nor the woman yet.'

'But you said . . .' Masters began but was interrupted.

'I know what I said,' Albatha smiled to take the sting out of his words. 'But the fact is there are no photographs, no descriptions. Only vague unsubstantiated rumours. With their wealth and influence they could have a dozen passports, a dozen nationalities. The two of them can and probably do travel the world in complete safety.' He shook his head in a mixture of disgust and admiration. 'They have to be stopped.'

Alleysia Raduyev was in a melancholy mood brought on by her loneliness. Despite the fact that she moved in the same circles as the rich and beautiful she did not have a single friend – acquaintances by the hundreds but no true friend. Her father had been her constant companion. They had shared a friendship so deep it could not be replaced. The night of the coup she and her father had been at home, only the servants in the castle. The two of them had been sitting in the room her father called the library, playing chess. It was a large room, lined with books. In one corner stood an antique bar from which, from time to time, she had taken a bottle of superb French brandy and refreshed her father's glass. They sat in front of a roaring log fire, for the night was cold, and he took the opportunity to relate something of the organisation. It was part of his training programme for her and had been going on since she was a little girl. Since she had proven herself by killing her husband, he knew she would be a worthy successor.

The door opened to reveal a nervous looking servant. 'Sir, Sali Gabot seeks an audience.' Sali Gabot was her father's right-hand man. A few years his junior, he was a vicious, amoral thug who carried out her father's wishes without question. Alleysia had never trusted nor liked him.

Her father had frowned and said to her, in German, so that the servant could not understand, 'It must be important for him to come here on such a wild night.' He switched to Russian and answered, 'Ask him to please join us. Alli, get a brandy for our guest.'

She had stepped behind the bar and was reaching for a glass when, not one, but three men entered unexpectedly. She was suddenly afraid.

Her father had looked surprised. 'What is the meaning of this, my friend? I expected only you.'

'Pardon the intrusion,' said Gabot with a slight bow, the sneer on his face making a mockery of the gesture and his words. 'I have come to deliver a message of the utmost importance.' As he spoke he put his hand in his pocket and, without removing it, shot her father three times. The brandy glass slipped from her father's fingers as he slid, dead, down the leather armchair.

Alleysia's heart stopped for a second and then began to race, pounding, causing her to feel breathless. Gabot withdrew the gun from his pocket and stood with it pointed at the floor. 'I am now in command.' He had looked at her with cold eyes and said, 'Is that clear?'

She had nodded.

'Get me a drink. I will have a slivovitz.'

She picked up the bottle of clear, dry plum brandy and poured a few inches into a glass, her hand shaking. She looked at the neck of the bottle rattling on the glass and was suddenly awed to find that it was not fear that caused her hand to shake but hate. She looked at the other two men who had been standing behind Gabot. They both had their hands in their pockets but now they withdrew them, empty. She placed the glass on the bar and looked at the other two.

'Can I get you something?' She had kept her eyes averted from her father's body in case she broke down and cried. Tears would come later.

'Whisky.'

'And for me, a beer.'

She had nodded and reached under the bar, bending out of sight for a moment. As her hand closed around the Uzi she heard the shout. Too late, Gabot had remembered it was there.

She had not stood up but unexpectedly stepped around the bar. Finger pressed tightly on the trigger she hosed the men down, not stopping until all thirty rounds of bullets had been used. The men had crashed across the floor, blood splattering everywhere. When the magazine was empty she returned to the bar, found a second magazine and reloaded the gun. She still had the servants to deal with. There was at least one traitor in the household, the man who had let them in. She cursed herself for not having recognised the expression on the servant's face.

She poured herself a brandy but still could not look at her father's body.

It had taken a week. In that time she had identified those in the organisation who had been loyal to her father and who were prepared to transfer that loyalty to her. The man who had proven the greatest help was the Englishman, Maximillian King-Smith. Those who had actively supported the coup against her father she identified and eliminated. King-Smith had dealt with six members of the household servants. The rest was history and had passed into the folklore of time. Exaggerated, embellished, distorted, the coup had made her a legend in her country. People spoke of her with awe and immense fear. Then she faded into the background but her malign influence continued. She allowed King-Smith to become the figurehead of her organisation. Even now few people really knew or understood where the real power resided.

She had not allowed herself to grieve until her father had been buried, ten days after his murder. She had only cried once – late at night on the day of the funeral. No one had heard her sobs.

12

'The departures are on the monitor above your head,' Hunter continued. 'The next Iberian Airways plane is in fifty minutes. And there's a British Airway flight in an hour and ten. I think . . .' he broke off suddenly, his face split into a wide grin. Ruth followed his gaze and saw him staring at a beautiful woman dressed in a pilot's uniform. He gave a yell and rushed towards her, grabbed her around the waist and kissed both cheeks. The pilot gave a yelp of pleasure and surprise and hugged him back. As she introduced him to her two companions, both sporting four stripes on their sleeves as opposed to her two, she hung onto Hunter's arm. Then she slid a possessive arm around him and gave him another hug. Hunter said something and nodded towards Ruth. They all turned and looked in her direction. Ruth felt a surge of jealousy wash over her as she looked at the other woman. She was beautiful – raven-haired, tall with a fabulous figure beneath her uniform. Ruth disliked her on sight.

The group came across to her and Hunter began the introduction. 'Louise darling, this is Ruth. Ruth, this is Louise – my little sister.'

'I'm very pleased to meet you,' said Louise, holding out her hand. Ruth shook her hand gratefully, her jealousy evaporating as quickly as it had risen.

'I thought you were on the Trans-Atlantic run,' said Hunter to his sister.

'I was. Heathrow to Washington DC. But some of our pilots went down with some sort of 'flu bug and I was re-assigned to fly a 737 from Heathrow to Seville. Captain Owens is in command. I'm being checked out. This is Captain Clive Smith. He's the chief pilot at BA, the man who says whether or not I can fly a plane.'

'Not quite that,' said the grizzled, grey-haired Captain. 'I know you can fly just about anything,' he smiled. 'I've seen the reports about her flying the simulator. I'm here to make sure she flies safely. We don't want the passengers getting airsick.'

'And how am I doing?' Louise asked.

'I'll let you know when we get back. What brings you to this place?' he asked Hunter.

'Trouble. Serious trouble. I could do with your help.'

The two senior pilots exchanged glances and Owens replied. 'I don't want to involve British Airways in any shady business.' He was a short, dapper Welshman, immaculately groomed in his uniform, his hat sitting at an angle on his head.

'I wouldn't involve BA or any of you unless it was vital. I'm not being dramatic but this is a matter of life and death.'

'Hear him out,' said Smith.

Owens agreed with bad grace.

Briefly Hunter explained their predicament. Louise, who had heard some of her brother's stories in the past, was not surprised. 'Why is it,' she asked, 'you are always in trouble?'

Hunter shrugged and grinned, sheepishly. 'Just lucky, I guess. Can you get us on the flight?'

'I don't know,' Louise replied. 'Are there any seats left? I haven't seen the manifest yet.'

'The flight closed,' Owens said looking at his watch, 'five minutes ago. So it doesn't look as though you'll be able to come with us after all.'

'Come on,' Hunter protested. 'You're the Captain. Get us on. It's a matter of national importance.'

'Sure it is,' said a sceptical Owens. 'But once the manifest is closed that's it.'

'Sorry, Nick,' his sister said. 'There's nothing I can do.'

'Sure, Lems, thanks,' Hunter reverted to her childhood nick-name.

'It looks like we're on our own,' said Ruth, tucking her arm into Nick's and pulling him half a pace from the pilots.

'What will you do?' Louise asked worriedly.

'We'll think of something,' said Hunter. 'You'd better go and get ready for your flight.'

'But what will you do?' Louise repeated. 'I can't just abandon you.'

'Come along, we're running out of time,' said Owens. 'We have a flight to get ready.'

Reluctantly Louise turned away as well. She looked back at her brother who gave a rueful smile and a wave. Suddenly she walked back and said, 'Come on. This is ludicrous. If I can't get you on then nobody can.'

'First Officer Hunter, we need to go,' said Owens.

'First Officer?' said Hunter with a smile. 'I thought you were a lieutenant with those two stripes.'

'Very funny,' Louise said to him and then turned her attention to the Captain. 'You heard my brother,' said Louise. 'They're in trouble and we're ignoring it. We expect men like him' she caught Ruth's eye and added, 'and women like Ruth, to fight our battles for us. We don't stand up to be counted. Well, I'm not leaving them. You two can get the plane ready. I'll go with them to the BA desk. As soon as I've fixed things I'll join you.'

'If you do,' said Owens, 'I will put you on report. Your career will be jeopardised.'

Louise paused and looked at Owens for a second and then at her brother. 'Quite frankly, my dear,' she paraphrased the hero of *Gone with the Wind*, 'I couldn't give a damn.' She put her arm in Hunter's and dragged him away.

'Lems, you shouldn't have,' Hunter protested.

'Of course I should. I really don't give a damn. The little twerp tried to get me to sleep with him when we were in Washington and he didn't like being rebuffed.'

'What?' Hunter stopped, askance. 'I'll kill the little sod.'

'Nick, I'm no blushing virgin so climb down off your white charger and leave me to sort out my own mess. Men . . .' she

133

said with mock sorrow to Ruth who smiled in return. She liked Louise immensely.

At the check-in counter they discovered that there were plenty of seats and the manifest was quickly altered to include another two. Hunter paid to travel in tourist. Before they went into the departure lounge he turned to his sister. 'Thanks. One more tiny thing.'

Louise raised a quizzical eyebrow. 'We're carrying.' Her lack of response meant that she did not know what he was talking about. 'Guns. We both have guns.'

'What?' Louise went ashen. 'You can't be serious. Get rid of them for pity's sake.'

'How? We can't very well dump them in a rubbish bin, can we? I don't want them falling into the wrong hands. Can't you take them onboard?'

'That's impossible! Look Nick, I don't mind putting my career on the line but I do object to the possibility of a jail sentence if I'm caught with a gun. No, two guns,' she hissed, keeping her voice down.

'But surely you don't go through any checks?' Hunter asked.

'Of course we do. Aircrews are obvious suspects for drug runs. That's why we go through almost the same rigmarole that you do as a passenger.'

'Damnation. It looks like we'll have to get rid of them. Ruth, I'll take mine apart and drop pieces in various bins. Can you do the same?'

Ruth nodded.

'Okay, let's go. Thanks for everything. I'll see you onboard,' Hunter said to his sister.

A few minutes later, going through the security check and immigration, neither of them was aware of a figure hurrying towards a bank of telephones.

Onboard the airliner, Hunter was pleasantly surprised to find that his sister had arranged to have them upgraded to the first class section in the front of the cabin, separated by a curtain from the remainder in tourist. Both declined the glass of champagne offered prior to take-off. They listened to the usual announcements and safety advice and, once the plane was in level flight and the seat belt sign had been switched off, Hunter asked for a telephone, wanting to talk to Macnair.

'I'm sorry, sir,' said the stewardess, 'but we don't carry them on these planes.'

He nodded resignedly. Flight time was two hours and twenty minutes to Heathrow. Although Spain was on the same longitude as Britain the Spanish kept European time, which was one hour ahead of the UK. They would be arriving at 23.00, British Summer Time, all being well.

'Is there anything else I can get you?'

'Yes, please. Ask the First Officer if I can join them in the cockpit.'

'Certainly, sir.' She was aware that he and his companion had been bumped up to first class on the say so of the Chief Steward. She was away only moments before returning. 'If you come this way, sir.'

'I won't be long,' he said to Ruth, who nodded.

The cockpit was cramped. The plane had two seats for the pilots and a jump seat that folded down in the middle for a third person, sometimes a guest, most often a senior pilot checking out the routines in the cockpit. His sister was in the right-hand seat.

Her eyes scanned the dials continuously but she took time out to look up and smile. 'What can we do for you, Nick?'

Owens scowled while Smith nodded pleasantly.

'I need to talk to the General. Can you patch me through on a safe frequency?'

'Sure, no problem,' said Louise, knowing her brother well enough to realise that he would only ask if it was important.

Owens could no longer control himself. 'I'm the Captain of this plane and I won't allow it. You are here to fly the aircraft while I supervise you. This is against all the regulations.'

'Sir,' said Hunter, 'I don't know what your problem is but this is of vital importance. We've just spent the last thirty hours running for our lives with God knows who chasing us. The woman with me is a Mossad agent. I work for TIFAT. Check us out. Call Paul Meadows at Heathrow. He's Head of Security. Tell him I'm on the plane and that I want to talk to Macnair.' He could see Owens hesitate. 'Captain Owens, let me make myself clear,' he smiled at the frowning man staring at him. 'This really is a national emergency. This is not a game. For some reason the people after us won't give up. That doesn't make any sense. I don't know if we've been seen and if there will be a reception committee waiting at the other end. All I do know is that I have never seen such a well-financed and ruthless organisation before. Now, either call Meadows or let me call Macnair.' Hunter spoke coldly, his anger barely under control. He let the other man feel his anger and then smiled. 'Please.'

Which gave Owens the opportunity to back down. Gracelessly, he said, 'The radio is behind you. You can call anywhere in the world if you know the right frequency.'

'Thanks. I know the frequency.' Hunter keyed in the world wide, emergency call-up frequency for TIFAT and used his personal call sign. In less than thirty seconds he was patched through to General Macnair.

'Sir, Ruth and I are en route to Heathrow.'

'Roger that. There's a great deal happening and I need you back here. I'm glad to discover you're still in one piece. Be very careful. GCHQ intercepted a message two days ago that they have only just decoded. The cartels are demanding revenge against all those who are involved in hindering their trade. They've declared war against any law enforcement officers who try to stop them. Quite frankly it's hard to believe, but there have been so many incidents I'm forced to accept it. Police and Customs officers have been gunned down while carrying out their duties all across Europe. The cartels are displaying a barbarity previously unknown. The governments of the Western world are in virtual chaos. They just don't know how to respond. We are battling against a huge amorphous army we can barely identify. There are so many foot soldiers that we can't fight them all. We need to get to the heart and brains of the organisation as a matter of urgency. We're working on it right now. Over.'

'Roger that, sir. Can you tell Paul Meadows we're arriving? I would like to enter the UK unobserved. Over.'

'Roger that. Out.' Macnair broke the connection.

Hunter replaced the receiver deep in thought. He had heard the anxiety in Macnair's voice and Hunter knew that he was not a man to scare easily.

The armed patrolmen at Heathrow airport were hyper-alert, although their demeanour did not show it. Activity in every airport in the world had been stepped up as the Bikini State had been increased to Black Alpha and then Amber. They were in contact with their control room and each other on individual, scrambled frequencies. When the call came over the patrolman's radio Fergusson was startled. He had never expected it to happen.

'This is Lauder. Do not broadcast, just double click the transmit button.'

The blood drained from the patrolman's face. Luckily his partner was looking around, watching the crowds, searching for trouble. He made the two clicks.

'A man and a woman will be leaving the aircraft arriving from Seville, Spain, with the aircrew. You cannot miss them. They will be wearing plain clothes while the remainder are in uniform. They are to be killed. One hundred thousand pounds for one dead, an additional fifty thousand for the second one. Do I make myself clear?'

He made two clicks, feeling sick. It had finally happened, after all this time. For three years he had been paid one thousand pounds a month as a retainer. It had been very useful money, helping with his gambling debts, paying for the nicer things in life. He had always known that he would be called upon one day to earn it. But he had never expected . . . this. He had thought he might have to turn a blind eye to something or be in the wrong part of the airport at a crucial moment. He had not, even in his wildest dreams, anticipated murder. *Dreams? Nightmares.* His thoughts turned to the money. There was a lot he could do with a hundred and fifty grand. But first he had to get away from his

137

partner. He looked at his watch and the arrivals board. He had over an hour.

He walked across to his partner. 'Sorry, Martin, but I feel lousy. I'm going to the loo.'

'Okay. I'll wait here. What's wrong?'

'I think it's this flu everybody's getting. I don't know. I just feel sick. I'm hoping I'll be okay. Give me five.'

'Okay. I'll call in.' His partner radioed the control room to report on the situation.

The patrolman stayed away for nearly fifteen minutes by which time his partner was getting edgy. When he returned, he said, 'Sorry I took so long, but I feel like hell.'

'You don't look too good. What do you want to do?'

The dab of water on his forehead looked like sweat and as the thought of what he was about to do made him queasy it was no big act to look ill. 'I'll stay for ten minutes and see how I feel. After that I'll go to the rest room. If I'm not up to it I'll have to call it a day.'

The two officers strolled along, eyes darting everywhere, missing nothing. Twenty minutes later Fergusson said, 'I've had it. I'll go in to the rest room. What will you do?'

'I'll give you ten minutes. Let me know how you're feeling. Then I'll report to control. They can decide.' Officers always patrolled in pairs and so if they split up for any reason whatsoever they had to report it. If a patrolman left or quit duty because of illness, his partner was either re-assigned another patrolman or was given a different job to do, one that did not require any back up.

A while later Fergusson returned from the rest room. 'Can you call in for me? I'm going to have to go home.'

'Okay. Leave it to me.'

'Thanks, Martin. I owe you one.' Returning to the rest room, he made his preparations.

The plane landed with barely a bump in spite of a heavy crosswind and pouring rain. Hunter knew that his sister had a rare talent for flying, one she had inherited from her great-aunt, Susan Griffiths, who had become famous during the Spanish Civil War. Hunter and Ruth stayed in their seats while the plane emptied. Louise joined them and with a smile said, 'I'm checked out. And even better news, Captain Smith has persuaded Owens not to say anything about you coming with us. So all is right with the world. Shall we go?'

Together with the cabin crew they walked down the steps of the plane. Hunter and Ruth walked on one side, both of them alert, watching, aware. The walk around the nose of the aircraft brought an itch between Hunter's shoulder blades. Louise had paused to let her brother catch up when the shot was fired.

13

He had been concentrating on Hunter and hadn't seen the woman stop. Hunter was crossing left to right and so it was a tricky shot. He followed Hunter's path until he was sure of his target and pulled the trigger. The bullet passed through the woman pilot and bounced off the tarmac. Cursing, he aimed and fired again but missed as Hunter and Ruth dived onto the runway. The remainder of the crew stood like startled rabbits caught in the headlights of a truck. Then he heard orders being yelled and whistles blowing. It was time to leave.

Hunter lay by his sister and called to the crew to get down. Finally, beginning to move, two of the stewardesses panicked and ran. Hunter ripped open his sister's raincoat and uniform jacket, oblivious to the rain pouring down his neck and soaking him. 'Lems, hang in there. Owens, go and get the first aid kit. Lems, can you hear me?'

'I'll get it,' volunteered the Chief Steward. He rushed away.

'What happened, Nick? I felt a blow to my shoulder and then I was on the ground. Hell, it hurts.' She grimaced and moved, in obvious distress.

'You've been shot. The bullet's gone straight through. I'll get a dressing on it. Help is on its way. Ruth,' he yelled, turning to look for her, but she was nowhere to be seen.

Help was suddenly all around them. An armed escort appeared from nowhere and an ambulance arrived at the same time as the Chief Steward brought the first aid kit from the plane. Louise

140

was placed gently onto a stretcher and carried to the ambulance. Nick went with her, looking around for Ruth but there was no sign of her.

'Will she be all right?' he asked the paramedic, anxiously.

'I'm sure she will be,' she replied in a soft, Irish brogue, deftly hooking Louise up to a drip while the other medic strapped pads to Louise's shoulder and then reached for a hypodermic.

Hunter had looked at both holes and he was relieved to see that she must have been shot by a titanium or steel tipped round. The kind used to penetrate body armour. When it had hit Louise it had sailed clean through as though her flesh and bone didn't exist. He looked at his sister who smiled weakly, sinking into unconsciousness when the medic injected her.

The doors were closing when he jumped out of the back and ran towards the terminal building. He needed to find Ruth. Reaching the door it opened and he found himself face to face with Paul Meadows, Head of Security at Heathrow. The two had last met when Hunter had led a team against terrorists who had hijacked an airliner at the airport.

They shook hands. 'You'd better come with me,' said Meadows. 'I got the message from Macnair and was coming to meet you. When the alarm went off I had to set certain procedures into motion.'

'Any sign of the killer?' Hunter asked.

'Killer? Is he dead?'

'Wrong gender. No, she's not dead but this was an attempt to kill Ruth or me. Have you seen her? Ruth, the woman who was with me?'

Meadows shook his head. 'Sorry. Nobody's come this way, I'm sure.'

'Is there another way in?'

Meadows thought for a second. 'Via the roof, I guess.'

Hunter cursed. 'Of course! The bullet wound was higher in the back and lower in the front. Ruth's gone after whoever fired the shot. Can we get up there?'

'Follow me.' Meadows led the way into the building, his swipe passkey allowing them access through the doors. Entering the main concourse, it came as something of a shock to Hunter to see that the rest of the world was carrying on normally. Passengers and staff were hurrying busily about, as plane after plane was loaded and sent on its way.

'It'll be quietening down now,' said Meadows. 'There are just a few planes at this time of night.'

'There's Ruth,' said Hunter, touching Meadows on the arm and pointing.

Ruth was slumped in a chair, like a weary traveller found the world over. They quickly joined her and Ruth said, not looking up, 'Sit beside me and listen. How's Louise?'

'She should be okay. The paramedics are rushing her to St. Bartholomew's hospital. What are you looking at?'

'The man over there. Sitting opposite the bookshop. Looks ill. He's carrying a gun. I'm certain he was the one I followed from the roof.'

'How did you get up there?' Meadows asked.

'I climbed a drainpipe. See him now those people have moved?'

'I see him. He does look ill,' said Hunter. 'Are you sure he's carrying?'

Ruth gave him a withering look and he held up his hands in surrender. 'Okay, okay. I only asked.'

'Hell, that's one of mine!' Meadow looked disbelieving. 'His name's Fergusson. He was on duty earlier but went off sick. What's he doing here, I wonder?'

'Shooting people,' Hunter bit out, hate flooding him. The bastard had injured his sister and could just as easily have killed her. He wanted him to himself for a few minutes.

'There must be some mistake,' Meadows protested. 'He's just been recommended for promotion to sergeant. He has an exemplary record.'

'I'm telling you he shot Nick's sister. I didn't make a mistake.'

'Your sister?' Meadows said, shocked, looking at Hunter. 'You should have told me.'

'I was in a hurry to find the gunman. Okay, we need to take

him without any trouble. We don't want him shooting any more innocent bystanders. Paul, if you . . .'

Meadows was looking at Fergusson who had suddenly looked their way. He jerked upright and walked away, looking back over his shoulder. His boss was talking to the target! How was that possible? Fergusson's instinct was to run but then a wild idea took hold. He could still earn his money.

'Damnation,' said Meadows.

'It can't be helped. Come on, we'd better get after him. Not too close,' warned Hunter. 'We don't want to spook him even more. Paul, can you contact your patrols to close in?'

'Sure.' Meadows unclipped a radio from his belt. Before he could use it another patrolman appeared beside him. It was Martin, Fergusson's partner.

'Sir, I've been looking for you.'

Suddenly, Fergusson was running towards the group, drawing his gun. *Too bad that Martin's in the way.* Hunter was the only one to react as people, seeing a man running with a gun, began to scream and scramble out of his path.

'What the . . .' Martin began, looking up to see his partner fifty paces away and darting towards them.

Hunter flipped the holster on Martin's right leg and drew the automatic, flicked the safety and fired in one fluid movement. Martin was still coming to terms with what he was seeing, his machine pistol still cradled across his front, uncocked.

Hunter's first shot smashed Fergusson's hands and knocked the gun away. His second blew away his left knee and he collapsed. 'Stay here,' Hunter yelled. 'I'll see he can't hurt anybody.' He ran to the prone figure.

Fergusson was glaring at him, the shock holding the pain at bay for a few seconds longer. 'Help,' he croaked. 'Get me a medic.'

'Shut up,' said Hunter as he stopped a pace away. 'If you don't tell me what I want to know you're a dead man.'

'Go to hell. I'll tell you nothing. You've shot a policeman, mate. You're in trouble.'

'The pilot *you* shot was my sister. I want to know who put you up to it.'

143

'Screw you. I'm telling you nothing. I want a solicitor. I didn't do anything.'

'Ballistics will prove otherwise,' said Hunter. 'So answer me. Who put you up to it?'

'I'm bleeding to death,' Fergusson gasped as the pain hit him in waves. 'I need help. You have to help me.'

'Alternatively,' Hunter replied. 'I can let you die.' He saw Fergusson's eyes flicker past him and Hunter risked a quick glance back. 'Stay away!' he yelled. 'He's got a grenade and is threatening to pull the pin.'

Some of the onlookers, who had been edging closer, screamed and moved further back. Ruth and Meadows exchanged wry glances. Meadows nodded approval. The last thing he needed was to be caught up in a long legal case about who did what and whether the force used was justified. *Had the first shot stopped Fergusson? Why was the second shot fired? Was it attempted murder? Define "reasonable force"*. The thoughts tumbled through his head, even as he watched Hunter in action.

'I don't have a grenade, you bastard. Get me some help. I demand help.' Fergusson took a deep breath as though he was about to yell.

Hunter knelt beside him and dug two fingers into the man's gut, forcing the air out of him. He looked back at Meadows and the others. 'Stay away, Paul. I'll ask him for the grenade.' Hunter said in a low voice, 'You have about two minutes to make up your mind. At the rate you're losing blood you'll be past the point of no return very soon. Even if the paramedics get to you, there'll be nothing they can do with a plasma drip. You need a large infusion of blood and quickly.' It was true. Fergusson was losing blood fast, lots of it.

'You can't just let me bleed to death,' the man croaked, fear drying his mouth as he looked into Hunter's eyes.

'Don't bet on it.'

'Not in front of all these people. You'll be done for attempted murder,' he gasped.

'I'm a TIFAT operative. I'm licensed to stop scum like you. It won't get past the CPS.' Hunter hoped he was right. The

Crown Prosecution Service could feasibly decide against him. Unfortunately, a live Fergusson would be very embarrassing.

Fergusson believed his bluff. 'All I know is a code word. I got the message on the radio this evening. I swear I know nothing. It was the money. They pay me. Every month. Into my bank.'

'Which bank?' Hunter moved and cradled the man's head, as though he was trying to comfort him.

'Same as my pay check. Barclays. South Kensington branch. Please, get me some help.' Fergusson watched the blood oozing out of his shattered leg and hands. Each passing second the pain grew. He would say anything to stop it.

Hunter's eyes were pitiless as he looked at the man's pale, sweating face.

'Please, get me help,' Fergusson croaked.

Hunter leaned forward. 'I can't do that,' he whispered, 'because it's too late.'

Fergusson's eyes opened wide in shock. He tried to open his mouth to yell. What came out was a last, rattling sigh.

Hunter looked up and yelled. 'He lied. There is no grenade. Get help.'

Hunter gently placed Fergusson's head down on the ground and stood up, regretfully. Hunter knew that he'd had no option. He had no intention of getting caught up in a trial. Being called as a witness, having the defence twist the truth, blame him instead of Fergusson for what had happened. Fergusson claiming he was running to help or to give himself up. Or that he had picked up the gun after chasing the real perpetrator when he saw him on the roof. The possible defence scenarios played through Hunter's mind like a bad film. This way the incident would go to the CPS and no further. General Macnair could arrange it, he was sure. Hunter had more important things to deal with. Like getting those who had ordered the shooting. Because now they had a lead. A bank account with a paper trail to follow.

Meadows stood alongside, having already radioed for screens and further back up. Staff arrived and placed the screens around the body, hiding it from sight. Listening to Hunter's reasoning, Meadows nodded agreement. 'You did the right thing. I'll try and keep your name out of it. Shot by armed guards after shooting a pilot and threatening me. Right, Martin? That's for the newspapers. The CPS will be more awkward.'

The policeman nodded, staring at the body, fascinated.

'Thanks,' said Hunter. 'I think Macnair can take care of it. You don't have any doubts that he was about to shoot us, do you?'

'Good Lord, no. What about you Martin?'

The patrolman licked his lips. 'Uh? Yes, sir. I mean, no, sir. No doubt. Sir,' he looked at Hunter. 'I'm sorry. We train continuously but it's not like the real thing. When I saw Fergusson running towards us I froze. If it hadn't been for you . . .' he trailed off.

'That's okay,' said Hunter. 'I still remember my first time. You'll be okay if it happens again, believe me. Paul, can you get us on the next flight to Scotland?'

Meadows nodded. 'No problem. But it'll be in the morning.'

'That can't be helped. Can you get us onto the plane without going on as passengers?'

'I don't see why not. I'll get you a couple of BA uniforms and you can be crew taxiing to Scotland. That do you?'

'Sure and thanks.'

'You can also stay in one of the VIP suites for the night. It's where we put the rich and famous when they get stuck. It's easier that way.'

'Thanks. Now I need a phone.'

Meadows led them to his office and indicated the phone. Hunter's first call was to the hospital. To his relief he was told that Louise was in no danger. She was comfortable and sleeping. His second call was to his parents. He broke the news. Once they were assured that Louise would be all right they reacted in their usual competent manner and made arrangements to fly to London the following morning. His final call was to Macnair. Hunter briefed the General on the latest events.

'Good. You did the right thing. I'll see you when you get in. Have a good night's rest.'

The following morning, dressed in BA pilots' uniforms, they caught the shuttle to Edinburgh where they were met by a staff car. They arrived in Macnair's office forty minutes after landing.

The General was reading a signal. He looked bleakly at Hunter and Ruth. 'Sam York was killed by a car explosion in southern Spain yesterday.'

Hunter and Ruth both looked shocked. 'He was a hell of a nice guy,' said Hunter. 'Was anybody else hurt?'

'A staff nurse by the name of Susan Waterstone has leg injuries. Serious but not life threatening.'

'Poor Susan,' said Ruth.

'You know her?' Macnair asked.

'We met once. A very nice woman,' Ruth replied. 'Do we know who did it?'

'Yes. A message was sent to the Governor's residence in Gibraltar. It said that revenge would be taken against anyone who tried to interfere with the commercial operations of their enterprises.'

'Whose operations?' Hunter frowned.

Macnair replied. 'They called themselves Colombia International. We understood the message. It's being repeated all over Europe and reinforced with shootings, stabbings and explosions.'

'So what are we going to do about it?' Hunter asked.

'Fight back wherever we can,' said Macnair. 'We need to get to the inner core. If we can get the leaders we might be able to bring the situation back under reasonable control again. It was bad before and worsening. Now it's becoming a full-blown catastrophe. The level of drugs and violence involved is far greater than anything we've known in the past. This ruthless use of vulnerable people who are forced to leave their own countries and resettle across Europe as immigrants is a sinister turn of events. Chaos is reigning across Europe. Have you seen the latest edict from the Court of Human Rights in Strasbourg?'

Hunter shook his head.

'A notorious French drug boss was arrested three years ago and sent to prison for twenty years. All his wealth, which was proven to be based on his drug dealing, was confiscated. He appealed the sentence but it was upheld. The appeal went to Strasbourg. France is a signatory of the Convention of May 1974. You know about this?'

Hunter nodded. 'Some. It was part of a staff course I did a couple of years ago. Some countries have signed up to certain protocols but not all. The important ones are numbers one, four, six and, I think, seven.'

Macnair nodded. 'Well, France signed up to protocol number seven, which is split into five articles. Article number four is the right not to be punished twice. A ruling came down yesterday that a prison sentence plus the confiscation of all worldly goods was a double punishment and hence should not be carried out.'

'You're kidding,' said Hunter. 'Whose side are these imbecile judges on? The people's or the criminal's?'

Macnair shrugged in frustration. 'In this case it doesn't mean the criminal will get his money back as the punishment has been meted out. What it does mean is that future cases won't carry the same punishment. Luckily the UK hasn't signed up to that particular protocol but it still brings moral pressure to bear on future judgements. The criminals are winning and we seem determined to let them.'

'It beggars belief,' said Hunter. 'Can't government ministers question the decisions of the judges? After all, what's democracy for if it isn't to protect the ordinary law-abiding citizen?'

'It's worse than you think. In this country a judge has years of working before the bar prior to being offered a judgeship. The men and women who are given a sinecure in Strasbourg are frequently political payoffs. They don't have the ability or the training to pontificate on the complex matters that come before them. So believe me, Commander, it's a lot worse than you can possibly believe. Now we have a new problem.'

'What's that, sir?'

'The Convention of 1950 has fourteen articles. Article two is the right to life. Article six is a right to a fair trial. Article seven is no punishment without law. Three days ago an application was made to the court by an organisation calling itself Fair Trials International. It claims that under the Convention or Protocols of

148

the court the human rights of the people we are fighting against are being *systematically abused*. That we should be arresting the criminals and bringing court action against them. In principle I agree. But under the present circumstances I don't think we have a choice.'

Hunter wisely said nothing, merely nodded. When the General was on his hobby-horse it was best to let him have full rein.

He continued. 'It's all a matter of political will. There are many people who believe that the Court of Human Rights is obsolete and should be wound up. Unfortunately, it has taken on a life of its own and is expanding, not contracting. There are now forty-one states signed up to the Convention. There are forty-one judges although not from each state. Add to that the required bureaucracy to run such an organisation and you'll understand that there are huge interests vested in its continuance.'

'I can appreciate the problems,' said Hunter, 'but what are the solutions?'

'We need to change, even strengthen the law. Isobel has had a team analysing some of the judgements made at the court. I've passed what she's learnt to Leon Sautier in Paris. We agreed at the INL briefing that he would lead the fight against corruption in the European judiciary. If he finds anything he may be able to trace the source.'

Macnair watched as Hunter helped himself to a coffee and offered them each one. Both declined. 'The problem is one of absolutes,' said Macnair.

'Sir?' Hunter paused, coffee-pot in the air.

'The law is one of absolutes. A case is argued, the law applied and that's the ruling. As it is now, the judges will have to come down on the side of the criminal because of the way the laws have been drafted. Changes in the law would be anathema to the liberal minded of the western world.'

'Why is that?' Ruth asked, fascinated by Macnair's argument.

'We currently have laws that protect the rights of the individual. Agreed?' They both nodded. 'Right. And those laws protect the individual from the biggest threat to personal liberty. Do you know what that is?'

'Sure,' said Hunter. 'The State.'

'Precisely. Our laws have been developed over the centuries to protect us from the power of the state. It started with the Magna Carta in 1215 by King John at Runnymede. It was drawn up at the demand of the barons and represents the first document in English history to secure personal liberty and civil rights. Since then practically all the major laws that have been passed have been for the same reason. As a result we've gone too far in the wrong direction. The power of the State is no longer absolute and hasn't been for many decades. Notice I say decades and not hundreds of years. It has taken almost until today to achieve the aims of all right thinking people throughout the centuries. Unfortunately, those same laws are now being turned against us. We need a balance and we seem incapable of achieving it.'

'Incapable or unwilling, sir?' Hunter asked.

'Good question. In truth there are no real absolutes in this dilemma yet the law acts as though there are. So we don't get shades of grey, only black and white. Inevitably in court it will be argued that we are abusing the human rights of the people we are hunting down. The fact that we act for the greater good, or that we can prove the crimes committed by the cartels, will be of no use. *We* will be deemed to be the lawbreakers. And I don't mean just us here at TIFAT. I mean every law enforcement agency that is fighting these criminals using our methods.'

Hunter nodded. Macnair painted a bleak picture.

'That's all. I have a hundred phone calls to make.'

'Yes, sir.' Hunter and Ruth left the office. Despondently they walked along the corridor. 'It doesn't look good, does it?' he said.

'No, it doesn't. The question is, what do we do about it?'

'First of all I'm going to introduce you to Isobel. She's our specialist Head of Department for IT. While you two get to know one another I'm going for a run. I find the exercise makes my brain work better. After that I'll introduce you to some of the others. I've never asked but – do you have a reserve rank?'

'Sure. We all do, in Israel.'

'As you're Mossad, I assume you're an officer?'

Ruth smiled. 'No. Actually I'm a corporal in the intelligence corps.' She shrugged. 'Does it matter?'

'Not really. It would have been neater to have you seconded here from your reserve occupation. Everybody working here is military with the corresponding rank. I'll speak to the General and see if he can't make you a lieutenant for your stay. It makes life easier, that's all.'

'In what way?' Coming from one of the most egalitarian countries in the world Ruth couldn't understand his concern.

He looked uncomfortable for a moment. 'It makes fraternisation with you that much easier.'

'Fraternisation?' Ruth burst out laughing. 'Is that what you call it nowadays?'

Hunter grinned. 'It's what the armed forces call it. It's stupid and old-fashioned but it's fraternisation between ranks. I can tell you that there are still some who regard it as almost as big a sin as fraternising with the enemy. Come on, let's find Isobel.'

Half an hour later Hunter was in running kit and working up a sweat. A cross-country path led him through a small wood and around the perimeter of the base. On the parade ground he picked up another runner, someone he did not know.

Hunter grunted hullo, received the same response and picked up his pace a little. The other runner easily kept up with him. He speeded up again with the same result. Hunter began to stretch every sinew, forcing the pace, but to no avail. The other man kept alongside him, smiling. By now the sweat was pouring from Hunter as he ate up the miles, determined not to be beaten. They had done more than a half marathon when Hunter decided to give in. He could not shake the other man. Both men halted, panting, regaining their breath. Hunter was glad to see that the other man was sweating as much as he was.

Hunter held out his hand. 'Hunter, Nick Hunter.'

The other man was as tall as Hunter, thinner but wiry. Piercing blue eyes looked out from under a thatch of blond hair. A determined chin with a deep cleft gave him movie star good looks. 'Matthew Dunston. Call me Matt.'

'Where are you from, Matt?'

'Lately the SAS. Before then the Paras.'

'Glad to have you onboard. Fancy a workout?'

'Katas?'

'Sure. What style are you?' Hunter asked, referring to the type of martial arts the other used.

'I think eclectic describes it best.'

'Same here. Tae kwon do, a bit of kendo and some karate.'

'Throw in some aikido and that's me as well. Ready?'

Hunter nodded his head in a small bow and they squared up to one another. Hunter had decided to take it easy on his opponent but after two moves he changed his mind. It was obvious that Dunston was taking it easy with him! They fought in complete silence. Total concentration the order of the day as they parried and thrust, moved and counter-moved. Each time they stopped just short of connecting although a few blows got through in spite of their superb co-ordination. Hunter was aware that if he had been in a competition his opponent would probably be winning by points. If it had been for real, he would have been hard pushed to stay alive or prevent the other man from seriously injuring him.

They used hands, elbows, knees, feet and fingers. For ten minutes they went at it until Dunston asked, 'Had enough?'

Hunter replied, 'Yes. How about you?'

'Yes, thanks.' They both stopped and bowed. 'That was some work-out.' Dunston flexed his arms and legs and rubbed at the odd bruise or two that Hunter had accidentally landed.

Hunter did the same, smiling. 'It certainly was. You gave me a run for my money. Only the PTI can hold me like that.'

'So I heard,' said Dunston. 'He was telling me exactly the same thing yesterday. Shall we jog back to the changing rooms?'

Hunter nodded in agreement and they set off at a gentle pace, easing aching muscles. The endorphins, which had surged through Hunter's body, had done the trick. He had a few ideas to discuss with the General. In the changing rooms Hunter showered and put on his uniform. Dunston took longer in the shower and was beginning to get dressed as Hunter was leaving.

'You're a sky pilot!' Hunter exclaimed, watching in amazement as the other man fitted his dog collar in place.

'Didn't you hear I was joining?'

Hunter burst out laughing. 'I had no idea. When did you get here?'

'A few days ago. The General thought it was time you had someone here to look after your souls as well as your bodies.'

'But . . . but the fighting. Your fitness . . .'

'Don't look so bemused. I joined the army before I took Holy Orders. I left to enter the church and then rejoined. I'm also a qualified paramedic. It comes in handy at times.'

'You're a useful guy to have around. I'm glad you're here. Are you coming to the wardroom for lunch?'

'I'll be right behind you.'

Hunter found Isobel and Ruth in the bar, each sipping an orange juice. Hunter ordered the same, drank it in one long swallow and asked for another. He was glad to see that the two women were getting along so well together. Dunston joined them a few minutes later and Hunter introduced him to Ruth.

'You aren't much use to me, I'm afraid,' said Ruth, with a smile.

'Oh? Why not?' Dunston asked.

'I'm Jewish.'

He laughed. 'He's the same God. We just approach him from different directions, that's all.'

'I suppose you're right,' said Ruth, 'only don't let a rabbi hear you say that.'

'Or a Church of England bishop, or a Roman Catholic cardinal or an Iranian ayatollah,' said Dunston with a smile. 'Bigotry is bigotry no matter where it raises its head.'

'I agree,' said Isobel. 'What do you think, Nick?'

'I couldn't agree more, although I'm a barely practising believer who only has the odd chat with his God when he needs Him. That's enough theological debate. What about the worldly? Have you anything new for us?' he asked Isobel.

She nodded. 'Some. Ruth gave me the details about the

affair at Heathrow. I should have some information this afternoon on Fergusson's bank account. I'll start the paper chase then.'

'What do you expect to find?' Dunston asked.

'It all depends. It could lead us to a master account that is used to pay many more Fergussons around the world. Or it could be an account that is put in funds, in cash, for the one recipient only. Although I doubt that, as it means a great deal of work for someone. Also, it would represent a cut-out which we can't circumvent. We just have to see.'

'How,' Dunston frowned, 'do you get permission to do that?'

Isobel smiled sweetly. 'I don't. I just get on with it covering up my trail as best I can.'

'You can do that?' Dunston asked, in awe.

'That and more,' Hunter answered for her. 'She's a computer genius.'

'Hardly that,' said Isobel. 'It's just the application of certain systems and a mind that tends towards the nefarious.' The others laughed. 'I've also two expert helpers who leave me standing when it comes to certain things. They're the real brains behind the hardware. Together we make a good team. We've now got twenty analysts working with us and so we're achieving a lot more than we used to. All in all, I'm pretty satisfied that we can deliver whatever the General needs.'

'I'm glad to hear that,' said Macnair, appearing behind her with Major Carter. 'Meet me in my office at fifteen-thirty hours for a staff meeting. All of you.'

'Aye, aye, sir.' Hunter answered for them all.

Macnair and Carter walked together along the corridor leading to their offices. Isobel came rushing after them.

'Sir,' she called out.

Both men stopped and turned to look at her.

'Sir, Sarah is on the phone. She says it's urgent.'

'Thank you. I'll take it in my office,' said Macnair. He closed the door and sat at his desk, sweeping up the receiver. 'Hullo, Sarah,' he greeted her. 'How's life at GCHQ?'

'Fair to middling,' replied Sarah Fleeting, a senior manager at the famous establishment in Gloucestershire. 'Malcolm, we've got a big problem.'

Macnair gripped the telephone tightly. 'Tell me.'

'We intercepted a signal forty-eight hours ago. It had a low priority for two reasons. The first was the ultra-high frequency it was sent on and the second – it was sent in Morse.'

'Why does that make it a low priority?' Macnair was intrigued.

'Nobody uses Morse nowadays and I can't remember when that particular frequency was last used. The only radio equipment to my knowledge that can use that frequency and send in Morse is Russian.'

'Russian!'

'Mmm. I'm more interested in the content. The sender is not a radio operator. His or her fist is too clumsy.' A radio operator's "fist" gauges how well that person sends and receives Morse code. When Morse was in common use his or her fist could identify a radio operator.'

'Go on. What was the message?'

'Three nuclear warheads are being sold by the Russians to a crime syndicate.'

Macnair sat bolt upright. 'What? Are you sure that's what the message said?'

'Of course,' Sarah replied with some feeling. 'What we cannot be sure of is how accurate it is. However, based on how we received it, how it was transmitted and the way it was phrased, I'm as sure as I can be that the information is genuine. Somebody in Russia is trying to send us a warning.'

'Yes, but who and where are they exactly?'

'I've no idea,' was the honest reply.

14

Throughout the day the teams returned from numerous operations across Europe and Britain. Team Green was the last to arrive. They had flown by helicopter and plane from Turkey. Masters carried information from Albatha that he was sure Macnair would want in a hurry.

Meanwhile, Hunter was sitting with Ruth in his office. 'I think I'll put my thoughts down on paper before the meeting. Give me a hand, will you? I'll use this flip chart. We write all our ideas down no matter how ludicrous. We then prioritise them. '

There was a knock on the door and Hiram Walsh put his head in, a beaming smile on his face. 'I thought I'd say hi. Hullo Ruth, you're looking as lovely as ever.'

'Hi, Hiram. I wish I could say the same about you.' They had met during an operation in Israel when Ruth had met most of the team.

'Always a kind word. What are you guys up to?'

Hunter explained. 'I want to do this in time for the staff meeting with the General at fifteen-thirty.'

'Need a hand?'

'Sure. Why not? Glad to have you onboard,' said Hunter. 'Okay, let's get started.'

During the next half an hour they were joined by Lt Douglas Napier – SBS, Capt. Burghard Schwarzkopf – German Airforce, Major James Carter – Catering Corps, and Capt. Joshua Clements – American Delta Force. The brainstorming went well. By 15.00 they had dozens of facts and ideas written down. Ruth began to type the information into a computer in some order of priority but unfortunately they were running out of time. At 15.35 Hunter's intercom buzzed.

'Sir?'

'Commander, you were due here five minutes ago.'

'Yes, sir. Sorry. We've just been finishing a brainstorming session. I wanted to present a paper but we didn't get it finished in time. I'll be with you in two minutes.'

'I'll come to you,' said Macnair and broke the connection. A few moments later he entered the room. 'I wondered where you'd all got to.' He looked around the room at the flip chart with its scrawled writing, ticks, crosses and question marks. 'We'll continue here. I see what you're doing. It's not what I had planned but I'll join you. It'll help me to clear my thoughts. Oh,' he turned to Carter, 'ask Isobel if she'll join us.'

Macnair was impressed. He knew that the men and women he had selected to join TIFAT were exceptional and so it was proving. They thought clearly and concisely and were prepared to present their ideas no matter how far fetched. The flow chart showed a clear understanding of the international political position, as well as the legal problems they faced. It also showed a willingness to look at the unthinkable and respond accordingly. Nobody underestimated the threat facing the civilised world. If the criminals who ran the huge international drugs and terrorist cartels were not stopped then the future looked extremely bleak.

The problems identified were lack of resources and the reluctance to fight back. Armageddon was a biblical prophecy, a great battle between the forces of good and evil that would occur at the end of the world. Was that what they were facing? Looking around the room, Macnair knew that he could rely on the people there to do their bit, but could they rely on him? It was a daunting thought. The battle before him was the biggest he had ever faced.

Isobel's assistant, Gareth, entered the room a few hours later to speak to her.

'Is it the trace?' she asked.

He nodded in reply.

'Tell all of us.'

Gareth, tall and weedy with a ponytail, was uncomfortable in front of people. Computers were his medium. He coughed, blushed and spoke hesitantly. 'We've . . . we've traced the money to the bent copper. It leads to an account in London. To Coutts.' That caused a stir of surprise, as the bank was one of the most prestigious in the world and looked after the money of the well heeled or the well connected. 'We had some difficulty there as their systems are better protected than most banks. However, we got round them eventually. The account is fed by telegraphic transfers from an account in Paris, which in turn is fed from a bank in the Cayman Islands. The Cayman account has over ten million dollars sitting in it at any one time.'

'Do we have any names?' asked Macnair.

'Yes . . . sir, we do.' He handed over a list. 'These are the people who are the recipients of the money.'

There were ten names on the list, one of which meant something to Macnair. 'Did you put traces on all the names?'

'Yes, sir. I have the information here.' He handed over a second list.

'Can we trace the other users of the account?' Macnair asked.

'Yes, sir. I have,' Gareth said. 'Leo is working on where the money came from to get to the Caymans. It looks like Russia but we aren't sure yet.'

'Good. If it is, then it ties in with other facts we have. Anything else?'

'No, sir,' replied Gareth.

'Right. Thank you very much and well done. And thank Leo from me.' He dismissed Gareth who was glad to leave the room. 'We have a large number of investigations to carry out and we're going to need help. When we've put together what we need, I want the information delivered personally to certain people, not mailed. Jim,' he turned to Carter, 'can you make the arrangements?'

'Yes, sir.'

'One more thing before we break for the night. The Colombian tape transcript from the dead CIA agent, Guy Glover, suggests some sort of customer acquisition plan by the cartels. It's hard to decipher from the tape how they are going to do it but it will involve huge sums of money. We need to keep a look out for that money. Langley are still working on the tape but don't hold out much hope that they'll learn any more. We appear to have a deadline,' he checked the date window on his watch, 'of nine days time. What will happen then is anybody's guess. Right. It is now after twenty hundred hours so we'll call a halt. Tomorrow we'll meet immediately after colours. Any questions?'

There were none. They knew what was expected of them. They would need the co-operation of half the security forces in Europe and there was always the possibility, or rather the probability, of a leak. They needed luck and planning in large amounts, but luck, Macnair believed, was manufactured. He would fight the cartels with every resource that he had available and damn the consequences.

As soon as the meeting was over Hunter telephoned the hospital where Louise was being treated. He was put straight through and was pleasantly surprised when she answered the phone.

'Nick! Hi!'

'Lems? Are you okay?'

'Healing fast, Nick. No permanent damage. The muscles and tendons will be as good as new with just a small scar to show for it. David's arranged for just about every top surgeon of this and professor of that to have a look and they're all singing from the same hymn sheet.' Louise was referring to their cousin, Sir David Griffiths. He was very fond of Louise and Hunter could imagine him pulling every one of his considerable strings to help her.

'Thank God for that,' said Hunter, unable to prevent tears of happiness springing to his eyes. His sister, as he would have admitted to anyone who asked, was the dearest person in the world to him. Looking up and seeing Ruth smiling at him, he realised it was no longer the case.

'I'll be up and about tomorrow,' said Louise.

'So soon?'

'Yep. And I should be out the day after. There's been a little bit of surgery but nothing much.'

'Are you sure?'

'Nick, dearest, of course I am. So stop fretting and get on with whatever you're doing. Saving the world, presumably.'

He laughed ruefully. 'You got it, Lems.'

Louise chuckled.

'Are Mum and Dad still there?'

'In London. They've gone to David's. They'll be back in the morning. Do you want me to give them a message?'

'That's okay. I'll phone David. Take care.' He broke the connection and dialled his cousin. 'David? Nick.' They exchanged pleasantries and Nick then spoke to his father. 'Hi, Dad. I've just been speaking to Louise. Thank goodness she's on the mend. I'll be at home tonight. Ruth will be with me.'

'That's fine, son. Tell Ruth we're looking forward to meeting her.'

'Sure, Dad.' He said goodbye and hung up.

'Where is home, incidentally?' Ruth asked.

'A little village in Stirlingshire called Balfron. We can get something to eat on the way. Ready?'

'I'll need to buy a few things. Where are the nearest shops?'

'Stirling. It's en route.'

A short while later he drove them out of the front gate near Rosyth dockyard and turned left past the old naval married quarters' housing estate. Gunning the engine of his MGB, they went up the hill past *HMS Caledonia* and out onto the A985. Crossing the bridge at Kincardine they took the M9 to Stirling. An hour's shopping gave Ruth most of what she needed. Half an hour later they arrived at the picturesque village of Balfron. Picking up a superb curry from the local pub, the *Pirn Inn,* they carried on to his parents' house at the bottom of the hill. Minutes later they were sitting in the Aga-warm kitchen with a glass of lager, eating their meal.

'This is a nice house,' said Ruth, looking around appreciatively.

'Thanks. That's all my mother's doing. Out the back there,' he nodded at the kitchen door, 'is an extension where I stay when I'm here. It's new and self-contained. Right now it's a bit of a novelty for me and my parents, as I left home to go to the Royal Navy at the age of eighteen and only came here for holidays and visits. Now I'm with TIFAT, I stay here whenever I get the opportunity. Of course, I've got a cabin in the wardroom as well.'

'This curry is delicious.' She raised her glass of beer. 'Is this the best of both worlds? Commuting sometimes, staying in Rosyth at others?'

'Not really,' Hunter frowned. 'My parents are getting on a bit, although they're both fit and hearty. With Lems being away so much as well, coming here whenever I can seems to be the right thing to do.'

'Why do you call Louise, "Lems"?'

He laughed. 'Oh, that. It's a legacy from my father when Louise was young. He started it by saying something daft.'

'Which was?'

'Which was "Louisey, Peasey, Lemon Squeezy". Total nonsense of course, but then he started calling her Lems for short. And she answered to it. So I sometimes call her that. It's from the Sooty show.'

Ruth looked puzzled and Hunter laughed. 'It's a hand puppet. A bear that does magic.'

'A bear that does magic,' Ruth repeated, smiling, shaking her head in disbelief. 'You're obviously a close family.'

Hunter laughed. 'You don't know the half of it. We belong to the Griffiths family on my mother's side. We have a family motto: "The family, first and foremost". It's been ingrained so far into our psyche that it has become a way of life.'

'Your way of life?'

Hunter sipped his lager before replying. 'What I mean is, we help each other whenever called upon to do so. Any member of the family will help another, no matter what's required.'

'Provided it's legal?' Ruth queried.

Hunter shrugged. 'Not necessarily. It all depends,' Hunter said, enigmatically, 'on your definition of legal. The family, you should know, is immensely rich.'

161

'It is? How intriguing.'

'There's a very interesting history about them, written by my father three decades ago. He was nominated for a Pulitzer for the work.'

'Wow! Your father's a writer?'

'Before he went into the family business. I thought you should know . . .'

'You did? Why?'

Hunter shrugged, uncomfortably. 'Know what you're taking on.'

'Taking on? I didn't know I was taking on anything.'

'Well,' he cleared his throat. 'That is to say . . .' he trailed off.

'That is to say, what?' Ruth was enjoying herself. If he was trying to say what she thought he was trying to say, then she wouldn't help him one iota.

'You know what I mean.'

'No, I don't,' she smiled.

He caught her smile and suddenly grinned. 'Yes, you do. I know we haven't known each other long, but, somehow, you're just right.'

'You mean I fit? Like an old glove?'

He leaned forward and kissed her, gently. 'I love you,' he finally managed.

'I love you too, Nick.'

'In that case, will you marry me?'

Pleased she said, 'My immediate answer is yes, of course I will.'

'Good,' he smiled, raising his glass.

'But . . . I think we need to think more about it. We're old enough to recognise this isn't love's young dream. There are all sorts of practicalities to think about.'

'Such as?'

'Such as, where do we live? What about our careers? I'm Mossad. You're a member of TIFAT. Neither occupation carries a guarantee of a long and fruitful life.'

'Sure. Those are problems . . . wrong word . . . challenges, that we can sort out. We've a number of choices,' said Hunter seriously. 'You stay with Mossad and protect Israel while I stay with TIFAT and save the world.' He smiled self-deprecatingly. 'Or you join me in saving the world. Or we both leave and start something new.'

'Or I stay at home and have babies.'

'Or I stay at home and rear them,' Hunter quipped. 'See what choices we have? Emancipation all round. Isn't it wonderful?'

'Idiot,' she thumped him. 'There's plenty of time to make decisions, isn't there?'

'Sure. All the time in the world. Let's go through to my place and we can talk about it.'

In the self-contained flat behind the house he lifted a bottle of Cava vintage sparkling wine from the fridge and took it with them into the bedroom. There was not a lot discussed that night.

The following morning they were up with the dawn and arrived at Rosyth in time for breakfast. They easily made the 08.05 meeting.

The next two days were taken up with planning. They came to understand the enormity of the task ahead of them and, equally importantly, the complexity of it. Piece by piece the information they were collating painted an increasingly bleak picture. Their objective became crystal clear – to inflict as much damage to the cartels as possible. From Glover's tape they knew that a meeting of senior members of the Syndicate was scheduled to take place but at an unknown location. The Colombian Summit Meeting had been small compared to what they thought was going to happen next. Tentatively at first, but with growing confidence, a plan took shape. It would mean taking the fight to the enemy and fast, but there was no choice. If they delayed too long, then the legal and political powers could, and would, step in to stop them. Macnair had spent the previous evening, after the others had departed, speaking to his contacts across Europe. The men he trusted absolutely he took into his confidence, explaining his requirements and his intentions. Without exception they agreed. The forces of law and order would fight back harder than ever.

A brief conversation with Ruth's boss in Tel Aviv had cleared it for her to remain and help. She was now officially seconded to TIFAT.

15

The General deployed members of TIFAT across Europe, with the sections of the plan relevant to each location. A huge operation was being mounted without the knowledge of the politicians who, on the whole, were not trusted by the men and women of the security forces. In isolation, each section of the plan was not excessive. Which explained why the heads of the various security organisations felt untroubled by the actions they were taking. It was within their remit to do so. Only when the plan was put together did the sum of the parts become greater than the whole. Only then would the scale of the operation become evident.

One of the most difficult and delicate tasks was given to Leon Sautier of the French Bureau of Information. The bureau did not give out information but amassed it. It was one of France's most effective anti-corruption departments with many successes to its name, including the downfall of the corrupt Commissioners of the European Union, who had thought themselves above the law. The job Macnair asked of them was one they relished.

Sautier had assigned one of his best teams. It consisted of Jacques Withier, a small, dapper man in his early forties, who was a linguistic genius and Ferdinand Flika, thirty years old, tall, tough, born in Algeria and as black as coal dust. The third and final member of the team was Yvette Lahours. A pretty, dark-haired, forty-year old woman from the South of France, she hid her astute brain behind a veneer of bubbly froth.

'You understand what needs doing?' Sautier asked them.

'Yes. It is perfectly clear,' replied Yvette. 'And, I must say, long overdue.'

'We all agree with you there. The committee we are specifically interested in is composed of two men and a woman.'

'Committee?' queried Flika.

'Yes. The court is divided into four sections. The composition of each section is fixed for three years and presided over by a President and two Section Presidents. Are you with me so far?'

The three operatives nodded.

'The chambers, as they are called, vote by majority rule and sit for a twelve-month period. The chamber we're investigating voted on three of the most important anti-crime cases ever.'

'How do we know?' asked Yvette.

'Good question,' replied Sautier, standing and breaking government rules by lighting a cigarette. The other men followed his example with alacrity, while Yvette pointedly opened a window to let in some fresh air. 'A very good question,' he repeated and smiled. 'Because I have just received this from General Macnair.' He waved a docket in the air.

'From TIFAT?' queried Flika, blowing a long stream of smoke through pursed lips.

'The same,' replied Sautier.

'Heavy duty,' said Flika. 'Those people don't fool around.'

'Let's say,' said Sautier, 'that they have a more elastic mandate to operate than we do. Macnair's leading the fight we're all engaged in.'

'What's in the report?' asked Withier.

Sautier continued. 'I've visited TIFAT headquarters and seen what they are doing. They have a state of the art computer system. Where on earth Macnair gets his funding from is beyond me. However, he's downloaded every single European Court ruling over the last six years.'

'Why six? Why not longer?' asked Yvette.

'That's the term of office each judge is elected for.'

'Who elects them?' Yvette frowned.

'The Parliamentary Assembly of the Council of Europe, ostensibly. I say ostensibly, because judges are nominated by each state and are usually passed on the nod. It is, as usual, as corrupt as the other institutions we've been saddled with.' The others nodded. 'What is interesting is the thread of voting that runs through many of the chambers. May I remind you, each committee or chamber is only set up for twelve months. So decisions have to be taken within a relatively short timescale.'

'What does that mean?' asked Flika.

Sautier shrugged. 'Some of the law passed has been good law. The problem is much of it has been bad. Seven judges in particular have made some incredible decisions, a drip feed of changes that has gradually shifted the law in favour of the criminal.'

'Any examples?' asked Yvette.

'There are any number, but I'll give you a few. The original Convention of 1950, article six, states a right to a fair trial. On the face of it this is reasonable. The problem is, it's been twisted to practically handcuff our police and security forces when dealing with violent, vicious criminals of the sort we're fighting. As many as fifteen judgements have gradually undermined the law.' He broke off, seeing the looks on the faces before him, 'You don't need me to spell it out. Then protocol number six, article one, is the abolition of the death penalty. You know that this has been changed to suggest that a shoot-out with police and other forces is against this protocol. And the *pièce de résistance*, protocol number seven, article four, the right not to be tried or punished twice. You are aware of the latest judgement?' He made it a question.

They all nodded.

'Do you know what article five of the same protocol says?'

This time they all shook their heads.

'Again, on the face of it, it seems reasonable enough. Equality between spouses is enshrined in law. So how has this been interpreted? The same drug dealer has a wife. She claims she knows nothing about how her husband makes his money. As far as she is concerned he is just a successful businessman. She demands half his wealth. She can claim that to take all the money from him as a punishment is punishing her as well and she has done nothing to deserve punishment. Her life

167

style and that of her children is placed in jeopardy, yet she is innocent.'

'Surely,' Yvette protested, 'nobody believes that . . . clap-trap.'

'You would think not,' Sautier continued his lecture, 'but the evidence says differently.' He gave a Gallic shrug, 'Look at the voting pattern of these judges.' He handed out copies of the information he had received from Macnair.

The agents studied the information for a few minutes until, one by one, they looked at their boss, incredulity written large on their faces.

'It's . . . it's unbelievable,' said Yvette.

'Isn't it? Each law has undermined the last . . . No! That's the wrong word. Each new judgement has bent the last to the point of travesty.'

'What are we going to do?' asked Withier.

'We are going to find out why these three judges have sold out,' replied Sautier. 'Okay, you know what we need to do. Once we get anything, I'll pass the information to General Macnair and at the same time I will leak the information to the newspapers.'

There were nods all round. The same method had been used to break the European Commissioners. The force of public opinion eventually proved too great to resist.

Macnair, Hiram Walsh and Jim Carter sat in a corner of the ward-room, drinks in front of them, and discussed their achievements to date. Macnair sipped his whisky, barely diluted with a few drops of water, with relish, reasonably content that he had done everything he could.

Carter said, 'That's it. The whole package has been sent to the people we can *trust*.' He caught his boss's eye and amended his statement. 'Okay, sir, whom we *think* we can *trust*.'

Macnair nodded. 'There's a huge difference. I didn't like doing it, but having Isobel check out their financial situations was the best we could do. We have to place our hope somewhere.' He took another sip, enjoying the flavour. He was a connoisseur of whiskies and was renowned for his ability to identify the distillery a particular whisky came from. Even so, he rarely drank. It was the hobby that appealed to him.

'Did you read the report from Sautier?' Macnair asked. There were nods from the other two. 'It makes sense. Of the seven suspected judges, we need to concentrate on the current three from one particular chamber. You've seen what Sautier's planning. Any comments?'

Both men shook their heads. Walsh said, 'Sir, it seems to me they've covered all the bases. I agree with Leon. We don't have time to go after all seven. He agrees the three we identified originally have been responsible for the most damage.'

'That's only because the other four have not served as long,' said Carter. He took a healthy mouthful of gin and tonic.

Macnair said, 'I think we can warn off the other four. The three Sautier has in his sights are a different matter.'

'I thought,' Walsh frowned, 'that the idea was we would go public. Maintain TIFAT's security,' he hastily added, 'but leak the story along with the proof.'

Macnair nodded. 'That was my original intention. Sautier agreed with it. In fact, he relished the idea. However, I've had second thoughts. It isn't our job, or indeed our intention, to destroy the Court of Human Rights. Just to get it to act against the criminals, be that an individual or a state. We need the place to put its house in order and weed out any corrupt officials. I think that we need to take a different course of action.' He proceeded to detail his plans.

Sautier liked Macnair's new idea even more than the first one and was prepared to go along with it. Although the idea of shaming the Court of Human Rights into oblivion had appealed to him, it was, on further reflection, also true that the Court did some good. But it desperately needed cleaning up. The sacking of the EU commissioners for corruption had been a coup. Sautier estimated that it could take anything up to ten years before the same level of corruption was reached again. Sadly, he had no doubt that it would be reached.

'A slight change of plan,' he announced. 'We discover their motives and hand the information over to Macnair. He'll take it from there. No disclosure to the papers.'

'What will he do with it?' asked Yvette.

Sautier shrugged. 'I don't know,' he prevaricated. 'He just says to leave it to him.' Lighting a cigarette, he dragged in a lung full of much-needed smoke and exhaled a long white plume. 'Right, this is what we'll do. Yvette and Ferdinand will take judge number one, Jacques and I will concentrate on number two. Number three we will leave until a later date.'

'Why?' asked Withier. 'Why leave her until last?' he repeated.

'She'll be the easiest to crack,' was the enigmatic reply.

Yvette and Ferdinand Flika sat in a small office, each holding a copy of the file originally supplied by TIFAT but now thickened by their own enquiries. Judge Number One was a Dane. Poul S. Hellundssen, age fifty-six, was a crook. Bank accounts totalling over twenty five million French Francs had been found in his name. Yvette made a notation in the margin querying if there was any more. Hellundssen had gone to university in Copenhagen where he had barely scraped a degree. He then spent five years in law school, two longer than usual, to qualify as a lawyer. Luckily, he came from a well-to-do middle class family, one that owned a string of bakers' shops across Denmark. When he eventually qualified he went to work for the lawyer's office that handled his family's business. The contract was too lucrative not to give young Poul a job, even if the senior partner lived to regret it. Until Poul found politics.

Or rather, politics found him. He met Lotte, a beautiful blonde activist who made it clear that she could only be interested in him if he too became politically active. To everyone's surprise, including his own, he found he was good at it. Late-night meetings over beer and salami in bars and halls all across Copenhagen were the spice of life to Poul. And night times brought their own rewards with Lotte. By the time the excitement of politics had worn off for Lotte, Poul was hooked. He dumped her when he went to work for the Danish Conservative Party. For five years he was a gopher before he was asked to become a magistrate in Århus. Always in the background, never in the limelight, he rose in power within the party. He was able to pull more than a few irons out of the fire when individual party members found themselves in trouble, particularly with the press. He eventually married, had two sons, and then divorced – acrimoniously. The truth behind the break-up was mired in innuendo and lies. He had a string of mistresses. Then came his political pay day – he was offered the job in Strasbourg. Sautier's team discovered he had been paying his ex-wife more than he could afford in what should have been a reasonable divorce settlement. By the time he arrived in Strasbourg, Hellundssen was up to his neck in debt.

'You know,' said Flika, leaning back in his chair and putting his feet up on the desk, 'their vetting procedures for the judiciary are pathetic.' He put his hands behind his head, deep in thought. 'It was time to pay him off. That's what this has all been about right from the start. Somebody has been paying him, one way or another, his entire career.'

'I agree,' replied Yvette. 'Have you read the bank details yet?'

'Just finished them. We'll use the financial evidence to embarrass him. Prove what's going on.' Flika smiled and dropped his feet to the floor, sitting forward, his hands now on his knees. 'Our objective is to reform the court. We're going to start finding all the dirt we can on Hellundssen. A visit to the ex-wife is called for. We need to go armed to the teeth with information. We have to prove the rot started with the inadequate vetting procedures and the political payoffs.'

'Right. Where's the wife?'

'Hillerød.'

They flew to Copenhagen the next day. They had no official capacity and so were masquerading as journalists. They arrived at the airport to the south of the city, to be met by wet and windy Scandinavian weather. Hiring a car, they drove towards the capital. Coming from France, Yvette was unused to the politeness of the Danish drivers, and applied her usual appalling driving etiquette, cutting off other cars, blowing the horn and making

171

rude gestures. Flika persuaded her to calm down, but not before she got them lost twice by the simple expedient of disagreeing with the directions he gave her. They eventually found route 201 to Hillerød and Flika was able to relax and enjoy what scenery he could see through the curtain of the pouring rain.

Hellundssen's ex-wife lived in a four-storey, terraced building in a smart part of the town. Finding a hotel nearby, they checked in. At six o'clock that evening they drove round to the house. They rang the doorbell and a few moments later a striking, middle-aged lady, whose fair hair was streaked with grey, answered it. Madame Hellundssen must have been a beauty in her younger days.

'Yes? May I help you?' She spoke in Danish.

Yvette answered, first in French and then in English.

'Madame, I am so sorry to trouble you. We are looking for Madame Hellundssen.'

A wary look passed across the Danish woman's face. 'That was my name. What can I do for you?'

'We would like to interview you. About your husband,' replied Yvette.

'I am sorry. But I do not give interviews.' She went to close the door.

'Please, Madame, it's important. Give me a few minutes and I am sure we can persuade you that is in your best interest to talk to us.'

Madame Hellundssen looked from one to the other, sighed and said, 'You may come in for a few moments.'

She led the way along a wood-lined hall and into a large, well-furnished living room. Photographs dominated one wall, from left to right. They showed a history of her boys' lives. On the right were photographs of their weddings and others with children.

Madame Hellundssen indicated a sofa for them to sit on while she sat opposite, a long, low table between them. 'You said it was important.'

Yvette and Flika exchanged glances and Yvette nodded. 'It is. We would like to know about your husband.'

'Why is it important? And why in my best interests? He is a judge in Strasbourg. And please do not refer to him as my husband. We have been divorced for many years.' She spoke bitterly.

'We understand,' said Yvette. Experience had taught her not to waste time with niceties. She came straight to the point. 'We intend to expose his corruption. When it is made public, you,' inspiration struck and Yvette looked over at the wall, 'and your children and grandchildren will be tarnished. Our story is so powerful you will be hounded by hordes of newspaper and television reporters. If they don't get you they'll go after the other members of the family. And you must know that you can't hide forever. They'll dig and keep digging.'

Madame Hellundssen had turned deathly pale, her hand going to her throat, her mouth opening and closing as the enormity of Yvette's prediction sunk in. She was about to argue, to plead, but looking at the implacable faces before her she wilted, tears welling, reaching for a dainty handkerchief. 'Swine! You're all swine,' she whispered.

'Madame, I am truly sorry,' said Yvette. 'But you do have an escape route.' She dangled the bait before the distraught woman.

'I knew that one day it would come back to haunt me,' she spoke venomously, 'He's evil. Depraved. Disgusting.'

Barely managing to hide her delight at this disclosure, Yvette decided to follow it up. 'What do you mean? Depraved?'

The older woman seemed to age before them. Her head sunk to her hands and she sobbed for a few moments. Yvette and Flika let her weep, exchanging satisfied glances. They knew they would get what they wanted. Madame Hellundssen sat up, and composed herself. 'First I want to know about my family's way out.' There was determination in her voice as she faced up to what the future could hold for her and her family.

'You give us an exclusive exposé. When we go to press I will arrange for my newspaper to send you away for a few weeks on holiday. I can give you two weeks notice before we run the story. We will pay for all your family, if you wish. By the time you return it will be old news. And if there is nothing more to write about, nobody will bother you.'

Madame Hellundssen stood up, straightened her dress and stalked out saying she would return in a moment. Yvette also stood and walked along the length of the wall, looking at the photographs. There was not a single picture of Madam Hellundssen's ex-husband. Ten minutes later Madam Hellundssen returned.

'I accept your offer. At least with your help I may have a chance of avoiding some of the embarrassment. With others, God alone knows. But I want an agreement in writing.'

They talked for an hour. When the two agents finally left they thanked Madame Hellundssen profusely, promising her that the necessary arrangements would be made for her and the family to leave the country for a while. Naturally, they were lying.

Leon Sautier and Jacques Withier had a different problem. Their target was an Austrian named Karl Gautlich. He was a sixty-two year old widower whose wife had died eleven years earlier, leaving him with a teenage daughter just starting at university. Gautlich had been devastated by his wife's death and taken years to come to terms with it. Only when his daughter Lisa got into trouble over drugs at the university did he come out of his self-made shell and begin to function as a human being again. He rebuilt his law practice that had been allowed to wither away and was doing well when he was offered the judgeship. Eminently qualified, he sold his practice to his junior partners and went to Strasbourg. Financially independent, the salary he earned was, in effect, a bonus. For a year his decisions were those expected of a senior judge passing laws which affected hundreds of millions of people across Europe. Gradually though his decisions changed. Only a determined scrutiny revealed a pattern. Individually his pronouncements weren't significant. Analysed and taken as a whole the results were startling. For the last four years he had been twisting the law to aid the criminal. Not just certain individuals, but known cartels and terrorist groups.

The information supplied by Macnair, though accurate, had not shown the effect on Gautlich himself. He was once more the shadow of his former self, just as he had been following his wife's death. For the judge was not corrupt. TIFAT found no trace of unusual activity with either of his bank accounts in Austria or Strasbourg. His investments continued to grow at a reasonable rate and his life style was almost non-existent. When Gautlich had first emerged from self-imposed exile he had enjoyed a social life. His daughter had finished university in Vienna with a degree in computer science and then matriculated at the Sorbonne with a further degree in business studies. She had a high powered job with a small but dynamic software company in Germany. Gautlich had gone to Strasbourg. And a year later everything had changed. Why? What had happened? Sautier posed the question to Withier.

'It seems to me that Gautlich is a family man. He was devastated by the death of his wife and it was only the threat to his daughter that eventually rescued him from what appears to have been an early decline.'

'Agreed,' said Sautier, leaning back in his chair, feet outstretched.

'So what if it's his daughter again? Only this time he can't help her?'

'What do you mean?' Sautier sat up straight and leaned forward, his mind racing ahead.

'Look at the man. His business life as a lawyer has been exemplary. As a prosecutor he was definitely right wing. As a defender, consider the history of the people he defended. Again from the right. Then the death of his wife wipes him out personally. Only his daughter's brush with the law drags him back from the brink. According to the reports he was suicidal before Lisa needed him.'

Sautier nodded. 'And it appears he's that way again.'

'And he's making judgements which are out of character. He was never one to favour the criminal. One of the reasons he was recommended and eventually elected was precisely to balance other judgements made by the more liberal left-wingers. Agreed?'

'Somebody obviously has a hold over him. It can only be

175

through Lisa. Perhaps she's been taking drugs again. Or she's embezzled her company's money and is open to blackmail.'

Withier nodded. 'Nothing else makes sense. Organise a wiretap on his phone at home and I'll go and visit Lisa. Perhaps I can learn something.'

'We'll never get permission to tap the phone of a judge.'

Withier, knowing Sautier for over twenty years, gave him a look. His boss laughed. The tap would be illegal and not for the first time.

Lisa's company, Zellox GmbH, was headquartered in Frankfurt-am-Main in Germany. Withier hated flying and instead took a high-speed train. A short taxi ride from the Hauptbahnhof found him at his destination.

Zellox occupied the second and third floors of an old building with sixty or seventy employees crammed in the inadequate space. It was obvious that the company had out-grown the premises. Posing as a potential buyer of their manufacturing software, Withier had an appointment with one of their managers. He was shown into a small office containing a table big enough for four to sit around, two chairs and a sideboard that held a coffee percolator.

The room had an outside wall with a window overlooking another office block and a glass partition that let him see the bustle in the main office. It was depressing to realise how young they all appeared.

The door opened and a smartly dressed young man entered, carrying a folder. 'Monsieur Withier?' He held out his hand. 'I am Paul Sacker.' He spoke fluent English with barely a trace of an accent.

'How do you do, Herr Sacker?' Withier replied in German with a thick French accent.

Sacker switched to German. As he spoke, he handed over his business card, which announced him as a sales manager. Withier's fictitious card proclaimed him to be a technical director of a company based in Lille. They talked briefly about the software that Withier was interested in and whether or not Zellox could accommodate his requirements. A specialised application of software they already had could be modified within six weeks. Withier was looking for an opening when one was offered.

'How did you come to know about us, Herr Withier?'

'Eh . . . The daughter of a friend of mine works here. Lisa Gautlich?'

'I know no one of that name. Mind you, at the rate we are hiring that's hardly surprising. Is she new?'

'What? Oh, no. She has been here for three, maybe four years.'

The young man frowned and shook his head. 'That is not possible. Otherwise I would know her. I have been here over two years and when I first arrived there were only thirty or so people.'

Withier frowned. Perhaps they had made a mistake about the company. If so, it had been a wasted trip. And worse, a waste of time. 'Are you sure? I had hoped to see her.'

'Positive. *Augenblick, bitte.* I will check, in case I am wrong.' Walking quickly across the office to a desk near the door, he had a word with the woman sitting at a computer terminal who followed him back to the small office.

'This is Frau Wyssbrod. She has been here from the start. It seems I owe you an apology Herr Withier. We did have someone of that name here but she left three years ago.'

'You know Lisa?' Withier looked at the woman. He saw from her hand that she was married. Pretty enough and well groomed.

'Yes. She was a friend of mine.'

'Was? I don't understand.'

'She left suddenly. Didn't come to work one day. We thought that she was ill and expected a phone call or a message. But nothing. It was totally unlike her as she was always on time. More than that. She usually worked late as well. She loved her job. After two days I went to her flat. It was empty. So we thought that perhaps she had a problem with her father and she would contact us.'

'Did she?' Withier asked.

'No. But her father did. It was strange. When I took the call, he said that she had suddenly decided to leave. To go abroad. That was the last we heard.'

'Did you not make more enquiries?'

'Why should I? It is a free country.'

'But you did not know it was her father. It could have been anyone.'

'But I did. I had met him at least five or six times. So you see I had no reason to doubt what he said. I was surprised that she never contacted me but . . .' she shrugged. 'Life moves on. Have you seen her recently?' she asked, eagerly. 'If so, please give me her address. I'll contact her.'

'What? Oh, no. I last saw her two years ago,' he temporised. 'I had brochures about your company and I remembered that Lisa worked here and so I thought I would come here for advice and possibly meet our company's needs.' He stood up. 'Well, thank you both.' He shook hands and quickly left before any more awkward questions could be asked. None of it made sense. Where on earth was she?

16

When Withier arrived back at Sautier's office the next morning he found his boss listening to a tape machine. Sautier switched it off and looked enquiringly at his colleague. Withier quickly relayed all that he had learned at Zellox. Sautier nodded in satisfaction.

'It's as I thought,' said Sautier.

Withier sat down and reached for a packet of Gitanes, offering one to his boss. 'And what's your conclusion?'

'She's dead,' was the startling reply.

'You seem very certain.' Withier paused with a match to his boss's cigarette.

'*Ecoutez bien!*' Sautier pressed the rewind button on the cassette player and while the tape spun backwards he said, 'I got this late last night. From Gautlich's phone. Listen carefully.'

'Hullo, Papa. I hope you are still well and doing what they tell you. I am well. I will be home soon.'

'Lisa!' The anguish was all too clear in the judge's voice. 'Lisa. Tell them that if they release you I will give them all that I have. I must see you. I need proof that you are well. Lisa . . .'

'*Das geht nicht. Tchüss, Papa.*' The connection was broken but before the judge replaced his receiver the two men distinctly heard a sob.

'She has been kidnapped,' said Withier. 'She's not dead.'

'Listen again. Only carefully this time.' He replayed the recording. 'Did you hear that?'

'What am I listening for?' his subordinate frowned, puffing on his cigarette.

179

'The voice is mechanical. I think it's a synthesised recording of Lisa's voice. Take the tape to the lab and tell them it's a priority. I want to know immediately what they think.'

'You want me to wait and find out?'

'No. Come back here. If I am right then we have work to do.'

Knowing how Sautier worked, Yvette and Flika spent six hours putting together their report on Hellundssen. She collated the information while he typed it, his thick fingers flashing across the keyboard as quickly as a first class secretary. They were sitting in Sautier's office when Withier returned from the lab.

'Decision in one hour,' he said, nodding hello to the other two.

'Good,' Sautier replied. 'This is first rate work, you two. The facts are overwhelming. Hellundssen has been corrupt practically since the first day he started in law,' he said to Withier. 'Sexual peccadilloes aside, his proven criminal activity is enough for our needs. I'll tell General Macnair and leave it to him.'

'What about Gautlich?' asked Yvette.

Sautier brought them up to speed with the situation. 'Yvette, can you organise some coffee while I send this report to Macnair?'

Yvette had long ago learnt not to show any chagrin when asked to do what her male colleagues considered women's work. Like making coffee. Even so, she could not help flouncing from the room and slamming the door even though she knew that the only effect it would have on the three men would be to make them grin.

When she returned carrying four mugs she found them talking about rugby, a passion all three shared. There came a discreet knock at the door. A courier handed in a tape and written report to Sautier, who nodded his thanks. Ripping open the envelope he quickly scanned its contents. Wordlessly, he handed it to Withier, took his mug and sipped at the black, sweetened coffee.

Withier passed it to Flika who in turn gave it to Yvette. 'So she is dead.'

'It looks like it. Whoever killed her has recorded her voice

180

and manufactured a complete vocabulary. 'If you listen carefully to the recording there's a mechanical tone to the voice,' Sautier replied.

'Why didn't Gautlich catch it, then?' Yvette added, 'He should have known.'

Sautier nodded. 'I agree. I think he does know in his heart. I think he has been living in denial, hoping against hope that she was alive.' He shrugged. 'Who can blame him? Hope is a very strange beast to live with. We allow it to distort our vision of reality.'

'How should we proceed?' asked Yvette.

'We interview him. We need as many answers as he is willing to give. And if possible a signed statement about what he has been doing to pervert the law. Then we leave him be. It will be up to him. My guess?' he shrugged, eloquently. 'Suicide is not illegal in France.'

'What will we do with the information?'

'Pass it to Macnair. He's knows what to do with it.'

'What about judge number three?' asked Withier. 'The Dutch woman, Janice de Havilland.'

'I told you, she is easy,' said Sautier. 'Not only corrupt, but greedy. She also spends far more than she can afford. Tracing her money and its source was simplicity itself. At least Hellundssen had the good grace to appear as though he was living within his means. She makes no attempt. As though she were immune. Protected.'

'Maybe she is,' Yvette said, thoughtfully.

'What do you mean?' asked Flika.

'Just that. Have you read her file?' The three men nodded. 'She is forty-nine, no children, unmarried and has the looks and figure of a thirty year old. Her qualifications for the job are barely adequate and some of the judgements she has made are ludicrous. She's lost every judgement that's been appealed by the prosecutors. That's unheard of. She's careless. So who's protecting her?'

'That's a good point,' said Sautier, annoyed for not realising it himself. 'It shows how deeply the corruption runs. Right across the institutions. Just like with the Commissioners.'

'I agree,' said Yvette. 'Otherwise she would have been kicked out long ago.'

'I thought a judge could not be sacked,' said Flika.

'Not in the ordinary way,' replied Sautier. 'Not for incompetence, laziness or stupidity. But dishonesty is another thing. With her it is obvious, yet nothing is done about it. Yvette is right. She's being protected.'

'So what do we do?' asked Withier.

'Again, pass the information to Macnair. We've corroborated all the facts. He has absolute proof as to her guilt. It is up to him now. Jacques, it's time to call on Judge Karl Gautlich.'

The two men left the room. Yvette picked up the telephone and dialled. *Mon chèr?* I'll be home early. *Oui*. Supper and an early night. *Au'voir.*'

Flika looked quizzically at her. 'Anyone I know?'

Yvette smiled. 'A friend. Now excuse me, I've got work to do.'

Sautier and Withier met Judge Gautlich in his palatial rooms at the Court, beautifully furnished with light oak panelling and luxurious carpet. The furniture was rosewood and matched the maroon chesterfield and leather armchairs. Gautlich was sitting behind his desk, a haggard look on his face. Sautier noticed that even though the judge's hands were clasped tightly together on the blotting pad in front of him, they still trembled.

'What may I do for you *messieurs*?' the judge asked in fluent French.

'We come from . . .'

'Yes, yes, yes,' came the testy reply. 'I know who you are and what you do. What do you want?'

'It is about your daughter,' Sautier began without preamble and watched as the judge sat back, flinching, as though he had just been struck.

'Lisa?' The voice was a croak, painful. Anguished.

'Sir, my department believe she is dead.' There was no other way to tell him. Brutal, honest, soul shattering. Sautier felt sorry

182

for the old man but hardened his heart to the task ahead. 'We know she was kidnapped.'

The judge cried out as though to repudiate the fact, a denial forming and dying on his ashen lips.

'We believe that she was killed soon after.'

'No. *Das kann nicht sein.* I speak to her regularly. To keep me . . .' he stopped.

'To keep you doing what, sir? To keep you enforcing bad laws? Freeing criminals? Selling mankind down the drain?' Sautier's voice was harsher than he intended.

'You don't understand. My daughter . . .'

'We have a recording of Lisa's voice. It's been analysed. It's manufactured. She has to be dead.'

Sautier considered himself hardened, but what he saw then shocked him. The complete and total disintegration of a human being. Gautlich stood up, using the desk to help him and staggered across the room. He collapsed onto the sofa, curled up into the foetal position and keened. Sautier and Withier exchanged helpless glances.

'He needs sedating,' said Withier, 'and quickly. Before he flips over the edge. Put him out and let him come round slowly. Otherwise I fear for his sanity.'

Sautier nodded agreement and lifted the telephone receiver. He dialled one hundred for the operator. In less than an hour a heavily sedated Judge Karl Gautlich was in bed in a private room in a local sanatorium. Sautier pulled rank and had a gendarme stationed outside the door. He wanted to know as soon as the judge came round.

Macnair finished reading the report. Sautier had done a superb job. The paper trail was leading slowly but surely back to the source. Now, he needed to apply more pressure – those responsible would scream like stuck pigs. His biggest problem remained however. There was still no sign of the warheads.

His door was open and Isobel put her head round. 'May I come in?'

'Please. What have you got for me?'

'The more leads we have from Sautier the closer we get to the source. I lost Hellundssen in a bank in the Caymans but cross-referenced it to one for de Havilland and that led me to Liechtenstein. I've now set up a programme to do it for us. As we feed in the information the computer finds the connections and we keep going.'

'Where has it led to so far?'

'Georgia, in the old Soviet Union. A company there is heavily involved in what's called tolling.'

'What's that?'

'It's a way of laundering vast sums of money. The country's natural resources are sold below their market value to a middleman. The middleman sells them at the correct price and the difference pays off himself as well as the officials who were responsible for selling the goods in the first place. The balance is paid into an offshore account. Georgia has been robbed of vast quantities of wood and coal using this method.'

'Who's controlling it?'

'I think it's a woman named Alleysia Raduyev. I've traced a number of the companies we're interested in back to her. Most of them are dummies with no obvious trading but a few are legitimate. Even the legitimate ones make large sums of money from dealing in practically everything from legal drugs to ships.'

'Legal drugs?' Macnair frowned, puzzled.

'Yes, sir. Penicillin, anti-malaria drugs, even aspirin. It's a huge business.'

'I don't understand. I know what drugs you mean but how do they make money?'

'By buying up stock that is past its sell by date. Re-packaging them and selling on.'

'Good Lord! You don't mean to tell me that the major drug companies are a part of it?'

'Why not? It's not illegal. Provided the sale is made openly with the clear understanding that the drugs are, not exactly useless, but have a very limited shelf life. The manufacturers sell wholesale at a knock down price that suits them as they still make a profit. The people the drugs are then sold to still can't afford them. So they trade.'

'Trade what?'

'Illegal drugs, arms, people.'

Macnair nodded wearily. *What a screwed up world, he thought.* 'Why do you think it's this woman, Raduyev . . . ?' he paused and Isobel nodded, 'who's involved?'

'She owns some of the companies. It doesn't mean she is involved of course. She has her fingers in so many pies it would be easy for somebody else to be running the illegal side without her knowledge. And interestingly she has an Englishman working for her by the name of Maximillian King-Smith. And there have been a few references to an Englishman being involved at the highest levels of The Syndicate.'

Macnair nodded. He thought for a few moments, his fingers absent-mindedly tapping the desk in a military tattoo, or what passed for one in Macnair's head, before continuing. 'Concentrate on Raduyev. Find out everything you can. Also see what you can get on King-Smith.'

Isobel nodded and returned to the computer room. She called Leo and Gareth to her office and gave her instructions.

Yvette arrived home early. Her lover greeted her with a warm smile and a kiss. She sniffed the air appreciatively. 'Smells delicious. What is it?'

'Lamb casserole. Lots of herbs, spices and simmering vegetables.'

She kissed his cheek. 'What a lucky find you were,' she said, happily. She looked up adoringly into his deep brown eyes. He was a metre eighty tall, slim, broad shouldered, with dark curly hair. Born in Greece of Albanian parents he had immigrated a few years earlier to France. Yvette had met him at a night club several weeks earlier. She put her arms around him contentedly, smiling. They had been lovers almost from the beginning.

He put his hands on her shoulders and pushed her away gently, wrinkling his nose. 'Darling, your hair. It stinks of cigarette smoke.'

'Flika and the rest smoke non-stop even if it is against the rules. I'll have a shower while you pour me a drink. Cassis, vodka and lemonade, please.' Humming happily she went into the bedroom, stripped off and, as she entered the bathroom she looked at herself critically in the floor length mirror. *Not bad,* she thought, and then added the caveat, *for my age.*

She entered the shower and turned it on, full blast and hot, just the way she liked it. She sensed his presence behind her and feeling his palm on her back, she gave herself over to the luxurious touch of his hands as they washed her.

Later they lay in bed, the sheets crumpled, dinner all but forgotten.

'How was your day?' she asked him, sleepily, her fingers drawing a pattern across his back. She felt him tense and cursed herself. Wrong question!

'The usual. Who would have thought it was so difficult to find a job? I am a good chef. I need to find a backer and open a place of my own somewhere. Otherwise I shall have to return to Athens.'

'No,' she sat up, panic in her voice. 'Don't do that. Keep looking. I earn enough for us to live on. Something will turn up. I am asking all my contacts to help me out as a favour and God knows I'm owed enough of those.'

He leant on his elbows and looked behind him, at her worried face, and smiled. 'Maybe you are right, *Chèrie*, we will see. In the meantime I will stay as your houseguest.'

Relief flooded through her and she smiled in return. She bent her head to his. 'You are more than that,' she murmured. 'Much more.'

Later they sat at the kitchen table devouring the rescued casserole, she in a bathrobe, he in a T-shirt and jeans.

Sipping his wine, he asked, 'And how was your day? Did you save France yet again?' There was an edge to his voice that she chose to ignore.

'You know I cannot talk about work,' she began and then saw the truculent look that passed across his face. She sighed. It had been the same for the past few weeks. She had tried to make him understand that she could not talk about her job. At first he had found it amusing but eventually it festered to a sore. It was always the same. Unless she married somebody from within the department she would never be allowed to share with her lover. Dare she think about it? Security was all very well but not when it ruined relationships. It was hardly life threatening.

She smiled, put her hand on his, and told him all about her day.

On Saturday afternoon Hunter and Ruth were in Balfron, waiting for the return of his parents with Louise. His sister had a month's leave from the airline and she had chosen to spend it at home.

Ruth was nervous about meeting the family although Hunter tried to reassure her. She had proposed spending the afternoon preparing a meal but Hunter vetoed the idea. Instead he suggested they have a cheese *fondue* as it was more relaxed and conducive to talking.

It was after 6pm when the car drew into the drive and the three of them arrived. Louise had her arm in a sling but seemed cheerful enough.

Hunter gave her a hug and a kiss, pecked his mother on the cheek and shook his father's hand. He introduced his parents to Ruth, who was hovering nervously in the background.

Immediately sensing that there was something special between Ruth and her son, Hunter's mother tucked Ruth's arm under hers and led her away, ostensibly to show her the garden. Hunter and Louise exchanged long-suffering glances and then Hunter helped his father with their cases.

It was a wonderful evening. Ruth's delicious fish soup was enjoyed with a bottle of Chardonnay. Fondue, doctored with plenty of garlic, white wine and a spot of schnapps was served with cubes of crusty bread, glasses of Williams Pear schnapps and cumin seeds. Tea was offered but they chose to drink a chilled white Austrian Gewürztraminer, a fitting tribute to a simple meal.

Later, while the women chatted, Hunter and his father took the dog for a walk. In companionable silence they wandered down the hill towards the River Endrick. Winston, a golden Labrador, darted back and forth, his tail wagging, sniffing everything eagerly, happy to be out in the clear, cool air.

'So,' Tim Hunter began, 'what are your intentions?'

'Well, I'm pretty serious about her, Dad. But,' he shrugged, 'we haven't decided yet.'

'Ruth said she works for the Israeli government. Which branch?'

Hunter had never lied to his father before and he had no intention of starting now. He took a deep breath and said, 'Mossad.'

His father chuckled. 'I figured something like that. Her father is Deputy Prime Minister and so I suspect she's pretty well committed to Israel. Don't you think?'

'I guess so.'

There was a pause in the conversation as they stepped off the pavement and crossed the bridge to the other side of the river. They turned down the dirt track before Tim Hunter continued where they had left off.

'It's a big step. I can't see you living in Israel. Can you?'

Hunter thought about it for a few seconds before sighing. 'I guess not, Dad. So what I'm really saying is we have to live here.'

'Only if you stay with TIFAT. You can join the family firm any time. You know that. A big job with a big salary.'

'I know, but it's not really me, is it? Can you see me going into an office every day? Dictating letters, attending meetings?'

Tim Hunter smiled. 'I guess not, son. You're a throwback. You should have been a swashbuckler in the eighteenth century or worked with your great-grandfather during the First World War.' He clapped Hunter on the shoulder. 'You and Ruth will have to look at all the alternatives. Make a list and cross them out one by one until you're left with the only solution.'

'What if,' Hunter said bleakly, 'the solution is we only see each other occasionally?'

'Then so be it.'

188

On that sombre thought they dropped the subject and enjoyed the rest of their stroll.

Early Sunday morning the phone rang. It was Macnair. His message was brief. 'Commander, I need you to go to Bosnia.'

17

'Bosnia?' Hunter queried, when he arrived at Rosyth.

Macnair came straight to the point. 'Yes. I've received some useful information from General Mithoff which I want you to follow up.'

'The boss of GSG9?' Hunter wondered how the German Federal hostage release and anti-terrorist force were involved.

'The same. Do you remember the reports a few months ago about the misappropriation of a billion dollars from international aid and public funds intended for the reconstruction of Bosnia's infra-structure, following the ninety-two to ninety-five war?'

Hunter thought for a few seconds. 'If I remember correctly Bosnian leaders and the US State Department angrily refuted some of the story. Something to do with the Dayton peace accord.'

'Correct. The theft was exposed in a report by an American led, anti-fraud unit appointed by the United Nations Security Council. The State Department called the assertions false, unjustified and unsubstantiated. They maintained that such claims could seriously harm Bosnia when investment needed to be encouraged. Officials said, and wait for this, only twenty-one million dollars in international aid was lost and that was due to the collapse of Bosnia's central bank.'

'Only? It sounds a heck of a lot to me, sir.'

'Especially as it isn't true. Corruption and fraud are widespread, endemic. The actual figure is closer to half a billion.'

'Who's responsible?'

'We weren't sure. Until now. The State Department has categorically denied that there's any truth in the rumour. I didn't believe them so I asked General Mithoff to investigate. He sent a report through last night.'

'How accurate is it?' Hunter asked.

Macnair shrugged. 'The report's accuracy could be questionable except for one thing. Three of his men were killed getting it.'

'Do we know what happened?'

'They'd finished in Sarajevo and were preparing to leave. They had a disc copy of the report but they also sent one by e-mail via a sat-nav phone. Which is just as well under the circumstances. Within minutes of sending the report a massive bomb blew the hotel to smithereens.'

'I'd heard about the explosion this morning on the news. Do we know for sure that they were the targets, sir?'

'The explosives were placed under their room, on a wardrobe, directed at the ceiling. Six other people were killed and over a dozen injured without any discernible reason. No,' Macnair shook his head, 'the targets were the lads from GSG9.'

'What's General Mithoff doing about it?'

'That's the rub. GSG9 aren't allowed to operate outside Germany.'

'I thought that law had been changed years ago.'

Macnair shook his head. 'Their military units were allowed only to operate outside their borders, so that they could play a fuller part in the European Union. GSG9 were not part of the agreement. Mithoff sent his men there ostensibly on leave. He's in it up to his neck right now and doesn't think he can survive the political fallout.'

'What do you want me to do, sir?'

'Read the report. Then come back to me with your recommendations and suggestions. I want to save Kurt Mithoff. He's a friend and one of the few men we can trust one hundred percent. I also feel partly responsible for the predicament he's in. After all, if I hadn't asked him to help this would never have happened.'

'That's ludicrous, sir,' Hunter argued. 'He made the decision to help once he knew what was needed. He knew the risks. It goes with the territory.'

'Be that as it may, I still shoulder some of the responsibility. The problem was, we were too stretched to send our own people. And there was nobody else I thought I could trust enough. If we are to win this war then we need everyone. The loss of General Mithoff would be a serious blow to our efforts. And with the Turks being such a major problem in Germany, we need him working with Albatha.'

Hunter nodded. That made sense. The illegal immigrant problem in Germany was mainly Turkish based. Many of them were involved in the heroin trade and that in turn was causing a neo-nazi backlash across the country. Certain areas were tinderboxes waiting to explode. Some cities had no-go areas and were rife with drugs, prostitution and armaments. They were under the control of warlords known as *beys*. A *bey* was usually the governor of a Turkish province and so was a title of respect. The so-called *beys* of the drugs cartels and terrorist groups enforced their demand for respect with intimidation – beatings, stabbings, shootings and explosions. If the German authorities didn't fight back soon, it would be too late. Which was why Mithoff had agreed to send his team into Bosnia.

Hunter returned to his own office with the e-mailed report. He began to read. It was hair-raising stuff and a testament to the professionalism and bravery of the GSG9 operatives who had compiled it. The amount of money that had actually been embezzled was staggering. The dead German operatives had estimated it at anything from a quarter to half a billion US dollars. Their report also named a senior American State official as part of the scam. The corruption was truly awesome in its scale.

Because of their investigation into the embezzled funds, the GSG9 team had been able to identify three senior members of the Georgian cartel. One ran the cartel's narcotics business, a second looked after the illegal immigrants and the third, a particularly brutal man, took care of security. He used murder and intimidation as easily and often as he ate a meal.

When Hunter had finished reading, he sat back, deep in

thought. The GSG9 agents had gone to Bosnia Herzegovina with an advantage – one of them spoke Serbo-Croat. Hunter had heard enough television news interviews to know that the majority of the people in the region did not speak English and that their language was unintelligible to him, even though he spoke excellent German and passable French.

An hour later he had the bones of an operation put together. It was downright dangerous but, on reflection, could be done. The GSG9 operatives had been painstaking in putting together the report. It was all there, dates, places, people. Glumly, he thought, *aye, they were so good they got themselves killed*. He had no idea how accurate the report was – it looked good . . . but. He wondered who the senior British officer in SFOR – the Stabilisation Force – in Bosnia was, and whether he would co-operate.

Hunter returned to Macnair's office just as the General was replacing the telephone receiver. 'Damn! That was Jim Carter,' said Macnair. 'He's been told that an MEP is about to raise questions in the European Parliament regarding the operations we and the rest of the security services are carrying out across Europe. "Sentencing without trial" it's being called.' Macnair looked gloomily down at the Forth. 'They even work out their own sound bites nowadays. Saves the journalists the trouble.'

'What'll it mean for us, sir?'

Macnair looked bleakly at Hunter. 'A great deal of trouble, I should think. I was thinking about it earlier and in principle I agree with the MEP. We *should* be holding trials and sentencing the criminals to life imprisonment. The problem is that's not happening. Every security chief, senior officers of police forces and the military in Europe knows the problems we face, yet the politicians sit back and watch it happen.'

'It's called democracy, sir.'

'I know it is, Commander, but in this instance it isn't working. We need to regain control. Then let the rule of law reassert itself. Lord Acton maintained that power corrupts and absolute power corrupts absolutely, but does it?' Shaking his head Macnair said, 'We'll have the philosophical debate when this is all over.'

'Sir, when we find out who the MEP is we can do a background check. There may be an ulterior motive that we could find. If we expose it, along with the scandal about the judges, we'll be on safer ground.'

Macnair nodded. 'I've thought of that.' Macnair swivelled his chair around to face Hunter. 'We know the major cartels are meeting soon. We have to move quickly. We can't afford to have our hands tied at the moment. Once this is all over I don't give a damn if we go public.'

'If we can expose the corruption of the European judiciary, that could give us some breathing space. It might even be enough to spike the guns of the MEP.'

Macnair nodded. 'Jim Carter is trying to find out which Member of the European Parliament it is we'll have to deal with.'

Hunter hesitated a second and then decided to take the plunge. 'What if we find no ulterior motive? What if the MEP is acting out of sheer conviction? There is a solution.'

'Yes, I know. Fabricate something.'

Hunter nodded.

'No. I won't ask anyone under my command to smear someone who believes in justice. That's a misuse of power and completely out of the question.'

Hunter looked at his boss with relief. 'Perhaps we can try rational argument. That may persuade him.'

'Maybe. Now, Commander, what have you got for me?'

'Sir, the GSG9 boys did an excellent job. Their report identified three individuals who are senior members of the Georgian cartel and whose influence extends across Europe. I've numbered them, as their names are unpronounceable. One siphons money abroad but is normally active in drug manufacturing and smuggling. Two is involved with smuggling refugees across Europe. After all, it's an ideal place to be based – a crossover between East and West, rotten law enforcement, endemic corruption and smuggling routes too numerous to count. Number three is a real work of art. He's wanted for war crimes against the Croats and currently has three indictments outstanding against him. SFOR have standing orders to arrest and detain. So far he's escaped being picked up twice. Both times at the last second.'

'An informer?'

'It looks like it.'

'Did the GSG9 lads have a clue as to the informer's identity?'

'No, sir. When we go to Bosnia we'll keep a low profile. Stay away from our forces. Our biggest problem is the language.'

'I know. That's why Matthew Dunston is going with you.'

'The chaplain? Why?'

'He speaks a number of languages, including Serbo-Croat.'

'He's proving a useful guy to have around.'

Macnair nodded. 'He's a scholar of Latin and Greek. As a result he finds it easy to learn other languages. Western languages, that is. He is currently polishing up his German and French in order to become fluent. When I suggested to him that he might accompany you he was all for it and took himself off to listen to his language tapes.'

'That'll be a great help. The language barrier was a serious problem. I thought Masters and Badonovitch should come as well. We won't want too many. It's finesse we need, not overwhelming force.'

Macnair was shaking his head. 'Sorry, not possible. Neither is available. They've both got other jobs to do.'

Hunter knew better than to argue. 'My plan calls for four but I suppose I can manage with three. Do you really think a chaplain is suitable for this type of work? And what about one of the others?'

'I do, otherwise he wouldn't be going. Your number three will be Ruth Golightly.'

'Sir, I hardly think . . .'

'Commander,' Macnair held up his hand to stop Hunter, 'I am fully aware of your relationship. Ruth has been seconded here from Mossad. She is a highly trained, very tough and resourceful operative. So she goes. It's an order.'

Hunter wisely knew he should say nothing. There was no argument he could reasonably put forward. Except that he loved

Ruth and was horrified at the idea of her going into danger. He would need to change his attitude before they went into Bosnia.

Macnair's sat-nav phone rang and he picked it up. 'Macnair.' He listened for a few seconds and then added, 'Excellent. Thank you.' He hung up. 'That was Major Carter. The MEP concerned is Christine Woolford.'

Hunter grimaced. 'Never heard of her. Which party?'

'I don't know. I'll ask Isobel to get the details, along with the woman's voting record.' He pressed an intercom button and spoke briefly to Isobel.

'Be with you in a minute, sir. I'll get it off the Internet,' said Isobel.

Macnair finished speaking to her and turned back to Hunter. 'Right. Woolford is my problem, Bosnia is yours.'

'Who's OC our troops, sir?'

'Major General MacGregor. I know him. I'll have a private word and tell him what we need. I'm sure he'll co-operate and keep it quiet. We can't risk the informer getting to know about you. Currently Isobel is receiving information from around the world, which we're assessing. For once the various agencies are co-operating. Even the CIA, which must be a first. We know there are any number of undercover agents who have infiltrated some of the cartels. Very brave men and women who are risking their lives to discover what's happening. It's paramount that we protect them. What we need to know is where their next meeting is taking place. If we keep up the pressure we may panic the cartels' leadership. Panicked people make mistakes. That information is vital to us.'

'Has Isobel any leads, sir?'

'Some. But it's too early to tell where they'll take us. If we can hurt the Georgian cartel by attacking three of its leading members then we may learn something.'

'Yes, sir. When do you want us there?'

'The day after tomorrow. According to the tape from Columbia, the cartels will meet in eight days – but we still don't know where. Time is running out.'

Hunter nodded. 'I appreciate that, sir. Do we fly Crabfat Airways,' he referred disparagingly to the RAF, 'or go civilian?'

'Still to be decided. It all depends on the time-scale but you may even go rail/drive and have a car with you. Major Carter is working on a few things along that line.'

Hunter refrained from asking what they might be.

'There's something else you need to know. What I have to tell you is for your ears only. And that includes your team.'

If Hunter was surprised he didn't show it.

'The reason you're being tasked with these three men is their connection with the Georgian cartel. A few days ago GCHQ received a signal in Morse code stating that the sale of three nuclear warheads was being negotiated with a criminal organisation believed to be the Georgians.' Having begun with the shocking news, Macnair proceeded to fill Hunter in with what little he knew. He finished by adding, 'Nobody is to know about the warheads. I'm trying to keep the information as quiet as possible for as long as possible. If it should leak out all kinds of panic could ensue. Your main objective is to try and find out what has happened to the warheads. We think they'll be used for blackmail, which would tie in with a comment on the Glover tape.'

'We're dealing with criminals motivated by money so blackmail seems the most likely.'

'Agreed. Your targets may know something. If you get the opportunity to question them don't be gentle. We must find those warheads.'

'Yes, sir,' Hunter acknowledged.

There was a knock on the door and Isobel, without waiting to be asked, opened it and put her head through. 'Sorry to disturb you, General, but I've got the information about the MEP. I thought you'd like it immediately.'

'Yes. Thank you, Isobel. Right, Commander, that's all for now.'

'Yes, sir.' Hunter stood up, smiled at Isobel and left the room.

Macnair read the information handed to him, sat back and said, 'She seems to be a conviction politician, as I feared.'

'General?' Isobel looked quizzically at him.

'She does things out of belief. Her voting record is consistent. She cares about her constituents, she speaks up for what she thinks is right and that's everything from animal welfare to immigration and nuclear weapons.'

'She's a Labour MEP. Represents a constituency in Leeds.'

Macnair smiled. 'She's completely against nuclear weapons but has called for our troops to be better armed after the mess we had in Bosnia with faulty equipment. So she's not all bad.'

'She sounds like a thoroughly decent woman,' said Isobel.

Macnair looked at the photograph Isobel had pulled from the Internet. 'She is also attractive, divorced with a grown-up family.'

'What do you plan to do about her?'

'All I do know is that we must stop this debate. Arrange a meeting with her ASAP.'

Knowing the General as she did, Isobel did not argue. 'I have some other information,' she said. 'That bank account of Fergusson's, the policeman who tried to shoot Lt Cdr. Hunter. We've done some tracing back to that first account in Paris. It appears to be an account to feed corrupt policemen.'

'Damn. You said policemen, plural. How many?'

'So far, about fifty. Mainly constables, a few sergeants but . . .' she paused.

Macnair raised a quizzical eyebrow.

'One appears to be an Acting Chief Constable.'

'What!' Macnair was aghast. 'Which force?'

'Thames Valley.'

'Get me all the information you can.'

'In about an hour, sir.' Isobel left the office.

Hunter found Matt Dunston sitting in an office with earphones on, speaking out loud in an incomprehensible language. Seeing Hunter he switched off the machine and removed the earphones.

'Nick,' he smiled, 'to what do I owe the pleasure?'

'I'm here to talk about Bosnia.'

'I'm just brushing up on my Serbo-Croat. It helps to get my ear tuned in before I have to use it.'

'Good. I've got a file of info' here for you to digest. There are three targets we need to take care of.' Hunter paused, embarrassed about what he wanted to say next.

Catching his mood Dunston looked at him and smiled. 'You want to ask how do I reconcile being a Minister of God with what we need to do?'

Hunter nodded. 'Something like that.'

'It's not easy. The Scriptures are full of men who fought for Christ and God. Indeed, Jesus himself wasn't exactly meek and mild. He often lost his temper and lashed out. So, I take my example from the Bible and from history. We have a greater evil to overcome. We won't overcome it by turning the other cheek. In case you were wondering, I won't let you down.' His piercing blue eyes looked at Hunter who shrugged.

'I don't doubt it. Did you know that Ruth is the third member of the team?'

'Ah!' Dunston was surprised. 'No, I didn't. Are you comfortable with that?'

'A good question. Her training makes her ideally suited, but . . .' he paused, 'I'm not happy.'

'Understood. Let me read the file and I'll get back to you soon. Incidentally, I should tell you a little about myself.' He held up his hand to stop Hunter, who was about to stand up and leave. 'I trained at Sandhurst and went to Two Para for eighteen months. I was with Aitch at Goose Green.' An image flashed into Hunter's mind of the charismatic H. Jones, the most senior officer killed during the Falklands war, who was posthumously awarded the Victoria Cross. 'He was a great man and a great leader. I was affected by the war and after his death I resigned and took Holy Orders. But I couldn't settle in civilian life so I joined as a chaplain. I've kept all my old skills and added a few.'

'So I'd noticed. Fancy a workout during the dogs?'

Dunston looked quizzical. 'The dogs?'

'Yes. Sorry. That's RN watch keeping jargon. The first dog,

sixteen hundred to eighteen hundred and the last dog, eighteen hundred to twenty hundred.'

'Same as last time?'

'Why not? I'll see if Ruth would like to come along as well.'

Hunter left the room while Matt Dunston opened the file. Reading the report, he made notes, a few ideas coming to mind while he wrote.

That evening, after dinner, Hunter, Dunston and Ruth met in Hunter's office to discuss the operation.

'I'm aching all over,' said Ruth, with a groan. 'That was the toughest workout I can remember, apart from when I was training.'

'We'll have a few more,' said Hunter. 'We need to be in top condition. How about you, Matt?'

'Me? Never better,' said Dunston, not prepared to admit to the few twinges he was feeling. 'You?'

'Me? Great. No problems,' said Hunter, lying, marvelling at the other man's fitness. From their earlier conversation Hunter had realised that Dunston was at least eight or ten years older than he, but he was incredibly tough and gifted.

Hunter had used the computer to enhance the photographs they had of the three targets. He put them in order, numbered the photographs one to three and wrote their names in felt tipped pen. One was Momcilo Dimitrijevic, Two was Alexandar Stankovic and Three was Slobodan Ojdanic. 'You can see from the names why I've numbered them. They're practically unpronounceable,' said Hunter.

'Not at all,' protested Dunston. 'If you break the names down like this . . .' He proceeded to do so, making harsh, guttural sounds.

'Never mind,' said Ruth. 'Let's stick with One, Two and Three.'

'All I was trying to do was show you philistines that it is possible to speak the language if you try,' said Dunston.

'Thanks,' said Hunter, dryly. 'GSG9 did a superb job with the information. They've highlighted various weak spots for two of them. Three doesn't appear to have any.'

'He's the cartel's security man,' said Ruth, looking at her file. 'He's a nasty piece of work even if only half of what's written here is true.'

'In the summary, GSG9 stated that in their estimation the info' here accounts for less than ten percent of the crimes he's guilty of,' said Hunter.

'What!' said Ruth, flicking through the sheets of paper to the end. 'My God! Genocide, rape, torture . . . The man's a monster.'

'The others aren't much better,' said Dunston. 'Have you seen the quantities of heroin these people are thought to have dealt in? And look at the paragraph about the ship full of refugees they are said to have scuttled off the coast of Portugal! At least three hundred and fifty people were killed.' He shook his head, his lips compressed in fury. 'These men are evil. We have to stop them.'

'We're all agreed there,' said Hunter. 'It's just how and when. I spoke to Jim Carter this afternoon. He proposes we take our own transport with us. He's customised a Land Rover Discovery Tdi for us.'

'When do we leave for Bosnia?' asked Dunston.

'Immediately. Macnair's planning yet another co-ordinated attack across Europe. He wants the cartels off balance. He hopes they'll make a mistake that will lead us to their next meeting. Make them panic. It could give us the edge.'

'I agree with the ploy,' said the chaplain, 'but I don't know if it'll work.'

'Nick compared the cartels with the Hydra,' said Ruth, thoughtfully.

'Fanciful,' said Dunston, 'but apt.'

18

Macnair was having a rare brandy and soda. His private life had intruded a few hours earlier and he was wondering what he should do. He was a widower, his wife having died of cancer five years earlier. He supposed that he had loved her in his own way but, if he was honest with himself, it had been convenient being married to Bridget. She had been the ideal senior officer's wife, a good hostess at receptions and dinner parties, well connected, with private means. She had produced two girls who had grown up to be good citizens, one a lawyer, the other an accountant. Both girls were married although there were no signs of them making Macnair a grandfather, thank God. Bridget had not nagged him about his time away and had not made any fuss when some appointments had called for him to be accompanied – such as the post of military attaché in Lima. Home had been a large rambling house near Aldershot. This now needed his attention.

He had received an offer for the property and he was in a quandary about what he should do. The truth was, he felt no particular attachment either to the house or the town. He had spent little time there during the fifteen years they had owned it and he had been contemplating selling it now for months. He would make a handsome profit after he paid off the mortgage and he could stay in the wardroom for a while longer yet. Actually, he enjoyed mess life, most of the time. Sometimes it could be claustrophobic but most of the time it suited him. His meals were ready when he wanted them, the bar was open when he needed it and he could engage in conversation when he felt like it.

He sipped his brandy reflectively. The trouble was, he was too senior to be in the mess. The junior officers were intimidated by his presence and the staff was on tenterhooks whenever he was around. He could rent a house outside the base but that caused its own problems. He would need a housekeeper and he would have to cook. One thing at a time. He'd start by selling the house.

Putting his personal life on the back burner he thought about his forthcoming visit to the troublesome MEP, Christine Woolford. She had taken some persuading but she finally agreed to meet him. He had been prepared to go anywhere, anytime, and when she had realised his sincerity she had given in, albeit with bad grace. She had known who he was and had a good idea as to why he wanted to see her, although he had not been prepared to admit it on the telephone. The best she would do was see him that evening in Leeds. She had suggested a pub called the Castle and Peacock, on Armley Road, next to the Leeds and Liverpool Canal. There was a private meeting room she would arrange for them to use. Mentally he marshalled his arguments. He had to make her understand that there was no alternative to TIFAT's current operations.

Mere hours later, in Leeds, General Macnair sat at the table and looked at the woman opposite. Christine Woolford was a few years younger than he was. Her fair hair was cut short and swept behind her ears, with wisps of grey just noticeable if one looked hard enough. Of average height and build, with hazel eyes, she was an attractive woman. Wearing a smart blue suit, the short coat open, she casually displayed a tantalising figure. Macnair was acutely aware of her. He was also aware that she was fully cognisant of the fact.

'Can I offer you a drink?' he asked her, gesturing at the sideboard.

'Thank you. A coffee, please.' She smiled at him, showing even white teeth.

Macnair stood up and went across to the large flasks, one filled with coffee, the other tea. He gestured at the milk and sugar. She took it white with no sugar.

'Thank you.' She accepted the proffered cup. 'Well here I am, General. I did not wish for this meeting but as you insisted I decided I'd hear what you have to say.' She took a sip and replaced the cup in the saucer in front of her.

Macnair knew that it was going to be a difficult conversation. He neither expected nor hoped for a meeting of souls. Some understanding and open-mindedness was as much as he could wish.

He took a deep breath and said, 'Thank you for seeing me. I want to explain to you what we are up against and how difficult it is to,' he paused, 'not win the war but merely contain it.'

To his surprise she nodded. 'I understand that. But victory cannot be at the cost of the human rights of the individual. We are sworn to protect those rights. It is up to the courts to pass judgement. Not . . . not thugs in uniform.'

'Is that how you see us? Thugs in uniform?' Macnair was outraged and the conversation had only just begun.

'Yes,' she said defiantly. 'You shoot and kill innocent people, all in the name of protecting our country. I think that's a sham. A lie to . . .'

'Now wait a moment,' Macnair protested, holding up his hand, his anger barely concealed beneath a veneer of civility. 'I've had the privilege of knowing thousands of men and women over the decades who have fought courageously for their country and who have made many sacrifices that allow ordinary people to sleep soundly in their beds at night.'

'Oh, come, General, you don't expect me to believe that rubbish, do you? That's nonsense. Since the end of the Second World War the military has pursued its own agenda. It's a self-perpetuating, self-promoting club for buffoons. We squander a fortune on armaments that could be put to better use on our schools and hospitals.'

God, thought Macnair, *not that arrant nonsense. The woman was a blasted fool. He'd come all this way for nothing.*

'I'm not here to debate political and military theory with you. I am here to discuss the latest mischief you're creating in Strasbourg. Your interference – though well meant – is terribly dangerous. We have to stop the spread of drugs and terrorism across Europe or else our children – our future – will be lost forever.'

'That is for the courts to decide.'

'Look Mrs. Woolford . . .' Macnair began.

'It's Ms. I'm divorced and use my maiden name.'

'Look, Ms. Woolford, ideally I agree that we want the courts to handle the cartels. The problem is the courts and our political leaders are selling the honest, decent people of Europe down the drain. We have evidence of the corruption of senior court officials who have deliberately introduced laws with the specific aim of protecting the criminal. We can show you how the laws of Europe have been bent and by whom.'

'If you have proof, lay it before the courts,' Woolford said sharply. 'The so-called evidence can be examined and charges brought. If the law needs changing we'll be able to do it.'

'That will take years. By then it will be too late. The epidemic proportions of drugs flooding in through the illegal immigrants . . .'

'How dare you,' she hissed at him. 'How dare you suggest that the poor people of the nations that turn to us for help are bringing drugs into this country!'

'Not just this country,' Macnair protested, 'but all of Europe. Damnation woman, open your eyes. I came here to discuss the matter, to ask you to look at the evidence, but your mind is closed to reality. We can prove that the PPK are smuggling heroin into western Europe to pay for their war against the Turkish government. We know for a fact that the Kosovo Albanians paid for their arms with heroin smuggled into the West. We know too that Afghanistan, as one of the biggest poppy growing regions in the Middle East, is encouraged by the Taliban to process and smuggle heroin into Europe. It is estimated that over twenty billion dollars worth is ready for shipment. Even a fraction of that amount into Europe will cause huge difficulties. The mules are frequently the children of men and women already living here in Europe, claiming asylum, and asking that their children either visit or live here. Once granted a residence permit then they and their families regularly visit home to bring back supplies of drugs.'

'What utter, fanciful nonsense,' Christine Woolford jeered scornfully.

'It is neither fanciful nor nonsense,' retorted Macnair, 'but fact. The intelligence sources of Europe have mountains of proof but there is hardly a politician in Europe who will listen. Those who do are called xenophobic right wingers, madmen who should be ostracised. The reality is they are telling you the truth but you liberals won't listen. We've amassed volumes of information on drug related crimes from Chiefs of Police all across Europe and had the information broken down by gender and nationality.'

'That's illegal,' said Woolford. 'Since 1997 crimes by nationality can no longer be recorded. That was decided in nineteen ninety-three, to help race relations throughout the world. It took four years to get it to the statute books. The Chiefs of Police have broken the law by doing so. I'll . . . I'll subpoena the information and bring the culprits before the courts.'

Macnair knew then that it was no use. He might as well have saved himself the trouble and effort of talking to the woman sitting in front of him.

'Jesus wept, woman, don't you . . . can't you *see* the damage you're doing? I want the courts to protect us. I want human rights protection for every single person in the world. But first of all we need to re-stabilise the situation. We need to stop the spread of drugs and terrorism before it's too late. Turn it back until we have the situation under control and then let the courts deal with it. In the meantime we need to enact laws that will protect the majority of the people while at the same time protecting the rights of the individual. But we need time to do all that and we in the West are running out of time. Look, please, come and visit me at TIFAT HQ in Scotland and see the proof. Look at it with an open mind. Understand what it is we are up against and *then* make an informed decision about what you say in Parliament.'

She looked at him coldly. 'Oh, I will do that all right. I will make the speech. I will report what you have told me and I will demand that the appropriate authorities subpoena all your records. By the time I've finished with you, you . . . you'll be less than a corporal and that organisation of yours . . . TIFAT . . . will be a bad memory.' She stood up, quivering with outraged indignation. She was shaking with anger while Macnair looked calmly back at her. 'You're finished, General, finished.'

'If you don't believe me, perhaps these will convince you.' Opening his briefcase he threw a handful of ten by eight glossy photographs onto the table. They spilled across the wood, some ending up on the floor.

'What are they?' In spite of herself her curiosity got the better of her and she turned to look.

'Photographs of some of the victims. All children. Some have been killed while held in prostitution while others have died from drugs overdoses when condoms carried inside them have burst and pure heroin has seeped out. The deaths of all these children have been painful and horrific. This is the human misery end of what we are trying to stop. We cannot do it through the courts. Not yet. We need to regain the upper hand first.'

The MEP had glanced at a couple of the photographs and blanched. Now she looked Macnair squarely in the eyes. 'I agree this is why we have to stop them but it will be done my way. Not yours.' Still shaking she left. This time Macnair wasn't sure whether it was from anger or the effect of the photographs. Either way he'd lost the battle.

Sighing he stood up and followed her out into the early dusk. His driver was sitting in his car, patiently waiting for him. Macnair watched as the MEP walked away, her back ramrod stiff. She reached into a pocket for her keys and as she removed her hand a handkerchief fluttered to the ground.

Serves her right, thought Macnair and then, ever the gallant, he called after her. 'Wait!' He walked quickly in her direction and bent to pick up the handkerchief. He stood and handed it to her. 'You dropped this.'

She hesitated, a retort springing to her lips but then good manners came to her rescue. 'Thank . . .' she began, stiffly.

At that moment a car screeched to a halt next to them and a

well-dressed man stepped out of the back. 'Are you the MEP?' he asked in accented English.

He was looking at Macnair but Christine Woolford answered. 'Yes . . .'

The MEP got no further. Two guns were suddenly pointed at them from the car. 'Get in. Both of you. Don't make any sudden moves or noise.'

'What!' Christine began to protest. 'How dare you. Do you know . . .'

The noise of the hammer being pulled back on one of the guns caused Macnair to do two things. Scratching the lobe of his ear in time, he stopped his driver walking across to find out what was wrong while at the same time warning him there was trouble. Next he grabbed Christine Woolford by the arm and squeezed hard, shutting her up. She tried to pull her arm away as he helped to bundle her into the car.

'Be quiet. These men mean it. The guns are for real and right now I have no wish to die.'

The gunman said, 'We understand each other. Keep her mouth shut or we will kill you.' The car took off with a screech of tyres.

Hunter, Dunston and Ruth headed south. Hunter drove the new Land Rover Discovery Tdi automatic, with cruise control. It was a comfortable car and he set the speed at 80mph, a speed that would leave them unnoticed by the police. They needed to be in Bosnia as soon as possible. Dozens of incidents and operations were being co-ordinated across Europe, working to a deadline.

Ruth sat in the back reading a thriller, chuckling over it in derision, while Matt Dunston listened to a personal stereo playing a Serbo-Croat language tape. Hunter concentrated on his driving. He knew some of the General's plans but by no means all of them. Throughout Europe, intelligence organisations were even now re-tasking their operators to one specific objective. To find out where the next meeting of the cartels was to take place.

They were south of Carlisle and making good time when the car's phone rang and Hunter pressed the receive button.

Major Carter's voice came over the loudspeaker, 'Hullo? Nick?'

'Hi, Jim. To what do we owe the pleasure?'

It took a great deal of self-control not to react to his next words. 'It's the General. He's been kidnapped.'

There was a stunned silence for a few seconds as the enormity of the words sunk in.

'But . . . but . . . that's impossible. We just saw him this afternoon,' Ruth's voice was hoarse with shock.

Carter's disembodied voice filled the vehicle. 'I'm afraid it appears to be all too possible. Our only hope is that they don't know who he is.'

'Wait a moment,' said Dunston, 'that makes no sense. Why would anybody take the General unintentionally?'

'We don't think that he was the target,' said Carter.

'Then who was?' asked Hunter.

'The MEP Christine Woolford.'

'What!' exclaimed Hunter, indicating to the left and preparing to pull into the southbound services at Southwaite. 'But she's been making all the noise in support of the human rights . . .'

'I know that,' Carter interrupted him. 'Have any of you heard of an MEP by the name of Charles Woolforth?'

The occupants of the Discovery shook their heads before Hunter thought to reply. 'No. Who's he?'

'He is, for want of a better description, a right-winger of the old hang 'em and flog 'em brigade. Actually, I've met him a few times and he is not as bad as the press make out. He's been highly supportive of our aims and objectives, although he occasionally puts his foot in it and comes across too abrasively. It seems that the criminals who have taken the General have made a mistake. They appear to have mixed up C. Woolford with C. Woolforth.'

'But Woolford's a woman and Woolforth's a man,' Hunter stated the obvious.

'I appreciate you telling me that, Nick,' said Carter, dryly, 'otherwise I might never have noticed. She is also a northern-based politician while he is from Surrey and the Home Counties.

We have learned that Woolforth was visiting Leeds on some sort of fact-finding mission to do with the north-south divide and we think they've just made a serious mistake. Anyway, whatever the reason, the General has been taken along with Christine Woolford.'

'Do we know where they are?' asked Dunston.

'We're tracking them.'

'Was the General alone?' asked Hunter.

'All in good time. I see from the sat-positioning beacon you've stopped. Where? Southwaite?'

'Affirmative.' The sat-positioning beacon was fitted to the car and gave TIFAT a continuous fix as to where the car was at any time, day or night. It was one of the many modifications Carter had installed recently. In fact the car was a travelling arsenal.

'Good. I've made arrangements for you to go to Leeds to meet up with a Superintendent Locksby. He commands the ARVs for the north.' The Armed Response Vehicles were manned by some of the most highly trained policemen in Britain, if not the world. Each man and woman was an expert shot with all sorts of small arms and many trained with some of the special service units such as the Special Air Service and the Special Boats Service. They were the people whom the police relied upon when they were confronted by armed criminals. Formed as a direct result of the Hungerford massacre in the eighties, to date they had proven invaluable. At long last Parliament was considering the formation of more units across the country.

'Will Superintendent Locksby be co-operative?' Hunter asked.

'Yes. Actually, I've met him. He has officially requested that a number of his men come here and train with us. I told him a few weeks ago that we would be delighted. Nick, I should add he's a consummate professional and in command. You're there only to advise and assist, if required.'

'Sure! I've no problem with that,' Hunter announced, ignoring the raised eyebrows and looks that passed between his two passengers. 'Where do we meet the guy?'

'Head for Leeds and I'll let you know, depending on what's happening.'

'Was the General carrying his locator?' Ruth asked.

'Yes. We're pretty sure where they are and that they are moving slowly.' Carter finished.

'Provided the locator and the General are in the same place,' said Hunter.

'Precisely why we're moving carefully,' said Carter.

They broke the connection as Hunter started the car and headed back to the motorway. 'What's the quickest route?' he asked.

Dunston pressed buttons on the navigation display unit in the front and said, 'It's six of one, half a dozen of the other. We can take the A66 to Scotch Corner or carry on the M6 to junction thirty-six and then take the A65. The former is probably slightly quicker. Fewer towns and villages to go through.'

'Right. We'll go that way.' Pressing hard on the accelerator Hunter wound the Discovery up to 90mph. The radar detector fitted by Carter would warn him if there were any police around.

When they approached the outskirts of Leeds it started raining. The gentle shower quickly turned into a heavy downpour.

A short, guttural directive to the driver and the kidnapper's car slowed down.

'Is this your doing?' said the MEP, glowering at Macnair. Anger distorted her features. 'Is this your idea to persuade me to stop what I'm doing? This pantomime?'

Macnair looked at her incredulously. He could see that she meant it. The casual backhanded slap across her face from the man in the front passenger seat jolted her to reason, bringing tears of pain and shock to her eyes. Macnair shook his head, desperately willing her to shut up. For the first time she showed fear.

The man looked at Macnair and said, 'So, Mr. Woolforth, we have you at last.'

The statement made no sense to Macnair and so he kept his face straight. He looked at the man in the front seat through narrowed eyes. Guessing that the man was eastern European, the General thought perhaps he was Russian. The accent suggested the south. Georgian, possibly. Macnair looked at Christine Woolford whose eyes were wide open, staring at Macnair. The name seemed to mean something to her. Now he came to think of it, it meant something to him. Woolforth . . . Woolforth. What the hell was it? Then, he placed it. The MEP from the Home Counties. Yes! Charles Woolforth. He was a supporter of TIFAT and their aims. Macnair remembered meeting him after presenting the original paper at the summit meeting in Paris a few years earlier. Since then Woolforth had backed the idea of an anti-drugs, anti-terrorist force at every opportunity. These men seemed to think he was Woolforth.

As the realisation dawned on him so it did on Christine Woolford. 'You've made a mistake . . .' she began.

'Shut up, Christine,' said Macnair, harshly. He spoke just in time as the man turned to hit her again. The thug sitting next to her ground his pistol into her side, causing her to wince and gasp out loud in pain. 'What do you want? Where are we going?' he asked the man in front who was obviously in charge.

'Somewhere quiet. You will see.'

Macnair lapsed into silence. He was tempted to look behind him to see if his car was following but resisted. He did not want to draw attention to the fact that they were being tailed. Even if his car wasn't behind them the driver would be able to follow the homing signal contained in the heel of Macnair's right shoe. It was standard procedure for all operatives. He was sure that, even as they drove sedately along the motorway, action was being taken.

In the car behind, Macnair's driver was keeping out of direct sight. The bleeping contact on the small screen on the dashboard showed him precisely where the car was taking his boss. The driver was no ordinary chauffeur. There was no room for such luxuries in TIFAT. Instead the General used one of his highly trained specialists whenever it was expedient for him to do so. This time the driver was the SAS trained sergeant, David Hughes. He was one of the most resourceful and toughest men in Macnair's organisation and had volunteered for the drive to Leeds and back.

Hughes had been on the point of intercepting whatever was

going on when he had received the signal from his boss. Danger, stay away. He had slid back behind the wheel of the powerful 7 series BMW he was driving and prepared to follow. While he was doing so he spoke to the duty officer at TIFAT HQ and explained the situation. All that was necessary for him to do now was to follow the car in front, leaving enough space so that the other driver would not be spooked.

When the rain started the night came early and he switched on his sidelights. They were headed for Ilkley but turned right towards Denton. The road was a dead-end and stopped a mile or two short of March Ghyll Reservoir. Now they were bouncing along on a dirt track. Hughes slowed down, switching off his headlights as soon as they passed Denton. Courtesy of a pair of night-vision goggles he lifted from the glove compartment, the countryside was lit up like daylight. He saw the blip on the screen stop and he closed to within a mile. Switching off the engine and courtesy light he opened the door and went round to the boot. Opening it, he began to lift secret covers to compartments that contained a plethora of equipment. Within minutes he had changed into combat gear and had slung a Super Magnum rifle over his shoulder.

He used the sat-nav phone to talk to Major Carter. He brought him up to date with the situation and requested back up. He was not sure he was pleased to be told that a police ARV was en route.

Hughes locked the car and began yomping over the heath – trekking across the rough terrain to his target. The rifle he carried was one of the most powerful in the world. The AW 0.338 Super Magnum sniper rifle was British made and had become the favourite gun in use by the SAS. The weapon was capable of killing a man wearing modern body armour at a distance of a mile. Its bullets were specially manufactured so that they did not spread out on impact but kept their shape until their energy was expended and they finally stopped. Although the rifle was four feet long it weighed less than fifteen pounds and was fitted with a German Schmidt and Bender X10 rifle scope, one of the finest in the world. On top of the scope was a Norwegian Simrad

KN 200F image intensifier. A safety feature of the Simrad was a device to prevent the rifleman being blinded by an enemy using a laser to locate him. So far TIFAT had taken delivery of three of these awesome weapons.

Like a ghost Hughes flitted across the land, his destination over the brow of the next hill.

19

By the time Hunter arrived, observation posts had been established. Listening devices aimed at the ramshackle farmhouse meant there was no doubt that Macnair and the woman were inside.

He shook hands with Superintendent Locksby and immediately liked what he saw. The policeman was about fifty, tough looking, and had a no-nonsense air about him. He was an inch short of six feet and looked fit.

Without preamble Locksby brought Hunter, Dunston and Ruth up to date. Even as they spoke the team was unloading gear from compartments hidden around the Land Rover. They transformed themselves from civilians to soldiers before his eyes.

'We have the area contained,' Locksby was saying, 'with one of your men up on the ridge.'

Hunter nodded. 'Yes, I know. Sergeant Hughes.'

'He's brought along some sort of super rifle the like of which I've never seen,' said the Superintendent.

'A super magnum,' said Hunter. He looked at the policeman for a second before adding, 'Sir, it's your shout. We're here to advise and assist if needed. I know how well trained your people are but they're usually called upon when all negotiation has failed. If the people who've taken my boss and the MEP are who I think they are, there won't be any negotiating. They'll kill their captives and make a run for it.'

The Superintendent nodded. 'I agree. I've had a long talk with your Major Carter. I've an inkling of what this is all about and I think the sooner we bring matters to a conclusion the better.'

'What have you heard from the house?'

'Very little. We recorded a foreign language which we relayed to Major Carter and he's having it identified and interpreted for us. General Macnair tried talking to their captors but he was hit for his pains. The woman showed some spunk by protesting but she got the same treatment. They appear to be waiting for something.'

'Instructions, probably,' said Dunston.

'That's what I figure,' said Locksby.

'How many men do you have here?' asked Hunter.

'Eight in two teams. Two are women. They're probably my best shots.'

'Sir, do you mind if I direct operations?' asked Hunter. 'I'll clear anything I do with you.'

'No, you go ahead. Major Carter suggested I do just that and I'm more than happy. Just remember,' he added, 'the lives of my people are paramount.'

Hunter nodded. 'I wouldn't have it any other way, sir.'

They joined David Hughes on a mound over-looking the farmhouse. 'Hullo, sergeant,' Hunter greeted him.

'Hullo, boss.' Hughes did not so much as move a muscle. 'Glad you're here. Have you got any heat-seekers by any chance?'

'No. But the major is sending two complete sets. They should be here within the hour.'

'Good. If we have time we can move then,' said the sergeant.

If the policeman was surprised by the easy nonchalance with which an enlisted soldier and an officer exchanged views he didn't show it. He knew when he was in the presence of professionals and although his own people were highly trained they came nowhere near TIFAT's standard. He made the decision then and there that he would accompany his men when they went to Rosyth.

One of his men joined them. 'Sir,' he cast inquisitive glances at the three others, 'we've picked up some more speech. We've been patched through to some computer somewhere and we're getting virtually simultaneous translations. It appears the men are waiting for a phone call from somebody.'

'Good. That's what we thought,' said Locksby.

'Sir,' said Hunter, 'I want to move in. We don't know what the phone call will bring. It could be orders to kill them or leave them there unharmed. If it's the latter we let the gang walk out and take them alive. If it's the former we want to be in a position to move fast.'

'I agree. What do you propose?'

Hunter explained his plan and the Superintendent nodded. 'Good. Excellent. Let's make it so.'

Macnair sat patiently in the chair, his hands tied to the armrests, his feet tied in front of him. Christine Woolford was similarly bound, sitting in a chair next to him. Neither wore a gag but whenever Macnair tried to talk to their captors he was hit. After the third time he gave up.

Having absolute faith in his men, he had every expectation of being rescued. However he wanted to elicit as much information as possible before their three captors were killed.

Christine Woolford had rallied after the initial shock and now sat in the chair, contempt and anger vibrating from her in equal measures. Macnair was impressed by her fortitude. She either had guts or no imagination. He had no doubt that their abductors intended to kill them.

The three men sat nonchalantly at a table on the far side of the large room. Until recently the farmhouse had been a weekend retreat for a busy doctor, until the cost of maintenance outweighed the pleasure to be had from visiting the place. The house was in reasonably good condition, wind and waterproof, but had been emptied of all furniture save chairs and a table. There was no heating and the room, nearly nine metres long by six metres wide, was cold. The end wall faced north and had glass patio doors. The glass had been crudely painted over with white paint to prevent prying eyes looking in. Macnair knew how effective TIFAT's monitoring equipment was. No amount of walls and painted glass could hide what was happening inside the farmhouse.

A telephone rang and the leader of the three men lifted the mobile from the table. Listening for a few seconds, he mumbled a sentence and broke the connection. Placing the phone in front of him he stood up, reaching for his gun and loudly checked the breech to see it was loaded. Macnair knew what was coming and glanced at Christine Woolford. From the look on her face it appeared that she did too.

'Wait! Before you shoot us you need to know something.' Macnair spoke quickly. 'I am not a Member of the European Parliament. This lady is. Her name is Christine Woolford, MEP. My name is General Malcolm Macnair and I command TIFAT.' The kidnapper with the gun froze. 'Check it out. You're so slap-dash you've not even searched us properly. Look in my inside pocket. You'll find my identity card. I suggest you then phone whoever gives the orders for further instructions.'

The man stormed across the room, slapped Macnair a ringing blow across the face and reached into his pocket. He withdrew a plastic ID card and read its details.

'If I shoot you now, no one will know,' he said.

'Don't be stupid. Your bosses will know as soon as the real Woolforth makes his next speech. Believe me,' Macnair somehow summoned up the strength to smile, 'I'm worth more to you alive.'

The man's indecision showed clearly. Returning to the table he picked up the phone. Whoever answered told him to wait for further orders. He broke the connection and sat back at the table, his fingers drumming a nervous tattoo on the wood. Less than two minutes later the phone rang. He listened intently.

The man stood up and walked back towards his prisoners. 'It seems you are right. You are wanted alive. She is to be killed.'

Christine Woolford gasped in horror as the gun was lifted and pointed directly at her.

The bullet was a head shot.

The equipment was set up. The heat imager showed each person and the enhanced computerised picture cleared the profiles so that the normal red and orange hazy colour was obliterated.

It was like looking at a screen of clear ghosts, distinct but featureless.

The picture was carried by cable from the screen to the sight fitted to the rifle. David Hughes waited for the signal to fire knowing that Hunter was also listening to what was being said in the house. The attack when it came was co-ordinated to the nano-second.

Christine's assailant's head burst apart like a ripe melon being hit with a sledgehammer. The other two kidnappers died where they sat when Hunter and Ruth charged through the glass doors.

Christine Woolford leant forward and vomited all down her new suit.

Macnair turned to Hunter in typically sanguine fashion and said, 'Good to see you both. Did you get the phone numbers?'

'Yes, sir. Burg arrived with the gear just in time,' said Hunter, stepping over to his boss, slicing the ropes and freeing him.

Ruth did the same for the MEP and helped her to her feet. 'Let's go and find some water. You can clean yourself up,' she said, gently.

'Thank you. I . . . Thank you,' said the badly shaken woman. Ruth led her through the far door to look for a bathroom.

Superintendent Locksby arrived with his men and introduced himself to Macnair. David Hughes followed, the rifle that had killed Christine's would-be assassin slung over his shoulder.

'Thank you, sergeant,' said Macnair.

'Anytime, sir,' Hughes grinned back, relieved to see that his boss was okay. 'I'll just get the car.' With that he sauntered out.

Ruth returned with the MEP, now looking much better. The colour had returned to her face and her clothes had been sponged.

Macnair smiled at her and said, 'How are you?'

Christine Woolford tried to smile in return. She shook her head and said, 'I'm not sure, to be honest. When they were going to kill me, I felt anger, hatred. I wanted to break loose and kill them. I wanted to scream at them. I've never known such intense hate. I've done no harm to them. Yet it was as though I was nothing.'

'My dear,' said Macnair, trying hard not to sound condescending, 'to them you are nothing. As is every other life they ruin. They have no conscience. They have an attitude to life that is, quite frankly, alien to you and,' he added with emphasis, 'to me. That is why they have to be stopped.'

Like a religious convert Christine Woolford nodded. 'I believe you're right. God, what a fool I've been. My supercilious, holier than though attitude . . .' she broke off, shaking her head, unable to voice the feelings she was experiencing.

Macnair stepped forward and put a hand on her arm. 'I understand, I truly do. We have a great deal of work to do and you could help us if you will.'

'Me? What can I do?' asked the surprised woman.

'I'll tell you as we drive out of here.' He turned to the Superintendent. 'You don't need us, Locksby, do you?'

'No, sir. I'll do as you suggested and get every name I can. The sooner we round up these people the better.'

'Good. Let's wait outside for my car,' he said to Christine.

As the two of them walked away, Hunter heard the MEP say, 'I'm still concerned. Who will guard the guards themselves?'

Macnair chuckled. '*Sed quis custodiet ipsos Custodes*? Decimus Junius Juvenalis said those words around the year one hundred. But his fear remains my fear. I asked myself the question only a few short days ago. It is something we will have to address after we clean up the mess we're making of the twenty-first century. Right now I don't have all the answers.'

'Where did you learn Latin?' she asked, intrigued, her earlier animosity all but forgotten.

'I read the Classics at Oxford before joining the army. What about you? You quoted the translation exactly.'

'Nothing so grand, I'm afraid. I went to a North London Polytechnic . . .'

Hunter looked at Ruth and raised an eyebrow. She shrugged in return and they also went outside. Bosnia beckoned.

Yuri Voropaev watched as the Georgian staggered from the bar towards the toilets. He thought about following but dismissed the idea. He wanted more than one of them, if his plan was to succeed. The men at the other tables had drunk a good deal of wine but the woman's bodyguards hadn't touched a drop of alcohol. That fact alone impressed the naval Commander. He had bought two bottles of Russian champagne, which he had surreptitiously poured down a drain located under the bench where he sat. It was obviously there to aid mopping the floors at the end of the night. The vodka he had drunk earlier had long since dissipated and his mind was crystal clear.

It was the early hours of the morning before the party made signs of breaking up. Voropaev had rebuffed the advances of two prostitutes and a pimp, the latter with a look that suggested if he didn't go away Voropaev would make him regret it.

He paid the bill and left an additional ten-percent as a tip. He figured that was the lesser of two evils – to be remembered for giving a reasonable tip or for not tipping at all. As the Georgians moved towards the doors he stood up, slipped the empty bottles into his coat pockets and mingled with them unobtrusively. The bodyguards were too busy looking ahead to see him amongst them.

Walking across the foyer of the hotel, the black-haired woman was in the middle. No one stopped for a room key. They avoided the elevator, wisely not trusting it to arrive at its destination. Awkwardly timed electricity cuts were not uncommon in the hotel. Voropaev followed them upstairs but when they walked along the corridor to their rooms, he hung back. From behind a bend in the corridor he watched, noting who went into which room. Two of the bodyguards took chairs outside one of the rooms and settled down for a long night. Voropaev was satisfied. It was just as he expected.

Finding an empty chambermaid station Voropaev prepared to wait. He dozed, awoke with a start, and checked his watch. 03.00 – perfect.

Standing up, he worked the kinks out of his muscles and then carefully opened the door. Nobody was in sight. At the end of the corridor he located an old-fashioned electricity box containing the fuses and master switches for the floor. He prised open the cover and threw the switch, plunging the corridor into darkness. Walking quickly along the carpeted corridor he reached the turn and, singing softly to himself, he staggered along, swaying against the walls. In each hand he held an empty Champagne bottle. He made enough noise for the two guards to be instantly aware of him and one of them switched on a flashlight and shone it on him.

'Hey,' Voropaev paused, lifting his arm across his eyes, swaying drunkenly. He swore at them in Russian and told them to aim the light somewhere else.

Voropaev understood a little Georgian, having been taught it at school.

'A drunken Russian fool. Let him come near and we'll roll him,' one of them said.

'All right. Point the torch at the floor and let him pass us.'

The man holding the flashlight gestured with the beam and Voropaev lurched forward. As he passed between the two men who had moved to either side of the corridor he spun round, smashing a bottle onto each head, pole-axing both of them. The bottles smashed with the force of the blow. Voropaev checked their pulses finding one man still alive, the other dead. He dragged each of the bodies into the linen cupboard he had recently vacated. Using his feet he swept the bits of broken glass into a heap in a corner.

In the pocket of one of the bodyguards he found a British Spitfire automatic fitted with a silencer. *Only the best*, thought Voropaev, *for the thieving Georgians*. He thought about going into the black-haired woman's suite but of all the people in the party she had drunk the least and seemed the most sober. He'd try a different door.

Turning the handle of the room opposite he checked it was locked. Placing the gun to the lock he pulled the trigger. The cough was inaudible two metres away yet the clang of the bullet hitting the mechanism seemed to Voropaev loud enough to wake the dead. With a gentle nudge the door opened and he walked into the darkened room.

In keeping with the remainder of the hotel, the suite of

rooms on this floor was spacious, a sitting room leading to three bedrooms. His eyes were accustomed to the gloom and he could see a figure lying on a couch. Silently he searched for papers, money or passports. Finding a briefcase behind a huge television set he rifled through it. Under a flap at the bottom of the case he found a fistful of money. From the feel of the notes he guessed it was a hard currency, German marks or Swiss francs, the heavy textured paper instantly recognisable, unlike the flimsy paper Russian roubles were printed on. Shutting the briefcase he hefted it in his left hand while in his right he carried the silenced pistol.

The three bedrooms were unlocked and he searched each one silently. In each bed was a drunken body. The third man had one of the women with him. The copious amounts of champagne they had drunk ensured he did not disturb them. By the time Voropaev left the last room the briefcase was bulging. He was getting nervous and decided not to press his luck any further.

Walking down the service stairs he went through the dark kitchen and out the back of the hotel unobserved. Voropaev trudged homewards, the adrenaline that had kept him alert and pumped up fading fast. Fatigue was setting in. Forcing himself, he walked briskly. Dawn was breaking as he let himself back into his house.

Locking his door he made sure the curtains were drawn across the windows before he sat wearily at the table. Pouring the contents of the briefcase onto the table he began to make separate piles of his haul. Four passports, dollars, sterling, marks, Swiss francs, euros and roubles. There were papers written in an unidentifiable language. Unsure whether or not they were important he decided that the safest thing was to burn them. He studied the passports and was surprised to find that two of them were for the same man. One was German and the other was American. Voropaev had little doubt the American passport was a forgery. The owner had a similar build to him but with grey hair. The unsmiling face that looked back at him had his hair parted differently. Voropaev decided the German passport would do.

Finally, like savouring the best part of a meal until last, he counted the money. When he finished he did it again. He sat still, shocked to the core. He was rich! Nearly ten thousand dollars, nineteen thousand marks, seventeen thousand Swiss francs, six thousand pounds sterling, a year's wages in roubles and, the biggest amount by far, over forty thousand euros. *What temptation! With that money he could live like a king. A Czar!* Then he remembered the warheads. He knew his duty. He would put the money to good use and stop them if it was the last thing he did.

20

Alleysia Raduyev was satisfied. Although it had been late when they left the bar she was luxuriating in a hot tub, going over the last few days in her mind. She had finally concluded the deal to buy the nuclear warheads here in the putrid dump called Vladivostok. She had been warned what to expect but even so she had been shocked.

Vladivostok had been an important naval base and military area throughout the Cold War. A relatively warm water port, the sea rarely froze there as it did in the north. Nowadays it never froze because of the Soviet chemical pollution in the famed bay called The Golden Horn. The area was blessed with a bountiful amount of natural resources of timber, fish and furs. It had also had the benefit of vast amounts of military spending on the infrastructure. In 1992 when the veil of military secrecy was finally lifted the people dreamt of the area becoming Russia's Hong Kong. In reality, military personnel and their families, some 400,000 all told, remained stranded in poverty, unpaid and unwanted elsewhere. The end of the Soviet Empire had been tough on the sailors of the once mighty Pacific fleet. Its arms depots had been looted, its ships and submarines rusted away while admirals and generals built large dachas and stole everything they could. Now Chinese shopkeepers, Korean lumberjacks, Japanese fishermen and Vietnamese workers were infiltrating the area. Itinerant men and women from the Pacific Rim were exploiting work and jobs that could have been taken by the locals. The Russians had neither the skills nor inclination to stop them. So the high command dealt in the one commodity they still had access to and could still manufacture – arms.

Pouring herself a glass of champagne, albeit Russian, Alleysia continued her train of thoughts, gloating. It had been a stroke of genius to arrange a trip at her expense for the braver members of the jet set. After the fashion show in Monaco she had suggested they visited Vladivostok for a *petit divertissement*. Somewhere different for a change. The degenerates had leapt at the idea, particularly as she had made it clear that she would be footing the bill. All she needed to do was keep them fed with alcohol, drugs and sexual partners. The outcome had been perfect.

The deal she had concluded left her glowing. Twenty million dollars in hard currency for three nuclear warheads and the wherewithal to detonate them. It would have been cheap at ten times the price. And she had been prepared to pay it. *The idiots*! The world was full of fools, rich and poor. Idly she speculated on the carnage she could unleash with the weapons. Where would she detonate one? London? New York? Paris? No! She had a much better idea.

Sitting in the cramped living room of his house Yuri Voropaev held the photograph of his wife on his knees. Soyan had been beautiful, vivacious. She had died during childbirth, their son dying with her. They had explained it was nobody's fault. He still did not fully understand what had happened. He had heard the doctor's words as though from a deep well, echoing nonsensically around his head. Only the horror of the truth had any meaning. She was dead. They were dead.

He had gone to pieces. Only the patronage of the Admiral had saved his naval career and his life. Now the despair washed over him once again. He had been alone for six years. There had been plenty of other women, all trying to capture the dashing naval officer who, it was rumoured, had a bright future. But he hadn't been interested.

The collapse of communism had seen an end to all that. His rank was now a joke. He hadn't been paid in five months. The house he was living in was navy property, unheated as usual, the electricity not working for the fifth night in a row. Part of him did not blame the Admiral. Voropaev knew the money was to be used to help to rejuvenate the area. But at what price – national pride and honour? Besides which he didn't trust the Georgians. They were a deceitful, lying race. Many men, women and children could die if the Georgians were allowed to keep the bombs. He no longer owed a debt to the Admiral. It had been paid in full. It was time to do what was right.

And there, he hoped, he had an ally. His cousin, Jan Badonovitch, had written to him recently, telling him about his secondment to the new anti-terrorist organisation, TIFAT. He felt a pang of envy. Jan had become a Spetsnaz instead of joining the navy and becoming an officer. At the time he had thought his cousin crazy, but now he wasn't so sure.

He stood up, resolve coursing through his veins. Alone he could not stop the Georgians from taking possession of the warheads. They were too heavily guarded. But he could find out where they were going and tell Badonovitch.

Leon Sautier was in high spirits. They had achieved everything Macnair had asked of them. Tonight would be a celebration, his treat. They were to meet at the bistro on the corner of Rue St. Sulpice and Rue Bonaparte, near the Palais du Luxembourg. The bistro was small and intimate, selling a restricted but superb range of wines and offering a select menu that was changed daily. The price of the food was different for tourists than for the French. Especially if your name was Leon Sautier.

There were a dozen tables, all occupied. Withier and Flika were already there when he arrived and a short while later Yvette joined them. They had a pastis with slices of salami before their meal. The evening was a long and pleasant one, with a great deal of banter and joie-de-vivre. Although they imbibed a good deal of wine, they each had the typical French constitution for drinking, having been brought up on the stuff. It was nearly midnight when Sautier finally paid the bill.

Chairs scraped back as they stood to leave and coats were handed round. Flika placed his around his shoulders and adjusted the holster under his right arm. The Algerian boasted that he could draw and fire faster than a cowboy in the old American west. Sautier led the way out and they congregated in the light rainfall, bidding each other goodnight, looking for taxis.

A car came round the corner, speeding. Withier looked up, a sixth sense warning him before the others. The cry died on his lips as a hail of bullets smashed into them, flinging them down, smashing the glass front of the restaurant, hitting innocent people still enjoying their meal. Sautier died instantly, the bullets stitching a pattern across his chest. Withier was hit in the arm and neck, the blood pumping out in time to his racing heart. He bled to death within seconds.

Yvette was hit in the right shoulder and the left thigh. She was swearing, still conscious when she pulled open her bag and brought out her gun.

The car had stopped and four men had climbed out, leaving the driver. They advanced quickly towards the huddled bodies. Yvette, thinking she was the only one alive, waited until they were so close she could have spat on them.

Flika was lying under Sautier, unmoving, uninjured apart from a nasty crack on the head. Although his head was swimming he had the sense to keep still. His gun was already firmly held in his hand.

Yvette shot the first man through the head. Flika fired his automatic as quickly as he could pull the trigger, hitting two of the others before the gun clicked empty. Yvette lined up her pistol on the last man and froze as she looked along the barrel into the face of her lover.

'Hullo, Yvette,' he said, smiling, pulling the trigger, blowing her brains out. Next he turned to Flika who was frantically trying to struggle to his feet, to find another gun before it was too late. An arrogant, professional killer, Yvette's lover turned almost lazily to kill the last of them. His arrogance was his undoing.

Flika was three metres away and he knelt on one knee, throwing the revolver he was holding at the other man's head. All his rage and hatred were behind the throw and it hit the other man squarely between the eyes. Shock registered as the

228

man staggered backwards. The driver of the gunman's car was in a blind panic after the downing of his other colleagues. Seeing him reeling backwards he hit the accelerator hard. Yvette's lover staggered into the path of the car, bounced high off the bonnet and landed on his back. Both his legs were broken by the vehicle's impact and his neck broke as he landed on the street.

Flika grabbed a gun lying in the gutter. Turning his attention to the car he took up the sharpshooter's stance, both hands gripping the weapon, the gun held at arm's length, both feet planted firmly on the ground. Coolly he fired; the first shot missed; the vehicle was fifty metres away, accelerating, tyres squealing as the driver turned sharp right. Flika's second shot hit the driver across the top of the nose and took out his right eye. The car careened across the road, hit the curb and with a screech of metal fell on its side. Sparks flew as the car spun round, smashing into stationary vehicles, missing screaming pedestrians.

In the background the wailing of sirens could be heard. Flika turned to his fallen comrades, tears in his eyes.

21

The Land Rover's cruise control was set to 100mph and they sped down the deserted motorway. Thanks to Superintendent Locksby the police forces of the counties they would be passing through had been warned to leave them alone and they sped through the night down the M1 and onto the M25.

Arriving at Ashford, Kent, they were in time to catch an early morning train to Brussels. They drove onto the train, left the Discovery and went in search of the restaurant car. A cooked breakfast filled the journey through the tunnel, across the north-west corner of France and into Belgium. Soon, with Matt Dunston at the wheel, they were driving down the motorway towards Liege. From there they headed for the German border and Cologne. They had decided to stay on the motorways as much as possible. It meant a longer distance but a shorter journey time.

Driving south and east the weather cleared and became warmer. The cold front that had hit them in Leeds was a distant memory. The car ate up the miles. Frankfurt and Nürnberg were behind them when they finally pulled into Regensburg where they planned to stay for the night. The hotel was small, clean and cheap. They had an excellent dinner, a good night's rest and a hearty breakfast before departing the following morning. The in-car electronic display directed them along the motorways. On two occasions it highlighted delays ahead and advised them to take minor detours. Lunchtime found them approaching St Michael and the Gleinalm tunnel. They were about fifty miles from Graz.

Heading south and closer to Slovenia, the motorways began to deteriorate. They passed Maribor and although the night was closing in, they decided to keep going. In Zagreb they finally halted, booking into a major hotel near the city centre. The journey so far had been quick and relatively painless and now they had time in hand. Taking it easy the following morning, they headed for Banja Luka.

On a quiet country road they parked and changed the number plate on the car to an Austrian one. The British were less than welcome in the area, but it was also part of their cover. From now on Matt Dunston would do the driving and if they were stopped, all the talking.

Throughout the journey TIFAT sent, by sat-nav telephone, a continuous stream of information regarding the three men they had been sent to find. As of that morning the whereabouts of two of the men were known. Slobodan Ojdanic, or number three, was the only one missing.

Momcilo Dimitrijevic, number one, was in a small village in the hills to the south east of Banja Luka. It was called Podbrdje, on the river Vrbania and was a one street hamlet of less than a hundred houses. Everywhere they drove they saw signs of the military and were stopped on no less than six occasions by French SFOR troops. Their cover as an Austrian television film unit carried them safely through without any problems.

The file on Momcilo Dimitrijevic said that he was forty-two years old. Married with four children, he owned and ran the only restaurant and bar in the village. Driving slowly past the dilapidated houses, most of which looked ready to fall down, they saw old women dressed in black and grey sitting on rickety chairs outside their front doors, unsmiling, unspeaking. Children stopped whatever they were doing to stand and watch as the Land Rover passed. A few enterprising rogues ran into the street holding out their hands, begging for money, food, clothes, anything.

The day had turned warm, a light breeze keeping the atmosphere fresh. If they raised their eyes from the squalor of the people they could see the grandeur of the countryside. The mountains in

231

the distance stood starkly outlined against a blue sky, a few hazy clouds around their peaks.

'A beautiful place,' said Dunston, 'where only man is vile.'

Hunter nodded, not taking his eyes from the road in front of him, careful not to hit any of the children who appeared determined to be run over in their efforts to claim something of value from the car's occupants.

'I have to say,' said Ruth, 'that this does not seem like the natural habitat of a wealthy drug dealer.'

'I agree,' said Hunter. 'However, the information we have has been checked out thoroughly. Number one spends less than six or eight weeks a year in this hole. The rest of the time he's on his yacht in the Adriatic. He was the man behind the sinking of the ship off Portugal that killed all those people. Just because a Customs cutter hailed them.' At the time the atrocity had appeared in practically every newspaper and magazine, and was reported on every television and radio station in the world. The outrage appeared to galvanise the west into action against the perpetrators but then the fuss suddenly died down. Over the last few days, using the incredible computer systems now at the command of TIFAT, the full story had been pieced together. Bribery and coercion had convinced editors that it would be better for them and their families to drop the subject. The few who held out died in frightening circumstances. The world's media had quickly got the message. Other events quickly filled the vacuum and the issue was sidelined. Not forgotten by those in authority, but forgotten by the public at large – as fickle and hungry as ever for new, salacious gossip and great tragedies.

The idea to travel as representatives of an Austrian television news gathering company had been Jim Carter's. Dunston, with his good looks and Ruth, beautiful and articulate, were the reporters, depending on the subject being filmed, while Hunter was the cameraman. The specially padded container carried on the roof held their equipment. The camera was state of the art and actually worked. Some modifications had been made to it, which were certainly not usual by most people's standards. They came courtesy of a small band of specialists Major Carter had acquired at TIFAT. Furthermore, hidden in the solid looking foam packing were all sorts of useful items, such as detonators and firing circuits.

The last piece of information sent by Isobel had assured them that thanks to Echelon, the worldwide network of listening stations, Dimitrijevic was, without doubt, in the area.

Ruth had been the one to ask, 'Isobel, what's Echelon?'

She answered promptly. 'It's a top secret system of ten stations that operate around the world, capable of processing millions of messages an hour.'

'I thought we had that at GCHQ,' Hunter said.

'We do,' replied Isobel, 'but not like this. Echelon is really the civilised world's response to the drugs and terrorist problem. It's based in America, Canada, Australia, New Zealand, Germany and a few other countries, including our own. Ours is based at Menwith Hill in Yorkshire. I say it's top secret but in fact the European Parliament has launched an enquiry into Echelon's operations. Of course, we and the Yanks are denying it exists.'

'So what does it do?' asked Dunston.

'Effectively, it's like a huge vacuum cleaner in the sky that sucks up everything that's sent over the airwaves. Our computers select key words, just like they do at GCHQ, and sort the wheat from the chaff.'

'Why do we need it if it does the same job as Cheltenham?' Hunter queried.

'It's more effective on a world wide basis,' was the answer. 'Also we can key into the El Paso information centre in Texas and the Kronigen Centre in Denmark.' Each centre gathered data specifically on drugs and drug smuggling. The information collected was disseminated world wide to various law enforcement agencies.

'No more to it than that?' asked Dunston.

Isobel paused before replying. 'Actually . . . the politicians control GCHQ to a frightening extent. It still serves its purpose but not as effectively is it could. Echelon does not quite have that, what shall we say? Rigorous supervision?'

'You mean Echelon listens in where it shouldn't,' said Hunter.

'Not quite. A loophole in the 1985 Interception of Communications Act means intelligence officials can put organisations and individuals under surveillance without a specific ministerial warrant. It's proven very useful in the past.'

'I didn't even know it existed,' said Hunter.

'Good,' replied Isobel. 'A secret well kept. Although not for long. Not if the MEPs have their way. Still, we'll cross that bridge when we get to it. No doubt intelligence agencies all over the world are working on the problem.'

'What?' asked Hunter, smiling. 'Echelon Mark II?'

'Possibly,' was the enigmatic reply. 'In the meantime we will make maximum use of what we have. I'll keep you informed of reports relating to your end of the operation. Okay?'

The briefing was over and they broke the connection. It was only thanks to TIFAT's superb encoding equipment that they had learnt so much. After all, Echelon was listening to them. Stopping outside the restaurant, they climbed down from the car. Immediately urchins demanding money or goods surrounded them.

Hunter spoke briefly to Dunston who nodded. Picking on the toughest looking, about thirteen or fourteen years old, the chaplain said in Serbo-Croat, 'I will pay you ten dollars if you guard our car. Provided nothing is taken, when we come out I will give you your money.'

A grubby hand shot out. 'Twenty dollars and I want it now.'

'No chance. Ten dollars and you get it when we come out.'

The boy hesitated and then said. 'Okay. Ten dollars but paid up front.'

Dunston sighed and took out his wallet. Extracting ten dollars, to the shock of the crowd of kids gathered around, he ripped it in half. 'It's no use to you like that. But when I come out I'll give you the other half. Right?'

The boy scowled and then grinned. 'Okay. You can trust me.' He took the half note and stuffed it into a pocket. Immediately he began to order the other children to stay back. A few minor scuffles broke out but the boy had matters well under control. The three of them walked towards the restaurant.

Stepping inside, they stood blinking in the gloom, letting their eyes grow accustomed to the light. The establishment was less than inspiring. The dozen or so tables had stained tablecloths of different designs, bottles with an unlit candle stuck in the neck and small bowls of salt and pepper on dirty looking saucers. Even the salt looked grubby. The bar along one side was scarred wood and the stools looked as thought they would collapse beneath the weight of a grown man. The rows of bottles behind the bar appeared, on the whole, to be either empty or virtually so, and the barman looked as though he had not washed for a week, if not a month. It was a dump.

They immediately recognised the barman as Momcilo Dimitrijevic. Three of the stools were occupied by villainous looking individuals, all unwashed, needing shaves and with heavy moustaches. It was obvious that the team's entrance had halted a heated discussion and the four men looked at them angrily.

Dimitrijevic spoke harshly in Serbo-Croat. Before Dunston could reply Hunter said, quickly, 'We don't understand. We speak only English or German.'

In heavily accented English Dimitrijevic said, 'We are not open. Go away.'

'The sign says differently,' Hunter replied.

'I not care what the sign says. We are closed. Go.' He pointed a finger at the door through which they had just stepped.

Hunter stood for a second staring at the man and then shrugged. 'Okay. Have it your way.'

He led them outside. The car was intact and everything was as it should be. Dunston handed over the other half of the note, nodded his thanks and stretched up to unlock the roof container.

Hunter quickly took down the camera and set it alongside the Land Rover. In seconds he had on a pair of earphones and directed the camera lens towards the restaurant. Ruth stood in front. One of the men had come to the door and watched their antics. Ruth began to speak in English, describing the poverty of the area. Hunter tuned her out and the listening device attached to the camera began to pick up the conversation now being resumed in the bar. The conversation was taped and simultaneously transmitted by sat-nav telephone back to TIFAT HQ. There, the computers identified the language as Serbo-Croat but spoken with a local dialect, making it almost incomprehensible. However, after a few moments, the computer began to translate and relay the information back to the team. Dunston listened to the translation on a set of earphones sitting in the car. Given the way his hand was waving about and the dreamy look on his face, with his eyes half closed and his head thrown back, any observer would swear he was listening to a particularly melodious piece of music.

Hunter re-shot Ruth saying the same thing at least six times as he pretended that the recording wasn't quite right. Ruth, for her part, played her role well. They stopped recording when Dunston opened the car door and said, 'Time to go.'

Switching off the camera Hunter began to stow it in its container. While he did so the three men who had been sitting at the bar came out. They stood scowling, watching the team. Nonchalantly Hunter finished what he was doing, acting as though he was unaware of their presence. In reality he was coiled like a spring, ready to react should the three men try and cause trouble. As Dunston drove them away, he watched the men standing staring after the Discovery until they turned a bend and were no longer in sight.

'What did you learn?' Hunter asked Dunston.

The chaplain smiled beatifically. 'They are expecting a load of heroin tonight. It is coming by lorry from Tuzla and will be arriving about twenty-three hundred hours in order to beat the curfew.'

'How will they get a lorry of heroin past the roadblocks?' Ruth asked.

'A good question and the answer is . . . easily. The lorry is carrying old produce from the vegetable market in Tuzla. In effect, it's rotten cabbages and carrots. Have you any idea how bad rotten cabbage smells and how disgusting rotten carrots feel?' he asked.

'No,' replied Ruth. 'But I can imagine.'

'It's particularly vile,' said Dunston. 'During the Second World War the partisans carried vast amounts of guns and ammunition buried under the stuff right under the noses of the Nazis. Few soldiers are willing to search through the revolting mess. That's the disincentive. The incentive is heavy bribes.'

'It seems that old lessons aren't forgotten in this area,' said Hunter.

A few kilometres along the road they came to a track and Dunston turned onto it. The four-wheel drive vehicle easily climbed the steep hill, went over the brow and dropped down the other side, out of sight. He stopped the car and the three of them prepared to make camp. Within minutes they had a stove going and water on the boil. A council of war was called while they sat drinking coffee and eating cold meat and yesterday's bread. Eventually they agreed a plan of action.

They staked out the road from just after sunset. It was not busy. From their vantage point they could see a kilometre towards Doboj, the next large town, eighty kilometres away. None of them showed the slightest impatience. Each spent ten minutes glued to the binoculars with the light intensifier lenses. Longer than that and the mind tended to wander and precious seconds could be lost if their target came into view and was identified too slowly. A few cars travelled left to right, from Banja Luka towards Tuzla but the other lane was almost deserted. It was nearly midnight when a dilapidated lorry heaved into sight.

Dunston had the binoculars and hissed, 'This looks like it could be it.' He handed the glasses to Hunter who examined the target for a few seconds.

'I agree. Let's go.'

Like ghosts in the night he and Dunston flitted down the hill and along to the road. Ruth stayed in contact by radio, watching the target, looking for guards or other vehicles. They had discussed the possibility that there might be an escort but thought it unlikely. The smugglers' sole means of protection were bribes, threats and a rotten smell.

Over their personal radios both men heard Ruth say, 'The lorry's alone and there's nothing in sight from either direction.'

'Roger that,' said Hunter.

Dunston took the end of a wire and ran it across the road. The wire was carried under the Discovery, on a reel that was concealed inside a metal box the colour of the undercarriage. Tough, razor sharp prongs made a devastating barrier that would rip any tyre to shreds. It was only moments before they heard the vehicle. The wind was blowing along the valley towards them and, if they needed further proof that it was the right target, an all-pervading stench drifted in their direction. The lorry came into sight, belching diesel, leaning to one side on broken springs. The matt black wire was all but invisible and the lorry drove straight onto the barbs creating a loud bang and hiss as both front tyres collapsed. The lorry slewed out of control, the rear wheels hit the wire and it came to a juddering halt.

Hunter and Dunston stayed where they were, watching the cab. Nothing stirred. The night air was as still as a crypt. With the silence lengthening, the three men in the cab began to stir. Finally, seven or eight minutes after the tyres burst, the doors were flung open and the men dropped from the cab. One was on Hunter's side and two near Dunston. All three of them tightly gripped their revolvers.

Crouching nervously, the men looked about them. They could see and hear nothing. The man on Hunter's side looked under the lorry but it was pitch black. Kneeling by the front near side tyre, he felt it, cursing. Scrambling around to the other side he did the same. He said something to his companions but received no reply. Suddenly he was gripped by fear. Where were they? He tightened his grip on the pistol, sweat making it slippery in his hand. He heard a faint scuffling and tried to look behind him. The apparition he saw out of the corner of his eye would give him nightmares for many years as a blow to the side of the neck rendered him unconscious.

Dunston picked him up and carried him to where his two companions lay. He was quickly tied up and gagged. Hunter double checked their handiwork and stood up.

'So far, so good,' he said.

'Who's going to dig into that lot?' Dunston indicated the back of the truck.

'We toss for it.'

'Paper, rock, scissors,' said Dunston.

'Right, on three,' replied Hunter.

He held his hand in a fist in front of him and counted, lifting and dropping his arm as he did so. Hunter lost.

With a martyred sigh he scrambled onto the back of the lorry. The stench was revolting. He shoved the rotting cabbages and carrots over the back, onto the road. Within minutes he found what he was looking for. There were at least five, perhaps six, kilograms of heroin in sealed, plastic bags. He threw the bags down to Dunston who carried them over to the side of the road and made a small pile with them. Ruth acknowledged their situation report and they settled down again to wait. It was nearly 02.00 when Ruth gave a warning.

'There's a car, not showing any lights, coming from Podbrdje. It's moving slowly, about five minutes away.'

Hunter and Dunston readied themselves. The car stopped and four men climbed out including their target Dimitrijevic. Each carried a machine gun and moved warily, two either side of the road. Through their night vision glasses, Hunter and Dunston identified them from the restaurant. Two of the men trailed the other two by about five metres. Dunston and Hunter materialised immediately behind them and both men felt a breeze, a presence. The blows to their necks sent them into unconsciousness before they knew what was happening. Hunter and Dunston caught their prey and lowered them silently to the ground.

They followed the other two. One of the men looked back, satisfied when he saw his two companions a few metres behind. It took a few seconds for his mind to register what his eyes had seen. He began to turn his head but he was far too late. A smashing blow brought a grunt of shock and pain to his lips. Dimitrijevic was also too slow. Hunter almost took his head off.

They carried the four men to where the heroin was stacked. Dunston began talking to Dimitrijevic trying to elicit information. Dimitrijevic mustered his strength and spat at the priest. He missed. Dunston shrugged, made the sign of the cross, mumbled a prayer over Dimitrijevic and began to tie the other three securely. Hunter had no compunction about what he was to do next. He opened one of the bags of heroin and, propping open

Dimitrijevic's mouth, poured the pure narcotic down his throat. The body jerked, twitched and went utterly still. Forever.

Hunter found an old bucket on the back of the lorry and used his knife to smash a hole in the petrol tank. He drained off the petrol and poured it over the heroin. Setting light to it, he and Dunston sat and watched it burn. The heroin made the yellow flame of the petrol burn with an oddly blue tinge. Both men stood upwind, not wishing to inhale any of the noxious fumes. It took nearly ten minutes for the heroin to burn away almost completely. Almost, but not quite. When Ruth joined them, driving the Land Rover, Hunter telephoned Carter and told him what had happened. Carter relayed the message to SFOR. Half an hour later the place was crawling with troops and police. The restrained men were arrested and given a choice. If they refused to co-operate they would be set free unharmed. However, SFOR would ensure that information about the theft of the heroin was spread far and wide. The men were terrified of what could happen to themselves and their families. The information given to SFOR resulted in dozens of arrests across the region.

Macnair sat despondently at his desk. News of the deaths of Leon Sautier and his people had just reached him. His anger boiled over and it took willpower not to rant and curse. Jim Carter sat opposite him, his face ashen. He had taken the phone call from Ferdinand Flika, who had returned to his office before he called, using a secure line.

'Flika positively identified two of the killers from mugshots. He's going to follow up with his own enquiries. He's asked if there's any chance of back up.'

Macnair looked up from his desk. 'Where does he think it'll lead?'

'To a man named Peter Crackov.'

'Crackov?' Macnair repeated. 'Are you sure?'

Carter shrugged. 'That's what he said, sir. Why? Do you know him?'

'I certainly do,' said Macnair. 'He's Russian Mafia. An ex-general who has gone bad. The last I heard he was in Marseilles.

No!' Macnair snapped his fingers. 'In Tunisia. That's it! He's involved with heroin smuggling from Pakistan and India and definitely deals in cocaine from Columbia.'

'Flika says that one of the men he shot is Crackov's second-in-command. He's checking now. He says that Crackov is in a heavily guarded fort near Mahdia.'

Macnair nodded. 'Actually, we've got some details on file. I'll look them out. Tell Flika that we'll work to confirm where Crackov is. If he's at Mahdia then he can leave him to us.'

'He can?' Carter asked in surprise.

'He can,' replied Macnair. Grabbing the telephone Macnair speed dialled. 'Commander Hunter?' The General's voice was frosty.

Hunter acknowledged the General and broke the connection.

'A problem?' Ruth asked.

'A bollocking. The General told me in no uncertain terms that our task is the collection of information.'

'We tried to get information,' Dunston protested.

'Not hard enough apparently. We have to do better. Let's go.'

Target number two was named Alexander Stankovic and he was a lawyer. His offices were in Tuzla and there was no doubt that he had been the conduit for the heroin that the team had just intercepted. A few minutes before midnight on the following day, in the back streets of a run-down area, they found his address. Breaking into the building was simple. It was a four-storey block of old, rented offices. The lawyer had an office on the top floor, in a corner of the building, away from the street. Here the team ran into difficulties. The door was more securely locked than Fort Knox.

Dunston had used skeleton keys to open the front door. Here, none of his keys worked and after a few minutes he gave up.

'Not possible with what I've got, I'm afraid. These locks are far more sophisticated than I'd have expected.' Standing up, he shrugged helplessly. 'Only way is to blow them open.'

Hunter nodded. 'Ruth?' he spoke into his throat mike.

'Here, Nick.'

'We're going to have to blow the door. Is everything quiet your end?'

Ruth was sitting outside in the car, a few metres from the front door. The streets were quiet, a steady rain keeping all but the most foolhardy insomniacs at home.

'All's quiet,' she began. 'No! Wait! There's a patrol coming.' She watched the four man, SFOR patrol approaching. They were alert, carefully looking around them, checking for unwanted surprises. Such as an ambush by disgruntled Serbs.

Ruth sat still, as any movement could cause the car to rock. She knew that the tinted glass stopped anybody seeing inside but it was still disconcerting to watch while one of the soldiers came up close and tried to peer in. Ruth stared back, their faces only inches apart. Another one tried a door, shrugged, said something indistinct in French and the patrol moved on. Ruth watched them passing out of sight around a corner.

'Okay. All clear.'

While Ruth had watched the patrol, Hunter had kneaded small amounts of explosives around the hinges of the door. He put a detonator into each mound and set a fuse. The explosive he used was not the usual plastic. The detonator made a loud hiss rather than a bang. Instead of blowing up, the explosive burnt with an intense heat and cut through the metal hinges. They waited a few seconds for the temperature to drop and then pulled the door away from the surround, sliding the locks apart. Moments later they were inside.

After closing the blind across the only window, which looked out onto a deserted back yard, they took the place apart. They spent three hours going through everything they could find. Most of the files were old, redundant or unused. If Stankovic had enough clients to make a living it was not evident from the briefs they found. It was at least three years since he appeared to have had a real case. Although Dunston spoke excellent Serbo-Croat, reading it was more difficult but he knew enough to understand the gist of what he found. Finally, in a locked drawer, they hit pay dirt.

242

A box of floppy discs looked as though they were in current use. 'Perhaps,' said Hunter, 'Stankovic is taking the idea of the paperless office to extremes.'

'I doubt it,' said Dunston, sitting at a computer and booting it up. He began to work his way through the discs. 'Mainly transactions, though nonsensical ones.'

'What do you mean?' Hunter asked, leaning down and looking over the other's shoulder.

'Look at this. Delivery of two kilograms of apples, $20k.'

'That makes no sense,' said Hunter frowning.

Dunston pointed out similar transactions, translating with occasional difficulty from Serbo-Croat into English. 'Any ideas?'

'Sure. It's referring to different drugs.' Hunter pointed at the screen. 'Look at the amounts and the weights. Those are the wholesale prices for heroin and cocaine. I'll bet anything you like the remainder are for other drugs such as ecstasy and amphetamines.'

Dunston nodded. 'I wouldn't take the bet. Anything odd strike you about the office?'

'Sure,' replied Hunter, 'he has no staff. Not even a secretary. Nowhere for one to sit, no other room to use.'

'Exactly. It appears our lawyer likes to keep things to himself.'

'It certainly looks like it.'

Dunston said, 'This is interesting.'

Hunter looked again at the computer screen.

'I've traced the money. According to what's on here, Stankovic bankrolled dozens of jobs.'

'How can you tell?'

'I've married up information from this disc to another one. The figures tally and so does the information shown here. He's known about or participated in at least fifty criminal acts, any one of which should have landed him and his accomplices in jail for life. Look at this. A heroin shipment to Rome went wrong and the courier died when the condom she carried inside her burst. Their response was to threaten the family to supply another girl, this time the younger sister. Going as an *au pair* to somebody in Rome. I bet they're Mafia connected.'

'Probably. Why don't we download the whole lot via sat-nav phone to HQ and let them work on it? Isobel has all the facilities she needs. She may be able to lift the money from wherever it is.'

'You think so?'

Hunter smiled. 'I know so.'

'Okay. This won't take long.' Quickly setting the phone to e-mail, Dunston fed the floppies through the computer and connected his sat-nav phone to TIFAT. When the e-mail arrived at the other end the information was automatically stored and flagged. Work on collating and examining the files would start first thing in the morning.

'Come on. Let's go and find ourselves a slimy lawyer,' said Hunter. He needed to know about the warheads.

'So all lawyers are slimy?' asked Dunston.

'No,' said Hunter, straight-faced. 'Some are snakes.'

They placed the door across the opening and rammed it closed. Walking downstairs, they paused in the doorway. Ruth gave them the all clear and they stepped into the night, joining her in the car. She drove them away from the building to the hotel they had booked into earlier. During the twenty-minute drive across the city they were stopped three times by SFOR patrols. Their journalistic credentials got them safely through.

Yuri Voropaev watched as the police ran around like headless chickens following the discovery of the bodies and the missing money and papers. He took grim satisfaction in their ineptitude and lack of dedication. Why should they care? Life in Vladivostock rose barely above the poverty line for law-abiding citizens, while the criminals lived in unashamed luxury. If anything, the feeling amongst the police was that the partygoers had got what they deserved.

The clothes he was wearing were the best he had ever owned. He had actually enjoyed the hours he'd spent buying them. Careful as always, he gone from shop to shop, buying a shirt here, a pair of shoes there. Who said crime didn't pay?

Finally, using his own contacts, he had been able to establish that the Georgians would be leaving for Tokyo, only two hours flying time away.

They would be flying in a private jet; he would have to fly American Airlines. The flight stopped at Tokyo to refuel prior to making the long-haul leg across the Pacific to San Francisco. Although it pained him, after careful consideration, he decided to fly first class. He could use the first class lounge and stay hidden until it was time to depart. There was always the possibility that a serving or even retired member of the submarine service would recognise him or call attention to him. Either could be catastrophic.

Dressed in his new clothes, with hair gel plastered on his head and talcum powder rubbed in to create a grey tint at the sides, he left his house. Wearing an old, hooded coat over his suit, he kept the hood up and his head bent, not wishing to be recognised. He shambled along, another eccentric figure in a land noted for its eccentrics. Although it was the middle of the day few people were around to observe him and those that did took no notice. Decades of mistrust of neighbours were ingrained into the population and they still kept themselves to themselves.

In a back alley in the centre of town he dumped his coat and took a taxi to a travel bureau about two kilometres away. Having been promised five dollars when asked to wait, the taxi driver said he'd stay all day if necessary. Voropaev entered the bleak office, paused and strode across to the nearest desk. He sat down. The man behind the desk ignored him. This was part of the old communist ritual that rankled with visitors but was accepted by the inhabitants of the former Soviet Union from Smolensk in the west to Petropavlovsk-Kamchatskiy in the east, across nine time zones. Voropaev was preparing himself to wait when he realised that the dolt had not noticed he was a foreigner and that he, Voropaev, had better get into character. He was about to get angry when a fearful thought occurred. Perhaps wearing a few western style clothes did not change him enough. Hesitating, he looked across the room at the three other desks, each with an official behind it. No other customer was present.

Standing up noisily, scraping back his chair, he walked across to the next desk. He leant heavily on it, using the palms of his hands. 'Listen, bud.' Voropaev tried to speak English with an American accent, sounding like a bit actor in an American movie trying to sound Russian, 'I want a first class ticket to Tokyo. Are you going to get me one?'

The man looked up, startled. 'Yes. Yes, sir,' he stammered. 'Only . . .'

'Only what?' Voropaev snarled.

'Only you were being ser . . . served over there.' The man looked at his superior who was now glowering at him.

'That fool ignored me. You want the business or don't you?'

The man swallowed nervously and nodded. The commission was far too great to allow the customer to walk out. Shaking, he reached for his booking pad. 'I'll . . . I'll take the details. How will you be paying, sir?' It was always the first question. This time Voropaev enjoyed giving the answer.

His only luggage was the briefcase. Sitting in the bureau for the next forty-five minutes, the ticket was arranged, paid for and his seat confirmed. The man's glance at the American passport was less than cursory, giving Voropaev hope that the rest of officialdom would be equally as lackadaisical. He was now treated like an honoured guest, tea and coffee were offered and declined, along with a brandy and rum. When Voropaev finally left with the ticket in his pocket, he was nearly two thousand dollars poorer. But it had been worth it. The spin-off, which he had not even realised when he had decided to go to the bureau, was the fact that he had been allocated his seat and been given a boarding pass. His details had already been passed to the airline. He could walk straight through to airside without hanging around in a queue. Even passport control had a special entrance for first class travellers.

Climbing into the waiting taxi Voropaev ordered the driver to take him to the airport. He sat back in the worn seat as the old Trabant asthmatically wheezed its way along the highway, belching clouds of noxious gases out of the back.

Approaching the airport, Voropaev tried to act as nonchalantly as possible. Situated a dozen kilometres out of the city, it was a bleak place. The grey, uninspiring buildings formed a blot in an otherwise forlorn countryside. The control tower had once been painted white but now it was scabrous, the paint peeling on brickwork like pustules about to burst.

Alighting from the cab, Voropaev was in complete control. The only task he had left before he went through immigration and security was to ditch his pistol. The guns he had taken from the hotel were buried in the forest, hopefully never to be found. The gun he carried he would jettison at the last moment. First he had to cross the concourse.

He paid the taxi driver and added a second five-dollar tip. The effusive thanks he received embarrassed Voropaev. Hefting the briefcase in his hand he unconsciously straightened his tie, a habit many serving officers in any military service in the world developed when being called before a superior. Only this was worse – a lot worse. Suddenly he became aware of the fact that carrying a gun was futile. He would never use it against one of his own kind – a soldier or policeman doing his duty.

He pushed his way through the swing doors into a scene from bedlam. Throngs of people were pushing and shoving, passenger lines were snaking hours long. Touts and pickpockets infested the whole area. The policemen on duty were having a hard time controlling tempers – their own as well as those of the people waiting to leave Vladivostok. Fear erupted in the pit of Voropaev's stomach as paranoia raised its ugly, but often life-saving, head. Then he calmed down. According to the information board, the flights had been delayed due to an air-traffic control problem. Nothing unusual there.

Moving closer to Passport Control, he was struck by a thought. Perhaps the delay was really a ploy to stop whoever had committed the murder and theft in the hotel from escaping. Then reason prevailed. That made no sense. The police couldn't know he would try and leave through the airport. If the police assumed it had been local gangsters, then all they had to do was wait until one of them tried to spend the money that had been stolen. If they weren't local, then the sooner they left, the better.

Looking around he saw that there were definitely more soldiers and policemen in evidence than normal. But then, uniformed patrols weren't the problem. The danger lay with those who weren't wearing uniform. Ducking his head, he scanned the crowd, trying to identify the man or woman who was taking too much interest in the other passengers. Those who stood still, patient, oblivious of the noise and people, watchful and always wary. He kept moving, shouldering his way through the thick pack of humanity, stepping over and around suitcases, boxes and parcels. Four, he glanced to his left, no, five, he'd spotted so far. Perhaps his paranoia was working overtime for a good reason.

Looking behind, he bumped into somebody. Looking at the man, he felt a tremor of shock wrack his body. He hoped that his face did not show any emotion as he mumbled, 'Sorry,' in English.

The man gave him a strange look as Voropaev hurried towards the door to Passport Control. Staring at Voropaev's retreating figure, the man frowned. He was certain he knew whom he had just bumped into. That posture, the shape of the head. He smiled to himself. Wait until he saw Yuri! They'd have a laugh. Yuri Voropaev's doppelgänger had just passed him and headed for the first class section of the airport. The man chuckled. He knew Yuri well. They had served together for many years. Chuckling again, he walked away.

The first class ticket continued to weave its magic. Voropaev showed the ticket and boarding pass first and followed it with the passport. The immigration officer barely looked at it, waving Voropaev through, adroitly palming the German five-mark note tucked inside. Voropaev was approaching security when beads of sweat suddenly burst onto his brow. The gun! He still had the gun in his pocket! Mother of Christ! How could he have been so stupid? In his haste to cross the concourse, to get away from the prying eyes, he had forgotten the damned thing. He hesitated. The officials at the security desk were looking at him. He looked back, panic welling in his throat, trapped. One of them came over to him.

'Are you all right, sir?' he asked in Russian.

Voropaev nodded, croaked and then shook his head. Hesitatingly and he hoped, in bad Russian, he said, 'Came over . . . bad. Need . . . sit down.'

'Over here, sir. There is a toilet.' The man indicated a door behind him marked Staff. He pushed the door open and Voropaev followed. He nodded his thanks, went to a tap and splashed a little water onto his face and pointed at one of the cubicles.

The man nodded his understanding and Voropaev went inside, closed the door and sat on the toilet with a flood of relief. He was quaking. It had been a near thing.

There was knock on the door and a solicitous voice asked him if he was all right. It jolted him out of his reverie and he said, 'Yes. Yes, I . . . I'm coming.' He had to get rid of the gun! He looked about him. There was nowhere to put it. The cubicle contained a toilet and a paper holder. Nothing else. It was white tiled with a dirty concrete floor. He forced himself to calm down, to think. An idea was germinating. Something about the paper. Suddenly he grinned. That was it! Thank God for rough, tough, Russian toilet paper. Tearing off a strip, he wrapped the gun in the thick white tissue and took a second, longer piece, which he twisted lengthways. He passed the second strip through the trigger guard. Kneeling down, he carefully placed the gun behind the toilet bowl and tied the paper with a reef knot at the front. Tucking the paper up under the lip of the bowl he effectively hid it from sight. Satisfied, he let himself out of the cubicle. He smiled at the official still waiting for him, nodded, thanked him and handed the man a five dollar note. The man escorted him all the way to the lounge where Voropaev stepped through the door and into a different world.

The lounge was staffed and operated by American Airlines personnel who understood the meaning of the word service. There were a dozen passengers, eight men and four women. They were all loud Americans. He sat hidden behind yesterday's *Tribune Herald*, reading it not to be informed about world events, but to practice his English.

Fifty minutes later they were called and taken to the aircraft, a Boeing 747, and led onboard. Voropaev accepted a glass of

Californian sparkling wine, a half dozen canapés and a set of earphones. He sat in anticipation for the announcement to fasten seat belts and prepare for take-off. With each passing minute he became more concerned. Why the delay? To have come this far and be caught was unthinkable.

After what seemed an age the plane taxied to the runway, sat there for a further twenty minutes and finally hurtled down the concrete strip. The plane lifted effortlessly into the air and Voropaev sank back in exhausted exultation. He was out of Russia and hopefully still ahead of the Georgians – just.

22

Hunter and Ruth were watching the front door while Dunston moved into position around the back. This was no mere house; it was a chateau. Whatever the lawyer Stankovic did in his one-man office, he evidently made a great deal of money.

They had spent the morning in the hotel resting and the afternoon finding and watching the lawyer's house.It stood in its own grounds, set back a hundred metres from the road. It was, relatively speaking, an expensive area of the city, although each house could be bought for the cost of a one bedroom flat in Maida Vale. High walls, topped with barbed wire hid the houses on either side. Stankovic's was no exception.

Ruth and Hunter went in separate directions, carefully examining the walls and paying particular attention to the gateway at the front. It was like a fortress. They took their time, spending nearly half an hour recording and noting everything they could see. The infrared, palm-sized video cameras took pictures as clear as daylight even though by now it was pitch dark. The sky was overcast and not even a sliver of the full moon showed through the cloud. It promised to become a filthy night.

'Seen enough?' Hunter asked over the headsets. Receiving two affirmatives, all three slipped like ghosts back to the Land Rover. Plugging the cameras into the navigation console in the dashboard, they played the recordings they had just made.

'Look, there and there,' pointed Dunston.

'I see them. Damnation. I only saw one when I was look-ing.'

251

'Hence the cameras,' said Ruth. 'Look, isn't that a trembler assembly?'

The three of them stared at the picture and Dunston said, 'It certainly looks like it. Okay, good news and bad news, I think.'

Hunter nodded. 'I agree. His office is a front. The real work is done here. He also relies on mechanical protection instead of personal bodyguards.'

'So what's the good news?' asked Ruth.

'That is the good news,' replied Dunston. 'There's nobody there but him.'

'So how are we going to get in? This is just the perimeter wall. What's covering the grounds? Infra red beams? Transponders?' Ruth hoped they would not find any of the thin, line-of-sight beacons that transmitted a cobweb of rays to each other. If a ray was broken then an alarm sounded. They were difficult to spot as they could be hidden in flowerbeds and other foliage but still worked effectively as plant life did not affect the beams.

'Trembler pads?' Dunston suggested.

'All of those,' said Hunter.

'I agree,' said Dunston. 'So we go either over or under.'

'Or do neither,' said Ruth, 'and wait until the morning.'

'That's an option,' Hunter grinned, 'but we're here now and we may as well make the most of it.'

'So what do you intend doing?' Ruth asked.

'Going under means finding a drain or sewage pipe which I'm not keen on,' grimaced Hunter, 'for obvious reasons. So we go over.'

'We?' asked Ruth.

'No,' Hunter replied. 'Me. I've got the para-glider in the back. I'll use it to drop onto the roof.' As he spoke he was poring over a map of the city, 'I'll drive up to here. There's a monument on a hillock in a park area. Perfect.'

'Are you mad?' Ruth asked, aghast. 'That won't do any good. You'll never have enough lift to take-off. Para-gliders need height to drop down from.'

'Not this one,' said Hunter. 'It's more a wing than a glider and we have the technology to get us airborne.'

'Don't tell me,' Ruth sighed theatrically, 'a Major Carter innovation.'

'Correct,' said Hunter. 'Now, shall we get this show on the road?'

Dunston and Ruth climbed out of the car carrying their cameras. The cameras had a small viewing screen so the users could see whatever they were pointed at. The zoom lenses were strictly state of the art and once Dunston and Ruth were in position, hidden front and back, they focused the cameras closely on the roof of the building, seeking traps, looking for an easy way in.

Hunter, meantime, drove the two kilometres to the park, and stopped on the mound where there was a monument to an obscure poet. Climbing out, he stood listening. Nothing stirred except the leaves in the trees and bushes. The wind began to pick up from the west, bringing more storm clouds with it. Looking up at the sky he knew, with a seaman's instinct, that the rain and bad weather were only a short distance away. If he was to go then he needed to go now. Grinning mirthlessly he admitted to himself that he was actually looking forward to the flight.

He undid the case on the car roof and took out the ultra-light, reinforced carbon fibre frame. Each section was less than fifteen centimetres long and fitted and locked into place with a twist. He had done this on numerous occasions but never with quite so much urgency.

'Nick, it's Matt. Do you read me?' Dunston spoke into Hunter's headphones.

'Loud and clear, Matt.' Hunter continued, twisting the sections together effortlessly.

'I'm getting concerned about the weather. It's becoming marginal for flying, never mind hitting a small target.'

'Roger that. I'll just have to see how it goes. If it proves too difficult I'll veer away and we'll leave things until morning.'

'Okay. I can live with that. Out.'

I just hope I can, thought Hunter, finishing the framework. He slipped the microscopically thin fabric of the wing into place and checked the connections. Strapping on his fighting belt he prepared to launch himself into the sky. Even as he ran a few steps down the hill, into the wind, he was pressing the inject button on the handle. A canister released helium into the wing and increased the lift factor of the para-glider by nearly five-fold. Soaring into the air, swinging from side to side, Hunter stifled the yell of elation that sprang to his lips. His mission was too serious for frivolity but the surge of excitement was something he could not hold back.

Orientating himself to the city below, he surged upwards past the five hundred metre mark. He began to dump the helium as he took control of the flight and turned round in the sky, heading back towards the chateau. Ruth was beaming an infrared spot onto the roof of the chateau, which in turn was displayed on a small VDU in front of him. It indicated the distance still to cover, his height above the target and the speed at which he was approaching.

'Airborne and tracking,' he announced.

'Roger that,' said Ruth. She looked upwards, trying to spot him but the night refused to reveal its secrets.

Hunter settled onto a flight path that would take him straight at the target. The wind veered, lifted and increased in strength and he was thrown off course, spinning upwards, out of control. He dumped more helium, concentrating on getting back on course and back onto the flight path he needed for a safe landing. Under control again, he settled the para-glider for a straight run. Three-quarters of a kilometre to go. His height was three hundred metres above the target and he was closing at a speed of between twenty and twenty-five knots.

A down draft sent him tumbling from the sky, all lift gone. He was being driven straight at the side of a tall building. Adding helium as fast as he could, Hunter felt the glider pause in its downward rush and then soar upwards and to the left, as another up draft lifted him crazily into the air. Hunter again dumped helium for all he was worth. He missed the building by less than a metre, death by a nano-second. *This is crazy*, he told himself. The weather was now deteriorating fast and it was becoming more dangerous by the minute. *One more go*. After that he'd abandon the attempt. He lined up the glider on the target showing on the VDU. He was now less than a quarter of a kilometre away, a hundred metres high. He aimed at the target one last time. Any more problems and he would sail away.

The target bearing remained steady. He closed rapidly, the wind now carrying him at nearly thirty knots. Turning, he angled in for the zigzag he knew was necessary to come up into the wind and flare to a stop. He lifted his eyes from the VDU and looked at the landing spot. His night-vision glasses lit up the scene below him almost as clear as daylight. Unlike the old fashioned goggles shown on films, these were flat glasses controlled by a microchip. If a light suddenly burst on, the glasses immediately filtered it out, leaving his eyes unaffected. The old goggles left the wearer blinded for a few seconds, sometimes longer – long enough to get killed.

He could see the spot that had been chosen for him. It was the side of the roof, immediately below which was a flat roofed extension. He could see a skylight, ideal for his requirements. The para-glider flew smoothly through the night, the wind behaving itself for a few seconds. *Just a fraction longer*, thought Hunter, *that's all I ask.*

He was over the target, turning the wing into the wind, flaring upwards, stopping his forward momentum. At that moment the wind gusted straight at him, hit the roof and gave him a huge upwards surge just as he was about to land, his feet already touching the roof. Hunter's reflexes were phenomenal. He hit the release button on the harness even as he was soaring back up a metre higher. He slipped through the nylon webbing, landed on the sloping roof, dropped with a grunt onto his back and slid down towards the flat roof three metres away. His feet landed with a jar and he lay there for a few seconds, winded.

'Nick! Nick!' Ruth whispered anxiously into her radio. 'Answer me, damn you.'

'Okay, Ruth. I'm okay. Just getting my wind back. I'm on target. I lost the wing though.'

'Never mind the damned wing, as long as you're alive. All's still quiet.' Ruth and Dunston had listening-devices aimed at the windows of the chateau. By using the infrared camera they could aim tiny microphones at up to twenty targets and listen simultaneously. So far they had heard nothing. Either the chateau was empty or the lawyer was asleep.

As Hunter slid down the roof, his feet depressed tiny relay switches that set off an alarm connected to a wristband. Inside the chateau, Stankovic the lawyer was wide-awake, close to panic.

Hunter knelt next to the skylight and felt carefully around. 'It's as we thought,' he said softly. 'Lots of outward protection but nothing here.' He gripped the panel and pulled upwards. Two screws holding the lock in place came away and he was able to swing open the skylight. Looking down he saw a carpeted corridor about four metres below. He swung over, held himself at arm's length for a second and then dropped lightly. Standing up he heard the faintest click of oiled metal on metal.

Instinct saved him. He threw himself forward, desperately turning in the air, landing with a heavy smash on his back, sliding across the carpet and crashing into a table. Ornaments scattered and broke as he pulled his gun from the quick release holster across his chest. Stankovic fired an automatic machine gun in a continuous burst. The bullets sailed harmlessly over Hunter's head. Hunter fired only once, a silenced shot straight between the eyes. The lawyer flew backwards, the machine gun's shockingly loud staccato cut off. Silence fell, broken only by the drip of water from a broken vase. Its flowers lay scattered under the lawyer's body.

Rolling over and to his knees, Hunter answered the frantic calls for information, assuring Ruth and Dunston that he was uninjured. He listened intently. The house remained silent. Ruth confirmed there appeared to be no sign of life. *So much*, thought Hunter, *for modern technology*. The General was not going to be pleased. He had particularly wanted the lawyer interrogated.

Working his way from room to room, he checked for any other occupants. The house was empty. In the hallway at the front he found a locked cupboard. When he broke it open he found that it contained the control switches for the surveillance systems that protected the chateau. Turning off every switch, he opened the front door. A few seconds later, Ruth and Dunston joined him.

They began a systematic search of the house. During the night they received a phone call from TIFAT HQ. The duty officer called to tell them that they were now operating twenty-four hours a day and that work had already commenced on the information lifted from the lawyer's office. So far, it was useless.

'It makes no sense,' said Ruth. 'He must have a great deal of information somewhere.'

'But where?' asked Dunston. 'That is the question.' He eased his aching limbs into a seat and sat with his head thrown back, eyes closed, thinking. Hunter despondently lowered himself into another easy chair and also closed his eyes. Ruth paced the room.

Without opening his eyes, Hunter said, 'Is it your intention to wear out a hole in the carpet or just drop down into the basement?'

It was as if a frisson of electricity shot across the room. Dunston shot upright, eyes wide open, Ruth stopped pacing and Hunter smiled. 'Are we,' he asked, 'just plain stupid or cretinously, pig-headedly, stupid?' Opening his eyes, he sat up.

Dunston said, 'The latter. A chateau like this and we never thought of cellars! Come on. Let's find the way down.'

Easier said than done. An hour of fruitless searching led nowhere. Nonplussed, all three of them stood in the hall. It was a large space. A huge stained glass window on the half-landing leading to the upstairs rooms dominated the area. The entrance had a storm door and vestibule. The walls were wood-lined in ornately decorated dark oak and the hall was at least five metres wide and eight-deep. Halfway down, on either side, stood two complete suits of armour. Behind the armour on one side hung crossed swords that were at least four hundred years old. On the other, crossed lances hung, dating from the time of the Crimean war. The three of them had rapped, touched, prodded and felt every square inch of the panelling and had done the same in every other part of the house where a door was possible or even likely.

'Let's think this through,' said Hunter. 'We're agreed that the office was probably a blind. Right?'

The other two nodded.

'It seems reasonable to me,' he went on, frowning in thought, 'that with the way this place is protected there should be more here than just Stankovic himself. A cellar is an obvious bet. But,' he was warming to his theme now, 'if the organisation is as wide spread as we think it is then he would need help. He would need others to assist with the work. He wouldn't want them traipsing through the house. Ergo, there must be, somewhere in this room, a way down.'

Dunston paced the room, turned, stopped and shook his head in mock sorrow. 'We continue to be cretins.' He pointed at both suits of armour. Without a word he walked across to one and began to push and prod it while Hunter, with an oath, rushed across to kneel by his side.

Hunter knocked the floor with his knuckles, but wherever he hit, it sounded the same to him. Ruth, in the meantime, lifted a lance off the wall and used the shaft to rap the floor around the other suit of armour. Working steadily closer to the plinth, when she struck the floor next to it the echo was different. The two men heard it, stopped what they were doing, and joined her. They pushed and shoved but nothing moved.

'Stop a moment,' said Ruth. 'It must be simple to operate. If we're right then this statue will be moving regularly and therefore, easily. There must be a mechanism of some description.' She grabbed the left arm which was held across its body and lifted it. The arm bent at the elbow and the plinth moved silently on rubber casters, to display a metre square opening in the floor. A set of stairs, fully lit, led down.

'Like something out of a Boris Karloff movie,' said Dunston. He led the way. Ruth and Hunter followed closely, guns ready, expecting trouble, but finding none.

The cellar was huge, probably accounting for half the size of the ground floor. There were four medium sized offices along one side and a large corner office, well furnished with an illuminated window with an alpine scene dominating one wall. Three desks were in the main room. Each had the look of being well used. The lawyer definitely had a substantial operation. The question was, were the other workers a part of the criminal conspiracy or innocent employees?

'I doubt they don't know the truth,' said Hunter. 'It's impossible. You can't run this sort of operation and not have some information leak. Not in a place like this.'

'Well, let's get to work,' said Ruth. The three of them split up and went in different directions.

The offices were partitioned with half wooden, half-glass panels so that the occupants could see each other. Hunter took the large office which he was sure was used by the lawyer, if the photographs on the walls were anything to go by. Pulling open filing cabinet doors and looking through drawers, Hunter found nothing of interest. Sitting at the desk, he put his feet up and stared at the illuminated window. The mountain in the background, he was sure, was the Eiger. There were a few cows with bells around their necks, an old man with a walking stick and the obligatory peasant wench, looking like an idealised version of Heidi, with a milk pail in each hand. Her flaxen hair was in pigtails, her teeth were pearly white and her bosom would have made the Pope reconsider celibacy. Hunter hefted a paperweight in his right hand, looked again at the window picture and threw it at the girl. The glass shattered, startling the other two. Standing up, Hunter walked across the room to take a closer look at the safe he had exposed.

Ruth and Dunston joined him. The three stood looking at the behemoth. It was three metres high, four metres across and God alone knew how deep.

'It's a solid looking beast,' said Dunston with typical understatement.

'Any ideas?' Ruth asked. She looked at Hunter. 'You're the explosives expert.'

Hunter rubbed the side of his face. He sighed and said, 'If we used enough plastic to blow it open it'd probably bring the house down on our heads. We need to gouge the metal away, layer by layer.'

'How long will it take?' asked Dunston, glancing at his watch, noticing with a shock that it was 03.58.

'A while. It can't be rushed. Let me get started while you two finish checking the other desks and filing cabinets. There might be incriminating evidence out there as well.'

'Incriminating evidence?' Ruth repeated. 'What do we want that for? We know Stankovic is as guilty as sin.'

Hunter nodded. 'But think of the workers, his employees? The people who occupy those desks and offices.' He turned her around, patted her on the behind and said, 'A coffee right now would go down a treat.'

She looked over her shoulder and smiled. 'What did your last slave die of?'

'Boredom.' Grinning, Hunter took a closer look at the safe. On the right was a combination lock and turnkey arrangement. There was also a swipe card mechanism as well as two heavy handles. On the left the hinges were recessed and therefore immune from attack. It was a very formidable arrangement. He set to work. The first thing he needed to know was how strong the metal was. If it was reinforced tungsten then it would take half the day if he was lucky. If it was merely heavy iron with a steel door, then there was a possibility he could get through. Opening his rucksack, he extracted a small metal container, shaped like a beehive, a centimetre in diameter and two centimetres deep. It had three wire legs with feet that he could tape to the safe door. He filled the beehive with plastic explosives, fed the detonator into the opening at the top and taped the hive to the door. He set the fuse and stepped outside. Ten seconds later there was a satisfying explosion and he re-entered the office. The beehive shape had ensured that the whole force of the explosion was channelled at the door. The power of the blast was designed to focus one centimetre under the surface to give maximum effect for the minimum amount of plastic explosive. Examining the barely scratched but burnt paintwork, he had his answer. The door, as far as he was concerned, was impregnable.

Ruth appeared carrying a mug of coffee and a plate of biscuits. 'There's a kitchen of sorts back there,' she indicated. 'I found a percolator and switched it on. It'll be a while so in the meantime I thought you could use this instant.'

'Thanks,' he took the cup and swallowed. The hot liquid was welcome, reviving his flagging spirits.

'What are you going to do about that?' she nodded at the safe.

'Take out the walls and see if the sides are equally as tough. They aren't usually but then, nothing about this place is usual. Why do I get the feeling we keep underestimating these people?'

'What do you mean?'

'I was so sure they'd left the roof unguarded.' He shook his head. 'These are seriously tough and capable people, utterly ruthless, intelligent and determined. We might be the good guys but it doesn't mean to say we'll win as a result.'

'So how do we proceed?'

'We need to be more careful, less arrogant and a good deal more astute. Now, I'd better get on with this.'

Blowing out the wall was easy. When he pulled the first few bricks away he found a gap nearly half a metre wide running alongside the safe which, he now saw, was only a metre deep. Hammering more bricks free, finally he could step between the safe and the wall. Hunter repeated his performance with the beehive. The explosion created an almost perfectly circular hole, a centimetre in diameter and two centimetres deep. The sides of the safe were made of pig iron.

Starting at waist height, he lay a thin bead of plastic, shaped like an elongated triangle, the base firmly stuck to the metal, in a circular shape about half a metre in diameter. He set a detonator and fuse, retired to the kitchen and let it blow while he helped himself to another coffee, this time percolated.

Returning when the dust had settled, he could see that he had made a deep impression into the safe, about a centimetre and a half deep. He repeated the process in exactly the same place. After the third explosion, when he shone a torch on the deep groove, he saw patches of dark where he had broken through. The metal was six centimetres thick. Now he had to be more careful. If he kept using the same amount of plastic explosives he could easily damage the contents of the safe or even cause any inflammable material to ignite. So he varied the amount of plastic explosive along the bead, occasionally omitting some. It meant having to use four detonators as the explosive trail was broken, but at least he would minimise the risk to the contents.

After the explosion he saw that the ring he had cut was still held in place by two thin beads of metal, one at the top and another at ninety degrees. He put his back to the wall, placed his hands in the middle of the circle and pushed. The top bead snapped and then the lump of metal swung inwards and fell to the floor of the safe with a resounding crash. Switching on his torch, Hunter put his head and torso through the hole.

Dunston spoke into Hunter's earpiece. 'Nick, we've got company.'

23

Macnair listened to the briefing. The more he heard the more satisfied he became. It was going, if not exactly, then near enough to plan. Operational decisions had been made and agreed virtually world wide. The plan was finally coming together. TIFAT and their allies would hit the cartels and hit them hard. Their earlier operations were nothing by comparison to what was now going down. By releasing the information about the threat of nuclear weapons he had focused the minds of those fighting the cartels to a wonderful degree.

Isobel, Colonel Hiram B. Walsh and Major James Carter had done a superb job. But the final problem remained unresolved – where would the hierarchy of the criminal cartels bolt to when TIFAT and its allies went into action?

There came a knock on the door. Macnair called, 'Enter!' and Christine Woolford and Charles Woolforth appeared. Macnair had deemed it safer to have Woolforth at Rosyth where they could keep an eye on him. After all, there was no reason to suppose that the cartel would not try to kidnap him again. In fact, quite the reverse. Now that they had met a few setbacks, they were even more likely to want to cause damage. "Fighting like cornered rats" was the phrase that came to Macnair at that moment.

'I hope we aren't disturbing anything?' Christine Woolford smiled sweetly. Macnair hoped nothing of the pleasure he felt whenever he saw her showed on his face.

'No, of course not. We've just finished. Please, come in, both of you. Would you like some refreshments?'

'Not for me,' said Christine.

'Nor I,' said Charles Woolforth. A florid faced man, he was the epitome of the red-faced squire of the fishing, shooting and hunting set. Yet his was a classic case of appearances being deceptive. He had a double first from Oxford University in computer studies and mechanical engineering and had gone on to build a highly successful business. Having sold out at the age of forty, he had soon become bored and entered politics. After one term in the House of Commons he had realised where the real power was shifting, and had worked to become a Member of the European Parliament. He was popular with his constituents and often disliked by his fellow MEPs – both reactions stemmed from the same reason. Woolforth insisted on telling the truth, loudly. During the last three days Christine Woolford had come to appreciate the man – his encyclopaedic knowledge and his outspokenness. She had spent most of the last seventy-two hours in a daze as she re-evaluated and re-drew her principles, in shock at what she had discovered.

She smiled tentatively at Macnair. 'I've been such a naïve fool,' she said.

Macnair held up his hand and smiled in return. 'Not so. You believed in what you said and did. It's difficult to come to terms with the facts when you discover that much of what you believed in was based on a false premise. It shows great courage.'

'I'm not so sure about that. This was no single false premise,' Christine said.

'Yes it was. You believed in the innate decency of your fellow human beings. The shock was to discover that there are so many who do not share your views. Don't be mistaken. The majority of people are good, decent, honest and law-abiding. The minority is a significant cancer on the rest of society.'

'But such a deep-rooted cancer, spreading through the body we know as civilisation,' she said, 'is . . . is terrible. It has to be cut out.'

Woolforth cleared his throat. 'We agree, Christine. You and I must use our power in Europe to make the clarion call. We'll co-ordinate our speeches to hit every newspaper and TV station possible.'

'I can help there,' said Macnair. He then prevaricated. 'I have been in contact with some wealthy individuals who are fully aware of The Syndicate's machinations. They are prepared to buy advertising time in newspapers, magazines and television to tell the world what has been happening.'

'That's wonderful,' said Christine but then hesitated as she added, 'Of course it'll cost a fortune but even a little bit will help. Especially if we can then springboard the publicity into major news items, chat shows and political discussion programmes.'

'Leave that to me,' said Macnair. 'I can promise you significant coverage across Europe and America.' He did not tell them that he was prepared to use much of the vast financial resources TIFAT had at its disposal. This was one war they could not afford to lose.

'We've been working on our speeches,' Christine continued. 'We've collated as much evidence as we think will be necessary and we will circulate copies to every MEP in Strasbourg.'

'You can't do that,' said Macnair.

'Why ever not?' Christine asked in surprise.

'Because we know that eight, possibly nine of their number are in the pay of the cartels and a further four are possibly connected. We have proof. Let them have the evidence *after* your speeches.'

Christine looked shocked while Woolforth remained as phlegmatic as ever.

'We'll release the names to you before you leave. Incidentally, I want you to travel together. You will be escorted by three of my best men. Please do as they tell you and trust them. We must get you safely to the European Parliament and once there we must ensure your continued good health.'

'Is that really necessary, old boy?' Charles Woolforth asked.

Macnair nodded. 'I'm afraid it is. We've intercepted some disquieting telephone conversations that suggest that you two will be targets as soon as you leave here. How in God's name they found out where you were is another question we're trying to get to the bottom of. We need you to orchestrate the politicians, so TIFAT will move heaven and earth to keep you safe.'

'Is that the only reason?' Christine smiled warmly at him.

Macnair acknowledged to himself that she stirred his senses in a way no one had before, even his wife. 'I think we're both beginning to realise it isn't,' said Macnair gently. 'Right, let's get to work. I don't need to hear your speeches, after all, you're the professionals. What I do need to know is what corroborating evidence you intend using. I've a few ideas on that myself. Incidentally, tonight we'll have dinner here, in the wardroom. The next time either of you leave these premises will be by helicopter.'

Hunter acknowledged Dunston's warning. 'How many?'

'Four. Two men and two women. Nothing untoward looking. The men are in suits and the women in office garb. I think they're just coming in early.'

'Okay. I'll meet them in the hall. You stay out of sight.'

Acknowledging the order Dunston watched them approach. If one of the men hadn't pulled back his coat to scratch his side Dunston wouldn't have seen his gun. He warned Hunter.

Ruth also spoke. 'Nick, I've checked each desk. There is no way that the staff here could have been ignorant pawns. In one desk drawer I found reference to the ship we stopped in the Med. In another I found information about a heroin shipment using children. The whole damn lot of them are guilty.'

'Thanks,' Hunter said. 'Okay, let's take them alive.' He pulled a ski mask out of his pocket and slipped it on. Now only his eyes and mouth showed. He did not need to tell his team to do the same.

Standing behind the other suit of armour he watched the four employees enter through the front door. There was no surprise at seeing the offices open, as everybody tended to get in early. They operated on a world wide basis and often were called upon to work twenty-four hours a day. Indeed, Stankovic had recently hinted that they would be doing so again shortly. They were crowding around the stairwell when

Hunter stepped out from hiding. Nobody noticed him until he coughed.

One of the men looked at him, his curse causing the other three to swivel their heads in his direction. The man miscalculated when he saw Hunter's eyes flicker towards the others. Stupidly he tried to draw his gun. Hunter didn't hesitate but shot the man through the forehead. Falling with a crash into the cellar, the body slid down the wooden stairs, feet clattering all the way. The other three stood petrified, like statues.

The surviving man asked something in Serbo-Croat. Matt Dunston stood on the grand staircase and answered with barely a hint of an accent. 'Drop your guns. Nice and easy. Then walk, one at a time, down to the offices.'

The man did as he was told. Neither of the women moved. They glared at the two masked men. If they felt fear they didn't show it. Hunter had the distinct impression that if he gave them a millimetre either one of them would kill him. They were in their late thirties, perhaps early forties. Frumpish looking, in poor quality clothes, they had cold eyes and small mouths. Hunter wondered if they were sisters. They bore a strong resemblance to each other.

One muttered to the other. Over his earphone Hunter heard Dunston say, 'Sorry, Nick. I couldn't understand. They spoke a dialect that's incomprehensible to me.'

'Expect trouble,' said Hunter.

Ruth reported in from below. 'I've handcuffed him to a chair. Send the next one down.'

'Be careful. I don't trust these bitches up here.' Hunter gestured to the next one to go below. The two women exchanged glances and the one nearest the opening started down.

Hunter saw the smile on the other's face and he moved. Striding across the hall, he hit the woman in the side of the face with the barrel of his gun and darted down the steps. He was only just in time. The woman who had gone before him had Ruth by the throat and was reaching for a knife carried in a sheath fixed to the top of her thigh. Hunter's shot went into the woman's leg, shattering the bone, throwing her against the wall with a loud scream.

267

'Nick! Look out!' Ruth screamed.

Hunter jumped the last half dozen steps to the floor, turning as he did. The second woman had been only a pace away from thrusting a stiletto into Hunter's back. Dunston took her out. He came down the stairs in a flying leap and landed feet first on the woman's back. She was smashed against the floor with Dunston landing with his weight on either side of her spine. If he had kept a foot on her spine, it would have broken. As it was, he cracked four ribs on either side and left the woman gasping in pain, unable to draw a full breath.

'Christ,' said Hunter, 'these are dangerous people.'

'To say the least,' said Ruth, wiping her brow with a shaky hand. 'Nick, we did it again. We underestimated them. It's going to get us killed if we aren't more careful.'

Hunter nodded. The woman with the shattered thigh was moaning pitifully, her hands clenched tightly around the wound as she tried to staunch the flow of blood. 'Handcuff them both first, and then see to her wound,' Hunter ordered Ruth. 'Matt, back upstairs. We could have a few others arriving any minute.'

They waited until 09.30 to see if anybody else would arrive. Nobody did.

At last they were able to give their attention to what was in the safe. Hunter and Ruth worked feverishly, scanning papers, transmitting information to TIFAT, opening floppy disk files to view the contents. Some of the information was in English, some in German and some in French. That they could understand. Some of the other languages were beyond them. The translations they received from TIFAT confirmed that the lawyer had been an important conduit for information to and from the Georgian crime cartel. They had unearthed records covering many thousands of crimes from petty theft to the smuggling of heroin, cocaine, arms and immigrants all over Europe. Some of the crimes had price tags between ten and twenty million pounds each. The scale of corruption uncovered was terrifying. It involved thousands of bank accounts, tens of thousands of people world wide and was still growing. In the middle of the morning the team sat in one of the offices. By now they were functioning on instinct.

They were physically and mentally exhausted to the point of dropping.

Although Dunston had done his best for the woman with the bullet wound, giving her morphine to ease the pain, she was now moaning piteously where she lay, her head rolling from side to side. Dunston had tried questioning the others but had achieved nothing. Short of torture there was nothing more they could do. It was time to depart.

'What are we going to do with them?' asked Ruth.

Hunter shook his head. Usually so decisive, he was in a quandary. He did not stomach the idea of shooting them in cold blood but these were, as Dunston reminded him, evil people who preyed on the vulnerable and weak.

'All I can think of,' said Hunter, 'is to leave them here, just like this. All being well, we send in SFOR after it's all over.'

'Somebody could find them and set them free,' said Ruth.

Hunter nodded. 'We'll leave a present at the top of the stairs and shut the place down as completely as it was when we arrived. Come on. We've a few things to do before we get out of here.'

After checking their captives' handcuffs and ensuring there was no way any of them could break loose, he administered a large shot of morphine to the wounded woman and then he and Ruth comprehensibly trashed the place. Finally satisfied, he followed Ruth up the stairs. The surprise package he left was a pound and a half of plastic explosives, cunningly concealed. It would bring the roof down, blocking the way down to the cellar, until SFOR could arrive.

Resetting the alarms, they left the chateau. Back in the Land Rover, Dunston drove while Hunter sat shotgun and Ruth fell asleep in the back. Target number three still had to be taken care of, but they needed to wait for TIFAT to confirm Ojdanic's location.

Yuri Voropaev's situation was a far cry from his world of submarines. He had no training in special services and had never been in an army or marine outfit. His experience was

269

hunting wolf and occasionally bear. He hoped it would be enough to see him through what lay ahead.

He had stood on the observation platform at the top of the airport building looking for the Georgian cartel's aircraft, which finally landed an hour after his. He watched as the plane rolled to a stop and the steps were lowered. A few seconds later an airport limousine appeared and the woman descended the stairs and stepped inside the car, followed by three others. Voropaev saw the car pull up outside the building he was standing on, a distance travelled of less than two hundred metres before the passengers disgorged. He hurried inside, knowing that the immigration and Customs requirements would be minimal at best.

Reaching the ground floor, he saw them walk through the Arrivals hall as though they owned the place. He followed them across the crowded concourse and out to the taxi rank. He edged closer, trying to overhear anything they said. Suddenly a large limousine swooped out of nowhere, screeched to a halt beside them and they climbed inside. Voropaev was left standing helpless, watching the car disappear into the traffic.

Although despondent he admitted to himself that he had not expected anything else. They were hardly going to take a cab! After plan alpha he now had to put plan bravo into operation. Which, truth to tell, was not much of a plan.

Before returning to the observation platform he went into one of the well-stocked airport shops and bought a pair of binoculars. Back on the roof he focused them on the plane and watched the pilots walking around, carrying out their checks. Focusing on their uniforms, he guessed that the plane was on private hire and did not, as he originally thought, belong to the cartel. He concentrated on their arm and breast badges. He could see what looked like a phoenix rising into the air, in gold thread. Very stylish, he thought. Then Voropaev's luck improved. A young woman, wearing a similar uniform, stepped down from the aeroplane and walked nonchalantly towards the terminal building.

Rushing down the stairs once more, Voropaev stood next to the Arrivals door. A few minutes later the woman appeared and walked towards a coffee bar. He was right beside her when she sat at the bar. She asked for a cappuccino in English and he ordered the same.

When it came he lifted his cup, took an appreciative mouthful and said to the woman, 'That's better. I needed that.'

She smiled in return and nodded. 'Me, too.'

'Are you with an airline?' he asked her. He quickly appraised her. Pretty but with lips that could pout as quickly as smile, a nice figure, average height. Brown hair, worn short, peeped out from under a hat that sat at a jaunty angle. She had on too much make-up for Voropaev's liking but, on a cold night in Russia, he would not kick her out of bed.

'Nothing so grand,' she said. 'A small private charter outfit from Florida.'

Voropaev guessed she spoke with an American accent but it was hard for him to tell. 'You're a long way from home,' he smiled.

'You're telling me. And it'll be another ten days at least before we get back.'

'Oh? Are you going somewhere interesting?'

She appeared happy to talk for a few minutes. After a little while he knew the plane's itinerary, the daily rate to hire it and the phone number of the office should he require the same service one day. She seemed disappointed when he did not ask her for her own phone number but rather slid off the stool and wished her a bon voyage. He needed to get ahead of the cartel if he was to find out where those nuclear warheads were destined. He just hoped that they were still on the plane.

Hunter sat at a table in the busy restaurant sipping a coffee. The other two were out and about checking on the information they'd received from Macnair. Already the files they had liberated from Stankovic were proving invaluable. To date, Isobel believed she had found bank accounts containing in excess of five hundred million dollars with a great deal more still more to come. When the time was ripe those funds would also be "liberated" and put to good use. Mozambique, Sierra Leone and Madagascar, to name

271

but three countries, would benefit from the money. As would Ethiopia and India, he thought. The charities, which would receive the windfalls, were international institutions. He smiled, thinking about Isobel. Thank God she was honest! Reaching into his pocket he removed three photographs he had removed from the wall of Stankovic's office. He looked at the first one. It was a group photograph. A woman stood in the middle with five men either side of her. She was striking looking, black hair, a hard mouth. The men appeared to have been grouped around her. In the next photograph, Stankovic stood next to the same woman, a smile on both their faces. The smile softened her looks, making her appear more attractive. The third photograph had been taken while she and two other men leaned over the stern of a ship. The ship's name should have been easy to decipher. Unfortunately it was written in Cyrillic. Although the west deemed the letters Russian, it was actually an old Slavic alphabet, based mainly on ancient Greek. Having sent copies to TIFAT HQ, Hunter now knew that the name of the ship was The *Mermaid*. Details would be forwarded to him as soon as they were uncovered. He wondered who the woman was.

Voropaev arrived in Amsterdam an hour before the private jet landed. He watched as a limousine took the entourage away. This time, Voropaev had hired a car and was able to follow them. A meeting took place in a lawyer's office in the city centre. Whatever its agenda, it had left the men in a foul mood. The woman had stormed out of the building and stood on the pavement screeching at the men. Her relationship with them was puzzling him. Voropaev had no idea what she was saying although he heard every word. She was letting loose a verbal fusillade in Chechnyan.

24

Alleysia Raduyev was talking so loudly that people were beginning to stop and watch her. One of her aides, braver and smarter
than the others, signalled to the car and when it drew up alongside
he unceremoniously hustled her inside. She was till screeching
at the top of her voice. Her threats were awesome, her language
unrepeatable. When they arrived back at the airport Voropaev
was there to watch as the plane took off. He would have given
everything he owned to know what had put her into such a mood.
He took the next flight to Cagliari, the main town on the southern
coast of Sardinia. He wondered what he would find there.

Alleysia Raduyev's bout of temper was brought on by information she had received from her Dutch lawyer. Whilst she
had kicked her heels in Vladivostock, her organisation had been
under siege from all quarters and she seemed powerless to stop
it. Dozens of attacks had taken place across Europe and hundreds
of her people had been either killed or arrested. Not only had
the fools failed to kidnap the MEP, they had managed to get
themselves killed into the bargain. Which was just as well as
the death she would have meted out to them would have been
extremely unpleasant. She had also learned about the attacks
on those fools in Bosnia. *Christos, but she was surrounded
by incompetents*. The sooner Ojdanic returned and took charge
the better.

While the plane took off she sipped at a glass of vintage
champagne, her anger turning to ruthless determination. Her

273

hatred for those responsible welled up in her throat and she squeezed her hand tightly. The fragile stem of the antique glass snapped and in her fury she threw the pieces and contents onto the floor.

'Maria!' she snapped, pointing. Her maid immediately undid her seatbelt, stood up and poured another drink for her mistress. She then cleaned up the mess. Alleysia ignored her, her anger simmering down to a controllable level while she plotted. She'd show them it was unwise to interfere with her. The sustained damage her organisation was taking would soon have its effect. She needed to reverse the situation as quickly as possible. Well she had the means. Three nuclear warheads! Her original intention had been to ransom off each one at fifty million dollars a piece. Now she had a different idea. She would detonate one as a warning and then demand a billion dollars for each remaining warhead. The only question remained – where to detonate it? She drained her glass and held it out to Maria for a refill. She smiled. Of course, she would find out who was behind the attacks and detonate it in the capital city of the country responsible. She guessed the target would be America.

It was a beautiful warm evening when the plane landed at Cagliari. She ignored the obsequious attempts of the stewardess and two pilots to say goodbye. A car was waiting for her when she stepped onto the tarmac and it whipped her away, through immigration and down to the harbour. She took only Maria with her, leaving the rest to take care of Customs and the luggage, even entrusting the warheads to them. With the head of Customs and Excise on her payroll she never needed to follow the normal procedures.

The ship Alleysia boarded was The *Mermaid* and was identical to three other vessels, each bearing the same name. They were currently in various ports – Singapore, Rio de Janeiro and Helsinki. Her plans were now reaching fruition.

The *Mermaid* had one of the most comprehensive communications systems ever designed. While she was taking a shower and getting changed, Alleysia received an encrypted e-mail. It was in her own private code, known to very few. The information it contained sent her into another paroxysm of rage. Over two hundred and fifty million dollars had disappeared from her bank accounts. Unaccounted for, untraceable. Just like that. Gone. She went berserk, smashing everything she could lay her hands on. When Maria opened the door to see what was happening she got a fist in her face for her pains and she quickly retreated. Alleysia's rage was all encompassing, welling up from deep within her like red-hot lava, erupting again and again. She desperately needed to kill somebody, to release her anger before it blew her mind. Nobody went near her. She took a semi-automatic pistol from the drawer next to her bed and fired all thirteen shots into the mattress before throwing the gun into the mirror, shattering it.

Finally she was under control again. In the darkest recesses of her mind she was aware that she seemed to lose her temper more often and with greater fury. Her father would have been displeased – control his byword.

She began thinking about the forthcoming meeting onboard the *Mermaid*. Every senior person in her organisation would be there to see her welcome the heads of dozens of other cartels and their senior people. With Syndicate profits expected to start in excess of one hundred billion dollars and climbing rapidly she was sure of a full attendance. Picking up an internal telephone she called the bridge. The Captain assured her everything was in hand. Yes, a new name was being painted on the stern and bow of the ship. Yes, the port of registration was changed from Le Havre to Barcelona. Yes, the appropriate paperwork was taken from the safe and placed on the bridge.

When she hung up she wished for the hundredth time that Ojdanic was there. Still, he would arrive before departure. She always felt safer when he was around.

Although it wasn't his real name, Slobodan Ojdanic had been using it for so long that he had practically forgotten he had been born Steven Ojinski in 1950, in New York. He had skipped America twenty-five years earlier when a warrant for his arrest had been issued following the discovery of a murdered and mutilated family in the Bronx. He had been murdering and mutilating ever since, in one country or another. Now, after five years of hard work, he was the chief enforcer for the Georgian cartel. It was a job he took very seriously. All the necessary arrangements had been made and he had plenty of time to join the ship. He had left instructions that he was not to be disturbed unless it was a real emergency while he enjoyed a well deserved, long weekend. Slobodan was relaxing at home.

He owned nearly the whole of the island of Lastovo, a rectangular lump of rock, ten kilometres in length from east to west by five kilometres north to south. Ubli was its only village consisting of a few dozen houses, a church, a tavern and a small harbour. The island also boasted a deserted castle a few kilometres to the east of Ubli that Ojdanic had wanted to buy and renovate. Much to his chagrin he had not succeeded. The village and the castle were the only parts of the island he didn't own. Instead he had built his own complex, completed a year earlier, which sat right in the middle of the island, dominating the skyline from its position eight hundred metres above sea level. It had cost a fortune, every item required to build and furnish it needing to be brought from Dubrovnik, a hundred kilometres due east. To the north was the much larger island of Korcula, while from the patio, on a clear day and using powerful binoculars, he could see Italy, one hundred and ten kilometres to the south-west.

The staff house contained four bedrooms, one for each of his servants. These were all men, exceedingly tough and vicious men, who doubled as bodyguards. They were well paid to look after him and, when required, Alleysia. For years his dream had been that, when the timing was right, he would take over from her. It would not be a friendly take-over but he had to admit to himself that he was looking forward to it.

The main house formed three sides of a square, built around the sparkling blue water of a huge swimming pool. Changing rooms stood along one wall and in a corner there was a fully stocked bar under a thatched roof. Next to it was a charcoal-burning barbecue big enough to cook for twenty guests. At that moment Ojdanic had a Bloody Mary in one big fist and a pair of tongs in the other as he expertly turned over a steak. There were half a dozen nubile, naked young ladies in the pool, splashing and shrieking happily. His servant-bodyguards sat at a nearby table, large drinks in front of them, discussing the girls' attributes. They had only arrived a few hours earlier and there was a great deal of anticipation in the air – the coming night held great promise. Ojdanic enjoyed barbecues. He prided himself on the marinating of the meat, trying different recipes. His favourite was a whiskey and orange concoction in which he soaked chicken for at least twenty-four hours. A long table held bottles of wine and salads of various kinds. When they were finished with the girls, they would be given a handsome bonus and taken back to Pescara in Italy. There they would return to the university to continue their studies. They would, he smiled, be tired and sore but they would earn more in three days than they would in six months working in a bar or a hotel, trying to supplement their meagre grants. Besides, he liked educated young ladies.

Ojdanic was fit for his age. Six feet two of solid muscle, he took great care of himself. He worked out every day and he and the other four often practised their martial arts skills together. So far none of them had beaten him, although Ricky – he preferred to use an Anglicised version of Ricarovic – the youngest at twenty-nine, had come close on a number of occasions. His craggy face lit up at the thought that he could still take the younger man, using a few tricks he still had up his sleeve.

'Come and get it!' he yelled.

There were cries of delight and the girls swam to the side of the pool, climbing out, picking up towels to drape around themselves. Now, as the sun set, the wind was picking up and a storm threatened. They would have to move indoors shortly.

His men joined them, crowding around the hot coals, plates held out. Fun and laughter were the order of the day.

Hunter had reported to Major General MacGregor, the officer commanding the British troops in Bosnia. Their meeting was held in private. He told the General precisely what they had accomplished and MacGregor agreed to clear up after them. The General was a life long friend of Macnair's and thoroughly approved of TIFAT's objectives. He only wished that he could operate with a similar degree of flexibility. Hunter declined the offer of a whisky, pleading that he needed to get to Dubrovnik as quickly as possible. Their next operation only had a twenty-four hour window. After that, God alone knew where Ojdanic would be.

The General nodded his understanding. 'I can get you there by air,' he offered.

Hunter thought about it but then shook his head, reluctantly. 'Thanks, sir, but we need the equipment in the Land Rover.'

'I'll have the car taken as well. There's a C130 I can send. It has a genuine reason for going to Dubrovnik and you can hop aboard. It'll save a lot of time.'

Hunter's smile threatened to break his jaw. 'That's very good of you, sir. It'll save us a heck of a lot of time. Especially getting through the roadblocks and past the patrols. Thank you seems somehow inadequate.'

'Think nothing of it. Malcolm's been telling me what's going on. We go back a long way.'

Hunter stood up. 'Sir, I'll get organised. When can we go?'

'An hour suit you?'

'Perfectly, sir. And thank you.' Although he was not wearing uniform, Hunter saluted, about turned and marched from the room. The Herky Bird would save them hours of driving.

Ruth drove the car up the ramp and into the belly of the aircraft. Two air-crewmen stropped the car securely to the deck of the plane. Declining the offer to sit in the small cabin in the front of the plane, just behind the pilots, the team settled down in the Land Rover to grab some sleep. All three were only dimly aware of the plane taking off.

In less than an hour they arrived at Dubrovnik. Dunston drove them from the military part of the airport out onto Highway 2. When they arrived at the port, they easily found the marina and the marine broker's office. There they took possession of a thirty-five foot pleasure craft capable of reaching a speed of thirty knots.

Buying food and drink at a local store, they stripped the car of its extra gear and stored the equipment onboard the boat. An hour and a half after arriving, with the fuel and water tanks topped off, they departed.

It was a two-hour trip to the island if they travelled at full speed. But if they did, they would never arrive, running out of fuel a few miles short of their destination. It was a balancing act of endurance over speed. The hull could be pushed along, on the plane, at thirty knots, but at a prodigious rate of fuel use. At twenty-two knots the boat cruised at an acceptable speed while at the same time being comparatively economical with the fuel. They would be arriving with the tanks nearly a quarter full. The broker who sold them the boat assured them that there was a fuelling pontoon at Ubli.

Half way to their destination, with the island of Miljet on their starboard side, they were forced to slow down. A storm was brewing away to the west and bringing with it squally weather that turned the Mediterranean from a millpond into an uncomfortable, chaotic sea. The boat, speeding along so smoothly only minutes earlier, was now slamming from wave to wave. The sea was coming from an arc that swept from the south-west to the west. Not only was the boat bouncing but it was also corkscrewing. The motion soon had Ruth reduced to lying down in the saloon, wedged between a bench seat and a table. The two men sat in the cockpit, enjoying themselves, both awed by the display of brute force that was contained in the storm.

'I'll make some coffee,' Dunston yelled above the wind.

Hunter shook his head. 'No, thanks. I'd rather have tea. Coffee has unhappy memories of a storm-tossed sea when I was a midshipman. I only have to smell it during a storm and my stomach starts heaving.'

Dunston smiled and nodded. 'Okay. I'll see to Ruth as well.' Sliding open the hatch, he let himself below. Ruth lay curled up, her eyes closed, her complexion a pasty green.

Dunston pumped water into an aluminium kettle, fixed it with a clamp onto a gas cooker and lit the gas. He found mugs and as an afterthought traced the bread and salami they had bought.

A few minutes later he was back in the cockpit with tea and sandwiches.

'Excellent,' said Hunter, spying the sandwiches. 'A sea running as fast and high as this one always makes me hungry.'

'What speed are we making good?'

Hunter fiddled with the GPS, the American satellite system that told the user precisely where he was, what course he was on and what speed he was making. 'We're down to fifteen knots over the ground and,' he pressed another button, 'we're making good twenty knots through the water.' That meant the sea was running at five knots against them. 'We'll be there around twenty-two hundred.'

'I'll pull the Pilot for the area as well as the charts,' said Dunston, opening a drawer in the chart table. He rummaged around for few moments. 'Have you had a look at this?' he asked, frowning.

Hunter grinned. 'Yep, a few minutes ago. I'd hoped that with God on your side you might have found something I'd missed. I assumed, wrongly, that we'd have a complete set of books and charts. Look at the date of the one we do have.'

Dunston looked closely at the bottom right hand corner. 'Good grief! It's over twenty years out of date.'

'Makes approaching an unknown shore interesting, to say the least.'

Dunston sighed. 'That, old pal, is an understatement.' The boat started down a long, low roller. 'Get ready for a series of roughers behind it,' he said.

Coming to the end of the long wave the boat hit a series of short sharp waves that had the hull thudding heavily into the sea. They were in the middle of a typical Mediterranean blow, uncomfortable and highly dangerous.

Dunston stood looking at the radar, adjusting the gain, and reducing the background clutter. Checking the picture against the chart, he said, 'There are three vessels crossing right to left. The line of contacts looking like a stationary convoy is a string of rocks.'

Hunter raised his binoculars and scanned the sea. The storm

had brought an early twilight and the ships he was looking at were visible only because they were showing their steaming lights. He checked their bearings, to see that they would pass clear and settled back into the captain's chair.

When they finally began their approach to Lastovo they had a bit of luck. The wind began to abate and it veered to the north. The entrance to Ubli was from the west, and although it was partially sheltered, with a heavy sea and against a strong wind, it would have been dangerous. Passing a small island at the entrance to the harbour, the sea calmed considerably and the wind, though whistling overhead, failed to affect the boat. Ruth arrived in the cockpit carrying mugs of tea and looking a good deal better if somewhat abashed.

'Sorry about that,' she said. 'It just proved too much.'

Hunter smiled. 'I don't underestimate the effects of seasickness. It's a sod and can be very debilitating. But,' he took the offered mug, 'welcome back to the land of the living.'

Taking the engines out of gear, he let the boat idle for a few seconds while they looked around to find a place to berth. The harbour was a natural curve in the rock with a breakwater sticking out a hundred metres or so. There were a dozen fishing boats, moored stern to the wall, bobbing alongside each other like a floating catwalk. There was a space between the end boat and the breakwater.

Deftly, Hunter swung the helm and made a stern board towards the space. Dunston dropped an anchor and Ruth stood ready to jump ashore as the boat neared the wall. Line in hand, she leapt onto the wall and dropped the bight of the rope over a bollard. Hunter left the engines idling while he helped her secure the aft lines and then Dunston used the capstan to tighten up on the anchor. They were secured alongside, stern to, in a classic Mediterranean moor.

The housing that fronted the harbour started about fifty metres away and curved around following the lay of the land. Lights shone from a tavern about a hundred metres from where they stood. They could hear noise and laughter. Apart from the merrymakers there appeared to be not a soul around to witness their arrival. Below decks, with the curtains drawn to keep out any prying eyes, they made their preparations. They intended arriving at Ojdanic's house around midnight.

Changing into combat gear, they pulled on yachting foul weather jackets and trousers. Should anyone see them they would appear to be merely stretching their legs on dry land after a bumpy sea journey wearing, the ubiquitous yellow sou'wester gear beloved of yachtsmen. Once clear of the village they stripped off their jackets and trousers and hid them behind a rock. Each carried a bag, slung over a shoulder, containing their equipment.

Slobodan Ojdanic rose from the bed, leaving the two girls asleep. Padding across the floor to the bathroom, he paused to look out of the huge bay window that dominated the room. He looked towards the east, to the lights of the island of Miljet, forty kilometres away. The storm had cleaned the air, leaving it crystal clear, though a lot cooler than it had been earlier.

The buzzing was so faint that it seemed more imagined than real but even so Ojdanic was suddenly alert, his heart rate increasing, tension building. Somebody had broached his defences.

He dressed quickly in a pair of dark trousers and a black sweatshirt. The high-sided canvas shoes he slipped on were the same type worn by special-services personnel the world over. From the back of a closet he took out a shoulder holster and a Glock 17 automatic. Pressing the catch on the left side of the butt, he removed the magazine. He checked it was full and at the same time ejected the round in the chamber. Pulling the trigger on a loud click, he reloaded the weapon. It now held eighteen rounds of 9mm Parabellum and was ready to fire. He pondered for a moment on the advisability of using a silencer but then thought better of it. Three rapid taps and a scraping noise on the door told him his men were outside. He grinned. The night was turning out better than he had expected.

He opened the door. 'I've checked the monitors,' said Henri Alaccio, a Corsican whose hobby was killing and who worked for Ojdanic as it enabled him to fulfil his pleasures. 'There are three of them. They are coming in very slowly, very carefully. From the way they're behaving, I'd say they're professionals.'

Ojdanic nodded and walked towards the room that contained the surveillance equipment. He stood looking at the monitors for a few minutes. 'They've frozen the cameras and somehow managed to confuse the listening devices.'

'Agreed.' Alaccio spoke with a thick, guttural accent. His long arms hung by his sides, the fingers flexing, itching to place them around the necks of one of the intruders. 'The transponders are also falling off one by one.' The screen showing the transponder network was gradually blanking out as each transponder was taken out of action.

'Very professional,' said Ojdanic in admiration. 'Where are the others?'

'They've gone to take care of them.'

'I want one alive,' said Ojdanic, sharply.

'I've already issued the orders.'

'Good. Then we will go outside and help.' Lifting down a personal radio, he clipped it to his belt and inserted the earpiece. He established contact with the other three.

Ojdanic led the way. The only piece of surveillance equipment that was still operational was the infrared heat seeker. In his hand he held a palm-sized monitor that was a relay from the main screen. He watched as the three tiny dots of the intruders merged with those of his three men.

So far the black box sensor had found the traces of electrical circuits that had led them to the transponders. If lifted slowly from the ground, without breaking the beam connections, the batteries could be dropped from the bottom without setting off the alarm. One by one they had taken them out of the circuit. The cameras were equally easily dealt with. Over each lens they slipped an electronic cap that froze the picture electronically. Anybody watching the screen would see nothing untoward. Hunter spoke. 'Something's wrong. We're missing something.'

'How do you know?' Ruth whispered into her throat mike.

'It's just a feeling. Split up. Ruth, go right. Matt, take the left. The house is only another ten metres or so through the trees.' The path they had chosen to approach the house passed through a thick, wooded area. Although it was slower, it also meant that much of the normal surveillance equipment was either degraded or useless. They had found what they had expected but Hunter wasn't happy. Nothing else showed on the black box.

'Down!' Dunston said. 'I hear something.'

The other two stopped, squatted and listened. Hunter sniffed the air. The scent was from behind. Soap! He identified the smell and whirled around just in time to see a figure looming behind Ruth. Through his NVGs the tableau had a blue tint to it that dulled the glint on the knife held over Ruth's back. Hunter's snap shot hit the assassin in the head, blowing it apart. The silencer made a sound barely greater than a sheep coughing on a distant hill. The falling body made a nerve-jangling noise as Ruth whirled around to see what was happening. The blood drained from her face when she saw her dead attacker.

Hunter said, 'Careful. They know we're here.'

Ricky dropped from a tree and landed immediately behind Hunter. He had a knife in one hand and a gun in a holster at his side. Even as Hunter whirled around to face his young adversary the knife was raised and about to be plunged into him. Hunter threw himself backwards, knocking his head on a tree. He was dazed for a second, trying to collect his wits. Ricky reversed the knife in his hand and prepared to throw it. Hunter's head was clearing fast but not fast enough. He tried to lift the gun he was holding but the movement seemed to take forever. His arm wouldn't do what his brain told it. Suddenly the young man staggered, a look of alarm replacing his original smile. A second shot, again fired by Ruth, knocked Ricky to the ground.

'Thanks,' Hunter croaked. He stood up, shaking his head to clear it, flexing his fingers, getting the feeling back into his hand. In the fall he had also hit his shoulder pinching a nerve, temporarily causing a loss of sensation in his arm and hand. There was a sound to his left. Seeing two figures in a silent grapple he dashed through the trees to go to Dunston's aid. He needn't have bothered. When he got there Dunston was standing over the inert body. Hunter knelt beside it and checked for a pulse. It was faint but steady. The man would be out for some time.

'I saw him standing behind the tree,' said Dunston. 'I just stopped and waited right next to him. The rest was easy.'

Hunter nodded. 'How many more do you think?'

'No way of telling. Our information said there were at least five, perhaps as many as eight.'

'Ruth? Can you hear me?' Hunter asked. There was no reply. 'Ruth! Ruth! Are you there?' He spoke in a harsh whisper. Dread washed through him.

25

Macnair called out. 'Come in.'

'Malcolm,' said a smiling Christine Woolford, entering the office, 'I wondered what you were doing tonight.'

Macnair kept a straight face and shook his head. 'Nothing. Why?'

'I've waited long enough for you to ask me to dinner, so I'm asking you,' she said.

Macnair smiled back. 'I've been meaning to. It's just that . . .' he trailed off, unsure of himself.

'It's just that you didn't know what I'd say and didn't relish the idea of being turned down.'

He nodded. 'That's about it, I guess. I'm too old to suffer rejection.' He made a self-deprecating gesture of his hands and head.

The MEP laughed. 'You can command battalions but can't ask a lady to dinner. My God, what am I going to do with you?'

They let the question hang in the air. The tension in the office was suddenly electric as her implication sank in.

Macnair nodded. 'A great deal, I hope. Let's say drinks in the wardroom at seven thirty and then we'll go into Dunfermline. There's a restaurant there that sells food the right side of edible.'

'Is that the best you can do?' she teased him.

'Tonight it is. I need to be available. Matters are coming to a head. I'm only waiting for confirmation of the whereabouts of the crime cartels' meeting place. We know there are four ships, all identical, all bearing the same name. Three we've traced to Rio de Janairo, Singapore and Helsinki. The fourth is missing. We have practically every airport, every port of call and virtually every frontier crossing covered. Some of the men that are now working with the crime syndicates are well known international criminals who used to be independent. With the damage we've been inflicting on them and their organisations I'm hoping we'll panic them into making a mistake. When they do we'll be ready for them.'

'When will that be?'

'Within thirty-six hours,' came the certain reply.

'How can you be so sure?'

'The tape gave us an exact date. What we urgently need to confirm is where.'

The MEP nodded and smiled. 'Good luck. I'll see you later.' On that note, she left.

Macnair pulled a folder towards him, frowning. He began putting the finishing touches to his encrypted report that would go via the Ministry of Defence to Number Ten the next day. It was marked *Eyes Only, The Prime Minister* but Macnair knew that at least five people would see it. They would be the buffoon with the title of Deputy Prime Minister, The Secretary of Defence, The Home Secretary and, under the assumption that he had some knowledge of security matters because of his job, the Secretary for Northern Ireland. Of them all Macnair rated the Home Secretary and the Secretary for NI the most. In spite of the autonomy he had, General Macnair still had to report to his political masters. He would have been dismayed to learn that the circulation did not stop there. The remainder of the cabinet also read his reports, although sometimes as much as twenty-four or forty-eight hours later.

That evening Macnair and Christine Woolford were driven to the restaurant, with two men riding shotgun. Macnair felt that he should stay at his headquarters but he also knew that he needed to relax. To return refreshed and ready for whatever the next few days threw at him. One highly disturbing factor needed his attention. Attacks against the law enforcement services were occurring with worrying frequency. Furthermore, there was a disquieting pattern to them that suggested a highly placed spy was passing information to the cartels. Hopefully, his latest report to Downing Street would help to solve the problem.

The dinner passed very pleasantly. The food was good, pheasant for Christine and venison for Macnair. Although there was no need for abstinence, neither of them drank very much, leaving a few inches in the bottom of a bottle of fine Australian Shiraz. There was no need to hurry. Both were completely at ease in each other's company. As they were leaving the restaurant the ringing of Macnair's mobile phone shattered their peace. On answering he felt a surge of anger. The American DEA had just found the bodies of three of their operatives.

Ruth was on her knees with a gun held to her head. Ojdanic had ripped out the radio and was busy putting the receiver into his own ear. 'Hey, if anyone out there can hear me, I suggest you come on in with your hands held high. Otherwise the little girl will get it.' He spoke with an exaggerated American drawl, a parody of a cowboy. 'I'll count to three. One . . . two . . .'

'All right. We give up,' said Hunter in a loud voice, emerging from the undergrowth, his hands in the air. A second later Matt Dunston appeared from the other side of the garden, also with his hands up.

'Come and join us, gentlemen. At least, I assume you're men underneath your masks. Hey, Henri,' he raised his voice, 'anymore out there?'

'No, chief,' said Alaccio emerging from the house. 'According to the infra-red sensors we have two cooling bodies and these three.'

'Plus Paulo. How is he?'

'Very angry and with a sore head. I have sent him to do a perimeter search.'

'Don't bother. There'll be nobody else around.'

'How can you be so . . .' Alaccio trailed off when he saw the look on his boss's face.

'Okay, okay,' he shrugged. 'I'll tell him to come in.' He turned and went back into the house.

Ojdanic sensed the sudden tension in his captives and chuckled. 'Take it easy, gentlemen. I'll kill her before you move half a pace. Then I'll surely drop one of you before the other reaches me. Then the fun would start.' He grinned, hoping one of them would start something.

Hunter caught a flicker of movement up at one of the second storey windows and glanced upwards. He saw the curtains twitch back into place.

Alaccio returned, nonchalantly pointing a gun at Hunter, 'Paulo will be here in a minute or two. What will we do with these three?'

Ruth twisted her head painfully, her hair gripped tightly by Ojdanic, and mouthed "Sorry" to Hunter. In return he gave a slight shake of his head and a half smile. It wasn't anybody's fault, least of all hers.

'Lock them up. We'll deal with them after the girls have left.'

That was interesting. So there were guests as well. Perhaps one of them had moved the curtain, thought Hunter.

The man known as Paulo appeared and walked straight up to Hunter, careful to keep out of Ojdanic's line of fire. Stopping close to Hunter he looked him in the eyes. Without warning he launched a pile driver of a blow at Hunter's gut. Sensing the blow Hunter moved back half a pace. Even so he still took a hard knock that left him winded. A smash to the head threw him onto his knees, his ears ringing, his vision fading in and out. He saw the foot drawing back and as it landed he rolled with the kick, grabbed the foot and gave a mighty twist. The cracking of a bone was loud in the quiet night. Paulo gave a scream of pain and reached for the gun he had slung over his shoulder. Nobody moved as the barrel swung towards Hunter. Standing on one foot Paulo made a mistake. He placed the other on the ground and collapsed with a screech of agony. The gun was lying on the patio but still pointed at Hunter. Paulo's finger was curling around the trigger when Hunter managed to kick the barrel to one side. There was a loud bang as the gun went off, the bullet spending itself in the undergrowth of the garden.

'Enough,' said Ojdanic. 'Stop, I say.' He pointed his gun at Paulo. 'Go and see to your foot. We'll question them later and find out what's going on. I want to know who they are and who sent them.'

Paulo limped away cursing, looking malevolently at Hunter.

'Henri, lock them in the cellar. They cannot escape from there. We will get the answers in the morning. In the meantime we will look to our guests. Leave the other two until tomorrow. We'll get rid of all the bodies tomorrow night.' The last statement left the team in no doubt of the fate that awaited them.

'Strip to your underwear,' ordered Ojdanic to Hunter and Dunston.

The two men did as they were told.

'Take your shoes off also,' Henri said.

They stood in just their shorts and a T-shirt. Henri patted them down but found nothing.

All this time Ruth had been on her knees. Ojdanic yanked her to her feet. 'Now you. And hurry it up.'

Ruth slipped off her clothing until she stood in nothing but her bra and panties. If her near naked body had any effect on her captors neither man showed it. It was obvious that she had nothing hidden on her.

'You two,' said Henri, gesturing with his gun, 'come with me. If you behave the girl lives.'

The entrance to the cellar was nearby. They were prodded down a few concrete steps and through a door. A few seconds later Ruth was pushed in after them.

She stumbled into Hunter's arms. He gave her a smile and a hug. 'Nick . . . I . . . I'm so sorry. Are you all right?'

'Shshsh,' he placed a finger on her lips. 'It doesn't matter.' He put a hand to his head and winced. 'Luckily I have a thick skull. We're safe for the moment and all we have to do now is get out. Then we finish the job and escape from the island.'

She smiled wanly. 'Just like that. I love your optimism.'

While they had been talking Dunston had been searching the

cellar. He found a light switch and turned it on. The room was about fifteen metres by twelve, the floor was bare concrete, the walls rough stone. The whole space was completely empty. There were no windows and only the one door. The lock was solid, heavy and recessed inside the door. On the way through both men had noticed it was a double deadlock and practically impossible to break open. It was also cold and Ruth was beginning to shiver. Hunter took off his T-shirt and passed it to her.

'Put this on. I'll manage to keep warm.'

'How?' Ruth asked.

'Leave it to me,' he smiled. As usual, his eternal optimism buoyed her up.

'I've found this,' said Dunston, holding up a flat piece of broken steel shaped like an irregular triangle. It was about five centimetres along the base with one side four centimetres and the other about three. One edge was rounded and smooth but the other two were irregular and sharp.

'What is it?' Hunter asked.

'I'd say it's a piece of trowel. It was imbedded in concrete in the wall. It looks like it broke off and was left by the builders.'

'Well done,' said Hunter. 'Let me try it.' Taking the piece of metal he knelt in front of the lock and scored the wood using one of the broken edges of the trowel. It easily dug into the door. He began shaving the wood, digging deeper with every cut. After about ten minutes he rested, flexing his fingers.

'Here,' said Dunston, 'let me have a go. We'll take it in turns.' He knelt in Hunter's place. The trowel sliced into the door and he scraped a half centimetre strip of wood, running along the grain, from the top of the lock to the bottom.

They changed places every ten minutes. The lock was set about a centimetre and a half inside the door and was about twenty centimetres wide and fifteen-high. It was made of steel, painted a dull grey and as they stripped the wood clear it became obvious that there were four screws also holding the lock in place. After nearly two hours of finger aching work they had cleared the wood from around the lock. Dunston fitted the edge of the trowel into the screw and slowly twisted it. The screw moved easily. Within a few minutes the four screws were removed and the lock lifted out. Hunter gripped the door and gently pushed. It didn't move. He pushed harder, with the same result.

'Damnation! There must be a bar across the outside.' He and Dunston put their shoulders to the door and gave a mighty heave. Nothing happened.

'Now what?' asked Ruth.

'Now we keep digging,' replied Dunston. He took the broken trowel and continued digging. Hacking away, the trowel slipped, slicing into his finger. 'Hell!' He dropped the piece of steel and sucked the cut.

'Here, let me have a look,' said Ruth. She took his hand. 'Nasty. I'll rip a bit off your shirt and bandage it.'

While she did so Hunter picked up the trowel and continued attacking the door. The trowel slipped and went right through the wood and almost out the other side. Carefully, Hunter pulled it back, fearful that he might lose it. When he looked closely at the sliver of hole he was aghast to find, not blackness, but the dawning of a new day. Their labours had lasted through the night.

The discovery put added urgency into their efforts. To fail now would mean certain death. After all, Ojdanic did not need all three of them kept alive to find out what he wanted to know. Since taking away the lock they had been working on a long strip, from high up to the bottom of the door, a centimetre wide on their side but narrowing to the thickness of the trowel. By now the trowel was becoming exceedingly blunt, their hands and fingers ached and all three had more than a few cuts and splinters.

'Look!' said Hunter. 'Here and here. We're through but no light is showing.'

'It's the bars,' said Dunston. 'Do they lift or do they slide?' he asked, wondering aloud.

'They must lift,' said Ruth. 'The archway would prevent the bars from sliding.'

'A good point.' Hunter prodded with the trowel. 'It's not long enough. It won't reach the bar with enough left this side to effect a purchase. What do we do now?'

'Now,' said Ruth, 'I take off my bra.'

Macnair had not slept. There had been a further eighteen incidents across Europe. Customs officials and policemen had been killed although no more undercover agents' bodies had been found. The stakes had been stepped up to unsustainable levels.

Finally, almost falling asleep at his desk, he stumbled away to his bedroom. In the half-life between sleeping and waking the answer came to him. Macnair leapt out of bed. Dressing quickly, he made his way towards his office. His computer was still switched on and he sat down to review the work he had finished only a short time earlier. It was as he had thought. The traitor had to be someone in the government. The attacks on officialdom that had been occurring across Europe were too well staged to have been coincidences. In each case, the men and women who had been targeted had either just completed or were working on important operations against the crime cartels. The only person who'd had the complete picture of the operation was himself and he'd reported it only to the Prime Minister. The leak was from the highest level of government. He sighed. He needed to plug it, fast. An idea took hold and gripped him. He could put precious resources and manpower into finding the traitor or – or he could use the person, whoever he or she might be.

Reaching for the latest *"Eyes only"* report he had been putting the finishing touches to, he began to tap on his keyboard with his two index fingers. The irreverent thought that he should become a novelist flashed across his mind.

Ruth had modestly turned her back, reached under Hunter's T-shirt and removed her bra. She began unpicking it. From around the cups she removed thin copper wire that she handed to Hunter. Holding the two pieces, about thirty centimetres long, he proceeded to twist them together. While he was doing so Dunston scraped more wood away from the area above the bars. Bending the end of the wire back, Hunter made a hook that he fitted through the door and under the bar. Holding the wire vertically against the door, he carefully raised the bar a millimetre at a time. He lifted it as far as he could and stopped.

'What's the problem?' Ruth asked.

It was Dunston who replied. 'The bar's as high as it'll go. Possibly clear of the bracket, but if Nick pulls any further the wire will unbend and the bar will drop back into place.'

'Correct,' said Hunter. 'Try pushing it away with the trowel. Only, for God's sake, don't push too far and lose it.'

'I think,' said Dunston, 'it's more for our sake than God's.' Pushing at the bar, he felt it move. He pushed further and then said, 'Try lowering the wire.'

Hunter slid the wire down the door, feeling the bar sliding past the horizontal. The wire vibrated in his fingers as the bar slid through the hook and fell with a clatter onto the concrete outside.

They froze, listening intently, breath held as they waited for a reaction. Nothing happened, no yells. Nobody came to investigate the noise. They repeated the performance on the lower bar, only this time, when the bar was raised, instead of pushing it away from the door, they intended pushing the door open. Dunston could then reach around the opening and quietly lift the bar out of its bracket. But when the bar was raised the wire slipped and the bar again fell with a clatter. Their luck had deserted them. The bar landed upright near the edge of the door and toppled straight back, jamming between the first step and the door. When they pushed the door moved only a few centimetres and stuck. It was locked as solidly as when they had started.

'Damn,' Hunter said.

Gloom and despondency settled on them for a few seconds. Hunter composed himself and said, 'Come on. Never say die. We dig out the rest of the wood around the lock and get an arm out.'

'There isn't enough time,' said Ruth, dully. Even her belief in him was beginning to wane.

'Maybe. But I'm damned if I'm going to wait for Ojdanic and his thugs to put a bullet in us without trying.' Wearily he knelt by the door and began attacking the wood again.

Ruth, who had proven time and again that she had the acutest hearing amongst them suddenly said, 'Quiet. Somebody's coming.'

Hunter stopped what he was doing. Dunston took up a stance behind the door just in case he had an opportunity to attack whoever was approaching. They exchanged puzzled expressions as they heard a faint scratching at the door.

Ruth said, 'Who is it?'

A female voice responded softly. 'Who are you?' She sounded English and educated.

Hunter answered. 'We are NATO officers. We came to arrest Ojdanic. He's wanted for war crimes in Bosnia. Can you help us?'

There was a sharp intake of breath. By way of an answer there was the noise of iron scraping on concrete and the door opened. The face that was framed in the doorway was beautiful. The girl was tall and slim, her blonde hair cascading around her face like a shampoo advert. She was dressed in tight fitting jeans and a loose sweater, which did nothing to conceal her charms.

'I'm Linda Donovan.' She added, 'From Chichester. I over-heard some of your talk last night. I guessed you were British. I would have come sooner but I couldn't get away. We're getting ready to leave.'

'My name is Hunter, Nick Hunter. These two are Matt Dunston and Ruth Golightly. We're indebted to you. Now you'd better go before you're caught. These men wouldn't hesitate to kill you all, as well as us, if they found out you'd helped us to escape. In case we don't make it, when you get to wherever you're going telephone TIFAT HQ at Rosyth in Scotland and ask for a General Macnair. Tell him what you saw. Will you do that?'

'TIFAT, Rosyth, Scotland. General Macnair. Okay. I'll do it. Now, I must go.'

'Okay. And thanks.' Hunter smiled at her. 'You've been very brave.'

She nodded but whether it was in acceptance of the compliment or in agreement with it none of them could tell. She dashed away, a beautiful wraith in the strengthening light.

Dunston picked up the iron bar and hefted it in his hand. It would make a useful weapon. Hunter picked up the other one. Waiting a few minutes, they listened to the sounds of a new day. Finally Hunter led the way outside. By now the sun was beginning to creep over the horizon on what promised to be a fine, warm day. Stopping and listening, they sniffed the air, sensing their surroundings like animals approaching a trap.

'What shall we do with the door?' Ruth whispered.

'Push it shut and leave it,' said Hunter, quietly. 'The bars are too useful to leave behind.'

Ruth manoeuvred the door into position. In the shadows, it looked normal until one got up close. 'What now?' she asked.

'Now we finish the mission,' said Hunter, grimly. 'But remember we need Ojdanic alive. Hush!' He held up his hand and the three of them heard the sound of voices and girlish laughter. From the other side of the house they heard a car draw up. A voice called 'Taxi!' There were muffled sounds of laughter and squeals of delight and a few minutes later the car departed, taking the noise with it.

'Come on,' said Hunter. 'Let's go.' Darting up the few steps from the cellar, he led the way across the patio to a set of French windows. He tried the handle and the door opened silently. The three of them stepped into a tastefully decorated lounge with a bare, highly polished wooden floor and white walls with an abundance of quality pictures hanging from them. Along one wall was a leather sofa capable of seating four people comfortably and in front of it was a low occasional table of solid wood. Three matching leather chairs were placed around and in one corner stood a well-stocked bar. Across the room was a door that . . . was opening towards them before their eyes.

Hunter moved quickest. He stepped to one side and darted the half dozen paces to hide behind the door. Dunston stepped behind one of the chairs and knelt down, his arm extended over his shoulder, ready to throw the iron bar like a spear. Ruth stood at the window.

Alaccio walked through the door expecting to find the room empty. Ojdanic's henchman was two paces inside the room before he saw her framed in the dawn light and his jaw dropped in surprise. He stood stock still for a second, enough time for Hunter to push the door shut and smash the man across the back of his head. Henri Alaccio's last vision on earth was of Ruth, his last thought of how she had escaped. Hunter grabbed the body and dragged it across the room, stuffing it behind the bar. A quick search showed that Alaccio had been unarmed. With difficulty Hunter stripped the T-shirt off the body and put it on himself.

'By my calculation,' said Dunston, 'there are only two to go.'

'Agreed,' replied Hunter. 'But I'd feel a lot safer if we had a gun or two.' Even as he spoke, he was opening a drawer under the bar. It held only towels. A second drawer had various implements and rummaging around he found a sharp knife, obviously used for slicing fruit for different drinks. He hefted it in his hand, then threw it into the air, spinning and catching it by the handle. 'It'll do,' he announced. He handed the iron bar to Ruth. 'You'd better have this.'

'Let's go,' said Dunston.

Opening the door, Hunter saw that it led to a corridor. There were doors on either side. At the end, through an open arch, came the sound of somebody moving around, handling things, opening and shutting cupboards.

Hunter padded silently along the corridor. On the left he passed a wide staircase. Signalling to Ruth to stay on the other side of the stairs, he and Dunston approached the arch. When they got closer it became obvious the room was the kitchen and that there was one person inside. Hunter knelt down and looked around the edge of the wall. Ojdanic was busy preparing breakfast, breaking eggs into a frying pan, apparently oblivious to any danger.

Flicking oil onto the eggs, Ojdanic heard the beginning of a yell coming from the corridor and spun around. Paulo, hobbling downstairs, had seen Hunter and Dunston. Drawing his pistol, he was shouting a warning when Ruth smashed in his skull with the iron bar. His gun clattered onto the wooden floor, followed by his body.

Ojdanic had the reflexes of a leopard. He dived across the room, throwing himself onto the table, his fingers clutching for the gun lying on its surface. He almost made it. Hunter threw the knife with unerring accuracy straight into Ojdanic's hand, severing tendons and burying itself into the palm, the blade buried up to the hilt. Ojdanic screamed but still scrabbled for the gun with his left hand. Dunston stepped into the room and using both hands threw the bar like a knife. It slowly turned through the air, flying straight and true, smashing Ojdanic in the middle of his forehead. It was a killing stroke and Ojdanic slid limply off the table.

Dunston checked for a pulse. 'Damn, he's dead. Sorry, General.'

'Macnair won't be pleased but there was nothing else for it. That was too close for comfort,' said Hunter. 'Are you okay?' He looked back at Ruth.

She nodded, a little pale. 'Fine. What about you two?'

'Never better.' He turned to Dunston. 'That was some throw. Now let's find our clothes and equipment and take this place apart. We'll see what information we can find and send it to the General before we leave.'

Their search turned up the fact that a helicopter was due later that day to take Ojdanic and his men off the island. It did not say where the final destination was only that it would refuel at a small airport south of Rome before flying onwards. They passed the information to the General.

Macnair finished encrypting the report and sent it *Eyes Only* to the Prime Minister. Next, he contacted the senior officers of select security forces across Europe. He explained parts of his plan and enlisted their help. They leapt at the opportunity with alacrity. Finally satisfied that he had done all that he could, Macnair stood and stretched. The phone rang and he picked up the receiver. With a sinking feeling in the pit of his stomach he received more bad news. Bombs had exploded at police stations in cities across Europe. Then he took Isobel's call. It did not improve his temper.

26

'What do you mean they aren't on any of the ships we've been tracking?' Macnair snapped at Isobel. Lack of sleep was making him short-tempered.

'Sorry, sir,' said Isobel, stiffly. 'Just that. We've been checking and double-checking. There's been no unusual activity on any of the ships we've identified. The cartels are not using any of them.'

'Then it must be the fourth one, dammit.'

'Yes, sir, I agree.'

Her emphasis on "sir" was a hint to Macnair that he was out of order. He immediately calmed down and said, 'Sorry, Isobel. I didn't mean to snap your head off. I'm just a bit tetchy, that's all. Our whole strategy relies on us finding out where the heads of the cartels are meeting. With what we've confirmed we know the meeting's in less than thirty-six hours.'

'I'm aware of that, General,' said Isobel, her tone audibly less stiff. 'We are doing our best to find the fourth ship. The last we heard it was in Freetown. From there it headed north. The manifest said the ship was headed for Copenhagen but it never arrived. She could have gone into the Mediterranean or west to America. Right now we've no way of knowing.'

'What are you doing?'

'A few minutes ago we established precisely when the ship left Freetown. We're busy checking with every agency in the world that has a satellite up there if they have anything on the date we're interested in.'

'What then?' asked Macnair.

'If they have, we'll do our best to track it. We've got an aerial view of the other ships and they're virtually identical, as you know. So we can instruct the computers to follow one particular shape.'

'How long will that take?'

She sighed. 'Realistically, all day. And that's assuming we even get a sighting.'

'Is there anything I can do?'

'Such as?'

'Such as put a boot up somebody and get them to move quicker.'

'I doubt it. The government bodies such as NASA and GCHQ are being as helpful as they can be. The remainder I've contacted more in hope than expectation. In each case they said they'd put somebody onto it right away. I've given them the latitude and longitude we're interested in and so it will depend on whether or not they had a satellite looking in that direction at that time. We'll just have to wait and see.'

'There is one thing. Some information in from Lt. Cdr. Hunter. Apparently a helicopter was due to pick up Ojdanic and his thugs and take them via Italy to an unknown destination. Could that have something to do with the ship, do you think?'

'Maybe. I need to think about it. If it does then it points at the Med.'

'Agreed. Okay. Keep me posted.' He hung up, thought a second and dialled Jim Carter's number. 'Ah, Major,' he said when the phone was answered. 'We need to prepare a little surprise for some unwelcome guests.'

When Macnair had finished putting Carter in the picture, Carter chuckled. 'I love it,' he said. 'I'll issue a Bikini Red warning for the base. That'll ensure everything gets done quickly. Except we'll play it quietly. All checking will be in total secrecy.'

He finished explaining his ideas and this time it was Macnair who chuckled. 'Perfect. What time will our two MEPs be leaving?'

'Ten hundred hours. They'll be in time for the afternoon

session in Strasbourg. I'm sending a four-man and two-woman squad with them. I've made arrangements with the French police to provide another team when they arrive. In view of the recent attacks there were no objections.'

'Good. I'll see them before they go. Wish them luck and all that. Anything more from Hunter?'

'Not yet, sir. If we get anything else I'll let you know. I heard from Isobel about the trace on the ship. Let's keep our fingers crossed.'

'Anything more from the press?'

'No, sir. That reporter from the *Sunday Times* is still pestering us. She's asking a few astute questions but putting two and two together and making the usual five. What I think we need is to give a press briefing sometime soon. Off the record, non-attributable and all that. Feed accurate snippets of the battle that's being fought on behalf of the citizens of the free world. I've been working with Hiram on a few ideas in our spare time.'

Macnair raised an eyebrow and said, 'I didn't realise you had any spare time. Okay. Let me see what you've got later on. If need be I can have a word with the *Times* editor and see if we can hold them off for a while. If that doesn't work we can quote the official secrets act.'

Carter shook his head. 'That's like a red rag to a bull, sir. The official secrets act will ensure that the *Sunday Times* goes for the jugular.'

'Maybe you're right at that,' Macnair sighed. 'All right, leave it with me. I'll talk to Number Ten's press secretary. See what he can suggest.'

A short while later Macnair was interrupted by the arrival of Christine Woolford. Macnair cleared his throat. 'When this is all over . . .' he paused.

'Yes,' she prompted, smiling.

He cleared his throat. 'When this is all over will we see each other again?'

'Are you asking me for a date? Or are we embarking on more than just a friendship?'

Macnair appeared to blush. 'Much more.'

She stood up and for a second Macnair thought she was going to walk out. Instead she came round his desk and leant down. She kissed him on the cheek and again on the lips. 'Does that answer your question?'

Macnair smiled. 'By God, it does. However, we've a few dragons to slay before we can live happily ever after.'

She was suddenly serious. 'Live happily ever after?'

Macnair looked in her eyes and smiled. He stood up and embraced her.

She rested her head on his shoulder for a moment and then she pulled away. 'I don't believe in fairy stories but I do believe in fate. Maybe we can make it work. Now, I'd better go and find Charles. There are a few things I need to talk to him about.'

She left the office just as Isobel arrived. 'Good news and bad,' Isobel announced. She looked soberly at Macnair who was smiling at her. His fatigue had fallen away like a snake's skin and he was feeling decidedly happier. Isobel caught his mood and then saw the reason why. She took a Kleenex from her pocket and handed it to Macnair. 'You might like to wipe your cheek, General. There's a mark that bears a remarkable resemblance to the lady's lipstick just here.' She touched her own cheek.

While Macnair wiped away the telltale sign he asked, 'What's the news?'

'The good news is that there was a weather satellite looking at the target and we've been able to use it to start following the ship. The bad news is we lost it around the Canary Islands. We're still searching. What it does mean is that we can probably discount the Americas as a destination. So it has to be Europe, somewhere. As one ship is already in Helsinki I suspect the fourth one has entered the Med. I've set up a blanket search of the whole area. It may turn up something.'

'What other steps are you taking?'

'I've got two people working on following the trail but right now I've also programmed the computers to look at pictures supplied by GCHQ of the whole Mediterranean Sea. I'll have them compared to an overhead outline of the ship and see if anything develops. It'll still leave a lot to do as we have to add in the size and dimensions of the ship when taken from an exact height.' She waved her hand. 'In fact a whole raft of things need to be taken into account. If it's there we'll find it but not quickly.'

'Time-frame?' Macnair asked.

'Days not hours. We need a break and that could come at anytime. We just have to wait and see.'

'Thanks.' Damnation! They were running out of time. The warheads had to be with the cartel, but where?

Yuri Voropaev watched a seaman being lowered over the stern of the ship with a paint pot and brush in his hand. The ship's name was quickly painted out and the seaman hoisted back onboard, leaving the paint to dry. From his vantage point on the balcony of a small hotel overlooking the harbour, Voropaev was able to see nearly the whole of the upperdeck of the ship. He was astonished by what he saw. A dozen men were at work. A funnel was removed as though by magic, the after super-structure was dismantled and the stern had sections taken away, completely redesigning the deck. The shape of the ship was totally transformed. He pondered the changes for a few seconds and then understood. Satellite tracking!

He put binoculars to his eyes and focused on the woman stand-ing on the starboard bridge wing. As though sensing something, she looked in his direction. Her eyes seemed to bore straight into his. Like a peeping tom caught in the act of spying, Voropaev looked away. He wondered if she had really seen him.

It was time to make the phone call. He left the hotel and hurried a few hundred metres along the road until he found a post office. Inside was a bank of telephones. Entering the nearest cubicle, he lifted the receiver. International directory enquiries had no listing for TIFAT in Scotland. He hung up, defeated for the moment and went outside into the sunshine. Walking into the nearest bar, he ordered a beer. He sat nursing it, thinking what he could do next. A flash of inspiration rocked him. As a submariner he knew the important naval shipyards across Europe. Rosyth dockyard was near to TIFAT HQ. He drained the cold lager and returned to the post office. This time when he asked he was given the number of Rosyth dockyard. He fed cash into the telephone and dialled. He was answered immediately.

'Hullo,' he spoke in heavily accented English. 'Please to help. I am trying to telephone to TIFAT headquarters.'

To his pleasant surprise the operator said, 'Certainly, sir. Putting you through.'

The phone rang again and was answered straightaway. 'TIFAT HQ. May I help?'

'Please, I am looking for Sergeant Badonovitch.'

'I'll see if he's on the base. Can I say who's calling?'

'His cousin. My name is Yuri.'

'Please hold, sir.'

Voropaev fed more money into the telephone's hungry maw, impatient, desperate to talk to Badonovitch. He watched as the money drained away. Finally, the operator came back onto the line. 'I'm sorry, sir, I can't locate Sergeant Badonovitch. If you leave your name and telephone number I'll pass the message onto him that you called.'

'No! No, wait a moment. Get me the duty officer.'

'Yes, sir. Can you give me your full name, please?'

His name would mean nothing but his old rank might. 'Tell him it is Commander Voropaev of the Russian Navy. It is urgent.'

'Yes, sir.'

A few seconds later another voice came on the line. 'Lieutenant Napier. May I help, sir?'

'My name is Yuri Voropaev. I,' he was about to say "was" but changed it quickly, 'am a Commander in the Russian Navy. I have vital information to pass to you. I had hoped my cousin would be there. My English is not so good. I have much to tell.'

'Sorry, sir. Give me an idea of the information you have.'

'Three nuclear bombs are in the hands of a Georgian crime cartel and I think that they are on a ship.'

Napier suddenly sat up. He knew nothing about nuclear bombs but he knew all about the Georgians.

'Sir, give me your telephone number. I'll get a Russian speaker to call you back immediately.'

Voropaev read the number off the phone and added, 'That is Cagliari.'

'Where?'

'Cagliari. Sardinia.'

'Right, sir. We'll get back to you straight away.' Napier hung up, phoned Major Carter and relayed the information.

'Meet me in the General's office.'

When Napier arrived both senior officers were waiting. Macnair had Napier repeat the conversation.

While Napier was speaking, Carter lifted the General's telephone and dialled the communications centre. 'Major Carter here. Get Sergeant Badonovitch on his sat-nav phone and patch him through to General Macnair's office straightaway.'

Macnair was smiling broadly. 'If it's true then we may have the break we've been looking for. Isobel has been scouring the Mediterranean for the fourth ship but hasn't found it yet.' His phone rang and he swept up the receiver.

'Sergeant? It's General Macnair. Do you have a cousin by the name of Commander Voropaev?'

'Yes, sir. At least, he was a Commander. I thought he had left the navy.'

'Is he reliable?'

The question startled Badonovitch and he stuttered. 'Yes . . . I'd say he's reliable.'

'I'm going to three way you through to him and I want you to talk to him. I'll be with you on the call. I'll ask the questions and you translate. We'll also record the conversation. Have you got that?'

'Yes, sir,' came the prompt reply.

Macnair pressed recall and got a dialling tone. He phoned the number given to Napier and waited impatiently for it to be answered. After three rings a voice said, 'Hullo?'

'Commander Voropaev?'

'Yes.'

'This is General Macnair. I have your cousin. Wait a moment.' Macnair pressed recall followed by the digit three. 'You there, Sergeant?'

'Yes, sir.'

'Speak to the man on the phone. Make sure he is who he says he is.'

There followed a quick exchange in Russian and then laughter from Badonovitch. 'Yes, sir. It is my cousin.'

'Good. Get him to tell me his story in full. You interpret as we go.' Macnair's frown deepened as Voropaev's story unfolded. Nothing was left out, and at the end the General knew he owed a large debt to Commander Yuri Voropaev, formerly of the Russian Navy.

Hunter sent the information he had found in Ojdanic's house back to TIFAT HQ. It wasn't much. It appeared to be mainly banking transactions personal to Ojdanic. The American had not kept any records of his exploits but he had certainly been a wealthy man. Hunter hoped that Isobel would be able to liberate the funds.

Ruth had finished making the breakfast that Ojdanic had started while Dunston had carried the bodies down to the cellar. Hunter telephoned TIFAT to find that the General was on another call and left a message with Isobel. He was dozing on the huge sofa when his sat-nav phone warbled.

'Hullo, sir,' Hunter said groggily to Macnair.

'Commander, is everything all right?'

'A few aches and bruises, sir, but nothing serious. We finished the job a few hours ago.' He explained the difficulties they had encountered.

'All right. It can't have been helped. I've just been speaking to a Russian ex-serviceman. A submarine commander.' He gave Hunter the details.

When Macnair finished, Hunter asked, 'What do you want us to do, sir?'

'I've a helicopter on its way to you. It will refuel at Rome and then go on to Cagliari. A full load of equipment is being taken to Edinburgh. A Hercules will fly it out. I am liaising with all the relevant authorities so that there will be no delay. Commander Voropaev will meet you at the harbour. I'll give him your ETA when we have it.'

'Are we sure the warheads are onboard, sir?'

'As sure as we can be. Why?'

'What are we going to do? Sink the ship? Find the warheads first? What's the plan?'

'Right now, Lieutenant Commander Hunter, we don't have one beyond what I've told you. We are working on identifying the warheads and getting precise information on their construction. But don't hold your breath. The first reaction of the Russians will probably be to deny anything has happened.'

'Roger that, sir. When will the helicopter get here?'

'In about an hour.'

'What shall we do with the bodies of Ojdanic and his crew?'

'Take them with you and drop them into the Med. Let the fish eat them. It'll be easiest in the long run.' He paused, 'On second thoughts, leave them. I'll arrange for the police to deal with the bodies.'

'Incidentally, sir. You may get a telephone call from a young lady by the name of Linda Donovan telling you about our situation here. She saved our lives. Tell her we made it okay.'

If he was surprised, Macnair showed no sign of it.

When Hunter broke the connection he filled the other two in on the situation.

'Nuclear warheads?' Ruth said, aghast. 'God help us!'

'It appears to be the case. That's the end of our R and R. We'd better try and get some sleep on the 'copter.'

When the helicopter arrived it proved to be a Puma from No. 33 Squadron normally based at RAF Benson in England but on exercise in Italy. At a small military airfield outside Rome they refuelled and were back in the air in record time. They had broken most of the aviation laws regarding flight paths and flying times for pilots but they had been informed that wartime flying rules were now in force. The two pilots and the crewman had no idea what was going on but they made the most of it. At Cagliari, dog-tired, they set down in a corner of the airfield. There they were met by a small contingent of soldiers and their passengers were escorted away. The crew was ignored. They exchanged helpless shrugs and followed.

The team had managed to sleep on the helicopter in spite of the noise and uncomfortable seats. Even so they arrived at their destination barely refreshed. Each was bone weary and in need of a proper night's rest. There appeared little chance of that.

A car whisked them into town and dropped them at the hotel near the harbour, where they met Voropaev. He had arranged accommodation at the hotel and, after a refreshing shower, they all met in Voropaev's room. From the balcony, they examined the ship through the Russian's binoculars.

'How can you be certain that the warheads are onboard?' Hunter asked.

'I cannot be, how do you say? One hundred percent sure?' He received a nod. 'But I think so. I watch boxes loading earlier.' He paused, working out the English. 'They are right shape and size. That is all I know.' He shrugged. 'I am sure as I can be. Also, I see the woman who works for the Georgians. From all I see back home I think warheads are on the ship.'

'You could be right,' said Hunter. 'We can check it out when the plane arrives from Edinburgh. They're bringing a special type of Geiger counter that was designed for use during weapons' inspections.'

'Explain, please,' Voropaev demanded.

'When the UN sent in their inspection teams looking for weapons of mass destruction they were hampered by not knowing *where* to look. A new type of Geiger counter has now been developed which can penetrate buildings and even travel a considerable depth underground looking for traces of radioactivity. They're now working on a system to be fitted to satellites, although I understand that's a long way from completion. Once our people get here, all we'll have to do is aim and point and we'll know if the warheads are onboard.'

'If they're not?' asked Dunston.

'If they're not, we'll ask someone where they are,' came the enigmatic reply. 'Yuri, you've been watching the ship, has there been much activity?'

'Yes. A lot of people come here. I also see a lot of stores going onboard.'

'They could be getting ready for sea,' said Dunston.

'Yes, that is so,' said Voropaev. 'I speak to the harbour master. I ask him. He says the ship will sail tonight. At twenty hundred hours.'

'Does the General know?' asked Hunter.

Voropaev shrugged. 'I have not told him.'

Hunter used his sat-nav phone and called General Macnair on his direct line. 'Sir? It's Hunter. I've just learnt that the ship is putting to sea tonight at twenty hundred.'

'Have you confirmed whether or not the warheads are onboard?'

'No, sir. We won't know for sure until the others get here.'

'They won't arrive before twenty-two hundred hours at the earliest. Damn.' There was a pause before Macnair continued. 'It is of vital importance that we establish whether or not the warheads are onboard. I think Commander Voropaev is right but we still need proof. You'll have to find some way to delay them.'

'Yes, sir. That's what I was thinking. How much co-operation can we expect from the authorities here?'

'I think I've used up all the favours available. The Italian high command doesn't appear to have a great deal of influence in the area. And I'd rather not let the local police know you're there. I'll be very surprised if no one in authority is on the cartel's payroll. However, the American Sixth Fleet is operating about five hundred miles away. They're taking part in Exercise National Week Thirty-Five.'

'Any British ships, sir?'

'Only submarines. They form the attacking force. However I've been in touch with C-in-C Fleet and he's spoken to his opposite number at the Pentagon. In view of what's happening the fleet has been placed at our disposal.'

'The fleet?' Hunter repeated, awed at the idea.

'So I've been informed. Probably American over eagerness but who's to say they aren't right? Maybe there's no such thing as over reaction when faced with a situation like this.'

'Can we get some diving gear airlifted here? Oxygen rebreathers and all the kit? They'll know what to send. There's probably a SEAL team somewhere in the fleet.'

'There is. It's onboard the *Eisenhower*.' A nuclear powered aircraft carrier, the *Eisenhower* was one of the largest and most powerful ships in the world. 'Commander, if the ship has the warheads onboard then we need to allow it to sail. We can't risk a confrontation in harbour just in case they're mad enough to set one of them off. If that were to happen the devastation would be beyond belief. The fallout alone would kill hundreds of thousands. We need to neutralise the warheads before we attack.'

'What will happen if the ship sank and the warheads went off under the water, sir?'

'I'm trying to find somebody at Aldermaston who can give us the answer to that. So far I haven't had a proper reply. I keep getting "need-to-know" and "top secret" thrown at me. But I'll get what we want.' Aldermaston was where nuclear weapons were designed and manufactured for the British government – unless they were bought from the Americans.

'Okay, sir. It's dark here about nineteen hundred. I'll try and immobilise the ship for a while until our lot gets here. Once we know if the warheads are onboard we can decide what to do.'

'Right. Keep me informed.' Macnair broke the connection. His next call was to the Prime Minister. It was long and detailed.

At the end of it a shocked PM agreed. The possibility of a traitor had been one thing, proof that he existed was another. Calling an emergency meeting of the cabinet, he waited until they had all arrived before he dropped his bombshell.

'So you see, ladies and gentlemen, information known only to people in this room has been leaked to the Georgians.'

There was a shocked intake of breath. Murmurs of denial arose around the table. The Prime Minister raised his hand for silence. Sitting at the specially shaped table he was able to look each of the cabinet members in the eye – at least those who were willing to make eye contact. His next announcement was even more shocking. 'Information given to you all contained certain vital differences. We were ready at every opportunity to spring the traps we set. I'll give an example. I'm sure Gordon won't mind if I use him as the guinea pig.'

The Chancellor of the Exchequer shook his head. His conscience was clear.

'You all knew about the two planned raids in Paris and Berlin. When the security forces arrived, the cartels had abandoned each place. Gordon was told about raids in Madrid and Athens. They were carried out without any problems and a number of people were arrested or killed. The same goes for the other raids that each of you knew about, with one exception. There were raids on cartel premises in Edinburgh and Oslo that were unsuccessful because the criminals had been tipped off. We have sent information to the Georgians that the person who passed the information has turned Queen's evidence and is fully co-operating with the security services. That more arrests are expected any hour.'

There was a gasp and Angus Goldsmith, the First Minister for Scotland, looked up, fear etched in his lined, beak-nosed face. The sixty year old, normally so articulate and verbally aggressive, seemed to shrink beneath the looks of his colleagues.

The Prime Minister looked at the man with loathing. 'I expect your resignation immediately. The evidence we have is not sufficient to enable us to have you arrested and stand trial with any degree of possible success. We have been unable to establish a motive but we presume it is greed. We cannot prove anything but looking at you it's clear that you're guilty. Now get out.'

'I'm telling you it's not true!' Goldsmith could see from the cold stares on the faces of those around the table that nobody believed him.

'I suggest you hide somewhere,' said the PM. Then he lied. 'We will be passing the information to the Georgians and no doubt they will be acting on it as soon as they can.'

'That . . . That's murder,' said Goldsmith.

'You should have thought of the consequences before you decided to help them,' said the Prime Minister, his youthful good looks haggard in the knowledge of his colleague's treason.

Goldsmith got to his feet and swayed, holding on to the table for support. The enormity of his probable fate suddenly dwarfed the money he had been paid. Once the new Scottish parliament had finished its first term he had intended to retire with dignity to a remote farmhouse on the Mull of Kintyre and write his memoirs, safe in the knowledge that he had a fortune stashed away in overseas bank accounts. He could then indulge his passions by travelling abroad to areas of the world where abusing small children would not land him in prison with a heavy sentence. If a price was placed on his head by the cartels he did not even dare travel overseas. Staying quietly on the Mull there was a chance that he could escape detection.

He stumbled from the silent room, ridiculed, shamed. Eight months of total isolation would pass before he plucked up the courage to hang himself.

The Georgian cartel's tentacles had insidiously stretched across Europe and into the north. Their man in Glasgow, Mick McGrath, was arguing. 'Look, I don't care. Tell them there's nothing I can do. All the men are working. We've over two hundred hits going down tonight. That's nearly two million dollars of gear.' He was a highly efficient, well-organised psychopath.

He had been a loyalist paramilitary in Northern Ireland, a hard man who killed Catholics indiscriminately. Eventually his own comrades became so sickened by his perversity that they tried to have him assassinated. It was a botched job and McGrath escaped by killing the two men sent to murder him. By luck he was arrested at a roadblock, tried and sent to prison for life. There he was kept isolated for his own protection, as both sides of the divide wanted him dead. When the Good Friday agreement resulted in an amnesty a clerical error allowed McGrath his freedom. By the time the authorities realised their mistake McGrath had gone underground. Re-emerging in Glasgow, by sheer brute force he took over one of the gangs specialising in protection rackets. After three highly successful years, during which his power base consolidated and then expanded, he was recruited by the Georgians to run the enforcement section of their cartel in Scotland. He now earned more money in a month than he had done in a year. He took great pride in his work.

'Forget the hits. This takes priority. The Georgians want maximum impact tonight. Total wipe-out with everything you've got.'

312

McGrath smiled. That was exactly the sort of job he liked. 'Who are we hitting?'

'TIFAT.'

'TIFAT? Who's he? I don't know anybody of that name,' said McGrath.

'It's an organisation. The letters stand for The International Force Against Terrorism. They want them damaged and damaged badly.'

'Where will I find these guys?'

His contact sighed. McGrath might be good at what he did but he was as thick as two short planks. 'They have their headquarters in Rosyth.'

'Yeah? I was based there with the marines.'

'You were a marine?' The voice was incredulous.

'I did five years.' He did not say that two of them had been in a very tough military prison for attacking a sergeant instructor and half killing him.

'Right. In that case you'll know the place I'm talking about.' He gave McGrath further instructions.

'We'll go by boat. I know just the place.' Laughing out loud, McGrath hung up the receiver and began making calls of his own. He was considered a "thick Mick", a pose he worked hard at maintaining. Of course he knew who TIFAT were. To be ordered to attack them was a dream come true.

Hunter and two SEALs entered the water, did their checks, slid beneath the surface and flipped over to dive down to eight metres. They were using pure oxygen re-breather sets that left no telltale bubbles trailing in the water. Night was falling and under the water it was already dark. They were buddied to each other by two-metre-long straps, Hunter leading, using a compass and depth board, following a path that led straight to the ship. From across the harbour it was a ten-minute swim and all too soon they sensed the hull above them. Swimming its length, they located the two screws at the stern. The two SEALs carried a short length of extra-flexible, steel-wire rope, which they intended wrapping around one of the propellers. It was guaranteed to stop the ship for a few hours at least.

Hunter was aware of the throbbing coming from within the ship and frowned. It sounded as though the engines were running but that made no sense. Diesel engines only needed a short time to warm through. He checked his watch. It was fifty-five minutes before the ship was due to leave.

The two SEALs slipped the steel hawser over the shaft. They were passing the end of the hawser around one of the blades of the screw when the shaft began to turn. The divers were immediately thrown out of the way, tumbling in the water, trying desperately to stay clear of the blades. Hunter snatched a knife from the sheath strapped to his right leg and cut the buddy line, freeing himself from the other two and them from each other. The steel wire they had been draping across the shaft swung through the water and hit one of the divers on the side of the head, dislodging his goggles. Hunter saw his buddy grab him and pull him clear of the stern as the ship began to move away from the jetty.

Hunter shot to the surface, just behind the ship that was now beginning to edge forward. He took a small, compressed air gun from his diving pouch, aimed it at the stern and fired. A rubber coated three-pronged grappling hook, each prong five centimetres in diameter, shot out, flew over the guard-rail and landed on the deck. It trailed a thin, very strong nylon rope behind it, which he snatched into a special D-ring on his chest band and another at his waist. Pulling the nylon, he fed it through the two rings as fast as he could. When the grappling hook snagged on the top of the guard-rail he had a firm hold on the nylon and was dragged behind the ship at a slow speed. Working the nylon until he was up against the stern he hauled down on it while kicking upward with his finned feet as hard as he could. He literally swam halfway out of the water, falling back onto the nylon with his hands only inches from the deck. Reaching above his head, he grabbed the deck and pulled himself up. Casting a wary eye over the stern and seeing nobody, he hauled himself over the side. Staying low he ditched his diving set and weights and then used his personal radio.

'Matt, can you hear me?'

'Affirmative,' came the immediate response. 'We saw the ship begin to move and wondered what had happened to you.'

'I'm on the aft deck of the ship,' came the astonishing reply.

'What? Nick, get off. Right now. We'll track it and keep an eye on her until the rest of the team arrives.'

'Negative. I'm going to search the ship and see if the warheads are onboard. Got to go. Someone's coming.'

Hunter slithered along the deck and hid behind a lifejacket container. He was dressed in a neoprene wetsuit with an integral hood that he pulled off his head, making movement and hearing easier. Having ditched his diving set he still had his waistcoat, the pouches of which contained useful items. The compressed air gun that he had used to fire the grappling hook could also fire highly effective darts capable of incapacitating a man at twenty paces. If a dart hit the right spot, the temple or the heart, it could kill instantaneously. It had the advantage of being totally silent and the disadvantage of taking up to ten seconds to reload.

Two men approached but didn't see him. He debated with himself whether or not to kill them but then thought better of it. They might be missed. They looked like crew members, dressed in overalls, slovenly, unfit. Standing at the stern, the two of them watched the lights of Cagliari. The ship slowly worked its way through the harbour before reaching the open sea. There she picked up speed, heading out into the Gulf of Cagliari, turning a few degrees to port to pass nearer to Capo Carbonara.

Hunter needed a change of clothes if he was to pass unobtrusively around the ship. It was too dangerous to stay dressed the way he was. If he was challenged there was little he could do except fight. At least if he was dressed more suitably he might be able to bluff his way out of trouble. As was typical of the type of ship he was on there were storage rooms on both sides of the superstructure. In one he found a cardboard box containing blue overalls of the sort he had seen worn by the two men. Stripping off his wetsuit, he strapped on the waistcoat and pouches along with the webbing belt. He donned the overalls, hiding the items and his wetsuit from sight.

The best thing to do was brazen it out. Walking along the deck, he acted like a member of the crew. Over his shoulder he carried a heaving line. It served no purpose but the other men he passed accepted he was doing something useful and nobody questioned his right to be there. Hunter knew from Voropaev that about seventy or more men had arrived onboard during the last twenty-four hours. Their arrival had caused a rush of ostentatious activity and the crew had shown the "gentlemen" a good deal of deference. If the men were, in fact, the leaders of crime cartels from around the world, then it was safe to assume that they were gathered for the meeting that Macnair had been predicting.

Halfway along the deck he came to the first door leading into the bowels of the ship. Opening it, he stepped into a world of luxury. A deep pile carpet stretched ahead of him with doors left and right. The corridor ran the width of the ship. A junction on the right continued towards the bows, with more doors on both sides. Following the route he came to a grand staircase on his left which led down to another deck. Hunter went down the stairs and stepped into a huge room. It had cinema style seating for at least a hundred and twenty people. Half a dozen men stood there, preparing equipment to make a presentation.

One of them noticed Hunter and asked, irritably, 'What do you want?' He spoke a language Hunter did not understand.

'*Verzeihung*,' Hunter replied in German, 'I took a wrong turn.'

The man switched languages. 'Then get out. You know this area is out of bounds to all crew members. Now go, before I do something about it.'

Saying nothing, Hunter trotted back up the stairs. He retraced his steps until he was once again outside. It was now fully dark and the ship was showing its steaming lights and a few deck lights. Members of the crew were leaning on guard-rails, smoking, talking. Ignoring them, Hunter went aft. Around the other side of the ship he found what he was looking for. The entrance to the crew's quarters. When he opened the door he was facing a corridor lined with rubber tiles in the middle of which was a set of steel stairs leading straight down. On the deck below, on the same level as the presentation room, he found half a dozen doors. He tried each one but found them locked. He continued to the next level. As he stepped onto the steel deck a gun was shoved into his back.

Hunter didn't understand the harsh words. Another man stepped in front of him and rammed a gun into his stomach. The man gestured into the air. That he understood.

When the satellites picked up the conversation between McGrath and the cartel his whereabouts were quickly established and passed to the Strathclyde Police. As McGrath left Glasgow he was followed and the information passed to Colonel Walsh at Rosyth. It was nearly midnight when a large removal lorry and three people-carriers drew up outside the gates to the marina at South Queensferry. Twenty-four men manhandled three large inflatable dinghies to the slipway. They added boxes of stores and cradled their guns as though they knew how to use them. Most of the men were Kosovo Albanians and had learnt their craft fighting Serbs. They were tough, well trained and completely amoral. They represented the hard core of McGrath's enforcers in Glasgow.

The two plainclothes policemen who had followed at a discreet distance radioed the situation to Walsh.

'Roger that and thanks,' said Walsh. 'Now go home. I'll let you know what happens.' He broke the radio connection. 'Heads up,' he said over his personal radio, 'they're on the way. You all know what to do. Out.'

The three inflatables were powered by large Evinrude engines, modified to run quietly, capable of pushing the boats, fully laden, at twenty-five knots. Moving slowly in line astern, the boats were almost completely silent. The night was quiet with hardly a breeze, overcast and dark. The lights of North and South Queensferry faded behind them while the lights of the Forth Road Bridge flashed brightly a mile astern. The boats bobbed easily in the slight chop, the men preparing their equipment for the attack. Hardened veterans, they were looking forward to the next hour or two.

317

They were three hundred metres away when Walsh said, 'McGrath's in the first boat. We want him alive. Moby Dicks, lock on and fire.'

The Moby Dick missile was a recent development. It operated using compressed air and was considered one of the smartest weapons ever devised. The aimer used an infrared sight to lock on to the target. Aimer and rocket could be as far apart as a thousand metres, connected electronically. As soon as the missile was pointed a switch was thrown and the target locked in. The missile, two meters long and ten centimetres in diameter, launched vertically to a height of a thousand metres. It rose silently with no telltale flame showing it was even in flight. At the top of its trajectory it scanned the target and automatically made adjustments for detonation and target size. As it plummeted to earth, sensors adjusted the kill radius and height of detonation. It was a masterpiece of "fire and forget" technology. At the right height it exploded – soundlessly. The compressed air mechanism emitted hundreds of thousands of tiny particles of rough steel with a force so stunning that they shredded everything on contact.

The third inflatable was the first to be hit. At the right height the rocket shot out its payload and the boat and its eight men simply vanished. The largest pieces of their bodies left intact were their ankles with a few slivers of leg bone attached. Approximately two seconds later the second boat vanished. The muted noise of the boats' engines was sufficient to leave the occupants in the first boat totally unaware of their comrades' fate.

'Shooters,' commanded Walsh, 'an explosive round into the engine and take out the side men. That'll leave four.'

McGrath's boat was approaching the wall. Sitting at the wheel steering the inflatable towards the steps, he looked back to check that the other two were following and received the shock of his life. There was nobody there. What was happening? They'd been right behind him only minutes earlier. Turning his head around to see where he was going, he eased back on the throttle, slowing down, needing to resolve the problem. The heads of four of his men disintegrated in front of his eyes. The engine bucked and blew up, the loudest noise that night so far. They were less than ten metres from the wall when a spotlight arced through the darkness, bathing them in eyeball-searing white light. One of McGrath's men instinctively raised his gun to shoot out the light but died where he sat. The fusillade of bullets that struck the boat punctured every flotation compartment and it began to sink rapidly. There was pandemonium amongst the three surviving men. They dropped their guns in a desperate effort not to be dragged down into the cold, dark abyss. Within a few seconds they were floundering in the freezing water, gulping in the dirty river, spitting it out as they came up for air.

A boat appeared alongside and strong hands clutched their hair, dragging them over the side. They lay gasping, soaked, half drowned. McGrath raised his head and started mouthing a string of expletives, which were abruptly shut off when the butt of a rifle smashed the side of his face.

They lay half in and half out of the boat until they reached a slipway. There they were shoved back into the water. The Albanians shivered from cold and fear; McGrath did neither. He stood up and stepped out of the water.

'I want a lawyer,' he said.

Ten armed men stood around him. Another fifty continued patrolling the perimeter of the establishment, just in case an attack was coming from a different direction, a precaution dictated by their professionalism rather than expectation.

Hiram B. Walsh stepped forward, wearing full battledress, his colonel's eagles evident. He knew McGrath's history, having been sent the file by the Royal Ulster Constabulary only hours earlier. Walsh was unarmed. He stopped in front of McGrath. 'I have a few questions I want answered.'

McGrath responded with a mouthful of abuse and again demanded a lawyer. Walsh hit him hard and low. As McGrath's knees buckled Walsh caught him by the hair and hit him hard on the side of the face.

'Don't speak unless I tell you,' said Walsh. 'You think you're a hard man? You're a baby. A weak, pathetic coward who's only good at attacking people from behind. I've seen your record

319

McGrath. You're a psychopath and less than dirt beneath the feet of any one of the men standing here.'

Walsh got the reaction he had been hoping for. With a roar McGrath got to his feet and attacked the American. It was no contest. The colonel was like a ghost, insubstantial and untouchable as he darted and wove, landing punch after punch into McGrath until the ex-marine stood swaying, gasping and bloodied.

'I want to know who your contacts are in the Georgian organisation. I also want the names of every man and woman working for you anywhere in the UK. You will start talking now. You may then have your injuries . . .'

He got no further as McGrath started mouthing off again. When Walsh hit him this time he brought his hands together on either side of McGrath's head and broke three of his teeth. McGrath buckled, staggered, but stayed on his feet.

Walsh turned his attention to the other two men. One of them said, 'I no understand. No speak English. Want lawyer.'

Walsh nodded. 'You don't speak English?'

The man shook his head.

'He's no use to us,' he said to Sam McReady. 'Drown him.'

'Yes, sir.' McReady stepped forward and hit the man in the solar plexus. The man bent double, gasping for breath. Pushing him to the water's edge, McReady kicked the man's legs from under him and shoved his face into the water. The man kicked and struggled to no avail. As he grew weaker, McReady changed his grip and grabbed the Albanian by the hair and lifted his head out of the water. 'How's your English now?' he asked.

'I . . . I talk. My English is good.'

'What about yours?' Walsh asked the other man.

He nodded. 'I speak English.' The fear in his eyes told Walsh that the man would tell him all that he could.

'McGrath? Are you going to talk?'

'What happened to the others? My men? The boats?'

'They're dead,' said Walsh, 'All of them. Only you three are still alive. And you won't be for much longer if you don't tell us what we want to know.'

'How did you kill them?'

Walsh shook his head. 'I told you, I ask the questions. Are you going to answer them or not?'

McGrath took a deep breath and made his move. He thought that he was fast and tough. By comparison with the men he was up against he was an overweight slob. When he tried to take the gun from Sam McReady, the sergeant from the Special Boats Service let him put a hand on it and then moved. In a blur of motion he hit McGrath seven, eight times. McGrath stopped, took a pace and fell to his knees.

'Now are you going to talk?' Walsh asked.

McGrath nodded.

An hour later the information was passed to the Strathclyde Police. Across Glasgow armed police officers raided houses, clubs and warehouses. Vast quantities of heroin and amphetamines were found, along with over two hundred and fifty illegal immigrants. All male. In some cases their families were still abroad, hostages to the Georgians. Neither McGrath nor the other two men were ever seen again.

Hunter raised his hands and looked at the man in front of him and then glanced over his shoulder at the man behind. They were tough looking individuals. The guns they were holding unwaveringly were automatic pistols. If either of them fired, the bullet would pass through Hunter and hit the other man. It was some comfort to think he wouldn't die alone.

The man in front said something in a rough, guttural language.

Hunter shrugged. 'I don't understand. Do you speak English?'

The one behind said, 'What you do here? Not allowed.'

Hunter smiled in a friendly fashion and said in a nervous voice, 'I didn't know. I'm new. I got lost and wandered the wrong way.'

They weren't being overly hostile, merely doing their job. They had no reason to expect trouble when safely at sea, but their orders were to keep everybody away from that area of the ship.

'You go,' the man behind moved the gun away, gesturing with it, indicating Hunter should go back up the stairs.

Hunter nodded. The man in front stank of garlic and cigarette smoke. He was a few inches shorter than Hunter but burly, a lot of it solid looking muscle. The other man was already losing interest and turning away. He was a carbon copy of the first guard and was reaching into his pocket, taking out a packet of cigarettes. The gun was already back in its holster.

Hunter knew that if he returned later then it could be more difficult to get as close as this. It was likely the warheads were somewhere near and searching for them now was a priority. Lowering his hands, Hunter turned to leave. The man standing in front shifted his eyes and looked towards his partner. He still had his finger on the trigger and the gun cocked. Grabbing the gun, Hunter aimed it at the other man and jerked the weapon forward. The gun went off and the bullet hit the other man in the side, smashing through his left arm and penetrating his heart, killing him instantly. The man holding the weapon gaped in awe for a second, the longest of his life. Smashing him in the throat with the edge of his hand, Hunter twisted the gun around. The man let go when his index fingers snapped and Hunter snatched the gun away. He brought it down hard on the man's temple, killing him. Quickly he tried the nearest door. It opened to his touch and looking inside, he saw that it contained shelving full of boxes and other goods. He dragged first one and then the other body into the farthest corner, stuffing them out of sight. Removing the shoulder holster from one of the bodies he adjusted it and put it on under the overalls. He hid one of the guns inside his pouch and the other he placed in the holster. Closing the door to the store behind him he stood sniffing the air, checking for the distinctive smell of cordite. The air-conditioning had already dissipated the stench and now Hunter's only worry was whether or not somebody had heard the gunshot.

Dunston and Ruth helped the two SEALs ashore. One was dazed, spitting water, gagging for breath, while the second had only a few bruises.

'Are you okay?' Ruth asked the two men.

They both nodded. Superb athletes and fit to a standard not even the SAS could surpass, both men were recovering fast.

'Where's Nick?' she asked.

'Nick's on the ship,' replied Dunston.

Ruth was horror-struck. 'On the ship? Is he crazy?'

Dunston shrugged. 'That's not a word I'd use to describe him. In fact, quite the reverse.'

'We need to get help to him as soon as possible,' Ruth replied, the worry in her eyes betraying the fear in her heart.

'We will. Just as soon as the team gets here.'

'Is there nothing we can do in the meantime?' Ruth asked.

'Certainly,' said Dunston. 'We call General Macnair and have him contact the sixth fleet. They can keep the ship under surveillance. In that way we won't waste any time searching.'

'What then? We still need to know about the warheads. How are we going to get close enough to detect any radiation?' Ruth asked.

'That's a good question and one I haven't thought through yet.'

'You?' Ruth laughed, unkindly, fear for Hunter clouding her judgement. 'Matt, you're a sky pilot for God's sake. Let the tacticians work out the tactics.'

'What's a sky pilot?' asked one of the divers.

'A chaplain,' Ruth replied.

The two men goggled at her and then looked at Dunston. He was the oddest chaplain they'd ever met.

No one appeared and Hunter breathed a sigh of relief. Luck was with him. Apart from the door to the storeroom there were another three doors in the corridor. The first one he opened led down to the engine room. He shut it quickly, cutting off the noise of the diesels and generators. The second door opened onto another store. This time the shelves were stacked with cans of oil, spare parts and other engine room paraphernalia. The third door was locked.

Kneeling down, Hunter examined the lock. It was an ordinary key-turn mechanism, requiring the kind of large key that in years gone by equated to burglar proof. In this case it more than achieved its purpose.

Hunter was in a dilemma. There was no way to get inside short of blowing it open with plastic explosives. He searched the bodies of the two men but neither had a key. It was the proximity to the engine room that gave him the idea. He looked overhead. As with many ships, there was a highly efficient air-conditioning system. Being so low down in the hull the ducting was quite substantial, built to carry a high volume of air. A quick survey told Hunter that the duct running above his head was about half a metre wide and the same in depth. Into the ducting, at regular intervals, were *punkah louvres*, through which the air could be directed. Following the lines of the ducting he found that it passed through the engineering storeroom and into the locked room. Working on the principle that the guards were there for a specific purpose he hoped the warheads were next door.

He began a systematic search of the storeroom. It only took a few minutes to find a wide variety of tools stowed in a toolbox out of sight in a corner. Taking a screwdriver he started undoing the panels of the ducting. With his arms above his head it was tiring, muscle aching effort, unscrewing one bolt after the other. With eight removed from either side, he used the screwdriver to lever a gap. Gripping each side of the thin metal, he tore it, ripping the ducting from around the remaining bolts. He pulled away a metre long section before reaching the first join. The sheet came free and he placed it out of sight. The air continued along the ducting, passing across the space as though the sheet was still there.

Armed with a spanner and a pair of pliers Hunter climbed into the ducting, squeezing into the tight space, using his toes and fingers to crab forward. It was pitch dark ahead, although a faint halo of light came from behind him. Reaching the next split in the ducting, he was sure he was well inside the locked storeroom. He began to untwist the nut holding the bolt in place. It was easier than removing the screw, as the inside of the ducting had never been painted. With the nut off he gave the bolt a thump with the spanner and it fell free with a faint clatter, onto the deck below.

He began undoing the bolt opposite. It quickly went the same way and he began to make his way backwards, attacking each bolt in turn. Feeling the ducting move beneath him, he pushed down. The metal bent open but not far enough. He removed another six bolts and this time when he pushed, the ducting yawed wide. Not knowing what was beneath him, Hunter stretched across the gap and inched forward. He was sodden with sweat, his muscles were cramped and aching, his fingers on fire with the effort. He got his feet onto the loosened section of metal and now moved backwards, pushing down. The thin ducting bent and he felt himself edging over the side and into the compartment below.

27

Hunter lowered himself to the deck. It was pitch black, no hint of light from anywhere. Cautiously he felt his way around, like a blind man. He bumped into things, knocked his shins, hit his hands on items he could not even guess at but finally found a bulkhead. He worked his way along, trying to find the door and therefore a light switch. His hand touched a piece of metal, proud of the bulkhead and he felt around it, touching the retaining clips of the watertight door. On the other side of the door, precisely where he expected to find it, he found a serrated button. Turning it he switched on the strip lighting. He blinked rapidly, his eyes becoming accustomed to the sudden brightness. In the middle of the compartment, on specially constructed cradles, were three nuclear warheads. The yellow and black markings were unmistakable, used the world over to denote the same thing – radioactive material.

Hunter sucked in his breath. So they had been right. There was only one question that needed answering. What was he going to do with them?

The British Prime Minister looked at the bank of television screens. Each one displayed the face of a political leader in Europe and the last screen framed the features of the President of the United States of America.

'What we have here,' said the American President, 'is one of the biggest disasters to befall humanity. If this crime syndicate has nuclear warheads and intends to use them they have to be stopped at all costs.'

The BPM nodded. 'I totally agree. Which is why I believe we must come to an international agreement now. They must be stopped. So far we've abused just about every human rights' statute in the book. Once this is all over the lawyers will have a field day if we're perceived to have violated the "rights" of these criminals. We can throw them a few heads, a few token gestures, but the reality is Europe and America will be unable to preach human rights to countries such as China and North Korea, or Iran and Iraq, much before Doomsday.'

The faces in front of him nodded in gloomy acceptance. No matter what the facts of the matter, they knew he was right. They could mobilise public opinion behind them if they worked hard and used the press as shamelessly as though it were an election year. The problem was that they would never again win an argument in the United Nations against totalitarian states who would henceforth quote Europe's and America's "abuses" whenever their own were put under the microscope.

'What can we do?' asked the German Chancellor.

'We agree on certain things,' replied the BPM.

'What are they?' questioned the Prime Minister of the Netherlands, frowning.

'We must move quickly to bring in new laws with the Court of Human Rights,' said the BPM. 'It's all very well to suggest that World War III against the cartels has started but we must move with utter ruthlessness and determination.'

There was a sharp intake of breath.

'But what good will that do?' asked the only woman leader in Europe, the Prime Minister of Norway.

'It will mean that we use our military as well as civilian forces against the enemy. At present we are stretched to breaking point across the whole of Europe as we try and fight these people. If we use military force rather than police tactics we shoot to kill. TIFAT alone cannot do the job.'

'Your shoot-to-kill policy didn't work in Northern Ireland,' the French President pointed out.

'Granted. But this is entirely different. When the people of our respective countries learn that these people were prepared to use nuclear weapons against us what will their reaction be? Do you think that against the backdrop of such huge potential devastation they'll care about the human rights of a few criminals? I suggest that they'll thank us.'

'That may be so,' said the Italian Prime Minister, 'but the liberal press as well as the liberal lawyers who'll jump on the band wagon will slaughter us.'

'No, they won't,' said the President of the USA. 'We've worked that one out.'

There was a quickening of interest.

The British Prime Minister, looking older than his years, said, 'The time is right to disclose fully what we are up against. Public opinion must be mobilised in our favour. We must all act with a concerted voice across Europe and the rest of the world. We give interviews to every newspaper and television and radio show we can. If we're asked questions about civil liberties and the rights of those killed by our forces we counter the question with one of our own.'

'Such as?' one of the faces on the screens in front of him asked.

'Such as – Do we allow a nuclear bomb to explode in one of our cities with the deaths of hundreds of thousands of innocent men, women and children for the sake of the civil liberties of a few criminals? Attack at every opportunity! Make it understood that we, the elected politicians, are protecting our people from the crime cartels which are threatening the very foundations of our civilisation.' He paused and added, 'We declare all-out war and we act accordingly. We will use our military forces to the best of our ability to wipe out this scourge of the twenty-first century.'

'I have a problem,' said the German Chancellor. 'Our constitution does not allow the use of the military in what is basically a civilian problem.'

The US President came in then. 'It's the same for us. That's why we openly declare war against the cartels and circumvent the issue. At the end of the day we're skating on thin ice, both constitutionally and in regard to human rights. But we have to weigh that up against the rights of the majority.'

They went over the same arguments again and again, refining what they would say to their parliaments as well as to the press. With each passing minute the leaders of the Western world grew more confident. They were being forced to act. The theft and the very real threat of the nuclear warheads had changed everything.

When the video conference call ended excitement shone from the faces on the screens. At last they were being proactive instead of reactive. The stakes had been raised to such an extent they could now make a real move against the crime cartels. With additional aid promised to immigrants and real benefits being paid to those in need there was a possibility that a great deal of Europe's and America's ills would be taken care of. There were only two faces left on the screens after the farewells had been said. The British PM and the US President looked at each other.

'Good work,' said the President.

'The credit is due to General Macnair. He worked out the details.'

'Pass on my warmest and most sincere thanks.'

'I will. Although it's not over yet. And once the fighting has stopped we must capture the moral high ground and keep it. We have no alternative. If we can reduce the power of the cartels, crime rates will drop dramatically. We will then be the saviours of the West. Like you, I fear for the future if we don't prevent these criminals from invading every facet of the lives of decent, ordinary people.'

'Save it.' The smile took the sting out of the words. 'Use it in your speeches.'

The BPM grinned back, unabashed. 'Just practising. Did you get word from Vladivostock?'

'Yes. Admiral Gerenko insists he did not sell the warheads. Maintains it was the work of a lowly lieutenant. How in hell he managed it we don't know. Gerenko is full of apologies.'

'Do you believe him?'

'I'm not sure. According to Langley we have to work with the s.o.b., otherwise there could be more sales. The IMF will sanction soft loans up to five billion dollars as well as a grant of a further three billion. Admiral Gerenko will head the investment programme to revitalise the whole area. How are we doing with finding and stopping the warheads?'

'TIFAT is on top of it.'

Hunter stared at the warheads and wondered what to do next. The compartment he was in was bigger than he had expected. There were racks of engineering gear along one bulkhead and in a corner he found discarded diving equipment. He sorted out a pair of fins, a depth gauge and a set of bottles with an old-fashioned demand valve and a dilapidated mouthpiece and separate goggles. The rubber around the goggles was old and brittle, the elasticity long gone. There was rust around the top of the bottles but when he dug into it Hunter found that it was just surface damage. Along another bulkhead he found a bank of compressed air bottles with the purity stamp on the side showing 99.99%. Diving quality. They were the sort used to decant air into a diver's bottles if a compressor wasn't available. He cracked open one of the bottles and checked the pressure gauge. It showed that the bank was full. He opened the diver's bottles but found them empty. That presented a problem as the inside of the bottles had probably become corroded. Connecting the bottles to the bank, he filled them slowly, checking for leaks. When he finished he buttoned on the demand valve and mouthpiece and cracked open the main air valve. There was a small leak around the top of one of the bottles and the second stage of the demand valve was jammed open, causing a continuous stream of air, nothing that Hunter couldn't cope with. He hoped that when he escaped the last thing he would need was that particular set of diving gear.

In another corner he found what he was looking for. Warheads such as these required instruction manuals as well as special tools. The container he opened held both. Eagerly he lifted out the top manual depicting a picture of the warhead on its cover. With a

330

sinking heart he saw the writing was Cyrillic. But, he thought, what else should he have expected?

He flicked through the pages. Detailed diagrams showed the internal workings of the warhead and the types of fuses and detonators that were used to set off the nuclear explosion. He studied it for a while before turning his attention to the warheads.

Each one was nearly two metres long and half a metre in diameter. The propulsion part of the rocket was missing, otherwise they would have been impossible to transport with anything less than a low-loader. As it was, if the detonators could be set off, then the resultant explosion would devastate an area about a mile in diameter. Fallout would account for another five or ten miles and the devastation would be so great that billions or even hundreds of billions of pounds worth of damage was inevitable. Not counting the lost and injured innocent lives. *Surely they were meant for blackmail, not use,* thought Hunter.

The diagrams showed a firing mechanism that he was familiar with. The only difference was that the resultant explosion would be nuclear instead of high explosive. The actual method to start the process was the same as with many other similar bombs and warheads. In the box was also a complete set of tools, so what was he waiting for? He looked at the warhead and wondered about the nuclear material contained within it. It was ludicrous but somehow dismantling high explosive bombs didn't seem as dangerous as this. Either way, should he make a mistake, he'd be dead. This time he had the books to show him the way through the casing and into the mechanism. It was also evident from the diagrams that there were no booby traps, unlike with some conventional weapons. It was a simple case of getting in, removing three detonators, or more accurately, three firing devices, and getting out again. Easy. Straightforward. Nothing could be simpler. He hoped.

He selected an Allen key and began to unscrew the access panel on the side of the warhead. Six screws held the panel in place and they turned easily. Now that he had started his mind became crystal clear and he concentrated on the task in

331

hand. It might not be a difficult job but a slip would cost him his life.

With the panel removed he shone a pencil-torchlight into the opening and studied the mechanism. He compared it with the diagrams until he was satisfied that he knew what he was doing. Each firing mechanism was a round metal box, inside of which were two detonators that fed into a shaped explosive charge. When one detonator ignited, the second being a backup, it set off an explosion that in turn started the chain reaction within the plutonium. The other two metal boxes contained identical circuits, which in turn were backups to the first one. It was a system designed with so many backups a nuclear explosion was inevitable once the order to fire had been given. Three bolts held the first box in place. They were well greased and Hunter used a specially designed spanner to remove them. Sliding off the box, he cut the wires leading from the battery. He placed it carefully on the deck. Turning his attention to the other two he quickly removed them. When he had done so he replaced the cover. Looking at it, nobody would know that he had disturbed the warhead. He placed the three boxes on a shelf, out of sight. Checking the time, he saw it had actually taken fifty-five minutes to dismantle one warhead. *Doesn't time fly*, Hunter thought . . .

He began work on the second warhead. This time he was able to cut ten minutes from start to finish. He was about to commence work on the third when he heard a noise outside. Throwing the tools into a corner he turned as the door was thrown open. Hunter faced three men, one kneeling and two standing. All three had automatic weapons aimed at him. He raised his hands in the air.

A question was thrown at him in a language he didn't understand.

'I only speak English.'

'Who are you?' asked another man. 'What are you doing? How did you get in here?'

Hunter put on a thoughtful face and replied, 'I materialised from a star ship.'

The English speaker was about five feet ten, stocky, clean-shaven with long, straight, black hair. He was standing furthest back but shouldered his way past the other two. He stopped short of Hunter but to one side, out of the line of fire of the other guns. The action told Hunter the man was a professional.

'Wise guy, huh?' He held the automatic loosely in his hands and suddenly struck with the speed of a rattler. The gun butt was rammed into Hunter's solar plexus and though he was half expecting it, he still had the wind knocked from him and was sent flying backwards into the bulkhead. He lay still, pretending to be more hurt than he actually was.

'Get up. We're taking you to see the boss. He'll want some answers.'

Slowly climbing to his feet Hunter was pushed up the stairs and back to the auditorium. A number of men stood in a corner talking. They broke off and looked at the intruders as the phalanx of four approached them.

'Sir,' the English speaker said, 'we found him down below in the restricted area. With the warheads.'

The man he was addressing was in his late fifties, a few inches shorter than Hunter, wide shouldered and turning to fat. He had a bald pate surrounded by thick grey curls, was deeply tanned and looked like everybody's idea of a kindly uncle or a priest. Maximillian King-Smith frowned and said, 'Who are you?' he demanded in a cultured, upper crust English accent.

'My name is Hunter.'

'What were you doing with the warheads?'

'Introducing myself,' Hunter replied.

There may have been a signal but if there was Hunter didn't see it. The blow to his kidneys was excruciating and he gasped in pain. He stayed on his feet, his eyes narrowed and he looked over his shoulder at the man who had hit him.

'Do that again,' he said, 'and I'll ram the gun down your throat.'

'You are in no position to make threats, Mr Hunter. Now, answer my question. What were you doing?'

'Nothing,' he repeated. 'I entered the compartment and saw the bombs. That was when these three goons showed up.' There was no point in denying he had seen the warheads as they were

333

unmistakable and could be nothing else. He hoped that by calling them bombs they would assume his ignorance.

The man turned to the other three. 'Wasn't the door locked?'

'Yes, Mr. King-Smith, it was.'

'So how did you get in?' King-Smith addressed himself to Hunter who shrugged in response.

This time he saw the eye movement and moved fast. There was no possibility of anyone shooting him. A bullet from a high calibre gun at such close quarters would pass through more than one body. He turned, swept the gun aside as the butt struck at him and, using straight fingers, hit the man in the throat. Staggering backwards, the man gargled, gasping for breath, his hands around his throat, the gun dropping to the deck.

Even as he thought about diving for it King-Smith said, 'Don't bother, Mr Hunter, or you will be shot.' King-Smith turned his attention to the two men now holding guns aimed at Hunter. 'Search him and then take him below. Lock him up somewhere until we can deal with him. We have a great many questions to ask.' He looked at Hunter for a few seconds. 'The way you did that I would guess special services. Certainly special training. We have a presentation taking place here in a few minutes. It will last approximately one hour. When it is over we will be meeting again and I will be asking you certain questions. If I do not get the information I require you will find the experience extremely painful, I promise you. Now take him away.'

The two guards nodded and stepped aside, waving their guns, indicating the door they had entered by. He heard one of the men in the group address King-Smith. 'This is outrageous! Special Services on board. I am leaving. I was assured total security before I agreed to come. Alleysia gave me her word.'

There was a murmured reply, which Hunter did not catch. He ignored the rest. It was unbelievable but nobody had searched him in spite of being told to do so. Hunter's mind was in overdrive. The man he had downed was the English speaker. King-Smith had spoken English. The other two hadn't understood what he had been saying, only the gestures. There was still a chance. Halfway to the door he stumbled on a chair and gasped in pain. Placing his right hand on his left side he slipped his hand inside his overalls, grimacing. The men with the guns impassively gestured for him to keep moving. Keeping his hand there he inched the gun out of its holster. One other thing was in his favour. They wanted him alive for questioning. The guns pointing at him were more a deterrent than a real threat.

Keeping his hand inside the overall, he slid the safety catch off his gun. Using his other hand to hold onto the railing, he was prodded down another set of stairs and then another until Hunter guessed they were on the lowest deck. They stopped at a metal door and one of the men stepped around Hunter to unlock it, his gun pointing at the deck. Hunter stepped back to give him room, and the man turned his eyes from him to look at the door lock. Turning his back on the man who still had him covered, Hunter fired his gun through his overalls and under his arm. The shot hit the man between the eyes. The bullet seared Hunter's arm and side but the adrenaline masked the pain. Even as the dead man flew backwards Hunter drew the gun and shot the second man in the side of the head, killing him instantly. In such a confined space it was the safest place to shoot. The skull stopped the bullet from ricocheting around the metal bulkheads.

The noise was horrendous and Hunter grabbed the two guns from the deck, placing them in his pouch. If necessary he would try and shoot his way out. He had only one idea and that was to get off the ship or to die trying. Nobody appeared. All remained silent and it was with a sense of relief he realised that the shots had gone unnoticed. He breathed more easily.

Sitting on the bottom step, he pondered his next move. With a sigh he knew that his duty was to try and neutralise the third warhead. It was reasonable to assume that the bodies of the two guards he had killed earlier had been found. Presumably, that meant more guards had been stationed outside the compartment. He listened to his conscience. He really didn't have a choice. Sighing, he stood up and opened the door to what was to have been his prison. He dragged the two dead men inside and locked the door. He pocketed the key, intending to ditch it later. There was blood on the deck and bulkheads that would be obvious to anybody who came down the stairs. Reaching up, he smashed the light holder and then the bulb with a few smacks from the butt of his gun. Now the blood was barely distinguishable in the gloom. Ascending the stairs he broke another two lights and left the place in total darkness.

Returning to the stairwell that led to the warheads Hunter had to pass near the auditorium. The doors were closed and he heard a voice from within. His curiosity got the better of him and he approached. One of the doors moved and he quickly turned, retracing his steps. Stepping around a corner he stopped. The scuffle of feet on carpet warned him that someone was approaching fast. Kneeling down, Hunter pretended to be tying a shoelace. The person appeared and stepped around him. Seeing the man was about his size he made an instant decision. Standing up, he smashed the gun on the back of the other's neck. The man sank to the carpeted deck with barely a sound. Grabbing him under the arms, Hunter dragged the body through a nearby door. He found himself in a well laid-out cabin. There was a bunk, a tall wardrobe and a sink unit. The man he had hit was breathing steadily. Hunter began to strip him of his suit and shirt. Washing in the sink, removing most of the grime he'd accumulated during his exertions, Hunter dressed in the man's clothes. He discarded the diving pouches and waistcoat he had been wearing and transferred the guns into the pockets of the jacket. While Hunter was putting on the coat the prone figure began to stir. Hitting him with the butt of the gun he knocked the man unconscious again. He used strips torn from a sheet to tie him up and was about to stuff him in the wardrobe when he had a better idea. Placing him on the bunk, he covered him with a blanket and then smashed the light bulbs. The cabin was in near darkness.

Stepping outside he returned to the auditorium. At the door he took a deep breath and pushed it open, slipping through. He was counting on the fact that there were so many visitors he would never he recognised as a stranger. There were about a hundred people, mostly men, with a mere handful of women scattered throughout the crowd. On the stage were six men and one lone female. She was addressing the audience. Hunter recognised her from the photographs in the lawyer's office. Alleysia Raduyev spoke in accented English, a melodious sound that was simultaneously compelling and sexy. When she spoke she paused frequently, to allow what she was saying to be translated. Hunter watched as men and some of the women bent their heads whispering to their companions. Alleysia's next sentence left him numb with horror.

28

She looked at the audience evenly, her expression calm. 'The first warhead will be exploded in England,' she began.

'Make it London,' a voice called out. 'That way we can kill a few million English swine.' There was laughter.

'Wait a moment,' said somebody in the audience. 'I run London. It will cost us a fortune. We have tens of thousands of users we can't afford to waste. The losses will be staggering.' The speaker was a large black man, fat with a bald head. He was nervously tugging at the lobe of his right ear.

Alleysia Raduyev smiled. Speaking matter-of-factly, as though describing a slight storm brewing in the Atlantic and due to hit Britain in the next twenty-four hours, she continued. 'We will explode the warhead in Cornwall. I have all the details mapped out. This will enable us to put pressure on the Europeans to leave us alone and at the same time convince them to pay fifty billion pounds for each of the two remaining warheads.' The stakes had been raised.

Grotesque. It was the only word to describe what he was hearing. The Georgian woman was talking casually about the deaths of hundreds of thousands of people as though it meant nothing. Cornwall would be bombed back to the Stone Age. Britain and the West would be in total chaos. And she was presenting it almost like a marketing ploy of a large company trying to convince customers to buy its products. Fingering his gun Hunter contemplated shooting her from where he stood. Then he thought better of it. He'd die and somebody else would simply take over, of that he had little doubt. These people were hyenas, carrion eaters who would not hesitate to turn on each other if they thought it would do them any good. He had to get a message off the ship. Even as he moved she continued speaking.

'As you know, for the past two years there has been very little trouble between the different factions distributing drugs in Europe. Where turf wars have erupted we have settled them. That has been entirely due to my efforts. I, Alleysia Raduyev, have quadrupled the profits of the people involved and left the police forces of Europe floundering. I think you will like the figures we have been able to extrapolate once we work together on a world wide basis. Operation Siren,' she announced, 'began less than a month ago and is progressing smoothly.' From the seventeen at the original meeting there were now over a hundred cartel bosses from around the world in attendance. It was time for them all to know with whom they were really dealing. It was, she thought, a fitting memorial to her dear, dead papa. 'We will see the distribution of over five hundred billion dollars worth of heroin across Europe and North America in this full fiscal year.' There was little reaction from her audience until she added, 'For less than fifty million dollars cost.' There were gasps of amazement. She allowed the uproar to continue for a few moments and then raised her hand for silence. 'That is, at wholesale prices to us. The street value is infinitely greater.' Now there was bedlam. She stood quietly and let the noise abate. 'At the end of three months we estimate that we will have at least five million more users. Then we will simply turn off the supply and ratchet up the price. The inevitable crime wave that will sweep the world will completely overpower the forces of law and order. They will be so overwhelmed they will not even have an opportunity to look for us. This is a customer acquisition programme, the scale of which has never been seen before. We will create the first trillion-dollar industry in the world.' Her audience erupted into cheers.

Hunter sat in shock for a few moments. This tiny woman! She was the crime cartel's leader? He could hardly believe it. Taking advantage of the noise, Hunter slipped outside and hurried along the deck to the nearest stairwell. He took the stairs two at a time, acting as though he belonged, prepared for trouble but wishing to avoid it at all costs. There were two places he could send a message from. One was the bridge and the other the radio room. Outside the night was still, a heavy moon hung low and yellow in a clear sky and he stopped to sniff the fresh air. His thoughts turned to Ruth. He hoped his message would make her feel a little better. Provided he managed to send it, of course.

He went up the outside ladder to the bridge. A lookout was standing on the bridge wing, binoculars to his eyes, scanning the horizon from ahead, around the starboard side and aft. There were a few lights to be seen, ships passing in the night, but nothing of interest. The lookout lowered his binoculars and glanced at Hunter.

'Evening,' said Hunter with a smile. The other man nodded and ignored him, looking out to sea once more.

The door to the bridge was open and Hunter stepped inside. The bridge spanned the width of the ship and was about seven, perhaps eight metres from forward to aft. There were two chairs on either side of a central console, which contained the navigation equipment of a modern ship. A radar repeater, sat-nav and GPS displays and a combined UHF/VHF radio were part of the equipment. A digital compass showed the ship's heading and was linked to the automatic pilot. Next to it was the repeater display from the magnetic compass as well as the log showing that the ship was making good fifteen knots. The seats were occupied, a man sat in the port one, a woman in the starboard.

'I'm looking for the Captain,' said Hunter.

To his surprise the woman spoke. 'I am the Captain. Who are you?'

'My name doesn't matter,' said Hunter and froze her with a look. He was gambling on the fact that she was merely the hired help, used to doing what she was told. After all, he could easily be one of the cartel bosses.

'My apologies,' said the woman, nervousness showing in her voice. 'What can I do for you, sir?'

'I have been . . .' he was about to say "asked" but changed it in the nick of time, 'instructed to send a message to London.'

'Who instructed you?'

'Madame Raduyev.'

At the sound of the name the Captain seemed to flinch. As he had hoped, the ship and its crew were ruled with a rod of iron. Obedience to orders was as natural as breathing.

'Why didn't you go straight to the radio room, sir?'

Hunter realised that he may have made a mistake but recovered quickly and now poured on the charm. 'I personally believe that it is a courtesy to speak to the Captain of this or any ship before making a signal. Permission is sought and granted as a matter of respect. That is all.' He spoke pleasantly. In the gloom he could not make out the woman's features and had no idea of her age. To be a captain she had to be at least thirty years old, probably older. He just hoped that she appreciated a bit of old-fashioned deference to her position. She did.

'Thank you. You may use the bridge communications centre.' She nodded at the back of the bridge and Hunter saw a door he had missed earlier.

'Thank you,' said Hunter, crossing the deck. Opening the door he entered and closed it behind him. The room was two metres deep and three-wide. He was facing a bank of dials, knobs, handsets, displays and all the paraphernalia associated with a modern ship capable of world wide communications. A man sat in a chair in the middle, earphones on, smoking, oblivious to Hunter's presence. Three steps and Hunter was behind him, tapping his shoulder. Startled, the man looked up and Hunter jerked his thumb at the door. 'Out,' he said. The man left the room without a murmur.

A glance across the console showed him what he needed. A *Sperry-vec* satellite communications set was at one end of the display. Grabbing the handset, Hunter dialled in the correct frequency.

'Chess this is Rook, over.'

'Rook this is Chess,' came the immediate response from the duty communications operator at TIFAT HQ. If the man was surprised to receive the call he did not show it by so much as a change of inflection in his voice.

341

'Patch me through to King, please, over.'

'Roger, sir. Patching you now.'

A few seconds later Macnair's voice came over the radio. 'Rook, King, over.'

'Sir, I am onboard the ship. The three warheads are here. One is intended for detonation in Cornwall. The other two are for sale back to us. I've made safe two of them and will try and do the same to the third. The warheads are situated in a compartment about two-thirds of the way from the bows and below the waterline. The ship has to be stopped. Blow the bows out and she'll sink like a stone. We can recover the warheads later. Over.'

'Roger that, Rook. Can you standby on this frequency? Over.'

'Negative. Have to leave right now. Sir, we have to stop them at all costs. Do you copy? Over.'

'Affirmative, Rook. Out.'

Hunter, breathing a sigh of relief, replaced the handset and moved the frequency dial. Now all he had to do was fight his way into the compartment containing the warheads, dismantle the third one and escape before a warplane appeared over the horizon and blew the ship to pieces.

Macnair digested the information. He had been given operational control and ordered to take all necessary measures to stop the warheads either being used or being a threat. He knew what had to be done but his hand hesitated for a moment when he reached for the receiver. However grim, the truth was that one man's life was of no consequence in the scheme of the success or otherwise of the total operation.

He was patched through to Admiral Steinbecker, USN, onboard the American carrier, the *USS Eisenhower*. 'Admiral? This is Malcolm Macnair.'

'Hullo, General. What can I do for you?'

Macnair told him.

'Okay. I'll despatch *HMS Thunderer* immediately. We know precisely where the ship is but I have to warn you that it'll take a good six hours for the sub to get there.'

'I appreciate that. But there may be survivors. In the meantime will you do your utmost and have your lads blow the bows to smithereens?'

'Can do. How reliable is the information?'

'One hundred percent. I've no doubt about that. Hunter is one of my best men.'

'I sure hope you don't lose him.'

'So do I, Admiral, so do I.' Macnair broke the connection. It was time to give his political masters some good news.

A Tomahawk missile fired from one of the ships would have blown the target to tiny pieces. The danger was the faint possibility of a sympathetic detonation setting off one of the nuclear warheads. That had to be avoided if at all possible. The Tomahawk could be fitted with different warheads – nuclear, anti-ship, anti-runway, land attack or anti-personnel mines and was extremely accurate. However, the use of a Tomahawk would be overkill. The mission was to take away the complete bow section and sink the ship.

Three aircraft were tasked to do the job. They were carrier-based F-14 Tomcats, with a wide selection of possible armaments. In this case they would be using Sea Rays, normally fired by helicopters. They were small, inexpensive air-launched anti-ship missiles which didn't carry too much of a punch. Which was why each aircraft would fire four missiles. Twelve small explosions instead of one big one would reduce the possibility of sympathetic detonation of the nukes.

An E-2 Hawkeye was on station. It was a naval, carrier-based airborne radar plane used to monitor friendly aircraft and to search for enemy aircraft and vessels. In this instance they knew precisely where the enemy was to be found.

Preparations were made to launch the Tomcats. Launch time was one hour. Attack time was one hour and ten minutes.

Hunter thanked the Captain when he left the bridge, carefully closing the door behind him. Walking briskly through the ship, he headed for the compartment that contained the nuclear warheads. At the final stairs he paused. He had no strategy but he also knew he had no time left either. If Macnair worked at his usual speed and competence, Hunter reckoned he could expect a visit from an American aircraft in the next hour or so.

He whistled as he walked down the stairs, his hand at his side, an automatic gripped tightly in his fist. There was nowhere to hide and the two men on guard were standing by the door. They both looked at Hunter, reassured by the fact that he was wearing a suit and tie.

'Good evening,' said Hunter, cheerfully.

The two men looked at each other, not understanding. Hunter shot both of them. The first died instantly with a bullet through the heart. The second responded so quickly, Hunter was lucky to hit him with a snap shot into the thigh. Even as the guard was raising his gun Hunter fired again, this time hitting the guard's hand, knocking the gun away. The third shot was to the head, killing him.

Hunter ran up the stairs to a watertight door. Slamming it shut, he jammed over the twelve clips that were used to hold the door in place. The noise he had made this time was too great to hope that he had avoided detection. He dived into one of the stores that he knew contained rope, tackles and other rigging gear. Pulling the store apart he searched for something suitable. What he found was ideal for his needs – double-ended rigging screws. Grabbing them he dashed back up the stairs. Each end had a hook, which were joined by a long thread of solid steel, two centimetres thick. The thread fed into two sheaths that were tightened using a centre bar. He slipped one of the hooks over a door clip and the other over a clip opposite. Quickly he turned the bar until it was as tight as he could make it. The only way through the door was either to break it down or to cut it open with an oxyacetylene torch. He wasn't a moment too soon. The other clips were already being thrown back. The two he had fixed didn't move. Leaping down the stairs this time there was no finesse. Grabbing a long-handled jemmy he shoved it behind the door lock and heaved down. For a second or two nothing happened. Then, with his muscles straining and his eyes bulging, bolts sheared and the lock flew off.

Opening the door Hunter saw that nothing had changed. It

took only a few seconds to make certain that the detonators he had removed were where he had placed them before he started working on the third warhead. The hammering on the door above ceased and he was able to concentrate on the task in hand without the thumping intrusion. Because this was his third warhead, he told himself, he would go for the record – his record – and complete the job in half an hour. His fingers moved like greased lightning. He soon had the panel open and was able to start on the bolts. He removed the metal box and cut the wires. He placed the first one on the deck.

He heard a noise outside and went over to the door and looked up the stairwell. The sound was that of an oxyacetylene torch cutting through the door. Even as he watched he saw the flame cut a few centimetres of steel away. Grabbing another double-ended rigging screw, the last one, he rushed back up the stairs. He gently pushed two clips across, fitted the screw and tightened it. Outside, no one had noticed the clips moving, which wasn't surprising. With an oxyacetylene torch throwing off white-hot heat and a brightness that can blind, nobody would be looking at the door.

Back at the warhead he finished his task and removed the final detonator. He was about to replace the panel when he paused for a second or two. He had an idea. Checking the diagrams against the inside of the warhead he traced the battery compartment. He disconnected the battery and lifted it out.

Picking up the detonator boxes, he went outside the compartment. He was as low down in the ship as it was possible to go by stairs. However, there was a hatch, dogged shut, in the deck. Undoing the clips, he threw the hatch open and looked down. As he thought, it was an access hatch to the bilges, two metres below. He climbed down, making three trips, each time carrying a detonator box. Placing the boxes against the outside bulkhead, he connected the detonators in series and then to the battery. Climbing the ladder, he looked up the stairwell. They had cut through the corner of the door around the first two clips but the door still wouldn't open. Somebody noticed the other two clips and there were curses and heavier hammering on the door.

A voice yelled an order and the hammering stopped. The

unmistakable whoosh of the lighting of the torch came distinctly through the gap in the door. A few seconds later and the other side of the door glowed red and the tip of the torch burnt through. It was almost time to discourage them further, just as soon as he finished what he was doing. In order to set off the detonators he needed to complete the circuit. He ran two lengths of cable from the detonators up to the compartment. If he touched the wires together, in theory the detonators would explode, setting off the explosives in the boxes. Wrapping the ends of the wire around a suitable vantage point, he wondered how the theory would work in practice.

The oxyacetylene torch was now half way towards finishing the cut. Grabbing two guns, he flicked the safety from single shot to fully automatic and bounded up the stairs. He paused, calculated the probable location of the cutter and placed the barrel of one of the guns near the still warm hole. Reaching up to another hole, he placed the second gun and pulled both triggers at once. A stream of bullets erupted in the stairwell, some hitting straight into targets, others ricocheting off the bulkheads and deck, before tearing flesh apart, killing and maiming. There were loud screams and wild curses followed by the sound of feet scrambling out of harm's way. The oxyacetylene torch lay on the deck, hissing, a background of noise to the moans and whimpers that Hunter could hear. The guns clicked empty and he threw them away. Glancing at his watch, he reckoned it would be about another ten, maybe twenty minutes, before the cavalry arrived. If he was to survive, Hunter needed to have everything ready. In the compartment he began to loosen one of the deck plates. He finally removed the last bolt, inserted a screwdriver between the plates and levered it open. The bilges were beneath him. He was concentrating so hard on what he was doing that he didn't hear the door at the top of the stairwell being bent open. Nor see the armed men silently creep down the stairs. The first intimation he had of danger was when he heard a scuffling at the door and looked up. He was too late. The gun was aimed and fired before he could move.

*   *   *

'Target in sight,' said the Tomcat pilot. Both pilots on either wing acknowledged. 'Follow the leader.'

The Tomcat dropped to sea level and came in over the wave tops. It fired four Sea Ray missiles with a half-second delay between each and broke left, clawing for the sky. The second Tomcat was five seconds behind and firing when the first missile struck. Each one smashed another hole in the ship. The third aircraft got the surprise.

As it closed on the target a Phalanx CIWS – Close in Weapon System – opened fire. It was radar guided and fired 30 millimetre rounds from a Gatling gun and was used by many naval ships as a last-ditch defence against incoming missiles. The pilot in the third Tomcat didn't even have time to squawk "Mayday" before his plane broke apart. He and his radar intercept officer were dead before they realised they had a problem.

'Aircraft down! Aircraft down!' The pilot of the first Tomcat screamed over his communications net. The four men in the two circling aircraft watched, horror stricken. A few pieces of debris scattered across the surface of the sea. There was no sign of their two comrades but then, with no ejection, there wasn't likely to be.

They turned their attention to the ship and watched as it ploughed bow first into the sea. As the angle increased, the screws drove the ship downward towards the seabed. The diesels kept working until the air vents clogged with seawater and then they coughed, spluttered and fell silent. The ship continued down, settling upright on the bottom.

29

Hunter threw himself backward with such force that he hit his head on something hard, making him see stars. The bullet creased the top of his head and blood poured from the wound, blinding him as he lay, immobile. There was no strength in his limbs and, lying there, he knew he was about to die.

A woman's voice shrieked something he didn't understand. Through a fog of semi-consciousness, he sensed her standing over him. He was dimly aware that three other people had entered the compartment. Then the first missile struck.

The ship shuddered. In rapid succession another seven missiles hit home and with each one came a distant explosion as the bows were shot off. There followed the almost continuous chattering of a Phalanx CIWS, a sound that Hunter had last heard in the Gulf war. The deck canted and he slid along, away from the figures crowding into the space. Trying to open his eyes for a moment Hunter thought he had been blinded by the bullet wound. Then, through the sticky mess of coagulating blood, one eye flicked fully open.

The four others in the compartment were cursing and screaming. The door had swung closed and one of them lost his footing, cannonballing into the man standing next to him. There was a chain reaction and they all fell forward, crashing into one of the missiles, knocking over the cradle, taking the missile with them. The noise of further screams and snapping bones was almost lost against the backdrop of the sound of the dying ship. The decks and bulkheads groaned loudly as the pressure of water increased as the ship sank. Hunter, his wits returning quickly, crawled across the deck, now canted at thirty degrees or more to the horizontal. Water was already pouring in around the edge of the door and he knew that he only had seconds if he was to stop the compartment from flooding. The main lights had gone out and the emergency lighting had come on. Battery fed, they would last for hours.

Reaching the door, he grabbed a clip and pulled it over. Then he grabbed a second and a third. The amount of water pouring in reduced to a trickle but he knew it would not last long. Once the air was forced from the ship it would become completely flooded and either the water pressure would blow the door open or the sea would simply come up through the deck. There was only one chance.

He would fight for life to his last breath but he knew that if the ship went down further than forty, maybe fifty metres then nothing would save him. It would be all over in minutes. Even as the thought was forming, the devastated bow of the ship hit the seabed. The deck slowly dropped and settled at an angle of about five degrees forward and ten to port. The sound of popping rivets and tearing metal galvanised Hunter.

Leaping to the bottle bank, he cracked the bottles' valves wide open. High-pressure air flooded into the compartment. He prayed that he wasn't too late. Glancing at the deck he saw the seawater was seeping through and he tried to open the valve to the bottle bank even further. The four figures who had been thrown against the forward bulkhead were still there, though none of them trying to move. The woman held her hands to her ears and began screaming as the pressure built up steadily. King-Smith was watching Hunter, but made no attempt to use the gun still held in his hand. Hunter realised that both King-Smith's arms were broken and lay uselessly over the top of the warhead as though he was cradling it. Stepping across the compartment, without a word, Hunter removed the weapon from King-Smith's hand and dropped it out of his reach.

The depth gauge Hunter had found was showing twenty metres and increasing as the pressure inside the hull caught up with the depth outside. Water was still coming in around the door but more slowly. Taking hold of the clips, Hunter swung off each one, tightening them in turn. The water trickled to a slow seep at the bottom, where the door was slightly buckled.

The pressure inside the compartment equalised with the water pressure outside. The creaking and rivet popping reduced to an occasional noise and eventually even that stopped. Hunter looked at the depth gauge. Thirty-one metres. He had less than twenty minutes to get out if he wanted to avoid having to carry out decompression stops on the way to the surface.

Alleysia Raduyev, a woman feared across continents, stopped screaming. The pain in her ears had suddenly eased – both her eardrums had broken. She tried to move but couldn't. Her leg was trapped under the missile. She looked at it for a second and then, seeing the odd angle of her foot, she began to scream all over again.

'Shut up, you stupid bitch,' King-Smith said viciously.

She was so surprised at being spoken to like that she actually stopped screaming, looked at King-Smith and began to sob.

'You shouldn't have done that,' said King-Smith to Hunter. 'Now it'll take us longer to die.'

'But I'm not going to die,' said Hunter, with a grin, 'only you are.'

King-Smith laughed, a hollow sound. The water in the compartment was now about ten centimetres deep and slowly rising. The other two men with them were face down in the water and already dead.

Alleysia was recovering fast. She was beginning to think in terms of survival herself.

'Get me out of here,' she screamed, her cultured voice suddenly harsh in her fear. 'I will pay you a hundred million dollars.'

Hunter's reply was succinct. 'No chance.'

'Five hundred million. Pounds.' Alleysia Raduyev believed everyone had his or her price.

Hunter turned a bleak look on her as he touched together the two wires he had fixed earlier. He made no indication that his life probably depended on the explosion going off. There was a low bang, the shock wave travelling through the water into the compartment and he smiled.

'What was that?' King-Smith asked.

'My escape route,' said Hunter. He began to strap on the diving bottles.

'You can't leave us,' said the Georgian woman. 'You can't.' Her next statement made Hunter laugh out loud. 'It would be murder.'

'You filthy swine.' Hunter's face was distorted with loathing. 'You intended to kill hundreds of thousands of innocent people and for what? Power? Money? You don't need any more of either. There's nothing more to be bought or enjoyed.' He stepped towards her and she flinched. 'You'll die a slow and lingering death. If you're lucky the water will seep in deep enough for you to put your head under and hold it there. Your death will be relatively quick. If the water doesn't reach you then gradually you'll use up all the oxygen in the air and suffer a long, painful death.'

'For God's sake,' said King-Smith, 'don't just leave us. Take the gun and shoot us. Now.'

The same thought occurred to Hunter and Alleysia at the same time. She leant forward and grabbed for the weapon. Her grasping hand was inches away from the barrel and she stretched further. Trapped as she was, when she moved, a spasm of agony shot up her leg and through her body. Even so, she reached the barrel and was turning it in her hand to grab the butt when Hunter brought his foot down hard on her wrist. The bones snapped with a loud crack and she screamed in agony. Taking the gun away, Hunter then did a quick sweep of the rest of the area. The other guns were out of her reach.

Alleysia sobbed and moaned, cradling her arm to her chest.

'I've never begged for anything,' said King-Smith, 'but this is different. Please kill me.'

Hunter shook his head in bewilderment. 'The crimes you've committed are too numerous and depraved to count.' He checked his watch. Fifteen minutes had elapsed since the ship settled on the bottom. Time was running out.

King-Smith closed his eyes and laid his head back against the bulkhead. Hunter shot him through the forehead. King-Smith's blood and brains splattered across the compartment, spraying Alleysia Raduyev with gore. She screamed again.

'Now,' said Hunter, 'you'll live longer and die alone. A fitting end, don't you think?'

The invective she poured out at him was in her mother tongue but no less satisfying to hear for all that.

'Got to go.' He cheerfully placed the face mask on, cracked open the main bottle valve and fitted the mouthpiece between his teeth. It tasted disgusting and was as tough and unyielding as plastic. Before he left, out of sight of Alleysia Raduyev, he set the last timer on the side of an oxyacetylene bottle.

The last he saw of Alleysia she was sobbing quietly, her arm cradled across her body. He sat on the edge of the deck where he had removed the plate and glanced in her direction. When he looked at her, there was no pity in his heart.

He slipped into the water and swam down into the darkness. Quickly he found the hole he had blown in the side of the ship and felt around the edges. Not all the charges had gone off. The hole was too small for him to swim through.

Christine Woolford was nervous – an emotion totally out of character for her. She had the floor and the other Members of the Strasbourg Parliament were all looking at her with interest. They knew that she was about to make an important statement – the rumour mill had been cranked up beforehand.

'A week ago,' she began, 'I was kidnapped.' There was a stir throughout the chamber. Heads that had been looking at papers on desks suddenly shot up when the interpreters repeated her words. Omitting nothing, Christine related her ordeal. 'The kidnapping was ordered by the leader of a major European crime cartel whom we have not yet identified. All we do know is that the crime cartel has its roots in Georgia. At this very moment details of some of the cartel's crimes, compiled by The International Force Against Terrorism, are being deposited in each of your mailboxes. They represent only a tiny proportion of the cartel's activities during the past few years. We believe that criminal cartels from all over the world are planning to get together to act as one super cartel known as the Syndicate. Individually they deal in drugs, arms, terrorism, money laundering, illegal immigrant transportation, blackmail, armed robbery, prostitution, gambling – both legal and illegal. Think what they could do if they acted collectively. Recently they have begun to take minority shareholdings in medium to large sized companies with the express intention of using criminal methods to take control. Their wealth is staggering. Combined, they will control assets greater than the value of the stock markets of France and Italy and have an income as great as the gross national income of Finland, Sweden and Denmark added together.'

Her announcements were met by stunned incredulity by the other members of the Parliament. Delegates wriggled uncomfortably as the truth was laid out before them. When she continued, Christine laid bare the open secret of governments across Europe and the free world.

'We have failed the people of our great nations, of our continent. We, the elected leaders, are supposed to protect the children, the young and old, the weak as well as the strong.' Being an old campaigner she knew how to use highly emotive language even when speaking to a group as cynical as the one she faced. 'We are supposed to have laws that protect our people and punish the evildoers. It may be an old fashioned term but "evildoers" describes them best. I have been given evidence of the corruption of our laws on a national and international scale. That information is also contained in the files that are awaiting you. Men, women and children are being forced into helping the criminal cartels distribute drugs across Europe. We must protect the families who are coerced into the world of drugs either through fear for themselves or intimidation of their families.'

For fifty minutes she spoke to a packed, silent and incredulous house. At long last the truth was being told. The genie was out of the bottle and there was no putting it back. Action would have to be taken. Otherwise the problems that were currently wracking Europe would escalate. Christine paused and took a sip of water before continuing. 'I propose that we build on what TIFAT has already accomplished. My friend, Charles Woolforth,' her words caused another stir as the two were known to be political enemies, not friends, 'has written a paper on the action needed to take forward our fight. However, I propose that he takes the floor and outlines his proposals. All in favour?'

A vote was called for and arranged and the MEPs pressed their buttons. Over ninety-five percent agreed to Woolforth speaking. A recess was called immediately after the vote with the speech planned to follow. Europe's leaders stood, milling around, talking, and exchanging views. Three members of the chamber left the room. Christine Woolford watched them go. The third member who walked out caused Christine's eyes to narrow as she controlled her surprise.

Each of the three MEPs rushed to their offices. The first one, Maurice Blanche, the French MEP from Normandy, picked up the telephone and dialled a mobile number. It rang twice before he was connected.

'*C'est moi, Maurice.* The woman MEP, Christine Woolford, has stated here in the chamber that TIFAT is organising the fight against the . . .' He frowned. His phone had gone dead.

The second, one of the MEPs for Bavaria, used the extension in his secretary's office, not waiting to get to his own. The secretary had already left for the day. '*Grüss Gott. Hier spricht Ernst Schwarz.* The enemy is TIFAT. Tell . . .' He looked at the handset, perplexed. The connection was broken.

The third MEP sat at her desk and thought for a moment or two and then sighed. She had no choice. She was in too deep. She picked up her phone and dialled the number. '*Ciao . . .*' Carole Lombardi immediately realised that the line was dead.

In each of the offices the same scene followed. In Maurice Blanche's office two men appeared. 'I am Inspector Tisier, this is Sergeant Axel. We have here a warrant for your arrest. You will come with us, please.'

'How dare you!' blustered Blanche. 'Do you know who I am?'

'We do, sir. You're a traitor who has been selling the people of

Europe to the criminals. You have just phoned their organisation. We knew there were traitors in our midst and we needed to find out who you were. Which is why we had all your telephones tapped. Now,' the inspector leant forward and put his face inches from the MEP's. 'Stand up!' He yelled. 'You vermin.'

Blanche shot to his feet, shaking with fear.

'Now move!'

As he stumbled from his office he saw Schwarz and Lombardi also being led away. They were both ashen, Lombardi with tears on her cheeks, ineffectively wiping her face with her hands. Outside the building they were in for a complete shock. The area was packed with newspaper reporters, television cameras and interviewers.

30

Light bulbs flashed and microphones were shoved in their faces. Questions were yelled at them from all sides. Then came the most devastating moment of all. A bull of a man, with thick grey hair and a handlebar moustache stepped forward. Two metres tall and heavily built, he was well known. Sidney Hershell was the police commissioner for Strasbourg.

He held up his hand and called for silence. 'Ladies and gentlemen of the press, we have irrefutable evidence that these three people are in the pay of a major crime cartel in Georgia. They are, without doubt, traitors to their countries and to Europe. They have abused their positions of power for their own ends.'

It was Blanche who realised the meaning of the announcement. In triumph he yelled. 'I protest. We cannot have a fair trial if you denounce us to the world. It is illegal. No court in the world will be able to try us.'

The police commissioner smiled. It sent shivers down Blanche's spine.

'What this man says is true. However, because these three have been totally co-operative with us, have told us all we wanted to know, which implicates many others within the cartel's organisation, we have decided not to press charges. They are free to go with the full knowledge that we are very grateful for their help.'

There was a stunned silence. The reporters and the TV crews watched as the implication of the statement sunk in.

'No! No, it cannot be!' screamed Lombardi. 'They will kill us. They will have their revenge. No! No!'

The commissioner smiled again and said softly, 'I do hope so, madam.' He turned back to the press. 'Naturally, in view of the fact that these people have, in our opinion, been responsible for heinous crimes, we cannot offer them any protection should they be threatened.' He turned to go as the light bulbs flashed in another frenzy of photo taking. As one, the three MEPs ran for their cars.

None of them lasted twenty-four hours.

Charles Woolforth was finishing his speech. 'We must have an effective way of protecting the innocent people caught up in the web of crime. I therefore propose further that a task force be used to investigate any and all statements of intimidation made by asylum seekers. This task force will have the authority to investigate in the countries of origin. We will work to protect the families of asylum seekers on the condition that they tell us what is happening. Only by being honest with us can we help. We will be able to target Europe's resources to ensure a better and safer future for all . . .'

Christine Woolford tuned him out and thought about Macnair. She was looking forward to a visit to Scotland. Soon.

Ruth and Dunston got the message just as the team arrived. Thirty armed men ready to go and nobody to fight. The ship was reported sunk.

'We have to go out and look for survivors. Nick could have escaped, somehow,' said Ruth.

Dunston nodded and placed his arm around her shoulders. He didn't hold out much hope but he said, 'We will. If anyone can survive, it's Nick.'

Joshua Clements appeared. 'It'll be light soon. We'll find anybody who's still alive. Nick's one of the most resourceful men I know.'

Ruth nodded. It was true but she knew it was virtually impossible to survive a shipwreck where the ship sinks in only a few minutes. There was no time to take to the lifeboats. And anyway, he had been amongst the enemy. He was the last person they would allow to escape.

'Corporal Weir,' Clements shouted.

'Sir!'

'Let's get going. A submarine is racing to the spot and as soon as it's light we'll have helicopters in the air. We can beat them if we move fast.'

'Yes, sir. The inflatables are ready and we're just putting on the engines. Two minutes and we can go.'

'Right. Take side arms only. We shouldn't need the heavy stuff. If we do we can call up the airforce.'

'Yes, sir.' Weir turned to Badonovitch. 'Ready, Jan?'

'Yes. I've fixed the lights. We'll have search lights as well as the infra-red seeker.'

'Okay. Let's go,' said Clements, overhearing Badonovitch's comment.

They launched five boats. The inflatables were eight metres long and could carry thirty fully equipped troops. The two outboards were each 120hp and at full speed could achieve 50 knots. Away from the harbour they fell into a diamond formation and slowly picked up speed. At forty knots it felt as though they were flying, the V-shaped hulls skipping across the calm sea. Theirs had turned from an attacking mission to search and rescue. At least there was little or no chance of anybody being killed. Barring accidents.

Jan Badonovitch sat hunched over his equipment with David Hughes at his shoulder. The infra red seeking device was working perfectly and, in close up mode, he could distinguish each engine and each person on the boats. He moved the scale up and set it on two miles. The bodies around faded away into an amorphous mass and tiny dots of background "noise" showed on the screen. He turned down the gain and clutter switches and stared at a blank screen. Even something as small as a head would show up once they were within two miles range.

'Good work,' said Hughes, clapping his Russian friend on the shoulder.

'Thanks,' Badonovitch smiled and turned his thoughts back to his cousin. His brief meeting with Yuri had been joyous. He was looking forward to many beers and a few vodkas when he returned. They had a great deal to catch up on.

For his part Voropaev had volunteered to stay behind with two of the others to guard the mountain of gear stacked on the quayside.

Ruth and Dunston sat side by side, each immersed in their own thoughts. They knew that the chances of survival were so slim as to be out of sight. So far the helicopters which had been criss-crossing the skies with their searchlights had picked up six men. None of them Hunter.

Hunter checked his watch and depth gauge. He'd been at thirty-three metres for twenty minutes and he knew that he was running into serious problems. From memory he was as sure as he could be that he had about twenty minutes at that depth before stops were needed. The tables gave a certain amount of leeway, but not much. He probably had five or six minutes extra before there was a likelihood of decompression sickness. Even then, the bends would not be extreme. He was unlikely to be agonisingly or cripplingly bent, provided he started for the surface now. He could try and find his way through the ship or he could go straight up. If he went the former route God alone knew what delays he would encounter. He chose the latter.

He slipped the shoulder harness off and, holding the bottles, tried pushing them through the hole. It was no use. They were old-fashioned bottles and were broader than his shoulders. If he had time, he could take them apart but time had run out. He had to go now.

He worked his way feet first through the jagged hole. The metal had bent outwards and so the jagged edges were all on the other side. When he got to his shoulders he was stuck for a few seconds until he exhaled and curved his shoulders round. He slid through. He left the bottles against the hull, took a last mouthful of air, and started for the surface. He felt a gentle thud behind him as the oxyacetylene gas exploded in a fiery ball, sucking out the oxygen, incinerating the Georgian crime boss, Alleysia Raduyev.

It had been, he thought, an act of kindness where none had

been warranted. The explosion had been small but sufficient to cut through the metal of the bottle and ignite the gas. The oxyacetylene erupted in a fiery ball of intense heat that lasted less than half a second during which the total oxygen supply in the compartment was eaten up. The fire was self-extinguishing and was so quick that the metal of the compartment and the surface of the warheads did not change temperature by as much as a hundredth of a degree centigrade. Alleysia was inhaling at the time. The gas incinerated her inside and outside so quickly that she was a blackened skeleton within the same time scale. It was over so quickly that her senses did not even have time to register pain. Like the fabled Hydra of old, Alleysia Raduyev was consumed by the flames of a firebrand. Hunter knew a small sense of satisfaction – the means of death was somehow appropriate.

A free ascent is one of the most difficult disciplines a diver learns. Hunter's instinct was to hold his breath. His training told him he had to breathe out all the way to the surface. Rising at the same rate as the bubbles trickling from his mouth, he was heading up at approximately one foot a second. It would take about one hundred seconds to reach the surface, exhaling all the way. It was unnatural. It took tremendous will power not to hold his breath but if he did, even for a few seconds, he knew that there was a serious danger of damaging his lungs. So he looked up, pursed his lips, and relaxed his diaphragm. The change in pressure did the rest and air escaped from his mouth all the way.

He hit the surface with a gasp. Breathing in and out was a luxury. He took a few seconds to get his bearings but then, in the gentle swell, he was able to look around and see what was going on. About a mile away he saw helicopters flying back and forth, powerful searchlights shining down as they looked for debris and possible survivors. Above the clatter of the helicopters, loud and clear through the still night, came another sound. The deep pulse of large outboard motors driven in attack formation drifted clearly across the water. Hunter grinned.

Waving an arm above his head, he guessed they would be using the infra red search equipment. The noise of the boats grew louder and suddenly the first one appeared before his eyes, a spotlight illuminating him.

'Hi, boss,' said David Hughes, as though they met like that everyday.

'Hi, Dave. How're things going?' Hunter wasn't going to be outdone in the nonchalance stakes.

'Oh, not bad,' grinned Hughes. 'You know how it is. Saving the world yet again.'

'I think . . .'

The rest of the sentence was spoilt with a loud yell of delight. 'Nick!' Ruth called. 'Nick! You're alive!'

'Of course I'm alive. What did you expect? Give me a hand, somebody.' Ruth's boat nudged alongside him and he passed an arm over the smooth round gunwale. Finning like fury, he flipped out of the water and over the side, lying there gasping. That final effort had taken the last of his strength.

Ruth was by his side instantly. 'Nick! Are you really all right?' There was deep concern in her voice.

'Sure,' he said, beginning to shiver. The cold of the swim was finally getting through to him. 'I need a blanket. Or dry clothes.'

'You're hurt,' Ruth looked at the wound on his head. The sea had washed away the blood and a scab was forming.

Somebody broke open a medical pack and handed Hunter a thermal blanket, which he gratefully wrapped around himself as he sat up. Ruth used an alcohol swab to clean his wound and plastered gauze over it. 'Luckily it was your head,' she said, 'otherwise you might have been hurt.'

Hunter returned her smile.

'What's the score, Nick?' Captain Clements asked.

'I think most of them are dead. The ship went down so fast I doubt many could have got out.'

'And the warheads?'

'Safe. I removed the detonator boxes from all three of them.'

'Good work.'

'When are we going to bring up the warheads?' Hunter asked.

'As soon as it's light.'

'There's a short cut into the compartment where the warheads are stored. If we go back down and set shaped charges along the hull we can blow a hole big enough to bring the warheads out and straight up. It'll save a load of work.'

'Right, you get back to shore . . .'

'No way. I'm staying. I'd like to see this through to the end.'

Clements didn't argue.

They spent the remainder of the night searching the surrounding area. Between the helicopters and the boats a total of fifteen people were picked up, including Maria, Alleysia's maid. She had been on the bridge when the aircraft had attacked. She knew almost as much about the organisation as Alleysia Raduyev herself. Always around, unobtrusive, in the background, ignored and treated as though she was less than dust beneath the great woman's feet, Maria had a great deal of revenge to extract.

The submarine arrived as dawn was breaking. It hung around on the surface, supplying the men in the boats with sandwiches and hot drinks. Dry clothes were sent over for Hunter who was quickly recovering his strength now that he had food and coffee inside him. Preparations were made to dive down to the wreck and blow a large hole in the side of the ship. Hunter had wanted to do the job but was dissuaded by Clements and so Douglas Napier led the divers. They found the hole Hunter had blown in the side and set shaped charges three metres higher. They blew a hole four metres in diameter.

The men swam inside and fixed mine-raising bags to the first of the warheads. Cracking open a compressed air bottle, they filled the bag sufficiently to lift the first of the warheads off its cradle and push it towards the opening. Once in the open they let in more air and watched as the warhead floated to the surface. When the pressure decreased the bag rose higher, the volume of air increased and release valves set in the bag released the unwanted air. The warhead floated serenely upwards. To remove all three took over five hours. The warheads were taken onboard the submarine and, in accordance

362

with orders received direct from the Pentagon, taken back to the Sixth Fleet.

The four bodies were also removed. They would be needed for identification purposes as the law closed in on the remainder of the members of the cartels. The ship would also be searched for other bodies. There was a great deal of work to do but luckily TIFAT had finished its part.

Returning to Cagliari, Hunter said to Ruth, 'I don't suppose there's any point in us continuing our interrupted sailing holiday, is there?'

Ruth frowned. 'Maybe. The problem is, with you the excitement will probably be too much.'

Hunter laughed and Ruth joined in with a fit of the giggles, relieved to have him in one piece.

'We could so something else,' he said.

'Such as?' Ruth asked.

'Such as skiing in Colorado.'

'Wrong time of the year.'

'Fishing in Scotland?'

'Too wet and boring.'

'A quiet hotel on a beach where the service is superb, the sun is hot and the drinks are cold?'

'Now that,' said Dunston, overhearing what they were saying, 'sounds great.'

'You aren't invited,' said Hunter with a smile. 'Besides you have to collect the boat from Ubli.' Linking his arm through Ruth's they walked away with a wave.

Epilogue

The ship's surviving crew, including the captain, were arrested and ferried to an Italian jail. Only seventeen cartel leaders were found alive and were taken away by the Americans. After weeks of questioning they were summarily tried by a military court, in camera, and shot two days after sentence was passed. The seventeen men had given sufficient information to enable the American and European authorities to carry out over two thousand arrests, make drug seizures worth nearly a five billion dollars and to trace bank accounts with sufficient funds to wipe out the total debt of the third world. Drug smuggling dropped drastically and the street price of heroin, smack and cocaine went up astronomically as a result. New players began to move into the business, tempted by the possibility of huge profits. Only this time the game was much tougher.

Maria was taken by helicopter to the Sixth Fleet and then by aircraft to London. Her knowledge was of incalculable benefit and as each nugget of information was made available it was passed to the relevant agency of the country involved. In the end a thousand page report was given to every government world wide which had even a passing interest in the subject of the cartels. Seventy different countries were involved, a sign of how far and wide the crime cartels had spread. It took a year to extract all that Maria had to say. Her information exhausted, she was given a pension and a new identity.

*   *   *

Flika's revenge was swift. The American Sixth Fleet bombed Ex-General Crackov's fort in Mahdia out of existence. The Tunisian army followed behind the airstrip and wiped out the few remaining survivors. Crackov's charred body was identified when his fingerprints were matched with those kept on file at the headquarters for the Committee for State Security – *Committee Gosudarstvennoi Bezoopasnosti* – better known as the KGB, Moscow.

Eighty-six policemen and women were traced through the Barclays' account at Kensington. They were all dismissed from the service without the benefit of their pensions. Eight had the good grace to commit suicide. The Acting Chief Constable of Thames Valley, before he could be arrested, moved to Cuba with his wife and two teenage children. He wrote a best-selling book about the corruption of the West, which sold mainly in Cuba. Copies were bought via the Internet across the world. An international warrant for his arrest is still outstanding.

Commander Yuri Voropaev returned to his hometown and joined Admiral Gerenko in rebuilding the region. The lieutenant implicated in the theft of the warheads was shot when trying to escape from prison. He maintained his innocence throughout.

Jana Avramovic was given a bursary through the Griffiths' Educational Trust and began studying medicine at Edinburgh University. Her avowed intention was to qualify as a doctor and return home to help her fellow countrymen.

Isobel's talents again came in very useful. Using the information they had amassed, she and her team worked to repatriate hundreds of billions of dollars worth of cash and assets. The United Nations had a wonderful time debating who should be the beneficiaries of such generous largesse. In some third world countries the money found by TIFAT was used to eradicate poverty. In others, ignorance and greed prevailed and it was used to finance further wars.

*   *   *

Hunter and Ruth enjoyed their holiday but it was curtailed by two days. Macnair needed them for a crisis had developed in America. There were serious problems with drugs and terrorism in California and the finger of blame was pointed firmly at the Japanese.

A Million Tears

by Paul Henke

1890. Murder and intrigue have forced the Griffiths family to flee
their native Wales. They leave behind a village devastated by a
mine disaster and the oppression of the Victorian ruling classes.

Their subsequent adventures represent the American Dream. With
bravado born of necessity, Evan Griffiths builds a business empire
– retail, transport, banking, real estate – in the frontier town of St.
Louis. With an inherent sense of justice, and the support of his
beloved Meg, he forges a political career. But on his right hip,
Evan carries a gun. No one will ever hurt his family again.

In Wales, David yearned to travel, dreamed of discoveries.
Shipwrecked on a coral island in the South Seas, he discovers
himself.

His brother, Sion, dreams of flying, craves freedom and adventure. But will his dream – and Sion himself – die in the lawless
hinterlands of the Wild West?

Through meticulous research, author Paul Henke expertly braids
together fact and fiction, recreating the Frontier of America. With
consummate ease, he conveys a vivid sense of life at the turn of
the century, weaving the thread of history – and the lessons it can
teach us – through his narrative.

The vitality of Henke's fiction is mirrored in the energy of his
vibrant characters. On his vast canvas he captures their triumphs
and their tragedies. In 'A Million Tears' he unveils the portrait of
the remarkable Griffiths Family. A gem to be treasured.

ISBN 1-902483-00-6

The Tears of War and Peace

by Paul Henke

It is 1911 and David Griffiths is in Wales, bored and lonely. He travels to London at the behest of their family friend, John Buchanan, to start a new business in banking. There he gets caught up in the suffragette movement and falls in love with Emily. Against the backdrop of women's fight for votes and the looming First World War, the Griffiths build a vast, sprawling company encompassing banking, aircraft manufacturing, farming and whisky distilling.

The enmity of a German family follows them tragically throughout this period, leading to murder and revenge. At the end of the war, thanks to a change in the Constitution, Evan is invited to run for President of the United States. The family rally round for the most important battle of Evan's life.

With the Brown-shirts running rampage across Germany, David and Sion are soon involved in a battle for survival.

Sir David Griffiths is a colossus of a figure, striding across the world and through the century, a man of integrity and bravery, passion and dedication. Determined to win, nothing comes before the family.

The story is as compelling as ever. Historical fact woven into the fictional characters makes a breathtaking tale of adventure you will not want to put down.

ISBN 1-902483-03-0

Débâcle

TIFAT File I

A Nick Hunter Adventure

Following a summit meeting in Paris an alliance of interested countries form an elite fighting force to combat terrorism throughout the world. Based in Britain and under the command of a British General, the team is made up of Western, Russian and other non-aligned countries' special forces.

Without warning the terrorists strike. A group of bankers, politicians and industrialists are taken prisoner off the coast of Scotland and the new, untried force is sent to search for them.

The Scene of Action Commander is Nick Hunter, Lieutenant Commander, Royal Navy, an underwater mine and bomb clearance expert with experience in clandestine operations.

The enemy is one of the world's most ruthless and wanted terrorists – Aziz Habib! Hunter leads the team against Habib, backed up by two computer experts: Sarah from GCHQ and Isobel, hired by the General to run the IT for the new force.

While stock markets take a pounding and exchange rates go mad, the state sponsoring the terrorism is making a fortune. It has to stop. At all costs.

This is non-stop adventure from beginning to end. A riveting story told by a master story teller. You are guaranteed not to want to put it down!

Débâcle mixes fact with fiction which will cause you to wonder, how true is this story? Did it really happen?

ISBN 1-902483-01-4

Mayhem

TIFAT File II

A Nick Hunter Adventure

Israel faces imminent destruction, nuclear Armageddon. A series of kidnaps, bombings and senseless murders have left her isolated from her allies and threatened by enemies of old. Unknown to all but a few, the situation has been orchestrated by multi-millionaire Zionist, Samuel Dayan. His vision of a Greater Israel will be carved from the charred ruins of the Middle East.

But Dayan is up against the international anti-terrorist organisation, TIFAT, and our hero Nick Hunter. To the age-old struggle of Good against Evil, author Paul Henke adds state-of-the-art communications technology and computerised warfare. In a desperate race against time, Hunter and his team of hand-picked specialists deploy satellite intelligence and high-tech weaponry to track Dayan to his lair.

The plot twists and turns in a series of setbacks, betrayals and mind-blowing developments. Myriad minor characters deserve story-lines of their own.

Relentlessly building the tension, Henke strips his hero Hunter of all resources but those within himself – knowledge born of experience and the inability to give up. Hunter simply must not fail.

ISBN 1-902483-02-2

A Million Tears

The Tears of War and Peace

'Henke isn't just talented, but versatile too. His books are very convincing. As good as Stephen King, Wilbur Smith, Tom Clancy and Bernard Cornwell.'

Burton Mail

'Read them and weep.'

The Stirling Observer

'He's one of the best new writers we've had in ten years.'
The Burton Trader

'A family saga with non-stop adventure from beginning to end.'
Tony Cowell, *PressGroup UK*

Débâcle

'A gritty political thriller . . .'

The Times

'A rip-roaring thriller from the world of terrorism and espionage.'

The Wee County News

'The readers will be hard-pressed to distinguish fact from fiction in Paul Henke's latest blockbuster.'

The Press and Journal

'A political thriller that combines international terrorism, the military and high finance. A roller-coaster of a thrilling ride.'

The Sunday Post

'Has that absolute tang of authenticity – a rattling good yarn.'

Chris Serle, *BBC Radio*

'Non-stop action from beginning to end.'

BBC Radio Manchester

'A political thriller that rivals Tom Clancy.'

The Stirling Observer

'Move over Tom Clancy. Henke has turned his own amazing real-life experiences into blockbuster novels.'

The Sun

Mayhem

'A non-stop action adventure set in Scotland and the Middle East.'

The Edinburgh Evening News

'A fast moving tale of terror and destruction set amidst the charred ruins of the Middle East. An international force exists to fight terrorism. Terrific realism.'

The Stirling Observer

'The hero, Nick Hunter, embarks on a non-stop roller-coaster adventure from the Scottish Highlands to the Middle East. Henke is being hailed as the next Wilbur Smith.'

The Aberdeen Press and Journal

'Mayhem is a classic airport thriller. It's a veritable page turner and a cracking read.'

The Milngavie & Bearsden Herald

'A cracking good yarn. Non-stop action from beginning to end.'

Central FM radio

'Fiction becomes fact in Paul Henke's action thrillers. A superb read.'

The Northern Echo

About Paul Henke

Paul spent nine years in the Royal Navy and qualified as a bomb and mine disposal expert, specialising in diving and handling explosives. As a Lieutenant, he survived a machine gun attack by IRA gun runners in Ireland in 1976. Using plastic explosives he was responsible for blowing-up a number of Second World War mines found off the coast of Britain. He was promoted to Lieutenant Commander in the Royal Naval Reserve where he had command of various minesweepers and minehunters.

In 1979 he spent fifteen months in Nigeria where he was in charge of a saturation diving system prior to moving to the American Midwest.

He has travelled extensively, researching material for his work and is now a full time writer. He lives with his family near Loch Lomond in Scotland.

Author's Note

Thank you for reading my novel. I hope you enjoyed it. At the beginning of the book you will find my web site *and* my e-mail. I mean it sincerely when I invite you to write and tell me what you think of my books. I have had plenty of replies which, as an author doing one of the loneliest jobs in the world, I have appreciated very much.

Thanks again, and all the very best,

Paul Henke